I0669451

FORGIVING
Nostalgia

LAURA A MULLINS

Copyright 2023

original cover art by Angie Pike

This is a work of fiction. The characters and events described herein are imaginary and are not intended to refer to specific persons alive or dead. All rights reserved. No part of this publication may be reproduced, distributed, or transmitted in any form or by any means, including photography, recording, or other electronic or mechanical methods without the prior written permission of the publisher except for brief quotations embodied in critical reviews.

Dedication

This book is dedicated to all the people who have dreamed this dream with me. To all my muses, teachers, guinea pigs, and fellow writers- Thank You.

CHAPTER ONE

Before Nick Thomas, Emma felt alone. She didn't remember people in their lives. Trips, events, milestones were all lost in a fog. Brief flashbacks shined out like tiny shards of sea glass rolling in the tide but completely out of reach.

Since her treatment, Emma didn't know her husband, David, any more than she knew herself. She remembered him from their childhood but couldn't think why she would have married him. She had no idea how he'd talked her into having kids.

David's job required them to entertain clients on a regular basis. Emma didn't like dressing up and going out with people she had no interest in meeting but David didn't want to leave her alone in the house. She found herself frustrated that no one expected her to partake in the conversation. Not that she could have if she had wanted to. Emma had trouble forming thoughts and she knew her vocabulary was diminished from the ECT.

It was impossible for her to drink herself to freedom. Justifying it with his recital of all her medicines and their reaction to alcohol, David monitored her intake. Stressing the importance of taking her medicines at the same time every day, he would often push her pills to her under the table if they were still out.

David didn't understand that she got tired of being asked how she felt. She also hated feeling like everyone knew her medical history as though David had prepped his clients for interaction with her.

Usually after a business dinner, she'd run upstairs and straight to bed to avoid talking. Sleep was her only salvation.

Until she met Nick.

She had been playing tennis with some women at the country club and had gone to the restroom. Upon exiting, she'd momentarily forgotten where she'd been before and stood in the breezeway, slightly panicked. Nick was working in a flower bed eyeing her curiously.

"Happens to me all the time," he said.

"What?" she replied.

He stood erect and dusted off his hands as he walked over to her. He was obviously amused but his grin wasn't mocking or cruel. With a dirt-encrusted hand, he knocked on his head.

"Was in a motorcycle accident and ended up with head injury. I forget where I am sometimes."

"Well, I suppose you and everybody knows about me and my treatment. Do you get a bonus for making me feel better when I feel like an idiot?"

"You're not an idiot and I have no idea what treatment you're talking about. I just know the look and how it feels to suddenly not know where you are or what you are doing." He reached out and lightly knocked on her head. "Apparently your treatment is a lot like my head injury."

He turned before she could respond and strode off. Emma stood there for a long moment watching him go. His shoulders were broad and she could see the muscles strained and hard through the fabric of his shirt when he picked up a bag of gravel. He wore long khaki cargo shorts, with various tools and rubbish poking out of the pockets. She noted the sharp definition in his calves. Every part of him was covered in dirt and his blond hair was pulled into a ponytail. It wasn't until he was out of sight that Emma realized she'd been holding her breath.

From that day, she sought him out every time they went to the club. David usually played golf or joined his buddies at the club bar. Emma had lost interest in their friends because she had a hard time keeping up with the conversation and often forgot which husband and kids belonged to which woman. They didn't really try to include her and talked about her as if she wasn't there.

Nick didn't ask questions and was the only person who didn't treat her like she was compromised. He understood how lonely she felt around people. Since he hadn't known her before, Nick wasn't hoping that she'd go back to "normal". David was still hoping for that.

"The club has rules about fraternizing with members," Nick explained out of the blue one day.

They were ankle-deep in top soil after she'd abandoned her tennis game to help him plant shrubs.

"You can tell them that my therapist suggested that I use gardening as therapy. They'll be afraid of legal action if they try to stop me. Everyone's afraid of crazy." Emma noted how musical it sounded when he laughed.

"You aren't, you know."

"I'm not what?"

"Crazy."

It was then that she realized that he was the only one who could see her. He wasn't embarrassed when she forgot where she was or couldn't remember the words she needed to say.

"Thank you," was all she could manage.

Nick smiled but said nothing.

Emma knew then that she loved him.

Emma's father had also required her to look like a normal, happy child and sit still despite the bruises or lack of sleep caused by his own drunken rages. The weekly business dinners and outings to the country club reminded her of all the times she had to smile and pretend she was happy. She felt like a captive. Maybe her incident had been her mind's way of rebelling. At least, that was what Nick had suggested. He had a way of finding the good in every situation.

David was the one she ran to so she could escape her father's tyrannical fists. It hurt him that she couldn't remember them together. It was obvious that David wanted her back to normal, but Emma wasn't sure she wanted to return to that place.

Although not physically abusive like her father, David was a control freak. Every night he came home and made the rounds. He would call her phone to see where she'd left it. Once, he found it in the microwave. When she had no recollection of how it had gotten there, he got upset.

"What if something had happened to you and you needed me? Or what if I needed you? You've got to be more careful, Em."

She tried to explain or offer some humor to the situation. His worried face would not ever yield to any smiles, so she quit trying.

Emma felt like she had to prove herself every day. But there was no real way to prove she wasn't crazy. David didn't understand that most days she felt fine. His constant picking up after her, worrying, and gentle scolding just made her feel that nothing she did was ever good enough.

One of his favorite things was to get out old photo albums and flip through them, asking her if she could remember this or that. Emma recognized herself in the photos and agreed that they looked happy, but nothing was familiar. It pleased him when she asked questions.

"Was I funny?"

"Yes. You were so funny."

"Not anymore."

"That's not true, Em. You're still funny. You've just been through a lot."

With her memory spotty, she often started things and then got distracted. Emma had little projects started everywhere, which she suspected annoyed David. She decided to do something useful and clean out a closet. Once, she'd spent the day organizing and throwing things out, thinking he'd be proud of her for taking on a cluttered mess of art supplies and old clothes which were strewn all over the walk-in closet. She'd been careful not to throw away any of his things. When he came home, he stared in disbelief at the piles of junk she'd amassed. He never even noticed how she'd installed another shelf. Instead, he picked up random things from the pile, took them into their bedroom and shut the door. She bagged everything else by herself. Later, when she passed by, she heard him crying. Emma didn't know what she had done to cause it but it was starting to make her mad.

There it was again. Before the incident, she was whole and perfect. From what everyone else described, she was smart, witty, considerate, and pleasant to be around at all times. Now, she was less. At least, that was how everyone made her feel. Everyone except Nick.

David

CHAPTER TWO

There have been many times in our lives together that I thought the worst thing had happened. I was wrong every time until now.

Before all of this, we were the couple that everyone else wanted to be. We both equally commanded attention when we walked into a room. We laughed about it. It was as though we had superpowers. Sometimes I won over clients simply because we enchanted them together. Maybe we believed that we were invincible as a pair. Or, maybe I am the only one who thought that.

After the miscarriage, a psychotic episode, and electric convulsive treatment, Emma didn't want to go to client dinners with me anymore. She didn't remember any of our friends and had no interest in socializing. I didn't want to push her, but the doctors insisted that she get back to her regular routines because it would help her heal.

My job required me to entertain more than I wanted to and I didn't want to do it without my alpha mate. She was always way ahead of me when I casually mentioned a dinner out. I listened while she told me why she didn't want to go before I countered. She conceded every time, but I suspect it was only because she was tired of hearing me talk. It hurt even though I couldn't really be mad at her. It wasn't her fault that the ECT had left her with holes in her memory and difficulty with conversation. We were friends as children for a short time. Then, we reconnected in college and dated four years until graduation. Now, after thirteen years being happily married, I guess I thought she would want to go just to be with me. I was wrong about that too.

For months, I watched over her. It was overwhelming but I helped her keep track of her phone, medicine, and doctor appointments. I encouraged her to paint and coaxed her out to the country club, to exercise, and to social events. In my mind, I believed that this was going to help her get back to normal. It didn't feel like I was rushing her.

Again, I thought we had been through all the worst parts. I knew she couldn't remember us so I showed her pictures. It was encouraging when she asked questions and laughed at the stories. I thought we were making progress.

A month later, she dropped a bomb on me that I did not see coming. I was upset because she'd converted our nursery back to a media room. In addition, she gave away the baby furniture without even talking to me.

"David, I don't want to talk about it. It's done. I didn't see the need to keep all that, and all the other furniture was crammed into the guest bedroom. So, I brought it in here."

"Em, I know you're scared. There's no hurry. We can try again."

"You're not listening. You never listen. I don't want children. I lost…" She began to sob.

I reached out for her but she pulled away, headed downstairs, and slammed the door on her way out. I could see her through the window glaring up at me as she started the car and drove away.

The first time I noticed Emma talking to the groundskeeper at the club, I wasn't suspicious. Sure, he looked like Thor, with biceps chiseled from granite. Em had always assured me that she didn't like big muscles. His blonde mane was long, unkempt, and usually tucked under a cowboy hat. His eyes were the color of glacier ice. He spoke to everyone like they were his best friends. So, when I noticed that they'd exchange a few words every time we were there, I thought nothing of it. I should have paid closer attention.

Emma

After an intensely exhausting conversation with David about the former nursery, all she could think about was talking to Nick. She ran out of the house, got in her car, and headed straight to Nick's place, which was only a few miles away.

Thank God David didn't pursue her. How had she let herself be talked into this? After Hawaii, she promised herself to never again be a slave to appearances. She also vowed to never have children. Why had she abandoned herself?

Nick hadn't wanted children either. He had left home at seventeen after his motorcycle accident ended his football scholarship possibilities. He rarely spoke of his father but admitted that he had no basis for being a good parent and his head injury impaired his judgment enough that he felt he couldn't handle a child.

He was outside, building something, when she pulled up. When he saw her, Nick always smiled and never asked her if something was wrong.

"I could use a hand," he said and handed her some safety glasses.

For the next half hour, Emma helped him cut and hammer boards into place. He handed her the nail gun and watched silently as she secured the last pieces. Then, together, they lifted the window box and attached it to the side of the small house.

He turned to her with a knowing grin.

"Conversation with David?"

"He was upset that I painted the nursery and put the original furniture back in there. The thrift store people came and picked up all the baby furniture. It's hard for him to accept that I don't want children."

"My dad was the same way. He would always say things like, 'you weren't like this before' or 'you used to have ambition'. It was like he was mad because I was different."

"Exactly. Like before I was perfect and now, I'm a problem."

"They don't mean to, you know? They just have a different idea of what normal looks like and they want us to get that back."

"What if I can't go back to normal?" she asked, unsure if she was addressing Nick or herself.

Scratching his head, Nick thought for a long moment. He opened a bag of topsoil and scooped handfuls into the new window box.

"Most people view normal as a static thing. Like once established, it is set in stone." He pointed at the round bag of dirt. "See, most would say that this is a normal round bag of topsoil. But look what happens." He hoisted the bag up with ease, turned it upside down and emptied it into the window box. "See? From a full, round bag to a half-full rectangular box. Normal is like that. It isn't static but instead adapts. It's not a matter of getting back to normal. It's only about accepting a new normal. And that starts with you."

It started raining. Large, sloppy drops fell hard on them but neither of them moved for shelter. Instead, they both started stomping in the puddles already forming on the cement. Covered in dirt and soaked to the bone, Emma forgot about normal, David, and babies. All there was in the world was rain and Nick.

Later, sitting on his deck stairs with towels and instant hot chocolate, he pierced her with one of those looks. His pale blue eyes seemed to look through to her soul.

"He's probably worried."

"He's always worried," she said, more bitterly than she meant to.

Nick nodded. "Do you still love him?"

Emma had been waiting for this question. Truthfully, she didn't know how to answer. David had been a godsend when she was a child. He was her best friend. Now he was always kind and gentle despite his disappointment.

"I loved him when I was a kid. He loves me. But I don't really know how I feel about him now."

Nick sipped his cocoa with a nod. "You need to figure that out."

"You think I don't know that?"

"I can't deny that I am developing feelings for you. But I don't want to be the reason you leave your husband. I want you to decide what you want on your own."

She felt her irritation melt away as he spoke. Although she wasn't sure how she felt about David, Emma knew exactly how she felt about Nick. There were no words forming so she stood up.

Nick did not rise but took her towel as she handed it down from her shoulders.

"Thank you for listening," she said.

"Anytime."

The drive home was dreamlike. As she pulled into the driveway, she could scarcely remember getting there. Nick was developing feelings for her. It wasn't her imagination, and that felt good.

David was sitting on the front porch steps waiting for her. For the first time in the months since the episode, she didn't feel exhausted when she noted the sadness in his face. She felt a mix of affection and sympathy. Though she knew she should regret it, Emma knew what she had to do. A week later, Emma asked David for a divorce and moved in with Nick.

A month later, she was so much happier. She still used the studio at David's house. He seemed happy that she wanted to use the space, and Emma knew that he was hoping that she'd come back. She hated knowing that she was giving him false hope, but she needed the place to work. Even though she didn't remember designing it, this studio was perfect in every way.

As she put her finishing touches on the painting of a boy fending off a small dog from his melting ice cream cone, she searched the face of the child. In a way, this painting symbolized her life now, which often felt like a series of near misses and small triumphs. The sunlight was causing him to squint but his determination was evident in his grimace. Even the boy's shadow stretched behind him like a toy soldier readied for battle.

"Did you know that Carl Jung was the first to use shadow to describe the parts we repress or deny?"

"Hey, lady. Did you know that people think you're crazy when you talk to yourself?"

She whirled around to find Nick. Her heart was racing already at the surprise but it calmed when she saw him standing there with a hand-picked bouquet tied in twine.

"I am crazy. Haven't you heard? What's the occasion?"

Nick shrugged. "Do I need a special reason to bring you flowers?"

"No…" She bit her lip.

Nick took her in his arms and kissed her. His mouth was hot and tasted of cinnamon from the gum he chewed regularly.

"Thank you," she whispered.

"You're welcome. What time is your exhibition tonight?"

"Ahh. I knew I was forgetting something. It's at seven."

"Want to go get some food and then we'll get ready?"

She nodded, passing a glance over the studio and deciding she could clean up later.

"Sounds great."

He picked her up and carried her out. Emma buried her face in his neck. The smell of Nick's skin was always pleasurable to breathe in. Intermingled with his own natural musk, she could detect the mix of dirt, plants, and flowers. It was so intoxicating that she felt they were the only people on earth.

David

CHAPTER FOUR

Even though Emma moved out a month ago, I still let her keep her key and work in the studio. After not finding her in the house, I headed out to the studio. I have asked her a hundred times to make sure the front door was closed and locked. Leaving it open not only triggered the memory of the awful night she had her episode, it also made it easy for people to steal. No one had so far but it wasn't for lack of opportunity.

The studio door was wide open and the paint on her latest creation was still wet. Her dead phone lay on the coffee table.

"Explains why she didn't get my calls or texts," I said to the painting.

Crossing the yard, I glanced at the pile of logs I was supposed to have moved several months ago. She kept complaining about tripping over them but now she was gone so I had no motivation.

Back in the house, I headed upstairs and straight to my closet. Wanting to impress, I chose a black suit, charcoal vest and silver tie for the opening night of Emma's art show. Emma had always described me as James Bond in this suit. I rather hoped she thought that tonight.

After getting out socks, underwear, and cuff links, I headed for the shower.

The water poured hot and hard over me and I stood under the multi-head jets and breathed in the steam hoping it would renew my energy. I had experienced depression before and knew how it manifested itself as fatigue and muscle soreness. The anger helped to burn off the sadness but sometimes all the feelings combined and left me feeling exhausted.

I helped her new lover move her stuff out. I didn't even try to fight. There was no need. She had made her choice. It still made me grit my teeth when I thought of him smiling at me as we loaded their new bedroom suite.

I was still holding onto hope that she would change her mind. And I knew he'd be there tonight. I just hoped I'd have a minute to talk to her alone.

Later, driving down Highway 31, I smiled at the skyline of the city. The small outcropping of skyscrapers hadn't yet covered the horizon, despite the age of the city. Unlike places like LA or Chicago, we still had wide-open spaces, and I breathed in the air and sunshine as I raced along the winding road to the exhibit. I tried not to look at the hospital in which we lost our baby. I couldn't think of that now.

As I arrived minutes later on Lancaster Lane in Homewood, I spotted an empty space two doors down from the gallery.

Tonight's show was at Art on Lancaster, which was owned by longtime friends Joanna and Sophie Marsh. Emma's first exhibition in Birmingham had been here. Joanna's extensive connections had helped launch Emma's career. Her paintings had earned nearly a half million and she was featured in galleries on three continents.

The place looked like a Roman temple with high ceilings, columns, and marble benches. The light fixtures looked like torches and the ceiling glowed with constellations. The flooring was natural stone tile. Joanna had insisted that all this was necessary to set the mood. I wasn't sure if the costly design inspired people to spend money on art or made them feel like they were in a museum, but it was my favorite gallery.

Joanna met me at the door with a worried expression. She wore a blue, backless gown and her long, gray hair was swept up, spilling ringlet curls onto her shoulders. I'm not sure anyone would describe her as pretty. She was handsome. Her high cheek bones and square jaw looked sculpted. With razor sharpness, her blue eyes always reminded me of a hawk. She had taken Emma's memory loss hard because it wiped out their relationship too.

"Have you heard from her?" she asked, admitting me.

"No. Her phone was dead, at the house."

"I hope she'll remember. I have important business to discuss."

"I hope so too," I replied, not expecting to make her feel better.

"Hello, handsome," came a familiar voice at my back.

I turned to see Sophie in a silver and black gown, low-cut, with spaghetti straps and nowhere to hide the tiniest amount of body fat. Her skin was the color of caramel and her cat eyes were like black diamonds. Elegant and lithe, Sophie looked like a goddess had stepped out of a painting. Her flawless hands, belying her sixty years, were bedazzled by a perfect three-carat yellow sapphire flanked by two one-carat blue sapphires set in gold.

We hugged and she paid me a kiss on the cheek.

"You look like James Bond," she whispered.

"And you like Helen of Troy."

"Flirt," she accused.

"Guilty," I said and hugged her again.

We both turned and watched Joanna as she sailed about, making small adjustments to placards and trays.

"Do you think I should give her Thor's number?" I offered, saddened by the woman's constant frown.

"No," Sophie replied quietly. "We're working on her letting go. If she has another way to reach Em, she'll only use it as a crutch."

I was glad. It still stung that Emma had instructed me to call Nick if I needed to reach her. I couldn't think of an emergency dire enough to butcher my pride that way.

"Let me go help her. Find me later," she called over her shoulder.

As the other patrons began entering the gallery, I momentarily felt out of place. There were couples everywhere and none so formally attired. Sauntering to the far corner, I took up a glass of champagne and leaned against the wall. I was determined not to feel sorry for myself and concentrated instead on people-watching. Sometimes I trailed behind groups and listened as they described the stories they saw in the hues. Ironically, all of Emma's paintings included children. This was especially painful to me now.

It had been hard enough coming home to find her organizing her art supplies. In the pile of discarded things were boxes of journals. On top of them, though, were cards I'd given her and her wedding dress. They meant nothing to her, and when I realized that she meant to throw them away I cried.

A group of 40-something women to my right were admiring a painting of two little girls building a sand castle.

"She must have children," one was saying.

Part of me wanted to tell the lady she was wrong but how could I shatter someone else's illusion just because mine was gone?

Emma

CHAPTER FIVE

She marveled at Nick's truck. Normally littered with pallets, bags of soil, flowers, and various tools, he had cleaned out the bed until not even a speck of dirt or single petal could be found

. She stared, disbelieving, at the interior, which was usually the refuge for discarded coffee cups, chip bags, and copious gum wrappers. Her shock and delight made him laugh that deep, melodious purr she loved.

"Well, you are a distinguished artist, and this is your exhibition. I couldn't have you arrive in a junk mobile, now, could I?"

She turned to kiss him but stopped short. Nick didn't own a suit or single tie, but he cleaned up well. He wore his good jeans, meaning they had no grass stains or holes, and a pressed, black shirt. Instead of work boots, he wore black cowboy boots that were freshly polished. His long hair was down to his shoulders, brushed, and sporting product to keep it from going rogue.

Emma ran her fingertip over his chin and up to his ear.

"Did you shave for me?"

"I did."

"Hoping to get lucky later?" She rubbed his earlobe.

"Don't need luck."

"Oh? Why not?"

Emma ran her free hand up and over his flat stomach to his chest. Pausing on his nipple until it stiffened, she suppressed a giggle. His neck was red, although she knew it wasn't from embarrassment.

"Because either way, the most beautiful woman in the world is coming home with me."

He didn't give her time to react but instead kissed her, deeply and hungrily. It was enough to make her knees weak. His arms and torso felt like steel warmed by the sun and she melted into him as he picked her up and pressed her against the truck.

Both of them knew that they didn't have time but wordlessly they unbuckled and adjusted. All she knew was that she needed to feel him, as though it would ground her from all the feelings of anxiety that had been building all afternoon. He didn't rush but instead moved slowly, infusing her with his calm strength. Emma forgot about her anxiety.

A half hour later, they were driving to the gallery, holding hands and grinning. They didn't talk, and Emma was happy that they both were comfortable with each other's silence.

Silence was salvation for Emma. It meant she didn't have to think or feel. She had no idea if she'd ever tried meditation before her episode. If the point of meditation was to reach stillness and silence, ECT had helped her reach Nirvana, Zen, Ping-Pong, whatever it was called. Finding a partner comfortable with silence was the piece she'd been missing.

David was not comfortable with her silence. It made him feel that something was wrong. No matter how many times she'd smiled, he would always ask. Sometimes she didn't feel like smiling. It wasn't that she was sad or mad, she just wanted to feel free. Nick understood this.

She looked over at Nick, who was humming to himself. Since her treatment, she was keenly aware of smells. Even after showering, Nick always smelled like flowers. Emma was sure that the fragrance just oozed from his pores. She didn't mind, although sometimes it did trigger memories of the treatment room.

The facility had tried to make the experience of medicinal electrocution more pleasant by adding fresh flowers. Certain flowers, she didn't know which ones, would trigger nightmares and she'd wake covered in sweat, heart pounding and with a general feeling of nausea. She could feel the electrodes dangling from her scalp like Medusa's snakes, smell the faintest hint of urine and the sweet musk of leather restraints.

The first time it happened, Nick didn't touch her immediately. He got out of bed and returned shortly with a glass of water and a damp cloth. Then, helping her peel out of her wet clothes, he covered her with a blanket.

"Just breathe," he whispered.

He held her hand until she stopped shaking. When she wanted more than his arms around her, he instinctively wrapped her in a gentle embrace and laid them both down. They molded and intertwined until it was impossible to tell where one ended and the other began. Without words, Nick pulled up the covers and they both went to sleep.

She smiled at the memory of it and found him watching her. His blue eyes found hers and she was momentarily lost in their pale depths.

"What are you thinking about?" Nick wanted to know as he pulled into the spot saved for the feature artist.

"I love you," she said.

Nick reached over, gently took her hand and raised it to his lips. "I love you too."

Something inside the gallery caught her eye and she turned to see David talking with someone. He was in a three-piece suit. She knew he'd worn that for her. That made her chest ache. It still made her sad that David was hopeful.

David

CHAPTER SIX

Emma was wearing a simple broom skirt and tunic top. Watching her get out of the car, assisted by Nick, I held my breath. Joanna shot across the gallery like a cannonball as soon as they made it through the door. There was a series of whispers and then a burst of applause when the patrons realized that the guest of honor had arrived.

Even in the simple outfit, she looked like a goddess. Was she glowing? Beside her, Nick stood tall and unreadable like a watchdog.

Joanna was telling her some good news. I could tell because her voice was up an octave and eyes teary. I couldn't hear and felt as though my feet had been stapled to the floor.

As though in slow motion, Emma turned and made eye contact. I straightened and prayed that my face would not betray the plethora of emotions rolling through me like a thunderstorm. I thought I'd faint when she excused herself from the throng of well-wishers and her escort and made her way toward me. She walked up smiling, tucked her hair behind her ear and touched my arm.

"It was so good of you to come."

Her words caught me off guard. She hadn't expected me. Before all the chaos, I was the only person she needed. Now, I was likened to a long-lost high school friend at a chance encounter.

"I wouldn't miss it," I stammered, immediately regretting it.

She smiled and cocked her head quizzically. "I've just received the best news. A benefactor wants to buy all of my paintings for children's hospitals all over the country," she could barely contain herself. "And Joanna has offered me the upstairs studio. You've been so good to let me use the one at," she paused, "your house. But working here will make shipping easier. My new buyer wants several custom pieces."

I knew I was staring blankly. The words were clear, but my brain would not register their meaning. Mercifully, she ignored my stupor and continued.

"I'll be by tomorrow to start moving."

She looked back and gave an upward nod to Nick and Joanna to signal she was wrapping up. Her eyes found mine and I wondered if there was any intent to hurt me, yet I found no malice in her golden gaze.

"Thank you so much for everything, David," she said, tiptoeing to kiss me on the cheek.

And, then she was gone. I watched her hustle off to Joanna, presumably to discuss the details of the sales. It was extraordinary news and I'd be happy for her at some point.

Nick and I looked like chess pieces. All the other patrons moved around us but firmly planted, we stood still. I was willing him to turn and walk out of my sight but instead watched him grab two beers and amble toward me. I didn't know what to do so I straightened my tie with one hand and reached for my trouser pocket with the other.

He handed me a beer without preamble like we were old friends. Then, passing a glance and grin in Emma's direction, he looked back at me and leaned in.

"I'm not used to this kind of shindig."

I couldn't speak, I couldn't hit this guy, and I wasn't sure I still had testicles. So, I drank. Nick went on.

"I have to go in early tomorrow. The club has a new water feature project and I'm behind."

Drinking and motionlessly dancing a jig, I nodded and hoped it would give me enough time to talk to her.

I excused myself and retreated out of the back door. She hadn't even noticed the suit.

Emma

CHAPTER SEVEN

S he was glad that Joanna was so hyper because it gave her a reason to leave David. It felt so awkward knowing he had worn the suit for her. He did look very handsome, but she knew if she commented it would only give him more false hope.

Aside from the awkward feeling, this was an amazing night. She still felt the heat from Nick's touch before they'd arrived, and the deal she was looking at was a fairy tale. She stared at the contract in disbelief. Everyone kept telling her that she'd worked so hard for this opportunity. She just nodded since she didn't remember that part either.

"I don't know what to say," she heard herself speaking.

"Hand me a pen would be a good start," Nick mused over her shoulder.

Joanna burst into laughter, mixed with anxiety. The gallery was getting thirty percent of this sale, which would be substantial.

"The buyer, Mr. Aroosian, will deal directly with you on the custom pieces. He will buy any pieces you don't sell tonight and any you have in your studio, sight unseen, for that price.

Emma thought briefly of the canvases she had at her studio. It was a decent body of work.

"Hand me a pen," she said, winking at Nick.

She signed the piece of paper and handed it to Joanna, who was trembling.

"Oh, honey, I knew you were something special the first time I laid eyes on your canvases."

Emma smiled. She hoped there were no questions attached to the sentiment. It was a terrible feeling when someone wanted to reminisce.

Luckily, the woman sat down at her desk and began hammering out an email in response to the elusive benefactor.

"He'll wire the money. Half when he gets my response and the other when you ship the rest."

She pressed send and looked up with tears in her eyes. "I cannot believe it. I thought my own paintings would make me wealthy. I hoped, at least," she said with some bitterness.

"Well, now you can start painting again. Your own work can still make you wealthy," Nick said.

Emma looked at him, unsure of his meaning.

"She and Sophie are planning to retire to the beach and maybe open a small place there. So, Sophie can sculpt, and Joanna can paint. Isn't that right?"

Joanna stood up and hugged them both. "I've been promising her this for so long. You probably don't remember that we almost sold the gallery last year, but now," she pulled back and looked at Emma, "your benefactor is going to buy this gallery as well. You'll be a resident artist, or at least paint here while you work on his custom pieces. I can finally afford to retire. Thank you."

Emma was genuinely moved, and she leaned in to squeeze the woman once more. She was glad that this deal had profited them as well. She was equally moved that Nick had taken such an interest and remembered the details of their upcoming venture. Thank goodness one of them could remember things.

Even after such a fantastic event, Emma was glad when they finally made it home. She didn't know if these social gatherings were always so taxing and wished she could remember the secret of getting through them. Their small space was solitary and welcoming.

The portly owner leased the place that had originally been built as an in-law apartment on the backside of the main house to Nick in exchange for groundskeeping. His landlord's elderly mother had died some years ago, which left no use for the space.

With a magnificent view of the city, the back of the house included a large deck, French doors, and a stone patio with fire pit. Just inside the French doors was a dining area that flowed into the kitchen. The surprisingly modern design boasted a galley kitchen with cheerful yellow cabinets and white counter tops. On the other end was a small but cozy den with a gas fireplace, built-in bookcases, and a picture window. The 46-inch flat-screen TV was mounted above the hearth.

From there, a wide hall opened to the single bedroom with a walk-in closet that led to the master bath. Clearly designed with a spa theme, the bathroom had an enormous shower. Inside the glass door was a built-in ledge that was big enough for two. The multiple shower heads guaranteed a satisfying shower whether you sat or stood. The floors were natural pine throughout the residence.

Nick had been living with an inflatable mattress, bean bag, and folding chairs. Without any argument, David let Emma take one of the sofas from the media room, a tall kitchen table with two chairs, and a bedroom suite.

The couple by-passed the kitchen and den and headed straight for the bedroom. Neither of them spoke as they got ready for bed. When they were finally in bed, Nick put his arms around her.

"I'm so proud of you, Emma. I don't guess I've ever paid much attention to art but I know when it's good. I'm so glad that you're getting the recognition you deserve."

"Thank you. I felt really bad that I couldn't remember people that came up to congratulate me. And Joanna," she paused to wiggle closer to Nick. "She's so sweet and maternal. I'm sorry I don't remember her."

"Don't beat yourself, Em. It's not your fault that your brain got electrocuted."

She laughed and turned over to face him. "You have such a way with words."

He studied her a long moment. "Don't be so hard on yourself. It gets easier and your memories will come back. But it's not your fault you can't remember them and if they genuinely care about you, they'll accept that."

"I love you," she said, snuggling in to his arms.

"Love you too, baby."

Later, with Nick sound asleep beside her, she should have been able to go to sleep too. Yet all she could think about was all the paintings in her studio at David's. Nick had to get up early to go to work and she didn't want to wake him. Emma knew she wasn't going to be able to sleep.

Slipping quietly out of bed, she pulled on her clothes and retrieved her purse. With any luck, David wouldn't even know she'd been there, and Nick wouldn't realize she'd been gone.

David

CHAPTER EIGHT

The night I arrived home to a dark house—that fateful night I will never be able to forget—followed a crisp autumn evening, a month after we lost our son. Like many nights before, I'd worked late because I didn't know how to act around her. I justified it as making up for the time I was off. Masking my grief was getting harder and I didn't want to upset her. I also didn't know how to comfort her, and she wasn't talking about it.

The drive home had been unremarkable and seemingly automatic since I didn't remember arriving. The dark house mocked me as I turned off the engine, and I cursed myself for not leaving lights on.

I was relieved that Emma had planned to go out with her girlfriends. It meant I could get a shower and relax without feeling like I was walking on eggshells. There were no lights on inside or outside but I wasn't alarmed until I saw the front door standing open.

The darkness beyond the blackened doorframe looked like something malevolent was lurking inside. Without thinking, I dashed inside and mentally began to battle every possible scenario.

I yelled for her as I sprinted through the first floor like a madman. No voice called out, and I slammed on lights as I went. Finding no evidence of her, I heaved open the back door and ran out to her studio but found the door locked.

Yelling again, I scrambled back into the house, tripping over the coffee table. It took my breath but the fear and adrenaline that she might be hurt propelled me to my feet. I shot up the stairs without any weapon other than terror. Our bedroom was the first on the right but I didn't find her there. Our photo albums were scattered and strewn everywhere, and this only fueled my fear. The guest room was next but I found no sign of her there either. Then, something caught my eye as I stood panting in the hallway.

The last door on the left was the nursery. Even with the curtains drawn, tiny fragments of light etched in from the street lights outside. Emma had painted a mural on every wall and the bright colors gave the nursery a peculiar glow. It was not that way tonight.

Before I stepped inside, I could smell fresh paint. The walls were solid black. Paint fumes were so strong they choked me and made my eyes water. When I turned on the light, it took a few minutes for my eyes to focus. All gone. All the scenes erased, as though some black hole had swallowed us up.

It was then that I saw her. Curled into a ball, she stared unblinking into the void. I rushed to her side, touched her, but got no reaction. Pleading her name, I stroked her cheek and tried to rouse her. Her skin was cool to the touch. I could tell she was breathing but there was no life in her eyes.

After hours in the ER, a squat bald man found me and grimly introduced himself as Dr. Jergensen. After a monotone litany of medical terms, he informed me that Emma had suffered a psychotic episode and was completely catatonic. His heavy accent would have been comical in any other circumstances.

"What can you do for her?" I asked, not really knowing if that was the right question.

"We'll admit her and watch her. We will keep her safe and calm." He tried to smile reassuringly.

"That's all?"

The doctor emitted a little laugh, though I wasn't sure if from nervousness or amusement.

"For now. We must give her time and see if she returns from the catatonia on her own. If not, other measures must be taken."

Without another word, he spun around and tottered off, leaving me to wonder if I'd offended him or if that was his regular bedside manner. It was then that the guilt hit me like an anvil and I crumpled to the floor. Only a few weeks after our baby had died, I had left her alone.

Days later, she still had not eaten, and only took small swallows of water if forced. She didn't speak but would look around. After a week, she'd lost considerable weight and had slipped back into staring without blinking.

Sitting across from Dr. Jergensen, I had a sense of foreboding that made the hair on my neck stand on end. The doctor looked like an owl that had been caught in a hurricane. Tufts of hair, including his heavy eyebrows, were sticking up, and his pale, hazel eyes were bloodshot.

"She will not eat or drink. She will not take medicine or sleep. We explain to her that she must do these things but there is no response."

As he droned on, I felt like I was slipping into catatonia myself. It was surreal. My Emma, my artist, who was always full of life, was now being described as the walking dead. Finally, the doctor sat forward and drew me out of my stupor.

"Mr. Campbell? Are you listening?"

Everything had slowed down and I felt like my words were wads of gum stuck in my throat. I nodded.

He began to describe the treatment. Electric Convulsive Treatment sounded like a method used by the CIA on terrorists. The little man explained that they would give Emma some anesthesia, place electrodes on her scalp, and apply a finely controlled electric current that would cause seizures.

"She might be confused afterwards and lose some of her memory but it's perfectly safe. It will bring her back to herself."

I consented. What else could I do? I wanted my wife back.

After the events at the exhibit and the memory of finding her in the dark house, I knew I would not sleep. I opened the front door and turned on every light on the way to my room and peeled out of the suit and tie. Depositing the dress clothes on the floor, I pulled on athletic wear and my running shoes.

One of our favorite parks was a few miles away. Emma and I liked to run or bike once or twice a week, and we often went there. It had a beautiful lake, track, picnic tables, and a playground. It wasn't gated or monopolized by any club or community and it usually wasn't full of people, despite being rimmed by houses.

Raising a cacophony of barking dogs as I passed, I ran hard up my street, across Highway 31 and onto the quaint alley that led to the park. I was fleeing my thoughts. The tight row of houses, with their cheerful porch lights, and the staccato of feet pounding against the pavement were dulling the ache in my chest and obliterating the images in my head.

When I stopped running, I was standing at the edge of the lake. I sat down, breathing hard, and watched the crescent moon's light dance flirtatiously on the dark face of the lake.

I could see that the ground was wet so I looked for a better place to sit. Darting through the obstacle course of slides, monkey bars and small plastic animals on springs, I found the swings. It was dark now, and the small oasis of trees surrounding this playground obscured the light from the moon and streets lights.

Just as I started to sit down, a voice from the dark nearly caused me to yell in fright.

"That one is broken."

I searched the darkness and finally locked onto a dark form a few swings down.

The frogs and crickets had camouflaged any sounds she might have made but I couldn't believe I hadn't seen someone only feet away.

"Thank you," I finally replied.

"You aren't meeting someone, are you?" Her voice was low, soft, and familiar, though I couldn't place a face with it. I noted her hesitation. My mind searched for scenarios she might be imagining.

"No," I said and sat down in another swing.

"Okay. Good. I usually don't see adults out here at night unless they're meeting someone."

"Does that happen a lot?" Admittedly, I was entrenched in suburbia and had no idea what went on in parks at night.

"Oh yeah. They meet up here and leave their cars or sit in the car and do whatever."

"I guess that makes sense if people are usually scarce at night."

"Usually," she added with a hint of amusement.

"I'm sorry. Are you meeting someone?" I asked.

"I'm not. Just needed to unwind some."

"Tough day?" I asked.

"Not particularly. Just busy."

Something in the rhythmic whine of the swings and evenness of her voice finally enabled me to breathe deeply. I could not place her voice yet, but I felt comfortable with her. As she sailed higher and higher, she drifted through patches of light and I strained my eyes to see her face.

"How about you?" she questioned during her ascension.

"It wasn't busy. Just…"

It had been years since I'd been on a swing, and the last time was with Emma. Was there nowhere I could go to escape her memory? Unable to join my mystery companion, I just sat there, suspended.

"Just what? Don't leave me hanging." Playful yet insistent.

"It was a hard day," I admitted without hesitation.

"I'm sorry."

"Thank you," I responded automatically. I pushed back and swung forward a few feet.

"It gets old, doesn't it?" It wasn't a question.

"What gets old?"

"The 'sorry your life sucks' responses," she said quietly.

Her candor caught me off guard and I laughed. "It really does."

"People mean well but it makes it feel like you're reliving it over and over."

"No one ever says 'good morning' but instead asks 'how are you' yet never expects me to say something good."

"I know, right? If you have a good day, then you're doing something wrong because no one expects you to have good days."

She stopped swinging. We sat still in silence for a moment.

"I'm looking forward to the good days if those even exist anymore," I said, slightly ashamed to admit my lack of hope.

"Did she leave you or die?"

That made me chuckle though I didn't know why. None of this was funny.

"Both, I think."

She pondered for a second. "Mine died but I know what you mean. He'd already left in so many ways."

I wanted to say I was sorry but we had already covered that. Instead, I turned in her direction trying to uncloak her face from the shadows.

"How did you cope?"

"I went on with my life. It was hard and I cried a lot. If I didn't want to cheer up, I let myself experience my emotions. He was the one who'd died after all. I had to live. Plus, I had a baby who would never know his daddy. I had to be both parents."

That last sentence struck me in the chest like an arrow. I was a daddy who would never know his son. I knew I'd have to go on. Emma wasn't dead but all we had died with our child. Everything we'd dreamed of was gone in an instant. The world had spiraled into oblivion and we could do nothing to stop its unraveling.

"Thank you for listening," I said, suddenly aware that I'd been quiet for a long moment. "I don't even know your name," I added.

"It's Kellyn."

I suddenly remembered why she felt familiar.

"Like Helen with a K," I recalled.

"Or Kevin with an L," she replied.

This was the exact opposite of our first conversation.

"I wondered what happened to you when someone else was assigned our account," she said simply.

I floundered with words. Only moments ago, I'd been talking to a stranger on a swing. Now, there was a brief moment of history I felt I needed to explain.

Months ago, the managing partner at my firm had approached me with a low-maintenance account for a local bank. It was two weeks before Emma miscarried. I was not excited, but Bruce assured me that it was an easy account. I consented and met with the bank president, Kellyn, a branch manager, and two assistants.

Emma teased me that morning, saying that my wardrobe was void of color, and picked out a tie with pastel blues, greens, and pink to spruce up my otherwise dismal navy suit.

As I walked into the bank, I felt self-conscious about the choice.

Kellyn Frost introduced herself and we had the awkward conversation about her name. I was instantly drawn to her eyes, which were such a pale gray I wondered if they might glow in the dark.

As I was meeting her team, she whispered, "Nice tie."

"It's too much, isn't it?"

"No, it's a breath of fresh air," she responded, further reassuring me with a hand on my arm.

During the meeting, I had a hard time meeting her eye but couldn't resist looking at her. She wore her red hair down and the ringlet curls framed her face perfectly. When she wasn't moving, she looked like a painting.

Hours later, after we'd closed the deal, I went for a run. I'm not sure if I was running to or away from something. Ever since Emma and I married, I'd never been so mesmerized by another woman. She was powerful and intelligent, confident but still kind. Looking into her eyes was like looking into the galaxy, and I wasn't sure she couldn't read my mind.

I was so entranced by the memory that I wound up at this same park and had literally almost run into her as I looked back, surprised by my destination.

She skewered me with those pale eyes as I clumsily apologized for almost knocking her down.

"Miss me, did you?"

"I did. So I ran right over."

We laughed for five minutes and every time she touched my arm, I felt lightning run through my body. Our encounter in the park hadn't lasted long, as I suddenly felt I should run home to Emma.

Kellyn stayed on my mind for days after, and Emma even mentioned that I seemed distracted. It made me feel guilty and wrong. I even wondered if all that happened later was punishment for my stray thoughts.

Realizing I'd been silent for several minutes, I shrugged.

"We gotta stop meeting like this."

She laughed. "Or you might need to take up rowing instead of running. I told you everyone meets in the park."

We both laughed and she stood up.

"I have an early meeting tomorrow."

"Me too," I lied and hoisted myself up.

We walked in the direction I'd run from and I finally saw her face. Her square jaw and high cheek bones were regal and beautiful. She'd swept her long hair into a ponytail and I could see the red and gold strands mixed with a darker russet. The yoga pants and t-shirt did not hide her curves. We stood there for a moment listening to the cacophony of night minstrels, smelling the sweet earthy evening air.

"I'm glad to see you, David," she said and hugged me.

"We'll have to do this again."

She giggled. "I'm here a lot."

I wanted to tell her that I hoped to see her again.

"Where is your car?" I asked instead. There were no cars on this side of the parking lot.

"I live right over there," she pointed at the darkened row of houses that lined the park, but I couldn't tell which one.

"Okay, well, I'll run along then. Good to see you, Kellyn."

She smiled briefly. "Meet you next time."

I watched her until she was across the street and then turned toward my own home. I could still feel the warmth of her embrace and it should have made me feel better.

Instead, I felt anger and confusion. I never considered my life with any other woman. The softness of her body and smell of her hair had no place in my mind. They were different from Emma's hyacinth and jasmine musk. I didn't know how to process the lavender I'd detected.

It was nearly midnight when I got home. In addition to the lights I had left on, the backyard was lit up like a county fair. I headed from the front door to the rear French doors that led to the studio.

I could see the door to Emma's studio wide open and even caught a glimpse of her.

I figured she couldn't sleep and was reasonably sure she was alone. Taking up a bottle of her favorite pinot grigio from the fridge and two glasses, I walked out the door.

Emma

CHAPTER NINE

E mma was glad that there were so many paintings. Leafing through them, she pulled out the ones she wanted to add to her new client's collection. She dismissed the landscapes and flowers. Since Solomon Aroosian was only interested in the ones with children, she would put the others in the gallery.

A sound startled her and she looked up to see David standing in the doorway with a bottle of wine and two glasses. He was in sweats and running shoes, the telltale sweat stains on his chest and pits.

"I'm guessing I didn't wake you," she smiled.

"No. I just got home and saw the lights. How did the exhibit go?"

"We sold a few of the smaller ones but I can't really be upset since my new client bought all the rest." She heard the giddiness in her own voice and realized how badly she wanted to talk to someone.

"Wow. That's great, Em," David said, setting the wine and glasses on the bar. "We should celebrate."

Emma watched him open a drawer and remove the corkscrew. His movements were so precise, and she was momentarily enamored with the muscles in his forearms. Silently, she watched him pour the wine and hand her a glass.

"Thank you," she said accepting the glass.

"To you," he toasted.

"I'm pulling out all the ones with kids. Wanna help me?"

"Sure," he said and set his glass on the counter.

"Oh, I love this one," he said, holding up a painting of a little girl feeding her cotton candy to an elephant.

"I remember that day," she mused.

Her family had gone to a zoo that had elephant rides. She'd begged her father for an elephant ride but Bob Roberts was hung over from a bender and staunchly refused. Emma was sent to the car after she started to cry. From there, she watched a pretty girl with long brown hair lose her cotton candy to a large elephant with an obvious sweet tooth. The little girl with the bright blue ribbon in her hair cried at the loss of her treat but Emma laughed. The elephant looked as though it was smiling. The image had stayed in her mind for years after. Ironically, the painting was really about the elephant rather than the girl but that didn't matter now. Most people only saw the children.

"How many do you have?" David said from the next aisle.

"I'm not sure."

"I forgot you painted it," he said as he lifted another painting.

Emma watched him as he studied it intently. He turned it for her to see.

The painting was of David's childhood treehouse. David and Emma had spent many hours in that wooden refuge and it was one of the first places she ever felt safe.

"You should keep it."

David silently carried the canvas over and set it down against the bar like it was fragile. Emma could tell he was moved and turned her head to give him a moment.

"Where is Nick?" he asked simply.

She turned her attention to a whole section of canvases set in Europe. Emma wasn't sure why he was asking but she didn't detect any hostility in his voice.

"He has to get up early so he's at home asleep. I was too excited to sleep so I came alone."

She saw him bristle some over the word 'home', but he said nothing. Instead, he crossed to the bar and picked up the bottle to refresh their drinks.

"Thank you," she said, noticing his eyes travel over her.

In the last few months, she felt uncomfortable when David looked at her the way he was now. Maybe it was the wine or the fact that he looked ruggedly handsome, but she liked the feeling of his gaze gliding over her exposed skin.

"I'm so happy for you," he started. "You've worked so hard and I'm glad to see this happen."

"I know you've helped me get here and I appreciate you." She touched his arm.

He blushed and shook his head. "You're amazingly talented so you'd be here regardless."

"Well, thank you anyway." She paused. "For everything."

He carried his glass over and refilled it, holding the bottle up to see if she wanted more. She could already feel the effects so shook her head.

For the next few hours, they amassed quite a collection. Since she didn't remember painting them, it was easier to assess them based on the quality. David knew all the stories about the places or events that had inspired them.

"What about this one?" David asked, draining his glass and holding up the image of a boy piloting a small, motorized sailboat.

"That one is a keeper."

"We were in Holland when you did this one. The boy's name was Bram and he gave us a lesson on sailing."

"He must've been adorable," she replied regretfully.

"It was fun until his batteries died and I had to wade into the cold water after the boat."

David was getting somewhat clumsy. Emma was glad when he took a seat and watched her. She wasn't sure what she saw in his face.

"Was it really cold?"

"Cold and full of duck shit. I had to throw my shorts away."

They both laughed until she noticed how he was looking at her. She could tell from his face that he was about to say something she didn't want to hear.

"I love your laugh," he said, his eyes fixed on her.

She wasn't sure what to say so she smiled.

"Em, I—" He stopped dead, his eyes widening and focusing on something behind her.

She saw his eyes catch fire and turned to see Nick standing in the doorway. He was barefoot and shirtless, his long hair mussed from sleep.

"Babe, what are you doing here?"

He smiled that crooked smile that made his dimples more noticeable.

"Sorry to interrupt. I woke up and saw the time. Thought I'd come check on you."

She walked over, despite the arrows David's glare was launching, and put her arms around him.

"Looks like I'm missing a party," Nick said, laughing.

"David has been telling me stories about all my paintings."

She looked up at Nick and saw nothing but sincerity in his face. He wasn't threatened by her hanging with David.

"Sounds fun," Nick said softly.

A loud crash behind her startled them both. David had obviously tried to jump off his stool but the wine had long since stolen his balance. Nick rushed to help.

"Oh, hey man, let me give you a hand."

David, still grappling with gravity, pushed Nick's aid away.

"I'm fine," he roared and pushed himself erect.

"David." Emma started toward him.

"Congratulations, Em," he bellowed and gathered the treehouse painting and the wine bottle. "I'll just see myself home."

Emma watched him, worried and feeling guilty. As though Nick had read her mind, he trailed after David. She had never met anyone so willing to help and so completely unabashed by hostility. She watched them go. David's aggression made her feel small and she wanted no more drama.

David

CHAPTER TEN

Everything had been going so well that I'd forgotten about Nick and Kellyn. For just a brief time, it was like the last few months had just been a bad dream. Then, Nick showed up and ruined it. I was livid and my limbs were denying my simple desire for removing myself from the studio with dignity. She basically described us as two old friends hanging out. I had felt something genuine between us but once again it proved to be only me feeling it.

"Damnit," I said aloud.

I felt so stupid, and even more so as I trudged along like a zombie scarecrow. How many bottles had I had? I remembered returning to the house once or twice.

A hand touched my shoulder. "Whoa there, friend. Let me help you."

To my utter amazement, I whirled around and did not fall. Nick stood before me, smiling, his hands out toward me.

"You asshole. Do you have any idea what you've done? That woman," I pointed toward the studio, "is MY wife. You don't know her like I do."

I was yelling and I didn't care who heard me. He bobbed his head without taking his eyes off me. To add to insult to injury, he never stopped smiling, which was making me homicidal.

"You got me there, man. You have known her longer and have so much history. But let me ask you one question. Are you sure that the woman you know is the real Emma?"

I stared at him. Seconds ago, I wanted to kill him. Now, through the spinning feeling and spots in my eyes, all I could do was stare at him. Even in the expanding fog, my brain was screaming. What if he was right?

What if I had never known the real Emma? He started toward me and I clutched my painting. It was the last and only thing I had of us, and I'd be damned if I let him touch it.

"Let me carry that for you and help you into the house," he said.

I think I actually screamed like a child for him not to touch me and whirled back to make a dash for the deck. Before I knew it, I tripped over those logs I'd been meaning to move. It happened so fast but in slow motion.

I heard a snap, followed by something that sounded like fabric ripping. The pain that came next felt like someone had just shoved a torch into my side. Maybe I was the proverbial Adam and God was taking the rib back.

Then, the darkness came and the last thing I heard was Emma calling my name.

I can't say I woke. Consciousness slithered in like a snake stalking its prey and I became aware of sounds and smells. The pain in my side was pulsing and was unforgiving of even the slightest movement. It hurt to breathe, and the weight of my body in the bed radiated the ache through my entire torso.

I knew I was in the hospital but the rest was a blur. The smell of industrial cleaner and juice almost gagged me, though the thought of puking made me shudder. The smell was taking me back to the day Emma miscarried.

After receiving a phone call that Emma had collapsed, I'd raced to the hospital. My panic must've been apparent because random strangers guided me into the ER waiting room. The older receptionist buzzed me through the door and I stood there unsure of what to expect. The next few moments were seared into my brain.

The nurse led me back into the myriad of examination rooms, with their white curtains and metal cabinets. The place smelled like industrial cleaner, and varying degrees of groans rang out.

The doctor wore light green scrubs and was waiting at the end of the hall, hands perched on his hips like a school principal. I was struggling to breathe. He held his hand out as I approached.

"Mr. Campbell, I'm Dr. Lovitz." He shook my hand without any warmth. "I'm afraid I'm the bearer of bad news. Your wife has suffered a miscarriage. Has she been pregnant before?"

"No." I paused. "This was our first. Where is Emma?"

"She's in surgery now with my associate, Dr. Bellows."

"This can't be happening," I mumbled. "She was fine this morning."

Standing in the hall of the emergency room, I stared at the doctor blankly.

"It was a boy," he said. "She's going to be fine. A little sore and traumatized but health-wise she's okay," the doctor continued, looking at his watch as though he had something more important to attend.

We spent the night in the hospital with a view of the mall. Emma was heavily sedated and slept most of the night. I couldn't sleep at all. The smell of the cleaner on top of the gravity of losing our baby made me feel nauseated most of the night.

Even the nausea felt the same. Then and now. So much had changed and yet so much was still the same. Fighting the urge to vomit, I opened my eyes slowly. I was expecting the sterile, white walls and a mounted TV like they had been in Emma's room. The blinds were drawn and the room chilled. My heart leapt at the sight of Emma curled up on a tiny loveseat a few feet away. Like Icarus, I had a few seconds of warmth and elation. Then, my heart plummeted in my chest when I looked to my right and saw Nick sitting in the chair beside me. Why wouldn't this guy go away? At least he had a shirt on, I thought bitterly.

I lay there thinking about his question. The thought that I'd been married for thirteen years to a woman that I didn't know haunted me. It sounded like a bad cable drama.

There was a sound to my right, and I turned too quickly to see a nurse in the doorway. The pain ricocheted through me like a bullet. Nausea overpowered the pain and I felt the vomit welling up like lava. I must have groaned and cinched my eyes so tight that my eyelids felt like they were turning inside out. A voice in my ear and hand on my arm distracted me.

"Breathe through your mouth. Slowly. It will pass," Nick said.

I was in too much pain and on the verge of oblivion to fight. I followed his instructions as the nurse checked my vitals. He was massaging my shoulder as the nurse administered something into my IV.

"Is there a urinal?" I asked her, ignoring the image of Nick standing behind me at the toilet.

She nodded and handed me a small plastic jug. Thrusting the device under the covers and hoping it was aligned, I released the flow. Nick had stopped touching me and had moved away to afford me a shred of privacy. He sat back, chatting with the nurse called Sarah. They were talking about me but none of it registered.

"You're very lucky," Sarah was saying as she collected the urine.

"Oh?"

"Dude, you almost stabbed yourself in the heart," Nick responded.

"What?" I said but the memories were flooding back.

Apparently when I tripped and fell the bottle struck something and broke. The broken edge sliced open my side, the weight of my body split the wooden frame of the painting, and then the busted frame impaled me.

"What happened to my painting?" I asked, my heart hurting more from its loss than my self-administered staking.

"I'll paint you another one," I heard a soft voice from the foot of my bed. Her golden eyes were soft and warm.

I had spent so much time in the loving glow of her gaze but now it radiated pity. It was just as well that my last tie to her was ruined. The realization that she was never coming home, never returning to normal, and might not even be the woman I thought I knew felt like an elephant on my chest. I was glad when the drug started working and I couldn't keep my eyes open anymore.

Emma

S he had gone to find coffee and call David's partner, Bruce. The events of the past 48 hours had taken a toll.

Nick had been great, helping without being asked. Despite the fact that David growled any time Nick came near him, Nick never complained.

They took turns staying with David, leaving and going to work, and then returning. Even if they won the lottery, Nick would still work. He left earlier, installed the new water feature, and returned energized. She understood how it kept his head clear. Working did the same for her, and she was glad when it was her turn to get her paintings packed and crated.

Walking down the hallway with her coffee, she smiled at the nurses quietly perched like owls in their station. They all smiled back but she felt some judgment from them.

When she told the medical staff that she was David's wife, she didn't offer any explanation as to who Nick was. The judgment and speculation felt like a backpack full of rocks. Nick wasn't hampered by inquiries as to his relationship to her or the patient. He didn't feel the need to set the record straight and would just smile if someone asked. Emma, on the other hand, had no patience for nosey people. They were always there to ask questions but were only listening for the answers they'd already guessed.

Turning the last corner to David's room, she spotted a woman outside the door. Her black pencil shirt was stretched across her generous ass like a sail in a hurricane. She wore a silver, sequined top, and as she turned her body Emma recognized the giant breasts.

Something happened in Emma's brain. She couldn't hear the sound of synapses firing but, as the memories flooded back, she knew they had.

They were at a Christmas party. Suzanne Devlin was decked out in a slutty Mrs. Claus costume and kept making references to "real women" and their curves. Emma was a B cup at best. It wasn't hard to decipher the passive-aggressive attack on her womanhood. Every time Suzanne spoke, she looked over at David. It was hard to fathom a woman so brass that she was making passes at her husband before her eyes. At the end of the party, much to David's distress, the woman seized him under the mistletoe and kissed him. Everyone except David and Emma had laughed.

Emma couldn't say it hurt physically to remember but the emotions that cascaded through her body felt like razor blades. She didn't have to remember everything to know that David despised this woman. How dare she show up when he was the most vulnerable?

Charging in like a lioness, Emma jammed herself between Suzanne and David's door.

"You are not welcome here," she spoke without preamble.

Suzanne met her defiance with a cruel grin. "Neither are you, I imagine."

Momentarily taken aback, Emma wondered if her being here was causing David more pain. She recovered quickly, realizing that this woman was a practiced narcissist. She was nothing more than a bully, like Emma's father had been.

The memories were still coming back and she recalled the moment that Suzanne bragged about speaking fluent French. Unaware that Emma was also bilingual, Suzanne declared in French that she'd have David in her bed before the year was out. The crowd laughed at the novelty of foreign words without meaning. When Emma responded in French that David's flat-chested partner would keep him so busy he wouldn't have time to leave the bed at home, Suzanne's eyes almost exploded out of her face.

"Perhaps you will understand if I tell you in French," Emma growled, gripping the doorknob as she pushed closer to Suzanne.

"Oh, so you're protecting him now. That's generous, since your leaving has devastated him," the woman snarled.

"What happens between me and David is none of your concern, you pathetic slut. He doesn't want to see you, and I'll call security if you step one inch closer."

Emma waited for it. Her body was trembling from emotional exertion but it felt good.

In flawless French, she whispered how they had laughed all the way home when they'd left the Christmas party and how David had literally washed his mouth with soap when they got home.

Suzanne turned so quickly that she almost toppled over. As she huffed down the hallway like a hippo in heels, Emma called after her in a pleasant tone.

"Don't come back."

Suzanne shot her a bird but kept walking.

Emma watched the woman turn the corner and then quietly opened David's door. To her surprise, he was awake and staring in her direction.

"Oh hey, I'm sorry. Did I wake you?"

He smiled weakly. "I sensed a disturbance in the force."

This made them both laugh and David clutched his side. When the laughter subsided, he asked her if she would help him up.

"The nurse told me I have to get up and walk around."

"Oh Davy, I'm not sure I can hold you up if you start to fall. Maybe we should wait for the nurse or—" She stopped herself.

"Or Nick?" he squeezed through clamped teeth.

David rolled onto his good side so he could slide his leg off the mattress like the nurse had showed him. Emma watched him slowly edge the other leg off and then prop himself up on his elbow. He used his forearm to stabilize as he pushed himself upright. Emma darted forward and took a position on his wounded side just as he stood up.

"Where do you want to go?" she asked, hoping he'd forgotten about her hesitation. The ECT had taken away her filter and she hated that she often said whatever she was thinking.

"Right now, I want to pee," he said and took hold of the IV pole.

They moved slowly into the small bathroom, her maneuvering the pole as David leaned on the door frame to get into position. She mused over the gap in the hospital gown and his exposed buttocks. With some difficulty, he yanked up the front of the gown and relieved himself. Emma kept close enough to stabilize him if he started to fall but far enough to afford him some privacy.

He finished his business and washed his hands without speaking, then dried them without looking at her. She noticed he carefully averted his eyes, and when he turned ignored her outstretched hand. Instead, he reached for the IV pole and made his way out of the bathroom toward the door.

"It was really nice of you and Nick to stay with me. I'm sure you have more important things to do."

Emma felt a pang in her chest. There was an edge to his voice that she didn't recognize. It was important that David accept the situation. She wasn't sure that the coldness in his tone was acceptance or something else.

"I don't have anything to do right now. Let me walk with you."

Emma helped him negotiate the exterior door, unplugging the IV just in time. Then, she pulled the gown together and retied it so he wouldn't flash everyone in the hall.

She took his hand. He stiffened but didn't rip his hand away. They walked in silence.

They'd held hands through the entire summer as children. She remembered so distinctly their fingers interlaced and her dragging him off on adventures. Now, there was no warmth or comradery. She couldn't blame him for his anger. The cold was painful.

CHAPTER TWELVE

T he first time Emma held my hand was in my tree house. We didn't talk much but instead stared out at the dotted lights on the hills of Mission Bay. It felt innocent and exhilarating at the same time. After that, she would take my hand for no reason and we'd walk along without any sense of time or urgency.

Our walk in the polished hallways of the hospital did not feel like that.

We walked for nearly an hour, every movement painful and me pushing through it determined to show her and whoever was looking that I was strong. Afterwards, I collapsed into bed and accepted the offer of pain meds from the perky nurse named Brittany. Emma sat in the chair where Nick had slept and chatted with me as I drifted off.

I woke hours later hoping to have a few moments with Emma. I felt bad for not telling her that I appreciated her help earlier.

The hand holding mine was not soft, nor small. I opened my eyes to find Nick dozing beside me in the chair. He roused as I attempted to withdraw my hand.

"You kept calling out," was his explanation.

"Thanks," I growled.

I looked around but Emma was gone.

"She went to the gallery. Anxious about getting everything packed and shipped."

"What did you mean the other night?"

He shifted in his chair, taking a moment to pull his hair into a ponytail, using the holder he always had on his wrist. I could see him searching for words.

"Before my motorcycle crash, I was a different person. I was an athlete and wanted to play pro ball. After my head injury, I didn't care about football anymore. Remembering things was a challenge and trying to remember things under pressure was too stressful. I began to look for things that required a slower pace."

"I get having to adapt. You asked me if I knew the real Emma. That is different than adaptation."

He smiled. "True. After something like that, you have to adapt. But sometimes during that process, you peel back layers and find that you've become something you never really wanted to be. For me, slowing down helped me see that I wanted the football thing to win my dad's approval. That had been his dream, not mine."

"So, you're saying that Emma peeled back the layers and realized I didn't belong? If that is true, how did we make it thirteen years?"

"Look, man," he started again. "I'm not saying she didn't love you or that I'm better than you. I'm just saying that, whether from necessity or circumstances, maybe she suppressed who she really was and became something else. After ECT, her brain restarted and took her back to her true self."

"Why are you here?" It was more of an expletive than a question.

"We didn't want you to be alone. Emma still cares for you."

"Still cares? Well, that's great," I replied dryly.

Nick sighed and stood up.

"You want me to go?"

Before I could answer, the doctor knocked on the open door and came in. He was short and frumpy, in a wrinkled white coat. He looked to be in his fifties, wore thick glasses, and had a bad combover.

"Hi, David. How are we feeling today?"

"I'm good. Better."

"Have you been able to move your bowels?"

The doctor was writing on a small pad and looked up over the top of his glasses, expectant. Nick had sat back down and I could see him out of the corner of my eye. There was no preserving my dignity.

"Yes, last night," I forced myself to respond.

"What about today?"

"Yes, this morning," I lied.

"Excellent. I am thinking we'll let you get out of here."

"Great. When?" I said finally.

The doctor laughed and finished a note. "As soon as they can unhook you. I've written some prescriptions for pain and an antibiotic."

Then, he turned to Nick. "Will your partner be taking you home?"

Nick nodded, ignoring the reference. "Yes sir."

"Okay, good. There is a pharmacy on the main level so you can get this before you leave."

He turned back to me, ignoring my horror at the exchange between him and Nick. "If you have any problems, call us. Follow up with your primary doctor in a week. Do you have any questions now?"

I shook my head, still hoping this was a bad dream.

"Okay, Mr. Campbell. Take care and stay off the bottles." Then, he turned and left.

"Hey, man, that's great. Sleeping in your own bed will feel like paradise after being in the hospital."

Nick stepped into the hall and, from his tone, I knew he was talking to Emma on the phone. The nurse pushed past him and came in without a knock.

"Alrighty, Mr. Campbell. I have your discharge papers and prescriptions. I also have some pain meds for the ride home." She set everything on the tray and began messing with the tubing. I watched her in silence as she shot the meds into the IV. "I'll be back in a few and get you out of all this."

Nick stuck his head in the door as the nurse left.

"So Em is in the middle of something but will meet us at your place. I'm going to run get your meds so there won't be any delay."

I nodded. "My wallet." I pointed in the direction I felt my clothes might be.

"Don't worry about it. I'll be back in a bit."

The meds were already working and I watched him go in silence. The world seemed to spin slower and things sounded more acute but farther away. I closed my eyes and opened them again to find both the nurse and Nick had returned.

"There you go. Now," she turned to Nick with a stack of papers. "Let me get you to sign here and initial there."

Nick did, or I thought he did. It was hard to keep the minutes in chronological order. They concluded their business and both turned to me.

"Mr. Campbell, hospital transport services should be here in a minute."

Later, Nick and a young woman named Abigail helped me into a wheelchair. I complied with everything they asked, although my timing was delayed. The fog was expanding and the confusion came with it. They set a bag in my lap, and it took me nearly the entire ride to realize that inside were my clothes. Something in the bag was buzzing, and I was sure I was hallucinating when I retrieved my phone and saw the screen read "mother".

Emma

CHAPTER THIRTEEN

She sat on an empty crate with a glass of wine and watched the last of her paintings being loaded up. All morning she had packed and directed others, and she felt exhausted. Her back hurt from lifting but she loved the new space. There was natural light and the air smelled faintly of lavender and lemon.

Nick had called to say that David was being discharged. She was glad but the cold shoulder from the last visit had left her not wanting to face him. He would probably be in a foul mood and she didn't want to feel all the negativity. There was no choice, though, and she resigned herself to being at that house. It felt heavy there but she knew David had no one to help him.

On the bright side, she still had a few things to get from David's studio. She'd decided to leave the furniture since the new studio was furnished, and hoped that David would be glad.

Tidying up, she left the glass in the sink and corked the wine. The new studio had a full kitchen. Joanna and Sophie had stocked the fridge and pantry before they left for Florida. The entire top floors of the building were both studio and living space. She now had the run of the place but she wouldn't use it. Nick wouldn't want to move. He needed outdoor space to work on his projects and this location only had a small fenced parking lot in back. There was no grass, and Nick wouldn't feel comfortable without something green.

The drive to David's was quick and she got there in time to help get the patient up to bed. He could walk but was heavily drugged. Nick had his arm around him, so Emma ran up to get the door.

David looked startled when she popped up in front of him. There was no sign of anger, and he even smiled.

"My mother called," he said with a goofy smile.

Her first memory of David's mother was of her in a drunken rage. She wore a long, flowing nightgown and robe. Her long hair was loose and hung to her shoulders. She looked like a movie star in an old film and Emma remembered thinking that she was beautiful.

Most children would have been frightened when Lexie Campbell began throwing vases and books at David's father. Emma was fascinated. Most of the objects thrown simply crashed to the floor without ever reaching their intended victim. She was yelling but even her words were not that damaging. When Emma turned, she saw David crying and looking horrified. Emma didn't understand his distress. Her own father was far worse.

David yelled when Nick accidentally touched his wounded side trying to negotiate the stairs. It pulled her out of her stupor. She ran to help.

"Why did she call?"

David looked at her. A moment ago he was yelling in pain but his face was now full of some inner amusement. "I don't know. I didn't answer."

Emma simply nodded. She was reasonably sure the woman's demeanor had not improved over the years.

They helped David into bed. Nick set his meds on the chest of drawers, along with the paperwork. He told her he'd already set alarms on his phone so they'd know when it was time to give David his pain pills.

David was asleep as soon as his head touched his pillow.

Emma rushed over to hug Nick.

"Hey, beautiful," he said quietly and kissed her.

She sank into the warmth of him. His body was almost pure muscle but she'd decided the softness and warmth she always found in his arms came from his heart.

"I think you are wonderful. Thank you for all you've done."

"No worries. I was glad to help."

They crept out and headed for the studio. Once outside, Nick turned to her and kissed her passionately. Emma felt the kiss all the way to her toes. When they parted, she looked up at him.

Nick smiled, his eyes sparkling. "I missed you."

Emma stroked his face. "I missed you too."

Something caught Nick's eye and he turned, frowning. Emma searched to see what had caused that reaction.

"I'll get rid of those logs."

She followed his eye line and saw the troublemaking pile of logs. Broken glass and blood still littered the ground. Emma watched as Nick collected the half-shattered bottle and pieces of glass, and then deposited them in an empty trash can. He then collected all the logs and took them to the back alley where the city would pick them up. He returned shortly dusting dirt and debris from his clothes.

"What do you have left in the studio?"

"Not much. I'll take the rest of the paintings to the gallery." She shrugged.

A few hours later, after taking turns checking on David, they had loaded all the remaining supplies, trash, and paintings she was moving to the new gallery. Ironically, since her new client had bought all her paintings with children, her other pieces were selling like hotcakes.

Nick was sweeping. She wanted to leave it spotless and usable for David. After cleaning the bathroom, emptying the refrigerator, and wiping down the countertops, Emma was satisfied.

She sent Nick to the gallery to start unloading. It was time for David's meds so she headed upstairs.

He was asleep, and for a moment looked like the little boy she knew. Emma didn't want to wake him but she had no choice.

"Davy," she said, shaking his arm.

He was slow to open his eyes but finally focused on her.

"Hey, sleeping beauty," she smiled. "It's time for your pain meds. The doctor said you needed to stay on top of them."

"Did you just call me Davy?" His voice was low and laden with sleep.

"I did. Is that wrong?"

He shook his head. "You haven't called me that in a long time."

"Can you sit up a little and take this pill?"

She'd already collected his medicine and gotten out the next dose. Emma watched as David forced himself into a seated position and took the pill from her. Handing him the glass of water that Nick had left earlier, she felt guilty that she hadn't helped him sit up. She also realized that they couldn't stay with him as much as they had so far. He was going to have to do things for himself. She felt guilty about this too.

"Thank you," he said, and set the glass beside the bed.

"You're welcome."

Emma decided to sit with him until he went back to sleep. Nick made sandwiches earlier and wrapped them so that David would have something to eat. She checked the alarms on his phone one more time and set a note on the bedside table.

It was cowardly on her part. As soon as he was out, Emma slipped out of the room and down the stairs. She hoped he would find the note and that might soften being left alone.

David

CHAPTER FOURTEEN

A loud buzzing jerked me awake and the sudden movement took my breath. It was a struggle but I finally reached the phone and turned the alarm off. There was a note beside the phone in Emma's handwriting.

Still groggy, I attempted to focus on the delicate cursive. It always started out smooth and artistic and then got choppy as she began to hurry. This time the message was short.

If you need us, call and we will come. There are sandwiches in the fridge. The alarms on your phone are set for the intervals you need to take your meds.

I scrunched up the paper and threw it across the room. It was not like I expected her to confess her love and stay. The "us" part made me feel nauseated. I felt stupid all over again. When had I become so pathetic?

As much as it hurt to get up, I had to pee and find something to eat. The meds made me groggy and unsteady so I had to hug the wall as I made my way downstairs. Finally, in the kitchen, I found several sandwiches just as her note had described. I opted for a half-eaten blueberry bagel, cream cheese, and a packet of instant oatmeal.

As I was mixing the oatmeal, I noticed that the door to Emma's studio was closed and the lights were off. Gathering my freshly toasted bagel slathered with cream cheese and the container of oatmeal, I went to the French doors and let myself out. I didn't have anything to hold onto and I was sure I looked like a toddler staggering across the yard. The pile of logs was gone.

"Thanks, Nick," I sneered aloud.

The door squeaked as it opened. At Emma's insistence, we'd purchased the barn door from an estate sale. Even with new hardware, it always made noise. The door grumbled and moaned, which was the exact reaction I had when I flipped on the lights.

I stood dumbfounded surveying the emptiness. She'd left the furniture and coffee maker but all her supplies, clutter, empty water bottles, and paintings were gone. There was something on the counter so I tottered over to see.

A single sheet of paper and set of keys sat on the marble counter. I set my food down and sat on one of the stools. I wasn't sure I wanted to read the note that came with the set of keys because it seemed so final. Taking a bite of my bagel, I picked up the sheet and forced myself to read.

David, I really hope you will make this your new "treehouse" and use this space for something you love. Thank you for everything. Come see me at the new studio when you feel up to it. E

I was grateful that there was no 'us' reference. Sitting there in the clean, empty studio, I ate all of my food feeling slightly nauseated. It had been my intention to stop taking my pain pills as soon as possible because they knocked me out. Right now, I couldn't think of any state I'd rather be in than complete oblivion.

Grabbing the keys and my trash, I labored back into the house. I didn't bother to close the barn door behind me. There was nothing in there to steal, unless someone wanted to cart off an expensive expresso machine or the 800 lb. Italian leather sofa and chair. I didn't care. No, it was more than that. I was furious. Literally tossing my plate into the sink, I headed back to my room.

Hauling my meds, phone, pillow, and a glass of water, I headed for the guest room. I understood all the mechanics of her treatment. It wasn't her fault she couldn't remember 'us'—the original 'us'. But how could she not realize that the references to her new relationship were not immensely painful for me? Why would she continually mention them? Was she rubbing it in my face? The Emma I had known would have considered my feelings. Maybe the Conan the Barbarian lookalike was right. Maybe I didn't know her if this was the real Emma.

I took my pain pills and set everything on the bedside table in the guest room. Gingerly, I eased myself down onto the daybed and pulled the comforter over me. It felt like anger was boiling out of me like a swarm of bees. Right now, I didn't want to think of her or us or them. I also didn't want to sleep in THAT room or THAT bed where I'd declared daily that I'd give anything to stay in it all day with her.

Instead, I wondered if I'd see Kellyn soon and let the medicine carry me into darkness.

Emma

CHAPTER FIFTEEN

She felt accomplished as she surveyed the gallery.

After a few more chores, she headed upstairs to her new studio. She wondered how David was doing and if he'd found her notes. Her phone began to buzz and she wondered if it might be him calling.

It was Nick and she answered cheerfully.

"Hey, babe."

"Hey, beautiful."

"I'm almost done here. Should I pick up something for dinner?"

"That's why I was calling actually. Couple of the guys are grilling out tonight and asked if we wanted to come."

"Sure," she replied.

"I'll pick up some beer and steaks. Meet you at home."

"Sounds good."

"Great! Can't wait to see you," he said.

She told him she felt the same and they disconnected. In the months since they'd gotten together, they hadn't done much socializing. Nick had not complained or even mentioned it but she knew he missed his friends. She wasn't sure she was ready but she owed him this.

When she got home, Emma discovered that Nick had picked up some potato salad with the beer and meat. After they both changed, they got in Nick's truck and headed south. They arrived at a small house beside a lake forty-five minutes later. Ten trucks were already there, although she didn't know how many belonged to the owner. Jose Suarte was Nick's second hand in landscaping.

Maria Suarte was the first to greet her, taking care to hug Emma despite her pregnant belly. Her warm brown eyes shone from a tired face but her smile belied any exhaustion she felt.

"It is good to finally meet you. Nick talks about you all the time," she said in introduction.

Jose was next to hug her. He took the containers of potato salad she was carrying. He was short but solid muscle, with a military-style haircut and goatee. What struck Emma was his piercing, black eyes that were small and sharp like a cobra's.

"Welcome, Emma," he said in a much thicker accent that his wife's. "I told Nico that if he didn't bring you around soon, I'd start to wonder if you existed."

They all laughed, and their laughter brought forth a swarm of people from the back of the house. The hugs and greetings continued and were warm but overpowering. Nick put his arm around her and led her to the large desk on the backside of the house. Emma was grateful, sure he could sense her anxiety.

The sunlight reflecting on the water blinded her momentarily. She was immediately drawn to the silhouette of a small boy fishing at the water's edge. He couldn't be more than five but cast confidently and with purpose.

"That is our Miguel," Maria offered, noting Emma's observation.

"He's very determined," she replied, still watching.

"You're a painter, right?"

Emma turned to face the woman. "Yes."

"I recognize the look. My abuela was a painter, even after she went blind. She would get this intense look on her face as if she could see something we couldn't."

"She painted after she went blind?"

"Yes. Would you like to see some of her work?"

"I'd love to," Emma replied, noticing that Nick and the guys were already settling into beers and banter.

They went inside to find four dogs sacked out over as many couches. They perked their heads up but none of them made any attempt to check her out. There were two

Rottweilers, a pit bull mix, and a Chihuahua, which was the only one who growled.

Maria led her through the living room littered with shoes, backpacks and books.

"I'm sorry for the mess."

Emma waved it off. "You should see my place, and I don't have kids to blame it on."

Maria turned suddenly and her eyes were soft like melted chocolate. "I'm sorry to hear about your loss." Her hands slipped subconsciously to her belly.

Emma smiled. "Thank you."

Truthfully, she had no memory of carrying the baby or losing it. It was the earnestness in the woman's face that made her want to cry.

"Here is my favorite," Maria said, turning to point at a large, framed canvas. The image was of three youths moving horses across a dusty field. They carried whips and were barefoot. The details of the children and horses were astonishingly accurate and almost looked like a photograph. It was so lifelike that Emma could see the dust accumulating in the corners of the boys' eyes.

"Oh my God. And she was blind when she painted this?"

"Yes. She said she could still see in her mind's eye and used the visions from her childhood to recreate them."

Emma touched the brush strokes. They were smooth and sure and Emma wondered how on earth the woman had so perfectly captured the image.

"Here is the next one." Maria had moved down the hallway past a bathroom and plastic clothes basket full of toys.

The next was equally magnificent and depicted an old woman making a blanket with a hand-made loom.

"This one was painted when my abuela was very young. The lady in the painting is my bisabuela—great-grandmother."

The colors of mustard, burgundy, and brown were so vibrant that Emma was sure that the woman would move any minute. She could even see the slight breeze playing with the strands of long, gray hair.

"She was a beautiful lady," Emma remarked, turning to Maria. "I can see the resemblance."

And she could. The same strong angles of bone and cartilage, light brown skin, and deep chocolate eyes made both women striking.

"Thank you. My mother always said I looked like her."

"Wow. These are amazing. I would love to feature some of her work in the gallery if you had any you could part with."

"Jose built me a room to store the ones that aren't on the walls. I'd love to hang them all, but I don't have the wall space."

"All? How many do you have?"

Maria beckoned her to the closed door at the end of the hall. She opened the door and Emma didn't know where to look first. The colors and shapes overwhelmed her eyes. There were large canvases propped against the walls and smaller paintings stored in various boxes and crates.

"Would you consider selling some?" Emma asked, admiring a large piece of vaqueros on skinny horses moving a herd of cattle.

Maria considered, smiling and staring off, as if seeing something in the invisible distance.

"I think I would. My abuela never made much money on her work. She said she painted because she had to. When she died, she left them all to me."

"I'm sorry. I know they are precious to you. They're just so extraordinary. I didn't mean to be insensitive."

The woman brushed a tear away, sniffing and smiling as though to cheer herself.

"I believe she would be all right with me selling them. With the baby coming, we could use the money and the space."

For the next half hour, they pored over dozens of canvases of different sizes and themes but all vibrant. There was no hint that they had been painted by a blind woman. Emma was astonished that even the signature was perfect, and simply read 'Estella'.

"When did your grandmother pass?" Emma asked while admiring a painting of an old man feeding a hot dog to a scruffy one-eared cat.

"Oh, several years ago. She lived a long life and slipped away in her own bed at the age of 92," Maria explained.

"I wish I could have met her."

The two women smiled.

"Do you think any of these would sell?" Maria asked quietly.

"No. I think all of them will sell."

Her new friend's face blossomed with something like pure joy.

"You have no idea what a gift from God you are. We need this room for a nursery but

I didn't know what to do with my abuela's treasure. The money will help but the biggest help is having the space and knowing her paintings are safe."

Emma couldn't help but hug the woman, negotiating her giant belly, laughing. Emma felt something poke her and they parted to see a tiny protrusion.

"Estella approves," Maria said, placing her hand on the protrusion, which she explained was a foot.

"She will have a proud namesake," Emma said. She didn't reach out and touch the belly.

"You think we should join the men?" Emma offered.

"Yes. They will tease us. Jose always says that woman disappear into an alternate universe if they find something to talk about."

"He could be right."

They laughed and a few minutes later had rejoined their partners, several bachelors, and the other wives, who had perched on the edge of the deck to comment on the gathering. Emma and Maria agreed to hammer out the details regarding the art later.

The men were all laughing and drinking around the grill. Taller and blonder than the rest, Nick stuck out above the crowd. He spotted Emma immediately.

For a second, though, Emma saw a different image. Whether it was the fading sun or the sea of dark skin and black hair, she wasn't sure. It was a gathering similar to this one from her life in Hawaii. Instead of Nick's blue eyes and smile, she saw another tall boy she'd adored.

But he was long lost to here, and silently, she cursed her father.

David

CHAPTER SIXTEEN

I slept for days, barely eating or leaving the room. If I had been able to put it all out of my mind, I'd have sold my soul.

A week after being discharged, I finally got out of the house. It was only because I had to follow up with my doctor, but it was the first time I'd seen sunlight. I didn't have a primary care doctor, so I went to the walk-in clinic and asked to see the doctor on duty.

The doctor turned out to be a thin Asian man who looked twelve. He gave me a good report and cautioned me to refrain from anything strenuous.

I was leaving the clinic when a thought occurred to me. I'd built a small tool shed beside the studio. It housed my lawnmower and a few things that I had no other logical place to put. I gunned the BMW and sped the rest of the way to my house.

As I strode to the rickety shed door, I couldn't hold back the tide. Grabbing the one thing I knew would make me feel better, I walked into the studio.

We'd built everything in here ourselves. I raised the sledgehammer and came down with all my might on the first storage shelf. The pain rolled through me like a fuse had been lit at my side and traveled over my extremities. It was so intense that I couldn't hear the questions in my head from the thundering of my pulse. The more it hurt, the more I felt free. The boards cracked, splintered, and crashed, and each impact was like I was being stabbed all over again.

As I smashed my way though, I didn't wonder 'what if' this or that. There was no questioning my every action for the last thirteen—no, twenty-three—years. Now, there was only the mass destruction I was inflicting on nostalgia. Each time I brought the hammer down, I obliterated my ties to her. She was everywhere I went, everything I enjoyed, and the star of every frame of my memory. Maybe I was having a psychotic episode now but I didn't care.

In the end, I started dry-heaving and had to lie on the cold floor. The shattered and splintered wood, nails, and dust looked like an earthquake had destroyed everything around me. I'd wiped out all the storage shelves, a coffee table, and put a hole in the squeaky door. My side was beyond throbbing and now felt like a nuclear bomb had gone off in my torso. The power of each tiny explosion tore through my cells, reconfigured me for a split second, and pushed endorphins to every nerve. It was equally excruciating and intoxicating at the same time. I lay there drunk in my destruction until I passed out.

It was dark when I woke. The street lights shined in like a policeman's flashlight and I half-expected someone to be standing in the doorway demanding answers.

There was no one but the neighborhood gray tabby. The cat was sitting on the sofa surveying me with intense disinterest. Emma was always battling Constantine, who snuck in whenever the door was open for more than five minutes.

"Enjoy. You're welcome to the House of Destruction anytime."

The cat looked away as if to say he didn't need my permission. I forced myself to rise, surveying my work and trying to avoid the nails and splinters. The counters, with their marble tops, and the cabinets had escaped annihilation. I'd spared the expresso machine and the tiny bathroom.

Something caught my eye amongst the debris. It took some effort but I finally picked my way through the splinters and nails to turn on the light.

The tightly woven, brown bag was stamped with "Kona Coffee" in red on the side. It wasn't heavy but the shape of its contents told me if wasn't coffee. My hands were shaking, so trying to untie the knots in the drawstring was nearly impossible. There was no telling what Emma had squirrelled away out here. I looked at where it had been and determined she must've pried a board up and hidden the bag in a secret compartment. I wasn't surprised. Emma loved to hide things.

The first time I learned this about her was when we were kids. I'd spent the day in my treehouse reading Robinson Crusoe and daydreaming about pirates and the high seas. While practicing my air-sword fighting skills, I noticed a board on the top end of a cabinet that was sticking out. The cabinet was about four feet tall and comprised of two top shelves, a tiny counter space, and two large compartments underneath. I'd watched my dad frame it and lovingly cut each piece to the exact fit. It seemed odd that he would have left anything askew so I investigated. The board near the top had been pried up with something that left impressions on the wood beneath. I couldn't see into the tiny crevice so I gingerly worked my fingers into the tiny space. At first, I thought that I was mistaken, and then my fingers grazed something. Whatever it was felt velvety and my first thought was that it was some kind of creature. When it didn't move or bite me as I poked at it, I determined it wasn't an animal but some kind of pouch. Retrieving a small hammer from the tool box my dad gave me, I worked the claw under the board and pulled down until the edge of the board was free. Inside was a small, emerald-green pouch with a drawstring tied into knots.

As though I'd discovered a pirate treasure, I fought with the knots eagerly and finally opened the bag. Inside were two crumpled dollar bills, a tarnished half-dollar coin, three plastic gem stones and a note. Breathless, I unfolded the paper and recognized Emma's handwriting.

"Whoever removes this treasure is cursed."

Now, peering down at the coffee bag in my hand, I wondered what curse I had just incurred in finding this treasure. I was twelve when I'd found the first one, and I had put the contents back into the green velvet pouch, shoved it back into its hiding place and hammered the board back into its place. I'd taken care to leave the edge the way I'd found it. Today I was tempted to drop the bag on the floor and leave it there in the ruins. Instead, I took it with me and stumbled back into my house.

Afraid to look at my side but worried about the self-inflicted damage, I tossed the bag into the box with Emma's journals and headed into the bathroom to see what I had done. Surprisingly, there wasn't any blood, and nothing more suspicious than some bruising. I took a pain pill, stripped my clothes off, and went to bed. The darkness was still filled with my own rushing blood, and the sound was nearly deafening in the silence. I had no idea where my phone was and I didn't care.

Emma

CHAPTER SEVENTEEN

After meeting Maria and seeing her grandmother's beautiful art, Emma expected to feel inspired. Her new studio was begging for action, yet nothing was coming together. She started and stopped, mixed paints, cleaned, and drank coffee.

At home, she couldn't sleep. She didn't want to close her eyes. There were too many things she was afraid to remember.

If no sleep and absolute zero inspiration weren't enough, there was the added expectation of her new client. She'd already received two emails expressing excitement over what she'd create for the custom pieces.

All she really wanted to do was hide from the world.

Unsure of where she was going when she got into the car, she started the engine. As usual, the interior was littered with empty cardboard coffee cups, extra paint brushes, receipts, and mail. It never ceased to amaze her, these days, the random piles of things she amassed. She'd recently found a dog collar, leash still attached, and hah no recollection of where it had come from.

She knew what was wrong. It was the flashback of Jake that had messed her up. Pulling onto the interstate on-ramp, she let herself go back to the night they'd met.

It was a warm July night and Emma and her friends had decided to surf. The moon was full and some of the boys had started a bonfire. Jake was a mutual friend of a boy in the group. He had black hair and golden eyes and had reduced her to mush with his dimples.

Somehow, Emma and Jake ended up sharing a board. She could still remember the power of the waves beneath them and the heat of his skin on hers. All the other kids were whooping and laughing but Emma and Jake didn't make a sound. It was almost like this was their church and they were worshipping. When they finally sat down on the beach, Jake turned to her.

"You're a natural," he said, holding his hand out.

"You think so?"

He nodded. "You need some lessons but you have good balance."

"Can you teach me?"

He nodded slowly. "Yes."

It was the perfect start. Their eyes were glued together and both of them blushed.

Maybe it was the way he spoke about how they were connected to the universe and the ocean but he made her feel safe. She hadn't felt safe since she and David retreated to his treehouse and talked about running away. But this was different. Emma had never felt this way about anyone before Jake. It was exhilarating and terrifying at the same time. She felt like she was flying every time he touched her, although he was respectful. She could see something burning in his eyes but the night ended with a simple kiss on the cheek.

An angry honk startled her back into the present. She checked herself as a car was passing her. The driver glared and was saying something. Emma assumed she had drifted into the other lane and she mouthed 'sorry' as the car sped by her. Looking around, she tried to figure out where she was.

It took a while before she saw a sign. Pulling off I-65 on the first Cullman exit, she had no idea where she was going but she turned right. The GPS in her car was pre-programmed with her home address so she knew she'd find her way back when she was ready.

For miles it was nothing but trees and a few houses that had seen better days. Emma finally found a clearing that turned out to be a sports complex consisting of a track, two baseball fields, and several outbuildings that Emma assumed were snack bars or restrooms. The parking lot was empty except for a dented Ford truck with mismatched tires. It didn't take her long to locate the vehicle's owner.

Emma parked, turned off the engine, and watched a man teaching a child how to ride a bike. From the clothing the child was wearing, Emma deduced the kid was male. The boy wore a helmet much too big for his head and seemed to struggle keeping his head upright. Emma giggled at the progression of the lesson. At first, the little boy seemed to think that his father was going to just push him around. He threw his arms out and let his huge head fall back against his father's chest as the man ran behind him while pushing the bike. That didn't last long and there was a conversation.

Totally enraptured by this scene and the freedom of the bike ride, Emma remembered the first time Jake picked her up on his motorcycle. It was Sunday and her father was home. She had to wait for him to pass out in front of the TV to sneak out. Running through the woods to get to the designated meeting spot, Emma tripped on something and fell. She must've yelled because it wasn't a full minute before Jake came busting out of the tree line. He helped her up.

Her knee was skinned and she had bitten her lip but she forgot about the pain the second she saw his expression.

"Are you okay?"

She nodded and stood erect. "You should know I'm naturally clumsy."

It was a lie but it was one she'd told her entire life. Having people think that she was accident prone covered unexplained bruises and reduced the questions she couldn't afford to answer.

Jake chuckled as he led her to his bike. Handing her a helmet, he smiled at her and Emma felt like she was melting.

"Well, I hope you can hold on very tightly. I wouldn't want you to fall off the bike."

Emma slipped her arms around him and pressed herself to him as though they were mounting a rocket. He was warm, solid, and strong and Emma didn't want to let go. When he started the bike and they took off, she wasn't sure if the sensation that they were flying was the result of the speed or her falling in love.

A loud crash and subsequent yelling forced her back to the parking lot. The father had apparently let go of the bike and the inevitable first crash had resulted with the boy and the bike on the ground near a large metal trash can. Emma watched the man comfort the child as he removed the giant helmet and hugged the boy. She could see the child was crying.

Reaching over in her front seat, Emma retrieved her camera and took a shot. Although she had not intended to drive around looking for inspiration, Emma felt relieved that an idea had found her.

David

CHAPTER EIGHTEEN

The next two days were hell. My arms felt like they were weighted with blocks. Streaks of fire shot through my body at the slightest movement.

There didn't seem to be any other consequence to my impromptu destruction of the studio. Maybe I was disappointed. It was hard to think of myself as an avenging titan, destroyer of memories and storage shelves, and only end up with some sore muscles.

Slipping behind the wheel of my BMW was tricky but I managed it. A run was out of the question, and the mere thought of collision between feet and asphalt was repulsive.

Instead, I drove to the park. It was bright and sunny and the drive seemed to clear my head. I didn't see Kellyn but then I didn't really expect to see her. I parked and walked the short distance to the lake. A small boy with a Spiderman kite and an older lady watching him were 50 yards away.

Carefully lowering myself to the ground, I enjoyed the embrace of the warm sun. Something was stirring beneath the dark waters and an occasional silver fish shot out and plunged back with equal speed. I made myself take some deep breaths.

What would I say to Kellyn? This was the question I had asked myself every day since our last encounter. I wasn't divorced yet. What did I really have to offer? It was too soon to be contemplating dating and yet I was here hoping to see her. Even though Emma had left me and was with someone else, we were still married. I'd been holding out filing the papers in case she suddenly realized that she'd made a horrible mistake. Turned out the horrible mistake was me holding on to hope like that.

A tiny noise from my right side caused me to jump. I cursed aloud because it hurt.

Instantly, I regretted that when I saw the tiny boy sitting beside me. He'd abandoned his kite and was instead content playing with a long blade of grass. His dark curls and long eyelashes made him look like a doll. I had no idea how long he'd been sitting there, patiently waiting for me to notice him, or if he'd just sat down.

"Hi," I said finally. "Please excuse my use of bad words."

"Hello. It's okay. Are you sad?"

"Do I look sad?"

He shrugged. "Sad people usually sit by the lake."

"Oh yeah? What do happy people do?" I laughed.

The boy thought a moment. "Play on the playground. Fly kites. Throw frisbees. Lots of things."

"Why do you think the sad ones sit by the lake?" I asked, curious to know his philosophy.

"There's so much water that nobody notices if they cry."

"Well, that makes sense."

"Did you bring your kids?" he asked.

His question caught me in the throat as effectively as a punch. In his world, adults mostly came here with kids.

"No. I don't have any."

"Why not?"

"My son died." It came out shorter than I meant it to and I hoped he didn't notice.

"I guess he's in Heaven with my daddy then."

It was such an innocent statement of faith and acceptance, but it made the hair on my arms and legs stand up. I couldn't look into the blue eyes that seemed too old for the face. I felt the tears forming despite fighting them.

We were both sitting cross-legged. Without warning, he placed his tiny hand on my foot.

"It's okay," he said quietly. "Sometimes I cry too."

It was then that I heard a female clear her throat behind us. We both looked up and my complete humiliation punched me in the head. I'd been thinking of those gray eyes but this was not the reunion I'd envisioned.

Whatever emotions or questions might be swirling in those silver pools were indiscernible. I felt like a complete loser.

"What are you two doing?"

"Mom," the boy admonished. "Go away. We're talking about man stuff."

Of course this would be her kid. There was no way of saving my dignity. I just had to pray that she didn't think I was a pervert. Silently, I wished for death.

"Okay, buddy. Don't talk too long. I'd like to talk to my friend David too."

The boy flipped around and peered at me, questions clouding his cerulean stare. He waited until Kellyn walked away. I was almost out of breath from nearly having had a heart attack. Watching her approach an older woman, I deduced they were related. The boy was still watching me.

"David," I said, extending my hand.

He shook my hand. "I'm Wyatt. Do you like my momma?"

"I…uh. We're friends."

"She's pretty."

I laughed. "She is."

"You should like her," he said, attempting to wink but instead blinking both eyes.

I wiped my face trying to clear the tears and suppress a laugh.

Wyatt turned his head so quickly I thought something was coming up behind me.

"I gotta go fly my kite now."

"Okay," I said to the back of his head.

"See you later," he yelled over his shoulder.

I tried not to let the pain show on my face as I rose and walked the short distance to the picnic table where the women were waiting. Kellyn looked happy to see me.

"David, I'd like you to meet my mom, Tawnya."

Other than different color hair and eyes, they looked alike. The same cheek bones, jawline, and height. Like her daughter, Tawnya was pretty, and in good shape.

"Nice to meet you," I said, shaking her hand.

Her grip was strong and warm.

"Looks like you made a friend," Tawnya said, indicating Wyatt, who was trying to get his kite off the ground.

Wyatt's tongue was out as he concentrated, and his limbs were totally absorbed in his task. We all watched as he gathered himself and charged ahead while jerking the tiny Spiderman kite into submission. It sailed up briefly and then deftly crashed, skidding nose down as the child ran until he fell. He didn't cry but instead hoisted his little body up and tried again.

"I think I did," I admitted.

"I'll say. They were talking about 'man' stuff," Kellyn added.

"I'm not sure what 'man stuff' is but your son made me cry."

She laughed and touched my arm. "Man stuff is when males talk about emotions. I don't know where he got that but that's what he meant."

"He's remarkably articulate," I said to both of them.

"Oh, honey, that baby was born talking," Tawnya mused.

"I think his first word was encyclopedia," Kellyn explained.

"How old is he?"

"Four."

I started to reply when the dejected child approached the table, dragging Spiderman behind him.

"I like your kite," I said.

Wyatt smiled and gave the string a yank. "It's magical."

"Really? What can it do?"

"Well, I thought it would help me fly but it must not feel magical today."

"Maybe it'll feel magical soon," Kellyn offered.

The frowning child turned to his grandmother. "Grandma, do you think my kite has lost its magic?"

Tawnya crouched down in front of the boy. "It's not the kite that is magical, baby. It's you. Now, why don't you give it one more try, because we need to go in and get your magical behind in the bath and start some dinner."

The boy giggled and pulled back with big eyes and a froggy grin. "Me? I'm magical?"

"Yes, baby. You are my favorite magical boy in the whole world."

The child hugged his grandmother fiercely and then turned abruptly and ran away from us. We all watched silently as Wyatt shoved his thumb into his mouth, drew it out, and thrust it into the air. Then, he rolled up the excess string and prepared for takeoff.

I watched him as he was giving himself a pep talk. I couldn't hear what he was saying but he seemed earnest. The sunlight fell on the crown of his head like a halo and I felt the knot in my throat growing.

As I silently prayed, a burst of wind came just as the boy started running. We all started cheering. His body was not in concert, his arms flailing out of rhythm with his pumping legs. The kite rose slowing and I held my breath as it finally soared upward. Wyatt turned and watched his kite and then gave us all a thumbs-up.

"I'm flying, I'm flying."

Tawnya had started gathering her things from the picnic table.

"We've been in the park for a while. I'm going to take him in and start dinner. Good to meet you, David."

"Nice to meet you too, Tawnya."

Kellyn and I watched in silence as the woman collected the reluctant boy, whose unsupported kite had already descended. He wasn't happy to be leaving but evidently something she said sounded great. They were almost at the parking lot when Wyatt pulled free. He ran a few feet back and waved at us.

Cupping his hands, he yelled, "See you later, David."

I waved with the hand on my bad side and winced.

"You okay?" Kellyn turned, her eyes immediately flying over me.

"Oh. Yes. I got hurt."

"Today? Was it Wyatt?"

I laughed. "No. Nothing like that. It was the night after the park."

"What happened?"

She sat on the tabletop, patting the place beside her. I sat down gingerly.

"Well, the long and short is that I tripped over some logs while carrying a bottle of wine and a painting."

"So, you impaled yourself on a broken bottle and a painting. Ugh! Should you be out of bed?"

"I was in the hospital for two nights and have been in bed ever since. Just had to get out."

"Probably stir-crazy, huh? Are you hurting now?"

"It's okay," I lied.

"I was wondering why I hadn't seen you. I was afraid I'd scared you off."

"I'm sorry. I thought about calling your bank. Then I was afraid it would seem weird."

She laughed and touched my leg. For a second, the sensation blocked the pain. "Silly, you should've called. I could have brought you food."

"Well, next time I try to kill myself I'll call you."

She stiffened and her eyes sharpened. I felt a pain in my stomach. She had said her husband died and from her reaction I knew how. Kellyn looked out at the lake.

"He called me the night he did it. He was in Afghanistan."

"Oh, Kellyn. I'm so sorry. Did you…? Uh, were you talking to him when he did it?" I asked, aghast.

She shook her head. "No. He didn't even sound depressed for once. He asked about Wyatt and asked me to tell him he was sorry he'd miss his birthday. It didn't dawn on me until later that he meant all of them. I just thought he was feeling homesick."

"Did he leave a note?"

"No. No email either. He just shot himself."

My impulse was to put my arm around her shoulders but that seemed like a bad idea. Before I could think of anything to say, she stood up.

"I'd better go get Wyatt in the bath."

I stood up too, nodding, and looking at my feet.

"Does she live with you?"

"Off and on. My stepdad is a truck driver and is gone most of the time. She helps me with Wyatt, and stays a bit, and then goes home."

"I feel like an ass. Please accept my apology."

She smiled warmly. "There is nothing to forgive. You didn't know and were just flirting."

Kellyn looked up at me with those eyes the color of the full moon. They were impenetrable. Her smile was dazzling and made me think she was challenging me.

"I was wondering if you would have dinner with me sometime."

"I would love to."

"I'll call you."

"That'll work. My mom is going back home and taking Wyatt with her." She paused and bit her lip. "Do you have your phone on you?"

I pulled it out of my pocket, swiped to unlock it and handed it to her. She navigated through all the icons, located my contacts, and entered her number. Handing it back after a moment, she smiled.

"Call me anytime. It won't be weird."

"I'm sorry I'm awkward. I just don't want you to think badly of me."

"She left you and moved in with another man. Why would I think badly of you?"

The surprise showed on my face and she laughed. *Psychic?* I hadn't told her that.

"No, I'm not psychic. I have my sources."

We started walking in the direction of the parking lot. She pointed at a beige house with white shutters and a blue door.

"That's mine," she explained.

"I know. I have my sources too."

I'd seen her mother and son enter through the blue door earlier.

"If by 'sources' you mean eyes…" She rolled her eyes as she giggled.

"Yep. They tell me everything I need to know."

She hugged me gently, careful to avoid my wound.

We parted slowly and she turned toward her house. I started toward my car, turning to watch her. She was already looking, and that made me smile. We both gave a little wave, looking back at each other a few other times before she disappeared into her house. It had been several months since I'd felt visible to another human being, and that felt good.

Emma

CHAPTER NINETEEN

After her impromptu road trip, Emma drove to the studio and started working on her new painting immediately. She concentrated on the images on her camera to help her escape her memories of Jake.

Hours stretched into meals forgotten and multiple cold cups of coffee strewn everywhere. Sometimes she'd nap on the couch for twenty minutes and then get up and start again. Today was no exception.

Jake still lingered in the corners of her mind, but she pushed herself on. When she finally reached a stopping place, she gathered up her supplies and headed to the sink. She was washing brushes when she saw the truck pull into the small lot in the back of the building.

Nick got out, covered in dirt but smiling like he was in a tuxedo.

"Getting a lot done?" he asked when she admitted him through the back door.

Emma folded herself into him with a nod. She loved the musky smell of skin and earth. Finally, she looked up at him and he kissed her.

"Let me show you my latest," she said, taking him by the hand.

Emma told him the story of the little boy and his bike. She could see by the look on his face that he was listening to every detail and was genuinely moved.

"It's beautiful, Em. And I feel it."

"Thank you. I almost cried when I saw them. It was so sweet how the man took the giant helmet off and the kid just fell into his arms. It was so raw and honest that I felt comforted."

"That's why people love your work, babe. You give them all the feels. This one speaks of comfort but also commitment."

"Oh? How so?"

Nick pointed at the father's profile. "You can see it in his eyes. He's looking forward, steeling himself for more crashes. But he's determined to help his boy conquer this bike."

Emma saw what he was talking about. She had not intended to convey that. She didn't know what that felt like, to have a father invested in his child.

"I love the way you see things."

"Well, right now I see a beautiful artist who probably hasn't eaten all day. You ready for some fresh air and food?"

She laughed. "Food and fresh air would be good."

After a short drive, they ended up at a food truck, choosing fish tacos, burritos, and chips with homemade salsa. This food truck was their favorite. The truck was run down and not aesthetically pretty on the outside but the food was amazing. The homemade salsa was one of the main attractions.

"This one is my favorite," Emma told Nick, as she pointed at the menu. The black bean salsa also featured corn, jalapenos, honey, onions, and tomato. It was savory and sweet, and Emma got it every time.

"I can't pick a favorite. They are all so good. I like the one with pineapple in it that I had yesterday."

"You went to the food truck without me?" she teased.

"It's Jose's fault. He was talking about something Maria cooked the night before and it made me crave it."

"Liar," she said, biting her lip.

"Okay, okay. You know I have a pineapple addiction," he admitted.

"The first step is admitting the problem."

They laughed and took another scrumptious bite of their feast. Without warning, Emma was transported to another time and place.

A small diner near the base was the only thing that Emma ever looked forward to after school. It wasn't a nice place, with mismatched furniture and dingy counters. The hotdogs, with fresh pineapple relish, were expensive but amazing.

Normally, her father wouldn't indulge the kids with takeout food. The owner, Stan, was her father's old shipmate so they stopped there weekly. Although he credited Stan for once saving his life, the story always ended by making himself seem like a hero for his financial support of the diner.

Emma wasn't sure that Stan did them any favors by saving her father's life, but the man did make an amazing pineapple relish. She couldn't bring herself to eat pineapple now.

Nick's loud mmmmm brought her back to the present.

"You need an intervention," she said finally.

"That was quite a pause. Where'd you go?"

"I think she put extra jalapenos in this time. My eyes feel watery."

Although Emma usually told Nick everything, she didn't want to talk about Hawaii. She also didn't want him to know that she was on the verge of tears. The day's trip down memory lane was weighing heavily on her.

"Well…" Nick stood up, gathering the trash. "Let's go work this food off and get you dirty."

Two hours later, they were knee deep in dirt and mulch. Nick was working on an irrigation system. Emma handed him various tools. She relaxed as she passed him things. They didn't talk much and that allowed her mind to drift.

Jake was a skilled surfer and built his own boards. Emma spent many afternoons just like this one but one afternoon he told her he'd be assisting her. From that afternoon, they worked for weeks on a beautiful board. Jake instructed her as she did much of the work herself. When it was finally completed, he gave her the board as a present and she caught her best ride on it.

Nick's swearing brought her back from her memories. His tool had slipped, causing him to cut his thumb.

"Mind if I give it a try?"

"Sure. I'm going to go get a Band-Aid."

She'd watched him do this dozens of times. Grappling with the tool and the PVC, she wiggled her hand into the narrow gap. She had uncommonly strong hands and had no problem tightening the joint, even with little space. Setting the tool beside her, she sat back to survey her success.

"That's good work," Nick appraised from behind her. "And a nice view," he added, chuckling.

Maybe it was all the memories of Hawaii, or the fact that she hadn't heard him return, but it triggered the memory of her father's knack for just showing up. Her heart shot into her throat. She felt the panic rising with it. Nick must have seen her terror because he eased forward and wrapped her in his arms.

"I'm sorry I scared you, baby," he whispered into the top of her head.

She felt like a bird caught in a snare. Her arms wanted to thrash but Nick had a strong hold. Desperate for something to pull her out of the clutches of her father, who always smelled like Stetson and whatever he was drinking, she forced herself to breathe deeply. The earthy musk of Nick's skin was grounding. Instead of pushing him away, she dug her fingers into him to pull him closer.

"You're okay," he was saying.

Later, though the regular rhythmic beats of Nick's heart were soothing, she couldn't sleep. Ironically, lying in the bed listening to heartbeats because of insomnia made her think of David.

The first time she'd spent the night with David was after her drunken father had abused her and passed out on the couch. Emma slipped out as silently as she could. Her heart nearly stopped as she was pulling her leg through the window when she heard a thud followed by a groan. Imagining him rushing at her, she got her leg snagged on something and fell the rest of the way to the ground. Popping up without regard to her cut or bruised shoulder, she peered through the window. The bastard had merely fallen off the sofa and was in an unnatural position on the floor. Emma hoped he'd broken his neck. She slid the window down and ran as hard as she could until she reached David's.

Surveying the trellis, Emma was fairly sure it would hold her since David snuck out this way and he weighed more than she did. Despite the cut on her leg, injured shoulder, and shaking hands, Emma managed to climb up and scamper onto the window box. The window was locked and she prayed that she had remembered correctly where David's room was located.

It took a few knocks on the glass before she saw his face, eyes wide and hair mussed. He was freaked out and Emma could understand why. They normally met at his tree house. She climbed wordlessly through his window as he opened it. He didn't ask questions when she climbed into his bed. She reached for him and he held her while she cried. Emma listened to his heartbeat, fast at first and then slower and steady. It felt grounding and made her feel safe. The next morning, he brought her cereal and toast and they sat together on his bed.

"I hate your dad," he said through gritted teeth.

"Me too."

David reached for another piece of toast. "Won't he know you were gone?"

She chewed her last bite as she crawled over David. Climbing through the window, she turned.

"Thank you," she said.

"For what?" His green eyes were warm and curious.

"Your heartbeat," she said and left.

Lying in Nick's arms now, she was as grateful for that heartbeat as she was for David's. She wondered if the feeling of safety had continued throughout their marriage. If it had, she could understand why she'd stayed with David so long.

Nick moved underneath her, murmuring something about rose bushes. She almost laughed but caught herself. His hand slid down and cupped her buttock, drawing her closer to him. She didn't care for insomnia but she liked the waking moments of listening to his list of tasks or dream conversations. She liked the feel of his hands on her. For those moments, nothing else existed and those old wounds stopped hurting. Emma couldn't know if she ever felt this way with David. She had with Jake. Right now, though, Nick wasn't just another person who made her feel safe. He was the human equivalent of belonging. She listened to his heartbeat and knew each one was for her.

David

CHAPTER TWENTY

My dad and I used to go look at cars. As a young man, he had dabbled with the idea of being a race car driver. The professional choices were limited for the son of an oil tycoon. I never met my grandfather but I believe he was a hard man. To him, race car drivers were akin to blue collar workers, and that was not an acceptable choice for a man of means. My father went to college and got a degree in business. He was to inherit his father's oil business and it was expected that he should have the requisite credentials.

Dad loved cars and building things. From the time I could walk, he had me with him.

We made furniture and my tree house, worked on cars, and went to look at properties for sale.

As I drove around, I had the strangest sense that my dad's spirit was near me. Without hesitation, I pulled into a car dealership and parked. Maybe it was the frustration of how my wound limited my agility, but my car suddenly felt too small.

"Don't look at the sticker," he'd say. "Look at the car, the quality of its construction, its lines and heart."

Like blood in the water, the sharks began to gather and circle. A guy aimlessly walking around a car dealership lot drew them into a feeding frenzy.

The first guy to reach me was a heavy, bald man named Richie. He was in his forties and carried a half-eaten donut.

"How ya doing today?" His accent suggested a northern origin.

"Hi," I replied simply.

"You looking with something specific in mind?"

"Not sure. Just looking."

He passed a glance at my parked BMW. It was three years old, paid for, and had no obvious defects.

"You thinking of trading?"

"Maybe," I said, pointing at a shiny, black truck loaded with leather and framed in chrome. For good measure, it had a huge red bow on it. "Can I see under the hood?"

"Yes, sir. Let me go get the keys. Hey, if you want, I can get my guys to look at your car."

I threw him the keys and watched him waddle off.

Less than an hour later, I had traded my boxy sports car for a brand-new, black truck. It felt massive as I turned out of the lot. Compared to the BMW, it felt like a tank. I could hear my dad's approval of my purchase. Pulling into my driveway, I felt like a king.

It also felt like someone had dropped an anvil on me. I let myself in, locked the door, and headed upstairs.

I woke up with my heart pounding and body covered in sweat. My dreams receded as soon as I opened my eyes but I felt specters remain from the shadowy depths of my nightmares. My hands hurt from clenching them and a knuckle on my right hand was bleeding from hitting something.

I didn't remember falling into bed. The guestroom had no windows and that made it disorienting. I picked my phone up and was astonished to find out it was morning. Inventorying my memories of the previous day, I remembered that I had asked Kellyn out and bought a car. It was the first time that I hadn't thought of Emma. It was good that I moved to the guestroom to give me a refuge from my memories.

Sitting up, I realized that Emma was everywhere in this room too. Precious Moments figurines covered the dresser and a floating shelf above it. Throw pillows I'd flung onto the floor were from a craft festival in Tucson, Arizona. The small oval carpet in the center of the room was a gift she'd bought herself in Spain on our first real trip. One of the pictures on the wall was from that trip too.

Without a second thought, I marched downstairs to the pantry. Quickly locating a box of 42-gallon contractor bags, I grabbed it and headed back upstairs like a madman. Ruthlessly, I ripped pictures from the wall and then began tossing in the Precious Moments figurines. It took two hours to exorcise Emma and our former life from the house. Despite the pain, I dragged bag after bag to the truck. I had removed clothes, pillows, trinkets and mugs, and anything that reminded me of her. I was shoving the comforter from the bed into a bag when I spotted a box of journals and the Kona coffee bag. All the other stuff was going to the thrift store, but when I grabbed the box, I intended to toss them to the curb.

I made it to my truck, hoisting the bags into the back. Walking deliberately to the spot where the trash was to be piled, I set the box down and turned to go back. Before I reached the door, my heart started aching. She wouldn't care, I told myself. When she'd moved out, she'd left all this stuff to haunt me. She was going to throw the journals away herself, and I was the one who'd rescued them. She was done with all of this so why shouldn't I be too?

But. What had she hidden in the secret compartment? It must be important. What if she couldn't remember where she'd hidden it? She might have forgotten about all of the contents of the box.

Something punched me in the gut and I sprinted to the curb like the garbage truck was idling down the street. As much as I wanted to, I couldn't throw the journals away.

Setting them in the same spot they'd been, I surveyed my room. It looked like it had been burglarized and vandalized. My back was hurting from sleeping on the daybed and I wanted my mattress back. If I were seeing a counselor, I was sure they would have told me to do this. The adrenaline I felt from succumbing to my anger should have made me feel tired. Instead, I felt energized.

After a quick shower and shave, I got dressed and collected my keys and wallet. I still had much to do.

The box of journals mocked me and I glared at them. I couldn't throw them away yet but I lied to myself and promised myself it would be soon.

Emma

CHAPTER TWENTY-ONE

She woke unable to breathe. The sweat poured down her body as if she was standing under a waterfall. There was only one thought on her mind. Where had she hidden it? All her secrets. What would happen if they were found?

Forcing herself to breathe through the panic, Emma tried desperately to remember. After a few long moments, Emma quietly got up, annoyed that Nick was so blissfully asleep. Since their place was small, she left a note and headed for the studio.

It was everything she could do not to drive directly to David's and search his house. How would she explain it if he was home? She could just tell him that she was missing some art supplies. She could also tell him that she was checking on him.

Turning to the gallery instead, she tried to focus. She didn't have to try to remember if she had told David anything. She knew she'd probably told him some things, but she knew herself well enough to know he didn't know the whole story.

Still deep in thought, Emma unlocked the door and let herself in. As she turned on the lights she noted that everything was still where she'd left it the day before. She started cleaning up and collecting trash.

Maybe David had thrown it away. That thought was comforting. She wasn't sure why she hadn't destroyed the thing years ago. It was not like she wanted to revisit all of that.

When she was a kid, she'd lie in bed dreaming of having a place of her own. Her dream was to have a partner and live far away from her father. If she was honest, being with Jake wouldn't have been far enough away.

He had planned to take her to another of the Hawaiian Islands or maybe Australia. They'd dreamed about teaching surfing and living simply.

That was another thing that was bothering her. Why all the thoughts about Jake? He wasn't just one that got away. He'd been dead for almost seventeen years. She couldn't help but wonder if the boy with eyes like melted caramel and long eyelashes would have made it to Australia.

After fixing a coffee, Emma stared at her painting. It had practically painted itself. There were a few finishing touches she wanted to add but it was finished. That made her smile despite her thoughts.

She'd been painting the night Jake died. They had planned to meet in secret but she never heard from him. The painting was of a small boy watching his father working on a surf board. The inspiration came from Jake's telling her of watching his own father and learning from a young age. He wanted to teach his own children, and his face lit up when he talked about it. He made her think that it was possible to create their own happy family.

Taking up a clean canvas and setting up her paints, Emma let her mind go back to Jake. The powerful shoulders and muscular legs stood out in silhouette as she pictured the setting sun streaked in orange and red in front of him. He was always looking for the perfect waves. The ocean's rhythmic song filled her ears and the sweet tang of pineapple and the coconut from the surf board wax filled her nostrils. The sand felt cold and squishy under her feet.

Closing her eyes, she thought of Maria's grandmother and wondered if her own memories could guide her. She was surprised to find that her hands knew where to go.

An hour passed and the image now burned into her brain included tall waves and surfers in the background. A seashell collector was hunched down to Jake's left. He had a small boy on his shoulders.

The tears came without warning but she kept painting. She could see clearly the wind in his hair and the boy's hands resting on the crown of his father's head. The child was looking back at something over his shoulder. Tiny tendrils of sunlight spun through the boy's curls and reflected off his long eyelashes.

She kept painting, grateful that she always laid her colors out in the same order. The feel of the brush stroke told her how much paint she had.

Even if this piece turned out to be a kaleidoscope nightmare, Emma was enjoying the process. Plus, she wanted to study Jake a while longer.

The time flew by without so much as a whisper. When she finally opened her eyes, the light was bright enough to burn her eyes. It took a minute to focus but when the tears relented, she was delighted to find that the painting was not a total disaster.

Her heart was hurting, though, and her mind swam in memories.

Emma's father and Jake had died on the same night. One death left her exhilarated and the other was devastating. If only she'd been able to get out of the house sooner. Maybe things would have been different. And then she remembered.

"You are an idiot," she said aloud.

The heart's internal calendar kept track of events, even when the conscious mind stopped. Exactly seventeen years ago today, they had died. It was no wonder she'd been thinking so much about Jake. At the time, Emma had felt so guilty about his death that she didn't go to the funeral. She couldn't bring herself to face his mother or family. They would all blame her, and the weight of regret would be too heavy to bear. They would never forgive her. She didn't have to hear their accusations to know that. What was more crippling was that she would never forgive herself.

Now it made sense that she'd woken up panicked. She needed to remember where she'd hidden it.

David

CHAPTER TWENTY-TWO

As I pulled into the parking deck at my office, I knew what I wanted to do. Collecting a few boxes from the bed of my truck, I strode into the lobby like I owned the place. The security teen looked up from his comic book and gave me a long look. I was in jeans and my hair wasn't combed. I hadn't bothered to tuck in my shirt, which was a throwback from a Dave Matthews concert. The thin material and worn-off letters made me resemble nothing of the polished professional that normally headed through the pristine marble lobby.

Taking the stairs two at a time, I reached the office doors like a fireman in search of survivors. My office is small, with less than 30 employees. We take up the entire sixth floor of one of the only buildings not part of the university.

I used to meander to my office, taking a minute to speak to all the associates but today, foregoing the usual banter, I made my way silently through the rows of cubes and file cabinets. Most of the associates had stopped knowing what to say to me anymore. I didn't know what to say either.

Emma was everywhere in my spacious corner office. The paintings on my walls were hers. One was the glistening catamaran from our trip to St. John. The other painting was the waterfront in Salem, Massachusetts, with its curious blend of history and whimsy. My sofa and chairs, covered in rich hunter green and burgundy fabrics with splashes of cremes and browns, were all chosen by Emma's sharp artist's eye. Books and tchotchkes lined the bookcases as tokens from our various travels.

Without delay, I taped up the boxes and collected my personal belongings. Without rhyme or reason, I dumped books, photos, and trinkets into them unceremoniously.

Most of the sales and executive offices were empty as I made my way to my managing partner's palatial workspace. Designed to resemble a boat, the office had wooden wainscotting on the ceiling, striped couches, model sailboats, and a marlin on the wall behind the desk.

Bruce was in his office and obviously surprised to see me. He smiled but his eyes gave away his anxiety. I set my boxes down by the door.

"David? You're on leave. What are you doing here?" He got to his feet.

"I quit," I replied simply.

"David, you aren't thinking straight. You've been through so much. Let's talk about this."

I laughed at this. "I'm not having a breakdown and I'm not on drugs. I just don't want this job anymore. I'm tired of appearances and having to put on a happy face. I'm tired of the fake smiles and judgmental looks and, all the while, the people in the office are working their asses off. But do you care? Does anyone care that Sandra's husband needs a kidney? Or, did you even know that Cedric is taking care of both of his parents who have Alzheimer's? Tracy had to come back after only 6 weeks of maternity leave and can barely afford childcare. No. You don't. And I'm just as guilty. I know these things and have done nothing to help. All that is important is money and appearances. I'm done. We'll work out the partnership stuff later."

I pulled out a folded, hand-written resignation letter that I'd hastily written on my shopping list pad this morning. He looked at me, lip trembling, and eyes wide with realization.

Not waiting for a response, I dropped my letter on his desk, turned on my heel, collected my stuff, and walked out. People in the office were standing like meerkats and speculating what was happening. I stopped briefly at the front doors.

"Some of you I know better than others. All of you know everything that happened. I want you to know that I'm okay but I'm leaving. I can't do this anymore. You guys deserve better, and I'm sorry for the part I played in the treatment you've received. If you need recommendations, email me and I'll be happy to help. Thank you for your kindness and prayers over the years. Goodbye."

Tears and hugs were followed by several people packing their desks. The one good thing about the reputation I'd worked hard for over the years was that all the competitors took me seriously. I knew I could get jobs for anyone who wanted one with any number of agencies or clients across the city.

Deciding not to take the stairs down while holding several boxes of stuff, I headed for the elevator. The doors slid open just as I stepped in front of them.

Suzanne was getting off the elevators. Emma had finally told me that the woman had come by the hospital and that had been the disturbance I'd heard outside of my room. I thought of all the times Suzanne had belittled Emma and disrespected me.

"David? What are you doing here?"

"I'm quitting."

"What? Honey, this is not the time to be making big decisions. I knew that little slut being at the hospital was going to mess you up. You aren't thinking rationally."

I stepped closer to her as though intending to whisper in her ear. "I apologize, Suzanne. You are direct and aggressive, so I understand why you don't respect me. I've been much too subtle."

"Oh, Davy boy, there is no need to apologize." She licked her lips as though expecting me to confess my desire.

"Oh, but I do. I allowed you to belittle Emma because I didn't want to make waves. I've covered for you full knowing you were sleeping with clients to bend them into submission. You are a mean, nasty human. You are not my friend. And, I wouldn't have sex with you if someone held a gun to my head. I never want to see you again. As for Emma being a slut, takes one to know one."

The shock on her face was comical with her mouth literally falling open. She recovered quickly and I saw the transformation. Her eyes narrowed and the smug snarl displaced the momentary dismay. She looked like a viper.

"I was trying to help you, David. Clearly, you don't want it. It's early yet. The loneliness hasn't quite set in. It will."

"Even death couldn't be that lonely."

She pushed by me and I watched her slither toward the office in a skirt and blouse made for someone three sizes smaller.

The anger had erupted out of me like ants out of a disturbed colony. I wasn't sure where I'd been bottling all this up but it felt good to get it out. Getting onto the elevators and watching them close on a chapter of my life, I didn't know what was coming next but I did know what I wanted.

Like my father, I wanted to build things. Somewhere along the way, I'd forgotten myself and become swept up in making my way up the corporate ladder. I thought I was building a future for me and my family. My office and paycheck, respectability and success, were only shiny facades and had made me a prisoner.

Now I was free. I had money. My trust fund and stocks had amassed to a large enough sum to afford me some leisure. My dad had explained what it meant to have money before he died.

"Just because you have money, that is no excuse not to work," he'd said.

I drove to my next stop thinking about this advice. Working didn't mean pulling a 9 to 5. There were charity organizations that could use a hand. Even if I gave away the furniture I wanted to build, it would benefit someone.

After Emma had announced she wanted a divorce, she'd quickly followed with the statement that she didn't want any of my money. She had her own account which she'd opened when she started selling her paintings. My paychecks had covered mortgage and expenses so she spent her own money on art supplies, clothes, and car. She was frugal and had taught me much over the years about stretching a dollar. In all 13 years, we'd only dipped into my trust twice.

Pulling into the parking lot of the hardware store, I took a deep breath. The adrenaline made it hard to breathe normally. I knew I was on the right path or, at least, closer to it. My dad would have approved. I told myself that as I made my way into the store and purchased the items I needed to convert the studio into a workshop. Luckily, they were willing to deliver everything.

From there, I headed to a chain home-goods store. I gathered up a new comforter set, sheets, pillows, towels, and a bath mat. None of it matched perfectly but I chose them for the comfort, not color. It was liberating not to have to consider what would go perfectly together with the color palette in my house.

My next stop was the only one that made me forget about my side and how tired I felt. The sign on the front door read: "They say you can't buy your friends but no one ever said anything about adopting one."

I opened the door and went in, only to be met by a yellow tabby with cool green eyes. A woman I guessed was in her 70s greeted me with a big smile, loose dentures, and drawn-on eyebrows.

"You here to adopt, honey?"

Her name tag said she was a volunteer named Brenda.

"Yes, ma'am," I answered, not able to determine why I was nervous.

She gathered up some papers and put them on a clipboard. Grabbing a pen, Brenda handed them to me.

"Fill these out and then go pick out your new friend. You can look first if you prefer."

She indicated a long bench, currently occupied by a large white cat with blue eyes. The eyes watched me closely but the cat made no attempt to flee.

"That's Felix," Brenda introduced us. "You here for a cat or dog?"

"Dog," I replied.

"Oh good. I hope you'll consider an adult. We have a few that don't have much longer."

"Much longer for what?" I wanted to know.

"If they aren't adopted soon, they'll be euthanized. If you see an orange card on their enclosure door, then they haven't much time left."

My heart raced as I walked through the kennels through a symphony of barks, yips, and howls. All eyes and calls were pleading for my attention. Paws and tails worked overtime for a second look. I'd never had a dog so I had no practical idea of what would be a good choice. There were numerous mixed breeds, and sizes ranged from tiny to giant.

It was like being trapped on those metal carousels on the older playgrounds. I could smell the fear and desperation and couldn't stop making laps. In a way it felt mean to give false hope but I guess I wanted them all to feel wanted. I stopped at each enclosure.

The last enclosure on the last row was occupied by a hound. There were several empty kennels around him and the stark white wall made the orange card stand out.

He wasn't barking or whining. The sober amber eyes watched me without expectation, and his droopy ears didn't prick when I read his card aloud.

"Hi. My name is Houdini. My master died and I've been here ever since. I get along with everybody but I'm really good at getting out a fence. I need a home with someone who will let me stay inside and who has energy to take me on walks."

The rest of the information described him as a mixed breed hound who was 4 years old, neutered, and house trained. He had all his shots. The orange card had a date that was only two days from now.

It was hard to say if the dog was white with brown patches or brown with white patches. His face was mostly white with a brown patch around his left eye. Smaller brown spots looked like freckles on his muzzle.

"You want to come home with me, Houdini?" I made eye contact as I spoke.

His tail thumped once and he picked up one foot, holding it suspended for a few seconds.

A young man with a bright yellow shirt walked up behind me. "He's a good boy."

"Can you get him out for me?"

The kid's face brightened. "I sure will."

Having been instructed to go to a small glass room, I watched as the boy slipped a makeshift leash on the dog. It looked like a noose to me but the dog didn't pull as they walked toward me.

I read the boy's name tag as he opened the dog. Kevin was barely twenty, with dreadlocks and bulging biceps. The dog wagged his tail as he walked closer to me.

"He's been here a few months. He has more personality but I guess he's kinda beaten down."

I reached out, palm down to let Houdini sniff my hand. Instead, he slid his big head under my palm. As I stroked his head and ears, he smacked his lips and moved closer, enjoying the contact.

"I think he likes me," I said finally. "I want him."

"Oh my God, man. I'm so happy. He's a great dog. Just needs a chance. Truthfully, I've wanted him myself but I've got no place to keep him. They won't let us keep dogs in the dorm and my mom would kill me if I bring one more animal there. What's your name?"

"David," I said and reached out to shake his hand.

"Good to meet you, David. I'm Kevin."

"Thanks, Kevin. It's nice to meet you."

"Okay. Do you want to get supplies here?"

I looked down at my dog, who was sitting calmly in front of me. "What size collar does he need?"

"Come on, man. I'll help you find the right fit."

Kevin led me to a small store in the front, full of toys, food, bowls, and an entire wall of collars, harnesses, and leashes. We picked out a respectable blue nylon collar and matching leash. Kevin also talked me into a retractable leash, dog treats, balls, chew toys, and a bag of dog food. Three hundred dollars, multiple hugs, and a few tears later, I left the building with my new dog and Kevin to carry all my supplies.

Houdini popped right into the back seat when I opened the door, and sat in the seat. Brenda had cried when she saw whom I'd chosen.

"Oh, you can see him smiling. He knows that someone wants him. It just touches my heart."

Glancing at the dog in the car, I thought he did look like he was smiling. I was glad that I'd got a truck with an extended cab. He lay there as we drove and I reached back at stop lights to pet him. He sighed loudly, and I took it to mean that he finally felt like he could breathe.

I wanted to feel that way again. My next order of business would be to call Kellyn. For now, though, it was nice to have another being that was glad to be with me.

Emma

CHAPTER TWENTY-THREE

Her mind was still stuck in Hawaii and she could almost smell the salt water. Why had she not remembered the date? She couldn't have forgotten all the terrifying things that lead to it. There was no amount of amnesia or alcohol that could wash the questions, suspicions, and guilt away.

Emma could remember the EMTs and MPs that responded to her mother's 911 call like it was yesterday. She watched them working on him, knowing that their efforts were in vain. Multiple authorities asked them about the blood on his shirt. Neither she nor her disheveled mother could tell them where it came from. They finally concluded that the commander had gotten into a drunken brawl. None of them asked about her mother's swollen eye or the bruises visible on her arms.

The next morning brought the tide of casseroles and sandwich platters, condolences, sad looks, and the ridiculous things that people say about people they don't know.

"He was such a good and handsome man," one officer's wife had said.

Emma had almost laughed out loud. She took the woman's tray and feigned a crying fit to get away. That was how she'd made it through most of the comments and hugs. It would do no good to tell them the truth. They just wanted to drop off their food offering and "pay their respects" without the burden of truth.

She was in the kitchen faking grief and trying to fit one more platter on the counter when a news report on the TV in her father's den caught her attention.

"Tragedy on Olomana."

Emma couldn't take her eyes off the screen. The reporter was live at the scene but she didn't hear anything that was said. In the background, she saw the familiar face of Jake's best friend, Kekoa. She knew the place they showed. Slowly, everything came into focus and her heart sank. She knew Jake wouldn't be coming. He was never coming.

Jake had been up on Mt. Olomana planning something for her. As she crumpled to the floor, surrounded by ham and cheese sandwiches, Emma was barely aware of anyone in the house. Her mother sent all the people away and sat on the floor with her for what seemed like hours. The tears would not come although Emma desperately wanted the release. When she finally did start crying, she couldn't stop and simply lay on a bed of tiny sandwiches until exhaustion finally took her.

Roused from memory, she took out her phone and stared at the screen for a long time. Finally, she scrolled through her contacts and hit send.

"Hi, Mom."

David

CHAPTER TWENTY-FOUR

I let the dog explore the house and yard. It hadn't occurred to me that he might be a chewer. Still, he seemed most interested in me as I retrieved my bedding and went upstairs.

As I folded the old comforter and laid it on the floor, I talked to him.

"Emma hired a designer to custom-make this one. It cost $1400 and now it is your bed."

The dog looked warily at the thick folds of cream and then back at me.

"It's okay. Try it," I patted the surface until he came to me.

Houdini's approach was cautious but I finally enticed him to lie down.

"Good boy," I said, rubbing his belly.

I pulled out my new comforter, which was navy and green plaid, and continued my conversation with my dog.

"Emma wouldn't let me buy a bed-in-a-bag, as she called it. She is the most frugal person I've ever known but she could have expensive tastes in some things. I got this for $49 since it was on sale. Not bad, huh?"

The dog groaned but I took it to mean he agreed.

"One thing left to do, boy," I said, enjoying having someone to talk to.

I grabbed a beer and one of the balls I bought for the dog and we went outside. I threw the ball and the dog looked at me like he'd rather have my beer. His expression made me laugh.

Sitting down on the outdoor sofa, I called him up to sit beside me on the thick cushions. He didn't hesitate and, after settling, put his head on my leg. I stoked his head and smiled to myself. I'd bought a car, spent thousands on new house goods and toys, quit my job, and adopted a best friend. It had been a busy day.

Pointing and tapping my way through my contacts, I located Kellyn's number and pressed send.

"You called."

"Is it weird?"

She laughed. "Not at all. What have you been up to?"

For a moment, I considered telling her everything. Thinking better of it, I told her about Houdini.

"He sounds adorable," she exclaimed. "Wyatt has been wanting a dog but I'm not sure he's ready for the responsibility at four."

"I don't know. He's not your average four-year-old." I laughed, remembering the boy talking to me by the lake.

"True. It's purely selfish. I just don't want the responsibility. Is that bad?"

"Terrible."

She reminded me that her mother was leaving and taking Wyatt with her for a few days. I remembered my offer to take her out to dinner, so I plucked up the courage and asked her again.

"I was hoping you might want to have dinner with me."

She paused for a long moment and my heart hammered in my ears so loudly I was afraid she could hear it.

"Would you consider letting me cook for you?"

In my mind, I was imagining dressing up and taking her to a fancy Italian place. I even had the place picked out. It was one of my favorites and one of the only ones Emma and I had never been to together.

"That would be great," I finally said.

"Not what you had in mind, though?"

"Well, no, but the thing I wanted the most was to see you. Are you sure it's not too much trouble?"

"No. I just want to wear my jeans and a t-shirt, have a beer, and eat a steak."

"And you're up for company? This is kinda last minute."

"Company is always welcome."

"What time do you want me?"

"Seven."

"Seven it is."

Emma

CHAPTER TWENTY-FIVE

Emma wasn't sure she should just blurt out her questions. Memories were swarming her brain like bees.

"Hi, honey." Ruth always emphasized the first syllable.

"How are you?" Emma asked.

"Is something wrong?" And she always knew.

Emma rested her head in her other hand and leaned forward as though she was hyperventilating. Her mother could hear distress even when it was masked in laughter. Ruth had endured years of abuse and cruelty. It was possible she didn't remember the significance of this day. Emma had called with the intention of discussing the events that had happened that night but she felt guilty for calling out of the blue to make her mother recall all of that. Had she always been this selfish?

"I'm tired, Mom. I just wanted to see how you are doing."

"Your stepfather is cooking dinner and pretending he has his own cooking show."

Emma couldn't help but smile as the male voice in the background attempted a French accent. She only knew him from her mother's descriptions. Glen was the complete opposite of her father. Bob Roberts would have never cooked anything and certainly would not have done anything to entertain his wife. Her mother described Glen as soft and gentle, an avid gardener, and a great cook.

"Sounds like fun. What's he cooking?"

"I don't know but it smells good. How are you, Em?"

Emma reached deep for the smile and tone she used for all the dinners with David's clients. It wasn't all fake. She did have some great things going on, so she began to tell her mother about all her good news.

"That all sounds great, Emma. I'm so proud of you. I'm glad you were able to help your friend and I hope you can sell all of the blind woman's paintings. Can I see them online? Glen has been teaching me how to use the computer."

"Oh wow! Yes, you can. I'll text you the web address."

"How are things with you and Nick?"

When she'd told her mother that she'd left David for Nick, her mother had only asked if she was happy.

"He's so great, Momma," she said, meaning it.

"That's great, baby. I wish you two would plan a trip to Hawaii. We'd love to meet him.

Your step-father is a master chef." She was laughing again. "He's just burned something up."

Emma laughed. "I'll talk to Nick about it and we'll try."

"Oh good! Listen, I've got to help Glen before he burns the house down."

"Okay, Mom. Good to talk to you."

"I'm glad you called and things are going well. I love you."

Emma got in her car after tidying up and locking the studio. She didn't know where to go but knew she wasn't ready to go home. Unsure of how she got there, Emma recognized a park that David had brought her to a few times. She parked on the far end, away from the playground and picnic tables. She felt unsettled and wanted to be around people without interacting with any of them. She definitely wasn't ready to see Nick. Everything felt bruised and heavy. She had no one to talk to about the worst day of her life and she was worried about her missing treasure.

Something in her peripheral vision caught Emma's eye. Even at a distance, she knew David's walk. Emma watched him stride up to a blue door with a bottle of wine. She didn't recognize the house but why would she? Emma could see him fidgeting and she felt somewhat breathless as they both waited for the occupant to admit him.

There was a small pang in her chest as the door opened and the female occupant hugged David. She wasn't sure which emotion pricked her.

She wanted David to be happy and find someone that could give him children. She had moved on so why shouldn't he? Was she feeling jealous? That didn't make sense. She had everything she'd ever wanted in Nick. Why would she care if David was trying to move on? Emma felt guilty for hurting him. But the weight on her chest didn't feel like guilt.

It wasn't jealousy, she concluded. Given the gravity of this horrible anniversary, Emma figured that all her feelings were amplified. Memories of her life with David were starting to come back. They were fleeting moments without context suspended in time but she knew that David loved her. Maybe she just wasn't ready for him to stop loving her.

In addition, memories filled her mind with montages of Hawaiian sunsets and Jake's smile. She saw the life that they'd dreamed of but never had. For a brief moment, she wondered if she was breaking down.

It didn't feel like the unraveling sensation she'd gotten before the first episode. Emma took a deep breath and tried to clear her head. While she already knew that she needed to cry and release the pressure cooker in her head, she had to focus. She did have something that she needed to do.

Emma looked up as though she was going to pray. The orange and red had already faded into a warm pink and the dark blue fingers of dusk were starting to filter the light.

"I miss you. I'm sorry that I forgot today was the day."

As she spoke the words, the images slowed and settled on the most joyous moment she had ever known. She squeezed her eyes tight, trying to capture the image for just a few seconds.

After the sweetness of that reunion memory passed, she remembered a bunch of random things she'd left in the storage closet. If she was lucky, David had not looked in there since she'd left. And, now she knew he wasn't home.

As she reached to start her car, Emma fumbled with her keys and her phone slipped between her legs. Her mind was too full of hope to notice that she was calling someone.

David

CHAPTER TWENTY-SIX

I remembered when she opened the door that she said she wanted beer. The panic must've shown on my face because she immediately asked me what was wrong.

"I've just remembered you wanted beer."

Her gray eyes gleamed like steel. "Gotta love a man who listens to the details."

She laughed and took the bottle from me.

"I'm sorry." I tried to laugh.

"Don't be silly. Wine is good too."

Kellyn was explaining how she loved a good glass of wine as I looked around. Her taste in decorating included neutral colors on the walls, with a dramatic splash of color on one wall, which was a dark claret color in this room. There were throw pillows to match, which served to tie the color to the rest of the décor. Her fireplace looked like an altar, with arranged candles of all different sizes in beige and claret. Emma also favored this use of fireplace and hearth.

Over the mantle, there was an oversized painting of a toddler on the back of a shaggy pony in a field. The long grass and pony's mane and tail, as well as the child's blonde hair, were backlit by the afternoon sun. I didn't have to look for the signature.

We had been traveling back from an impromptu trip to New York for a friend's wedding when Emma asked me to take a detour. We drove through states that neither of us had seen. For hours, we talked and dreamed, stopping only for gas, food, and bathroom breaks. Nights were spent in our car.

On the fourth day, somewhere in Tennessee, we pulled down a dirt road and literally into a field. I was exhausted and afraid I'd hit one of the thirty deer we'd passed at the onset of dusk. The air was chilly but we grabbed a blanket and got onto the top of the car and fell asleep under the stars.

When I woke the next day, I sat up to find Emma wrapped only in a sheet with her sketch pad. She looked like an angel as the sunlight spilled over her. I never asked if she'd actually seen a child on the pony.

"You want a beer or glass of wine?" Kellyn called from the other room.

I felt breathless and somewhat ashamed. What was I doing? I was not divorced, having dinner with a woman to whom I'd been attracted since before my wife left, and reliving the best road trip of my life with my wife. And what where the chances that my date would have my wife's painting in her living room?

"Beer is fine," I answered finally and followed her voice.

The next room was the den. It boasted a leather loveseat, a sofa in an "L" shape and a coffee table made from a lobster trap. The furniture looked expensive but showed signs of use. The rest of the room was tidy but it was obvious that a four-year-old lived here. Outcroppings of books or toys lined the walls and were neatly housed in plastic bins. In between two of the sofa cushions, I saw a tiny plastic soldier. The head and hand poked out as if requesting an extraction. On the wall opposite the sofas was a large-screen TV mounted on the stone accent wall. Beneath it was another candle altar in the small fireplace.

The wall behind the sofas drew me, with floor-to-ceiling bookcases. I browsed the books as an excuse to admire the craftsmanship of the bookcases. I was surprised to find everything from children's books and text books to novels and biographies. They were expertly arranged and in alphabetical order. I browsed through titles on sports, history, and finance. A large, well-worn collection of woodworking guides caught my eye.

Evidently, I was so captivated that I didn't hear her approach. I turned to find her watching me and wondered what she thought. She handed me a beer.

"You're kind of like a cat. Gotta look around before you get comfortable."

"I guess I am." I laughed.

"See anything you like?" she asked grinning, and sat down on the loveseat.

"You have quite a library. And the bookcases are magnificent."

They were. The oak was stained with a dark mahogany stain and the glass shelves were supported by bright, copper pegs. The lines were clean and perfect. I was already imagining the dimensions and list of supplies.

"Thank you. I made them."

"Wow. I'm really impressed."

"When I first got here, I didn't have much money. My stepdad taught me woodworking so I made a lot of my own furniture. I made this coffee table, the bookcases, kitchen table, and various other things in the house."

"My dad taught me too. I love woodworking. Do you still do it?"

She laughed. "I wish. Now my life consists of work, cleaning, cooking, conquering mountains of laundry, and stopping all of that to play with a four-year-old that never stops. Maybe one day."

"Sounds exhausting," I said.

"Oh, I'm well past exhaustion but that's the life of a single parent. How about you? Do you still do woodwork?"

"Funny you should ask. I'm about to start. I'll have some time on my hands."

"Oh? Extend your medical leave?"

This time I laughed but only because her expression invited it.

"No. Even better."

"Bought your partner out?"

I was enjoying the guessing game. We both took a swig of beer and looked at each other a long moment. Her eyes were looking into me and I could almost feel them penetrating my soul.

"Better. I quit."

"A fresh start never hurt anyone," she agreed without hesitation.

"I agree."

A sharp tone erupted from the kitchen and caused us both to jump.

"That'll be the bread," she said, getting up.

The kitchen was cheerful, with white cabinets, burgundy countertops, and various flowers. The backsplash was unique. It was made up of 5x7 tiles depicting vacation pictures of Kellyn and Wyatt in places like Disney World, the Grand Canyon, and snorkeling with dolphins. Framing them were smaller, multi-color glass tiles.

She retrieved a pan of bread. That aroma of garlic made my stomach growl.

"Good, I see you brought your appetite. I should probably check the steaks. Do you want to join me on the deck?"

I carried her beer and followed her through the sliding door.

Although it was small, the deck was inviting, with flowers, furniture, and bird feeders around the perimeter. The décor had been chosen with care. Bright blue irises stood out from yellow pillows in contrast to the dark wicker sofa and chairs. The birdhouses were tastefully bejeweled in splashes of claret, amethyst, and emerald. Several fairy houses hiding amongst the box shrubs offered both whimsy and charm. Hanging just beyond the railing on the stairs was a giant cluster of copper wind chimes, whose clangs and gongs were deep and soulful.

Kellyn was perched over a charcoal grill, which surprised me. She must've seen my expression as she looked up from flipping two rib-eyes and peaked into two foil patches containing vibrant summer squash, onions and diced potatoes. I could smell rosemary. I handed her the beer.

"There's nothing like a steak on a charcoal grill," she began while replacing the lid.

"I haven't seen one in a while," I admitted.

Taking a sip of beer, she shrugged and gestured toward a chair. I sat down, delighted to discover they were as comfortable as they were beautiful. My phone vibrated in my pocket but I ignored it.

"Did you weave the wicker yourself?"

This cracked her up and she said so. "Oh yes. It was during a trip to Jamaica. I got the inspiration from having my hair braided."

"Well, I can see you learned well. They are tightly woven yet comfortable."

"Thank you. You should see what I can do with beads."

"Is there anything you can't do?"

I didn't know if I hit a raw nerve ending but her smile slipped and I suddenly felt like a heel. She waited a few seconds to respond.

"Did I say something wrong?"

I wasn't sure if asking would help but her body language changed drastically. Her arms were crossed now and I could swear I saw a wall shoot up between us.

"No, you didn't. My mom is always telling me that men don't like women who don't need them. I guess your comment reminded me of her. I do a lot for myself. I can't wait for a man to do it for me. I guess, if she's right, I'll be able to build stuff, work on my car, and mow the grass for the rest of my life."

"I think it is cool that you can do all of that."

"Yeah, well, you might be the only one."

I was telling the truth but if I was honest, it was intimidating. Was her mother right?

Emma

CHAPTER TWENTY-SEVEN

It wasn't until the phone started ringing that Emma realized she'd called David by mistake. She nearly wrecked the car trying to hang up. Before she could retrieve the phone, the call ended. Emma was relieved but also somewhat offended.

Even though she'd called him by accident, she was surprised that David hadn't answered. He always answered.

After a short drive, Emma turned into David's driveway. Her heart was hammering and she felt breathless. It wasn't as though she was breaking into his house. He wouldn't care if she let herself in and searched through the closets.

Inserting the key in the lock, she passed a furtive glance in both directions as though she was expecting the police to pull up any second.

A loud growl precipitated a series of barks and frightened her so badly that she tripped back away from the door. Landing hard on her backside, she stared at the wooden door and imagined the beast within. She was sure the animal was peering out the glass window at the top of the door because she caught a splash of white in the pane.

Half crab-crawling, she scrambled to her feet and retrieved her key, and then ran to her car.

When had he gotten a dog? Emma brooded as she drove home. The headlights on the road ahead pulled her back into the present and she pressed the brake. A small sedan was pulling out of her driveway. As it passed, she got a brief view of the driver. Emma couldn't make out much but she could tell the vehicle's occupant was female.

Immediately, her mind flooded with questions. Who was this woman?

She resisted the urge to fly into the driveway. It had never dawned on her that she might not be Nick's only lover. For the past few months, they had been inseparable. What if he had met someone while she'd spent so much time at the gallery?

Although she knew paranoia was common after an episode, she recapped the fact that David, who always answered, had ignored her call. Then, a mystery woman was leaving her home. Pulling her keys from the ignition and hurrying to the back deck, she kept repeating to herself that everything was okay. The problem was that her heart was pounding and her head was full of treachery.

Nick was putting some papers away and straightening up their tiny living space. She could see him through the sliding door. He was dressed in a t-shirt and jeans. Anxious and suspicious, Emma stood there watching him.

He must've sensed it because he turned and saw her. He smiled and strode over to open the door.

"Hey, babe, glad you're home."

"Hey," Emma said finally. She was trying to remember the techniques that her therapist had taught her to slow her thoughts and focus on her breathing. It wasn't happening.

Had he seen the mistrust in her eyes? Who was this woman? How was she going to explain the scrapes on her palms and knuckles that she'd just realized were bleeding?

Emma wanted to hide from his kisses as he embraced her. She could tell he'd showered and she didn't detect any perfume.

"What have you been doing?"

"Work stuff. Just biding my time until you got home."

"Work stuff?"

He shrugged. "The club has a list longer than my arm of things they want me to do. I was just trying to get a handle on what I need to start with and whom I'll need to help me. What have you been up to?"

One of her palms hurt but she was glad. That pain was keeping her grounded instead of flying off into her head.

"Not much. I called my mom and talked to her for a while."

"How is she?"

"She's good. Glenn was cooking and making her laugh. She sounds happier than she's ever been. They invited us to Hawaii."

"Oh, wow. That would be awesome," he said, retrieving leftover steaks, coleslaw, and baked beans from the cookout at Jose and Maria's house. "You hungry?"

She wasn't but she nodded. They sat down outside with heaping plates. Nick ate vigorously but Emma was having a hard time getting the fork to her mouth.

Nick stopped eating. "Emma, what's wrong?"

"Who was she?" It came out flatter and colder than she'd meant it to.

Nick's eyes narrowed but only because he was thinking. Even this many years removed from his head injury, he still had problems with his short-term memory. She saw recognition dawn on his face.

"She's a work associate. We're working on a project together. She's a designer named Diane. I'm sorry I didn't tell you about her before."

His tone was low and even, and Emma wanted to look away. There was no real explanation as to why she felt so suspicious, like any minute betrayal would spring out like a jack-in-the-box. She wanted to tell him that she was reliving the worst moments of her life in her mind.

"I haven't heard from you much today and I saw her pulling out as I got home."

"I can see why that would seem suspicious. I'm sorry, Em. I should have told you Diane was going to stop by."

"I'm sorry. I'm just feeling anxious." She paused. "And having some flashbacks."

"There is nothing to be sorry for, Em. I'm sorry. I'll do better at communicating so you won't feel anxious. Do you want to talk about anything?"

She wanted to tell him everything but how could she? How could she possibly tell him that she was responsible for two deaths?

David

CHAPTER TWENTY-EIGHT

Kellyn was bent over the grill, tending some mushrooms and onions she'd wrapped in foil. I edged my phone out of my pocket and saw the name on the screen.

The four letters assaulted my eyes. My mind began racing over the reasons for the call.

Before Kellyn turned around, I shoved the phone back into my pocket. Emma would have to wait, whatever her problem may be.

Like an icepick to the brain, the thought seared through my cerebral cortex and rendered me paralyzed. Had Emma only been with me because she needed something?

I had no answer for that and my face must've drawn up like I was in pain. Kellyn started when she turned around and saw me.

"Oh my God, are you okay?"

"I'm fine. I just remembered something."

Her eyes were wide and a smirk blossomed on her mouth. "Was the thing you remembered about a body you forgot to bury? That look!" she teased.

"I was thinking about what you said about not needing a man. That made me wonder if Emma stayed with me because she needed something."

She didn't seem perturbed by the change in subject or that I was talking about Emma.

"That might have been part of it. But, David, you were together how long?"

"Thirteen years."

"I doubt her needing you was what kept you together that long."

"Those look perfect," I said, pointing at the steaks.

"Well, let's eat," she said and we got up together to retrieve the food.

I was grateful that the steak required chewing because it gave me time to reframe my thoughts. Everything was delicious and I told her so. The savory onions and spices were doing a good job of keeping me in the moment.

"For a long time after Seth died, I felt guilty if I was doing anything fun."

"What did you do to combat the guilt?"

Kellyn shrugged and chewed thoughtfully. There were a few long moments of silence until she finally set her fork down.

"You know, there really isn't a formula. I made myself do things. It wasn't always fun but I did them anyway. It takes time. You have to figure out what you feel guilty for."

"Just so you know, I'm not forcing myself to have fun right now."

She smiled. "I'm glad to hear that."

The rest of dinner and cleanup was lighter conversation about growing up and stories about Wyatt. I don't know why but I started feeling anxious as I helped her clear the table. We had stopped talking and for several long moments it was quiet. Too quiet. I wondered if I had blown this whole thing talking about Emma. The phone call was still on my mind and I wondered if Kellyn was going to say anything about the painting in her front room.

"Do you like jazz?"

"I do," I said, relieved at the break in silence.

"There is a jazz band playing at the neighborhood bar a few blocks from here. We could walk down there."

"That sounds good."

I waited by the door while she retrieved a few necessities. Armed with a blanket, she hastily shoved her arms into a moss-green hoodie.

The conversation got silly as we walked to the bar. Commenting on everything from the house with thirteen cars in the drive to the window with eight cats peering out, we laughed so much that my side was throbbing but I didn't dare say anything. I was having fun.

I paid the cover and got us a couple of beers. Kellyn picked a spot directly facing the stage but in the deeper grass. It was also far enough removed that we could leave without disturbing anyone. People of all ages were already camped out on blankets or camp chairs.

The outdoor stage was just big enough for a drum set, keyboard, bass, saxophone, and mic stand. The introductions were done by a petite blonde who turned out to be the keyboardist.

I felt antsy and uncomfortable sitting on the ground. She sat cross-legged, while I had my legs straight out in front of me. We didn't talk much in between songs but we shared several looks that made the hair stand up on my neck. Various body parts touched, sending waves of electricity through me like a lightning strike.

My inner narrator was laughing at me for the schoolboy experience I was having. *It's like you've never been with a girl.* I wondered if she could also feel the heat or it was just me.

The tenth song was a dreamy rendition of 'Someone to Watch Over me'. I felt as restless as a toddler. The steak was weighing heavily on my gut and I started to worry that sitting on the ground was building up gas.

"You ready to go?" she read my mind.

Looking over at her, I nodded, noting something in her eyes that I hoped wasn't disappointment.

We wordlessly gathered up the blanket and headed back toward her place.

We walked slowly, as if we both wanted to prolong the evening. She seemed sad.

Without thinking, I reached down and took her hand. She didn't seem hesitant or eager but slowly interlaced her fingers with mine.

"That was nice. Did you enjoy it? How is your side?" She sounded anxious.

"They are good. I really loved it. I'm sorry I was so fidgety. It's still hard to find a sweet spot that doesn't hurt."

"I'm sorry," she replied quietly.

"No, it's fine."

As she leaned her head into my shoulder as we walked, her hand suddenly felt so small in mine. Her silence made me wonder what she was thinking but something told me not to ask her.

My own thoughts were trying to take over the moment. How many times had Emma and I walked along like this? How many times had I assumed she was feeling the exact same thing I did? Maybe she had but then again maybe it was just me.

Kellyn pulled her head away and released her fingers from mine. We were standing in front of her house, although I didn't remember getting there. She turned to me.

"Thank you for a lovely evening."

"Thank you for cooking and taking us to a jazz concert."

"You're welcome. Thanks for indulging my jazz whim."

"Here I was thinking you're a romantic, but it's the music you crave," I teased.

Her eyes lit up like twin moons. "Guilty on both counts."

This was that moment. If there was going to be a kiss, this was it. I had started to sweat from the effort of holding a fart back. The pressure in my abdomen felt like it could blow at any second.

I took her hand and bowed slightly, praying the movement wouldn't encourage my intestines to sound a trumpet. Kissing her knuckles lightly, I looked up at her.

"Mademoiselle, you are enchanting and beautiful. I pray we can do this again soon."

I pulled the French accent from decades ago and hoped I didn't sound like a complete idiot. She didn't laugh. The smile was warm and I'd have sworn she blushed.

"I'd like nothing better, monsieur."

Letting her hand go, I stepped back. The window for the kiss had closed but the gas had reached meltdown. I could feel my abdomen expanding.

She turned toward the door and I knew I made a face of both panic and anguish. I didn't want to run to the car but I was afraid that the most memorable thing about this date was about to be an epic fart.

Turning at the door, she smiled at me as if she knew I had to go.

"Thank you, David. Good night."

I gave her a little wave, immediately chiding myself for being an idiot. She waved back and shut the door just in time.

If there had been a plume of neon-colored exhaust behind me, I wouldn't have been surprised. There was no trumpet but the smell was like a garbage dump and toxic waste site had combined. It was disappointing that my first date had ended this way. Instead of kissing a beautiful woman,

I was farting in her driveway. I'd felt like a loser before but this was an all-time low.

Part of me wanted to drive by Nick's place as I got in my car to head home. Pulling out my phone, I wondered if it was too late to call Emma back. She was a night owl, and it still bothered me that she'd called and I had no idea why.

Scrolling to the number, I poked the screen and listened for her voice. It rang several times and I should have hung up. Suddenly, the line was picked up.

"Hello?"

It was Nick. I clicked off and dropped the phone in the seat beside me.

To recap, I'd had a great date that left me with gas, pain in my side, feeling like a loser, farting in the driveway, and calling my ex after 10 p.m., only so her new boyfriend could answer.

I pressed the gas pedal and ran a light intentionally. I told myself I was angry at Emma but I knew it was projected. I was the one who'd worried all night about why she'd called. I was the one who'd worried enough to give myself an upset stomach. It was me who'd chosen to fake a French accent and kiss Kellyn's hand instead of telling her I wasn't feeling well. And it was me who'd called Emma after 10 knowing she'd be with him.

I pulled into my driveway faster than I meant to and almost hit the curb. Without straightening the car so it wouldn't look like I drunk-parked, I sprang out and sprinted to the door. Houdini was already barking incessantly, and I prayed he wouldn't bite me as I barged in. He didn't bite me or jump on me. The barking stopping as soon as he saw me and was replaced by a wagging tail.

"Good boy," I said and headed at high speed to the bathroom.

Emma

CHAPTER TWENTY-NINE

E mma usually felt warm wrapped in Nick's arms. Right now, though, she felt as though she'd been immersed in a frozen lake.

Slipping silently from the bed, she crept into the dining room and retrieved her keys. Once in her car, she felt like she could breathe again. She'd left him a note explaining she'd gone to the studio. By now, he was used to her midnight madness. Nick described her sudden and voracious need to paint like a werewolf's affliction over the full moon.

Creeping up the back stairs like she wasn't supposed to be there, Emma opened the door to the studio and turned on the lights. After turning on some music, she fixed some coffee and made her way to the sofa. Momentarily perched under a mass of blankets, she listened to the dulcet tones of Sara Bareilles. As she stared at a blank canvas on a solitary easel, an image began to take shape. It was cathartic to let her anxiety bleed onto the canvas in plum, indigo, emerald and yellow. As the image became clear, she forgot about all her feelings and questions, flashbacks and nightmares.

The child on the canvas was riding a carousel horse. Emma concentrated on the details. The glint of light on the horse's eye and flare of nostrils gave the illusion that it was real.

After the sun had risen, and hours of painting, Emma stopped to survey her canvas. She knew exactly what had inspired the image. The small boy with brown curls, head thrown back in delight, was riding a white horse with flame-colored mane. The toddler seemed undaunted by the angry snarl of the horse fighting his bit or the hint of mischief in the shiny obsidian eyes. This ride was one of abandon.

Sipping coffee and looking at her work in the streams of sunlight, she smiled. The carousel symbolized a nightmare. They always had in her mind. The horses always looked angry to her, running in endless circles, and to music that was loud and frenetic. It always reminded her of the futility of nightmares. All the angst and images spinning around and around and never resolving anything made her feel like being stuck on a carousel.

Why had she painted such a jubilant child on a symbol of anguish? To anyone else, he was a boy enjoying a cherished childhood activity. To Emma, it was the instruction to hold on and enjoy the ride or take the nightmares by the reins.

Exhausted, she burrowed into her covers, allowing her eyes to close and praying that her own nightmares would stay away. It was sometime later that she was nudged by gentle hands.

Nick looked concerned when she opened her eyes.

"Are you okay?"

"What time is it?"

"Three o'clock. When did you go to sleep?"

"I don't know."

He joined her on the couch and Emma was glad for his touch.

"Man, I was tired. I didn't feel you get up. I didn't even know you'd left until your phone rang."

"My phone rang?" she said, realizing for the first time that she didn't have it with her.

"It was David. He hung up when I answered so I guess he's okay."

The pain in her chest turned out to be caused by holding her breath. David hadn't answered while he was on his date but he did call back.

"I'm sorry he woke you. I'll call him back later," she said, kissing his neck. "And I'm sorry I got paranoid. You've never given me any reason not to trust you and I'm sorry I let my paranoia make me doubt you."

"Next time you feel this way, you'll tell me, right?"

She nodded, suddenly feeling little.

"I love you," he said.

Pressing her face against his neck, Emma worked to hide her feelings of guilt and shame. She was still thinking about Jake and all she had lost seventeen years ago. She felt guilty for that too. Here she was accepting the comfort from her new love while thinking about the old one.

"I love you too," she said.

David

CHAPTER THIRTY

While I was on my date, the adrenaline must've overpowered the pain. Now, it felt like someone was using me for a drum. Desperate for something to distract me, I looked around me. The box of journals caught my eye. I hoisted the box and brought it to my bed.

Staring at the books of different sizes and designs, I suddenly felt overwhelming guilt.

She left them, I told myself. Yet, I knew they were her private thoughts.

The desire to understand what happened to us was stronger than my guilt in the end.

I pulled them out one by one. She consistently wrote the date on the right side of the cover page. Arranging them in chronological order, I picked up the oldest one. It was purple with an embroidered teddy bear on the front.

The bear had unraveled some and the pages looked tattered. Gingerly, I placed the book on my lap and opened the cover. Staring at page after page, I felt more and more guilty. The tiny handwriting was faded but still legible, and I began to wonder if there was something wrong with my eyes. Either she had started doing drugs or this journal was in some kind of code. Letters replaced names and there were stretches of nonsensical prose.

My side and head were pounding so I reached for my pills without taking my eyes off the pages. Without much effort, I deduced that "D" was for her brother, Daniel. Multiple references to a butterfly made me think she was writing about her mother. They woman flitted around as though she had wings. A small entry at the bottom of the second page caught my eye.

"I found butterfly smashed on the steps. Thought dead but only hurt."

Another on the next page made my chest hurt.

"Hid butterfly in box. Safe until monster sleeps."

She had told me that she used to hide in a large footlocker in her bedroom but I didn't think I'd ever put it together. Ruth was under 5 feet tall and weighed somewhere between 90 and 100 pounds. It was heartbreaking to think of her balled up, with both kids, in a large footlocker meant for toys for a few minutes, let alone hours.

Page after page, the teddy bear told the story of broken bones and daring escapes. She literally had documented a year of terror in light, flowy descriptions of dragons, butterflies, and monsters. Page after page, I became more and more angry. How could anyone do that to his own family? The pain meds were working and my chest hurt from anger so I lay down. Sleep came for me and I dreamed about being trapped in a box.

Emma

CHAPTER THIRTY-ONE

She hated that the back of her mind was still shadowed in suspicion. It didn't make sense to be this comfortable in someone's silence but still wonder if you could trust them.

He got some sushi takeout and they ate it in the car on the way home. Emma didn't have much of an appetite but she forced herself to eat.

When they finally went home, they both piled into the shower. Watching the hot water rushing over Nick's skin, Emma breathed in his scent. Unyielding to the water, the hardened muscles forced rivulets to flow over carved topography until falling free to the drain beneath them. She was glad to have something to focus on and let her desire take over.

They ended up in a heap in the bed, covers strewn with the pillows across the room. Nick passed out with legs and arms splayed over all four corners. The sections of his brown skin were a sharp contrast to the white sheets. Normally, she'd be intertwined with him but she couldn't free herself from a sense of dread. Nick's phone was blinking.

It wasn't hard to slide out of the bed. She lifted his phone off the bedside. Grabbing a towel, she eased out of the room. One of the beanbag chairs in the living room had a blanket on top of it so she pulled it around her and settled into the pliable blob.

Opening his phone, Emma could see that the blinking was the notification that he had a text from someone named Brandy.

"Found Paradise. We'll talk soon."

She wondered if it was some kind of code. Who was Brandy? Much of what she'd done after the incident was question herself and whether she was operating from a rational mind. Like everyone else with her condition, Emma couldn't trust that she wasn't going to have another episode.

Emma knew it was wrong to look through Nick's phone. She couldn't stop herself, though, reading message after message from Brandy. Nothing seemed flirty or inappropriate.

It was a strange, ongoing list of exotic things punctuated by 'talk soon' or 'check in later'.

Maybe if she hadn't spent so much of her life writing in code, she would have dismissed this right now. He'd told her about Diane but not a word about Brandy. Why had she never heard of either of them or seen them at the club? Out of 159 contacts with complete names, there were only two female entries, Diane and Brandy.

Whether she was thinking with her rational mind or not, she had to know who these women were and why they were listed by first name only.

David

CHAPTER THIRTY-TWO

I woke with a clear picture of the things I wanted to accomplish. I pushed myself out of the covers, ignoring the stacks of journals. Part of me wanted to keep reading. The other part knew that I wasn't changing reality by delving into the pages.

After a quick shower, letting Houdini out, and toasting a bagel, I headed out to my first task.

Thirty minutes later, a cheerful bell over the door announced my arrival.

"Hi. Welcome to Pittman, Nichols, and Mack. How can I help you?"

"I have an appointment with Mr. Nichols."

I did. I'd made it online just like one would order flowers.

The receptionist was in her early fifties but sporting purple hair. She was overdressed for her post but the Anne Klein suit and Christian Louboutins did give the impression of success. She'd asked for my name, offered me a beverage, and instructed me to sit in the adjoining lobby. A re-run of a popular 80s sitcom was on, and I watched it while I sipped my coffee happily.

"Mr. Campbell?" a melodic tenor voice called from the doorway.

Turning, I saw a tall, thin gentleman with pale blue eyes and expensive glasses peering at me.

"Bill Nichols," he said and shook my extended hand.

"David Campbell."

"Let's get you divorced," he said with a smile.

Later, as I stood armed with two envelopes of paperwork, another bell announced my arrival.

The current installation was breathtaking. I read about the artist and was shocked to find that she had been blind. Her work was vibrant and evocative. One piece caught my eye and I stood admiring it so deeply that I didn't hear the footsteps behind me.

"David?"

My growing goatee, tousled hair, jeans, untucked shirt, and flip-flops must've been shocking because Emma's mouth was hanging open.

"Hi. This is amazing," I said, hooking a thumb in the direction of the painting. "Where did you find her?"

"She's the grandmother of one of our friends."

"Well, it's amazing. I'm sure it will fly off the walls." I paused and handed her the envelope. "Here's the divorce papers," I blurted out.

"Thanks," she said, half-smiling.

"I'm sorry it has taken so long."

"No problem," she replied, holding the envelope like it was fragile.

"Do you want to get some lunch?" I blurted the words.

"Sure," she said, and turned to retrieve something from the office.

Emma emerged with a sweater, her phone, and her hair pulled into a ponytail.

"Okay, I'm ready."

I shot forward and opened the door. She smiled and then waited for me to step out so she could flip the 'Open' sign to 'Closed' and lock the studio.

"Where to?" she asked.

"The Hole?"

"Sure."

The Hole was a local dive. It had originally been called Joey's Hole until residents complained that it sounded vulgar.

It was a short walk down the block. The bright sunshine with an occasional cool breeze felt good. We didn't talk much and I was okay with that. After reading about her childhood, I was feeling protective and had to fight my instinct to take her hand. I was just glad to be with her.

"How's the new benefactor?" I wanted to know.

"He seems nice but I haven't really had much contact with him. How are things with you? How's your side?"

"It's healing. Still hurts but I'm good."

"When did you get a dog?"

"Not long ago. He's friendly, er… well, I think he is. I adopted him from the pound. Did you come by the house?"

She nodded absently. "Last night. I was checking on you."

"Oh. Did he act aggressively? I'm sorry if he scared you."

"I started to unlock the door and didn't expect an explosion of barks. I never really saw him but he sounds big. At least you got a good guard dog. What were you doing last night?"

"Dinner with a friend."

She seemed amused. "What's the dog's name?"

"Houdini. Well, that's the name he came home with."

She giggled. "He's an escape artist?"

"So I've been told. He hasn't tried to run away yet, or pulled any rabbits out of any hats."

She laughed but her eyes looked far away. I ignored that and enjoyed a shared laugh. Was she sad I'd brought divorce papers?

The Hole was empty except for the owner and one of his sons. Emma navigated through the sea of white tablecloths, each with a small vase of fresh flowers, and got us a spot by the corner window.

"This okay?"

I nodded and we sat down. This wasn't a place where a waiter came to your table. Orders were placed at the counter. Today, Joey walked over to the table with menus and glasses of water.

He was in his fifties and looked like he'd been a bodybuilder since birth. Despite his 5'6" frame, Joey looked like a tough guy.

"I haven't seen you two in a long while," he said, vigorously shaking our hands. "Good to see you!"

We both told him it was good to see him too but Emma's averted eyes told me she didn't remember him at all. Luckily, he didn't pursue a conversation and left us to decide what we wanted.

I felt sympathy for Emma. She was staring at the menu bewildered. She had struggled with deciding on food since the episode. I could see the indecision in her face.

"You used to love the calzone here. Is that what you're thinking about getting?"

"That does sound good." She lifted her head and sniffed the air. "Mmmm, that smells good. What are you getting?"

"Meatball sub," I said shrugging. The smell of fresh beef, oregano, garlic, and onions, and Joey's top-secret sauce, had my mouth watering before we made it to the table.

"That sounds good too. Then, so does the calzone, and the lasagna."

"Does lasagna still give you indigestion?" I asked, hoping it would help.

She shrugged. "I don't know. I haven't eaten any lasagna lately. Did it use to?"

I nodded. "That's why you like the calzone."

"Thank you."

Joey interrupted my reply with a basket of fresh rolls. "Since there's no one here today, I'll take your order."

We both told him what we wanted and he nodded approvingly. "We'll get this right out."

I watched him go, envious. The guy had eight kids and worked his ass off. But he was happy and it was obvious. The restaurant was full of pictures of his family, and the one over the door was of him and his wife, Theresa, at their wedding.

Emma was grimacing when I looked back at her. She was pressing on her temple and had her eyes squeezed shut.

"Are you okay?"

"Yeah. I'm having a blinding flashback. Like I just saw Joey walking away but his hair was darker."

I inventoried my own memories. The gray seemed to pop up overnight. I only remembered because he'd gone on about how having eight kids should have made him gray in his thirties.

"That was about three years ago," I said.

What else was she remembering? I stuffed hot bread in my mouth to keep from asking.

She got a roll too. For several long seconds, we both just chewed away our thoughts. It wasn't clear if the flashback caused her pain or was just overwhelming. So, I asked.

"Does it hurt?"

She shook her head, still chewing the steaming roll.

"No. Well, not physically. Oh, this is so good."

On cue, her phone rang and Nick's face popped up on the screen before me. Smiling. What I would have given for my sledgehammer now. She didn't leave the table. There was no need since there was nothing to hide.

"Hey, babe," she said, more cheerfully than I'd hoped.

Listening to myself chewing, I tried to block out her recalling to Nick that I'd dropped by with the divorce papers and that we were having a celebration lunch. I gritted my teeth over the prospect of Nick joining us. To my relief, she concluded with how she loved him and would see him later. I could see the questions whirling through her mind plainly in her eyes. After all these years I knew the look. I doubted that any of them had anything to do with me.

"Everything okay?"

"Yes, sorry. Nick wants me to come by the club. What were we talking about?"

"I asked you if your flashbacks hurt and you said not physically."

She nodded. "Right. They're constant sometimes and seem to be out of order. It's exhausting more than it is painful."

"I'm sorry, Em. That doesn't sound like much fun. Is there anything I can do?"

She looked at me with those golden eyes for a long moment. "Was I hard to live with?"

"No. I mean, you have your quirks."

She laughed. "Well, at least some things never change."

"You know I'm here for you. Divorce or not."

"Thank you, David."

I knew she was lying. When we were kids, she'd climb into the treehouse with new bruises and I'd ask if she was all right. She always answered the same way by telling me everything was fine. Briefly, I thought about her journals. There was no use pursuing answers. She'd spent her life avoiding questions and keeping her thoughts to herself. I wondered how many times she had told me everything was fine when it wasn't. I had to know but I knew she wouldn't tell me now.

Emma

CHAPTER THIRTY-THREE

I t was good that he'd arrived when he had, although the last thing she'd expected to see was David with divorce papers in hand. The man standing before her wasn't the David she'd known for the last few months. He didn't look sad, and that relaxed her.

As they made their way through lunch, she tried not to think about Nick's phone. Maybe she'd jumped to a crazy conclusion and there was a legitimate reason he had those contacts.

It was sweet how David had steered her away from the lasagna. For the second time since the episode, she was really enjoying their interaction.

When Nick had called, her anxiety returned. She told him about the papers and that she was having lunch with David.

Nick asked her to come by work after lunch. She couldn't tell by his tone if he just wanted to see her, was excited about the papers, or something else but he sounded strange. When the call ended, she tried to focus on David.

"So, what made you decide to get a dog?"

"Oh," he paused and raised the last morsel of meatball to his lips, "I don't know. I wanted one as a boy and the house felt empty."

She ignored the pang. Was he trying to barb her or just being honest?

"What was it about Houdini?"

He fixed her with his green eyes in such a way that it made him look like a wolf. Emma felt panicked, as though he could read her thoughts. Could he tell that she was just making conversation but was miles away in her mind?

"He looked like he didn't expect anyone to love him. Like he'd accepted his fate. They were planning to euthanize him and it was like he'd given up hope. Plus, I'm going to be home more. I told Bruce that I'm quitting."

"I'm glad you got him," she offered.

"Yeah, me too."

He'd said something else. What was it? Everything seemed delayed.

"Wait. Did you just say your quit your job?"

David nodded with a slow smile. "Yes. I was wondering if you heard that."

Emma plainly didn't know if David loved or hated his job. She did know that he'd been predictable and cautious as a boy and she'd witnessed that in the months after the episode. This was like a whole new man.

"What are you going to do?" she asked.

"I'm going to make some furniture and rethink my life."

"What's your friend like?" The question slipped out but Emma didn't try to catch it.

He choked on his drink and began to cough. One hand signaling that he was okay, and the other on his side, he coughed a few more times. Emma hadn't meant to catch him off guard but she was curious about the woman. She still wasn't sure if she felt jealous.

When he finally composed himself, they both laughed. Dabbing his eyes with a napkin, he mused, "Apparently, I have a drinking problem."

Emma flashed back to the two of them on a beige couch watching the movie 'Airplane'. She didn't react outwardly this time. Instead, she just laughed and played along.

"Surely you can't be serious."

David's face brightened as he realized she got the joke. "I am serious," he started, then they both finished the line, "and don't call me Shirley."

Peals of uncontrolled laughter followed, and for a few seconds there was no past nor future. There was only the two of them, and it didn't matter what she could or couldn't remember. She couldn't give him hope but she could give him this moment. That felt good.

"She is very nice," David answered finally.

"Nice? Well, tell me about her."

David seemed reluctant but Emma pushed him. It was also nice to have something else to think about. The montage of memories of Jake and the worry about Nick were making her feel heavy.

"She's a single mom and a bank president."

"Wow. She must be really tired."

David laughed. "It does sound exhausting."

"Well, I'm glad you found a *friend*."

She saw it happen. It was like he'd suddenly remembered everything and clammed up.

"Ready to go?" David changed the subject.

"Sure," Emma replied, disappointed in herself for making the moment heavy again.

He walked her back to the studio after lunch and she was glad. The anxiety over Nick wanting her to come by had returned and brought friends. She had an acute pain in her stomach over the dread and self-loathing. Was this new? Had she always felt this worthless? She didn't know but she hung onto David's arm as they strolled back. She didn't want to let go. Then, she had a thought that made her feel even worse.

"That was fun," he said softly.

"It was. I needed to laugh. Thank you."

They had stopped in front of the studio. David handed her a business card with a lawyer's name and contacts.

"After you sign, either give me a call and I'll pick them up or you can drop them by the lawyer's office. It's not far away."

David looked to his right and an unlocking sound came from a huge, black truck.

"Did you get a new car?"

He laughed. "Yes. I got a truck, a dog, and quit my job."

They both laughed and she touched his arm.

"Careful. People will think my crazy rubbed off on you."

He frowned. "Em, you aren't crazy. You've never been crazy."

"I'm not so sure but thank you."

When he opened his arms, Emma filled them without hesitation. No matter what they had become over the years, he was still Davy. Still safe. Still protective. And she needed all of that right now. She didn't know what Nick had in store for her but she just wanted to feel safe before she faced him.

THIRTY-FOUR

I would have laughed if someone had told me that my best day with Emma since all this started would be the day I delivered her divorce papers.

She had remembered our long-time joke from the movie "Airplane". We laughed and talked with greater ease than we had in longer than I could remember.

On the one hand, I was glad. On the other, I had questions. Why now? Was she just relieved to be rid of me? What if Nick was some kind of narcissist, controlling her with his constant love? My stomach churned from the unsettling feeling that I was more confused now. Maybe it was Joey's meatballs. A thought struck me so hard I would have batted it like a wasp if I could have.

Pulling out my phone, I called the one person I knew that might have answers.

Sophie always sounded like she was about to purr like a cat.

"David, I've been thinking about you. I meant to call. How are you, honey?"

"I've just delivered divorce papers to Emma and then we had a great time at lunch. She looked sad when I gave them to her and then she told me she was glad I had a new friend. I had dinner with a woman the other night and probably blew that because I was worried about Emma. She called me while I was with Kellyn. I'm so confused. Sophie, do you think I'm a narcissist?"

She rolled into a gentle chuckle. "No, honey. You aren't a narcissist. You're just a man."

"I don't know what that means."

She chuckled again and paused. "It's your nature to fix things. Emma looks sad so you want to figure out why. Then, if she's happy about your new friend, you want to know why. But you want to fix her, to protect her. You probably questioned if Nick is a narcissist too."

"Okay. What do I do?"

I could hear her smoking and suddenly wished I was taking a drag with her. Probably out of rebellion against my predictability, I'd started smoking in college. After Emma and I reconnected, she didn't like it so I quit. During gallery events, though, Sophie and I snuck away and smoked together.

"Baby, there isn't much you can do for her if she doesn't ask for help. My great grandmother used to tell me, 'All you can do is live your truth and forgive nostalgia'. It took me a long time to figure it out. I think it means that you have to find out who you are, let others do the same, and stop using the past to define either of those things."

"Thank you. Sophie, am I predictable?"

"I would call you steady, David. Sometimes you are predictable, but aren't we all? Go do some things that scare the shit out of you. You won't feel predictable anymore."

She'd already told me I wasn't a narcissist but I felt like a selfish ass for calling her and not asking how she was doing.

"You guys doing okay, Soph?"

"You need to come down and visit. You won't believe it. We sleep in and go over to our little kiosk around nine. Unless it's busy, we close up at two. Cook dinner together every night. Waistlines are trimmer, blood pressure lower. Things are good."

I was glad to hear it and I told her. We both had worried about Joanna over the years, so hearing she was healthier was welcome news.

I was still taking in all that she'd said long after we'd hung up. I'd promised to come down as soon as I could. She understood that there were things I needed to do before I could. All I had to do now was figure out what these things were.

Emma

CHAPTER THIRTY-FIVE

S he drove like a NASCAR driver because she was consumed with her feelings. There was a list of suspects to blame. She was anxious, suspicious, annoyed, and scared. Thoughts were gaining ground so she sped up.

Nick had not said where he'd be and it would have made sense to call him first. It was a large country club with vast grounds so he could be anywhere. She decided she'd just wander around to find him.

Emma knew it was because she wanted to catch him unaware. Maybe he was like the Johnny character from 'Dirty Dancing'. Maybe this was what he did. She could be one of many.

She looked for twenty minutes, realizing with every step that she was being silly. At least, she thought so until she saw the girl.

Tall and leggy, the blonde was in shorts and a tank top. She looked like a cross between Bo Derek and Christy Brinkley in their prime. In fact, she looked like the female version of Nick.

Emma spotted her coming off a trail that led to an area Nick had been working on last week. Cautiously crossing to the trail, she felt like a detective about to solve a mystery. It was both terrifying and invigorating.

When she heard Nick's voice and pulled up short, Emma dodged behind a tree since there was no other cover. She strained to hear the garbled words. There was someone with him but she didn't recognize the other voice, only noting that it was female.

She could not muster enough anger to counter-balance the paralyzing fear. Emma wanted to catch him if there was a lie to be exposed but she also just wanted everything to be all right.

She felt stupid squatting behind a tree, and even more pathetic that she'd let all the feels drive her here like a crazy person.

Pulling out her phone, she called him. He picked up on the first ring and told her what trail to come to. He seemed happy.

She heard him tell the anonymous female 'thank you'. Dashing out of her hiding spot like a frightened rabbit, Emma ran hard to ensure he didn't see her hiding. Barely making it to the trail and turning around, she saw him walking up the path. He was clean and smiling. She was sweaty and breathing hard. Nick took her in his arms immediately.

"I love you," she heard him say but his voice was muffled. He was holding her tight.

When he finally looked at her, disheveled hair and sweat beads on her skin, he chuckled as he removed a piece of pine straw from her shoulder.

"You didn't have to run, babe. I would have waited."

His blue eyes were sparkling like the Mediterranean Sea and she'd swear he might've been crying.

Still consumed by her anxiety, she smiled. "I couldn't wait to find you."

That was actually the truth. She knew she'd feel awful later if this turned out to be nothing but she couldn't get it out of her mind.

"Well, you found me and I have something to show you."

It wasn't the words, but the feeling began to transport her. She didn't recognize it at first but as Nick led her down the path, the trees and plants fell away. In her mind's eye, she saw palm trees and hibiscus, plumeria and bird of paradise, with its sharp orange and purple spikes. She felt her feet moving over broken ground, and the hand leading her was soft instead of calloused.

When they arrived in the clearing, Emma was so enrapt in the past that she saw Jake, smiling and excited. She fought to return to the present but the past wouldn't let her go.

He stood tall and bronzed, curly hair teased by the wind, and warm eyes locked on her. Emma reached out as he slipped to one knee. The plumeria and hibiscus framed him in dazzling pink, red, yellow, and the palm trees seemed to applaud. She felt her heart pounding and she wanted to tell him to run away from her. This would only end in disaster. He seemed so alive and she couldn't speak. The tears came like a cyclone, blinding and unrelenting. She could hear his words, his voice with its soft, deep timbre as the flashback continued assaulting her.

Nick's voice reached through the time portal and snatched her away from Jake and the awful cliff behind him. The emblazoned Hawaiian sunset faded and she squeezed her eyes shut, trying to focus.

"Emma?"

When she opened her eyes she found the same palms, hibiscus, and plumeria but a different man on his knee.

Before she could respond, the curtain fell over her eyes and she felt herself tumbling into darkness.

David

CHAPTER THIRTY-SIX

Staring at the delivered piles of wood, supplies, and equipment, I knew I should work on my newly designated man-cave. After destroying all the bins and remnants of her, I'd made up my mind I'd make this place mine. Problem was that I wasn't any different than most people. All the commercials about DIY projects encourage buying all the supplies and end up with that feeling of accomplishment. The reality for most was hiring someone to finish the job. I wasn't planning on hiring anyone but I didn't feel like working on it right now.

I also didn't want to sit in my room reading those journals. Splitting the difference, I brought a few of the journals onto the deck and pulled up an Adirondack chair that Emma and I had built together.

The cover of the next installment looked like a distressed postcard of Route 66. The pages were faded and her tiny handwriting was hesitant as she described her new home and classmates. The dates told me that she was about nine. There were still sections written in gibberish, which I now knew was code for abuse.

The next one, with an ink furry Strawberry Shortcake cover, told me nothing.

Retrieving a bag of popcorn and a beer from my derelict man-cave, I sat down with the next.

The book was plain blue and I remembered it. I'd seen her writing in this when we were kids. My heart was beating fast as I opened the cover. This was the beginning of us, from her perspective. I had no idea what I'd find here but I was eager for good news.

I opened the beer while a detailed description of her clothes jumped off the page. She mentioned the pink sweater and striped jumpsuit I remembered like it was yesterday. It was the first thing I'd seen her in. I read about her mother bringing them to school. Halfway down the page, I read, *"Met a boy named David. He was nice. He made me feel calm."*

She'd always said that she knew from the first day that she could trust me and I wondered if it had something to do with the calm feeling. Did "calm" mean "safe" in a child's vocabulary?

Page after page, I learned what TV shows she loved, what movies she wanted to see, and that she wanted cream-colored Guess jeans with a button fly. The one thing that was missing was me.

I knew this period of time had produced late-night sneaking out. We'd spent almost every day together after school. I had never been tempted to keep a journal. If I had, there would have been pages and pages of Emma and me. Descriptions of our adventures would have used up pen after pen, like the time we went looking for pirate treasure and instead found a seal we named Little John. At the time, everything revolved around her, and my journal would have reflected that.

This was also the time frame for the night I got into a fight with her dad. Well, it wasn't much of a fight but I stood up to him to protect her. I still remembered the night like it was yesterday.

It was a warm night and the Santa Ana winds were blowing. We'd been pretending we were ninjas on a secret mission.

Suppressing laughter, we crept along the perimeter of the backyard, taking turns crouching behind bushes or doing a gymnastic move. We were so oblivious that neither of us noticed him waiting for her on the back deck. When we finally made it to the house, he rose out of the concealed spot and we both let out a little yell.

"Get in the house, Emma," he ordered, and she immediately started forward.

I grabbed her arm. "If you hurt her, I'll tell the police."

"You threatening me, boy? It's none of your business. Emma, get in the house."

I was terrified but I stepped in front of her. "I won't let you hurt her."

"I won't tell you again," he said in a low voice through gritted teeth.

I held my breath as she walked right by him and up the stairs without incident. I'm not sure what I was expecting but I was relieved he didn't grab her. I was naïve. Her face was so sad as she disappeared behind the door.

When I turned to go, he lunged for me. My brain told my legs to run but my legs were tired from ninja moves. I faltered for a few seconds too long and he grabbed me by the hair and yanked me back. I'll never forget how his breath smelled of alcohol and vomit.

"When your parents call you home for dinner, does it sound like money dropping into a piggy bank? Have you lost your silver spoon? You won't find it here. You stay away from my daughter."

He had me from behind, his claws digging into my shoulder. I wanted to hurt him. Reaching back, I struck him a glancing blow to his balls. It wasn't enough to hurt but just enough to get him to let go. Whipping around, I put my fists up in front of my face like my dad had taught me. Bob was still stunned from the flimsy assault but, seeing me readying myself like a prize fighter, started laughing.

I thought he was too drunk, but he was faster than I could've anticipated. The blow crashed into my left eye like a missile and I crumpled instantly. I'd been in fights with boys my age, although only once or twice. There was no experience that compared to the pain that radiated from my face, through my eye, and into my skull cavity. My ears were ringing, and I couldn't form a cohesive thought. He stood there for a minute and then labored off toward his house. Lying there, I heard a series of thuds and grunts followed by a loud bang. He must've started tripping up the stairs. I didn't see the process but raised my head in time to see him collapse onto the deck. As I pushed myself up and ran home, I hoped he was dead.

Not long after that incident, Emma climbed up to our treehouse and told me that her dad had gotten new orders.

"We're moving to Hawaii," she said with big tears in her eyes.

I put my arms around her and we both cried.

"We could steal a boat. I know how to sail. We could go far away. So far away that he could never find us," I offered through my own tears. "I love you, Em. You're my best friend. I'll figure a way to come get you."

She brightened. "You will?"

133

I nodded despite the fact that I was eleven and had no idea how I'd make that happen. "I promise, Em."

The day they left my dad drove like a madman to get me to their house. He stayed by the car but I saw the reaction on Bob's face. He leered at us but didn't try to stop Emma from running to me. She threw her arms around me.

"I tried the hunger strike but I couldn't do it," she whispered.

"We could run and get in the car. My dad will help us."

"Then he would get into trouble and go to jail," she said.

"I don't want you to go," I said, trying to dash away my tears.

"It'll be okay, Davy. You're going to come get me, right?"

"I promise."

She looked up with eyes like tiny suns and paid me a kiss.

"I'll never forget you," she said.

Houdini put his head on my leg and caused me to spill my beer on the deck. I wasn't mad at the dog. It was like he sensed me going down the rabbit hole and came to get me before I fell. I patted his head for a long moment and then returned to the journal.

Twenty pages after the first mention of us, I found a small passage that nearly stopped my heart. *"I had another dream about David. I wish he'd go away. If I ignore him, it will only make him try harder."*

The book magically transforming into a rattlesnake and biting me in the face would not have shocked or hurt me more that those words.

She wanted me to go away. Although she hid from her father at my place, she didn't want to be with me. Emma used to call me her best friend. Why would you want your best friend and refuge to go away?

Controlling the urge to throw the journal across the yard, I stared, unbelieving, as the pages resumed their mundane inventory of celebrity crushes and dream ponies. There was nothing else about us or me. Nothing else about the abuse, her spending time in my treehouse, not a single mention of us planning to run away and live in Australia, no details of her hunger-strike attempt, and no description of the fight with her dad. Nothing at all.

I made myself read to the last page to make sure. Why hadn't she recorded us? Trying to rationalize why she hadn't, I had one soothing thought. Maybe she was afraid to write any of that because her father might find the journal. Maybe she just kept everything hidden in her mind like I had.

My next thought was not as soothing. Maybe everything I remembered meant nothing to her. I certainly felt like something was wrong with me, being sympathetic seconds ago but now bitterly assuming that everything had been a lie. She couldn't record the day we found a field full of butterflies but she did write that she wanted me to go away. In seconds, I'd gone from understanding and protective to devastated and angry.

Really? After all of that, what I regarded as one of the most significant times in my life, she couldn't write anything positive? I get hiding details from prying eyes but a small "I like David" would've been nice.

The next few books detailed the move to Hawaii. There were longer passages in code and I didn't take the time to figure them out. I didn't count how many times she mentioned the *"waves battering passive sand"* but I knew it meant her father was beating his wife regularly.

Part of me was determined to find something that could wipe away all the doubts or confirm my worst fears. The other part of me was trying to justify burning the journals, forgetting about her, and pursuing Kellyn.

And there I was. Caught between the reality of the present and the nostalgia of the past, I could barely breathe. For the first time since my dad had died, I truly had no idea what was to become of me.

What was worse was that I wasn't sure I cared anymore.

Emma

CHAPTER THIRTY-SEVEN

When she opened her eyes, Emma had no idea whose face to expect. Jake had taken her to their special place and proposed. They were young but he'd promised her that he'd do whatever it took to take care of her and their family. He'd spoken passionately about getting a place and living on the land. Even now, it still warmed her to recall how he'd promised to rescue her mother and bring her to live with them.

After he died, she'd painted the place, with its palms and flowers, as a memorial to him. It was the only way she had to expel all the pain and love that hollowed out a place in her like rocks worn by waves.

She'd kept the painting and hung it when she moved in with Nick. When he asked about it, she couldn't tell him the whole story. She had explained that the spot, high in the mountains, had been her favorite place on earth.

Without explanation, she knew that Nick had worked to recreate that piece of heaven right here. She understood now why he had the numbers of those women. He'd told her about the designer. Emma was willing to bet that the other was a plant specialist or new employee.

The face staring down at her wasn't devastated or dejected. He was still smiling and his eyes were like stars in a cloudless sky.

"Hey, lady, if you didn't want to marry me, you didn't have to scare the crap out of me. You could have just said no." Nick stroked her face. "Are you okay?"

"Yes," she said. "I love you."

She'd said yes to Jake too. In addition, she'd listed all the reasons why he should run away from her. She'd tried to explain the obstacles and insurmountable odds that she and her mother would escape her father. Jake had not been deterred or crushed. He seemed more determined, and laughed when she told him that her father would destroy them. She had said yes but she knew they were doomed. And she was right.

"Yes, you're okay or yes you'll marry me?" Nick wanted to know.

Suddenly, sheepish and ashamed she'd doubted him, Emma had to force herself to look into his eyes.

"Both. I'm fine and I want to marry you."

David

CHAPTER THIRTY-EIGHT

Three things I should have never done. The first was start drinking before 10 o'clock in the morning. The second was buy $300's worth of toys for a dog who didn't play. Finally, trying to figure out what went wrong with my marriage by reading my wife's journals was a bad idea.

I forced myself to keep reading. Book after book, I numbed myself to the harsh reality that she didn't write about me. Meanwhile, I had been in California, missing and worrying about her.

In the thirteenth book, she began writing about her dream guy. I was surprised to find my name hidden amongst the descriptions. She wanted someone rugged like Tarzan, handsome like Pierce Brosnan, and kind like David. I shrugged as though there was an audience. Houdini lifted his head from the deck as though checking on me.

"She said I was kind," I explained.

The dog merely yawned and stretched, resuming his nap unimpressed. We had sat outside together all afternoon. After turning on all the deck lights, it would have looked to an observer that I was having a gathering. Had someone peeked through the privacy fence, they'd have found a single guy drinking beer, talking to his dog, and reading his soon-to-be ex-wife's journals.

Still, something in me had to know why I'd only been mentioned five times in thirteen journals. I needed to know why there was such a huge gap between what I perceived and what had really happened. Maybe my life was a M. Night Shyamalan film and I was about to find out that I was actually already dead and didn't know.

Whatever the issue, the other biggest epiphany was that I knew very little about my wife. She'd never told me that she could surf or that she'd seen people attacked by sharks. She never mentioned that she'd learned Polynesian dance or that she danced with a small troupe that included her mom, Ruth. Her father had started spending more time on the ship and this allowed them to do more things.

I finished the rest of the books and sat there perplexed. I had no more answers than when I'd started. Not only did I feel stupid but now I was depressed that I'd wasted my time and evidently nothing I thought was right.

Toward the end of the last book, Emma wrote about meeting her dream guy. His name was Jake and her night with him had been magical.

"He is everything I've ever wanted. We've just met but I know he's the one."

There were a few other passages but I could tell the relationship had been significant. The pages ran out before she revealed much else about this Jake. I had never heard her talk about him but something sounded familiar. Had I heard her say his name in her sleep? I couldn't remember. So, what'd happened to Jake? How did she end up with me? I stared at the book as though there might be more words hidden somewhere.

It was then that I remembered the Kona coffee bag she'd hidden in the bins. Where was that? Could there be more information there?

Not without some effort, I got up and went into the house. The dog followed me, staying at my side as I staggered upstairs.

It wasn't on the floor where the box had been. Looking behind the dresser and under the bed, I searched for the secret treasure that had seemingly disappeared as mysteriously as it had appeared.

"Where is the Kona bag, Houdini?" I asked the dog.

He looked at the floor and then walked over to his pallet and lay down. He wouldn't make eye contact with me, so I laughed.

"Did you eat it?"

The dog pawed his covers for a few minutes and I watched in fascination as he uncovered the bag.

When I jumped up, it scared us both. I almost fell, and the dog was expecting some kind of punishment. Maybe it was the alcohol but I was convinced my dog could understand English.

"Good boy," I said and retrieved the bag. I gave him a pat to reassure him and began working on the knots in the drawstring. It took a few minutes and I resisted the urge to cut them with something.

Finally opening the bag, I dumped the contents onto the floor. Another book fell out, and my heart started hammering. The cover was a picture of a dramatic drop overlooking the mountains and ocean below, framed in vibrant flowers and the Hawaiian sunset.

There was an inscription. "For J&K". The date on the upper corner told me she was 17 when she wrote this one. On the other corner, there was a drawing. At first, I thought she had just been doodling. Turning the page, I readied myself for the juicy stuff. All the questions I had were about to be answered. I was sure. I think I was salivating.

The book was full of numbers. Each page meticulously written in rows of numbers, complete with punctuation. Obviously, each row of numbers corresponded to words as these were clearly sentences.

Clearly, her cypher methods had gotten more advanced and that made me more curious about what she'd written. What part of her story was so covert that she had gone to such lengths to hide it? Turning back to the cover, I studied the drawing. She'd drawn this in pen. It was a circular zodiac chart with sharp details. I'd seen it before but there was one addition I didn't recognize. On the outside of the sign for Cancer, there were two vertical lines with three dots to the right of them.

I stared at it for a long time. It was undeniable that she wanted to make sure that no one could easily decipher what the numbers meant. I was no cryptologist but I had a basic understanding of how ciphers worked. Emma had always been fascinated by them. We'd made a special trip, years ago, to tour the National Cryptologic Museum in Maryland. Emma was completely enthralled while I was entertained that the museum was housed in a former hotel.

Completely thwarted, I dropped the book onto the Kona bag and that's when I heard a crinkle sound. There was something else in the bag. Disregarding the book, I hoisted the bag up and peered inside. My eyes wouldn't focus at first. Reaching in, I gingerly retrieved a Ziploc bag and held it up to the light. There was something white inside. It was folded and I thought it might be a handkerchief. I reached in and drew the item out, unfolded it, and sat on the floor completed dumbfounded. The mystery item was a tiny onesie with a surfboard embroidered on the front. It looked brand new.

The dog came over and nudged me. After multiple beers and reliving Emma's childhood and teenage years, I was exhausted. Knowing I couldn't break this code or decipher the mystery of the onesie tonight, I set everything on the dresser and headed back to the deck to gather up the other books.

"Let's go to bed," I yawned.

The dog was waiting for me on the bed. The mournful eyes watched attentively for signs of anger.

"It's okay," I reassured him.

I wondered if he could hear my thoughts thrashing around in my skull like a squirrel trapped in a mailbox.

What had happened when she was 17? And who did the onesie belong to? Why had she encrypted the journal and hidden them both in the false bottom of a bin?

I was in turmoil. All I could think about right now was that maybe Nick was right. Maybe I never knew the real Emma. I'd slept beside her for years. How could I know that she snored sometimes but not know about her life? Why did I think I knew her?

Emma

CHAPTER THIRTY-NINE

She dreamed of Hawaii all night and finally got up. She lay down on the sofa that she'd taken from David's house. As she pulled a blanket around her, she suddenly remembered picking out the sofa with David.

They'd moved through the showroom, sitting on every couch and loveseat. They'd commented on every piece in different accents. Emma giggled at the recollection of David sitting on a large leather couch covered in a faux bear blanket in his best Scottish accent.

After hours, they chose a beige couch with peacock blue pillows because it had the right depth in the seat and the arm rests weren't too high when you sat on it. The delivery was going to take too long so they rented a beat-up flat-top truck from the hardware store and moved it themselves.

David was so animated and funny in that memory. What she remembered from childhood wasn't this version of him. She wanted to rewind and watch it all over. He was handsome and romantic, and she felt something she hadn't felt since her incident.

In the wake of becoming engaged and receiving divorce papers, she was surprised to feel aroused over the memory of David. They'd had sex on this couch after the movie and laughed at how they couldn't have known in the showroom that it was the perfect size for sex.

Maybe she had just assumed that her life with David had been like the months after her episode, with him looking sad and checking behind her constantly. Now, she realized that his overbearing tendencies might have just been his reaction to what happened.

Could she trust her memory at all? That was the question that plagued her. Recollections of Jake and David had flooded back into her head but what if none of those memories were correct? What if her mind simply played them out the way she wanted to see them?

Her arms began to tingle as she recalled soft, warm skin. She felt the tears prick anew in the corners of her eyes. Jake's nose came clear in her mind now. It was pure and real, and Emma wished she could touch that face just once more.

Nick stirred in the other room and broke her trance. She felt a tiny pang of guilt. Suddenly needing contact, she pushed off the sofa as though it was covered in snakes.

She pulled back the covers and slid in beside Nick. His warmth radiated through the sheets raising goosebumps on her naked flesh. Trying not to wake him, she edged closer until the hair on his stomach tickled her lower back. Nick suddenly uttered a groan that sounded like a word and Emma was afraid that he would roll over away from her. Instead, his hand reached out for her hip and then snaked up the front of her body. He pulled her closer and into his warmth.

The effect was instantaneous. He was solid yet malleable and she pressed back to get more contact. Concentrating on his warm skin, she let Hawaii and David drain back into the shadows and drifted into dreamless sleep.

It was hours before she woke again. Surprisingly, Nick was still wrapped up with her. She panicked, glancing at the clock on her phone.

"Baby? It's 7:30."

Normally, he was up by five and out the door before six. He grumbled and pulled her tighter against him. Emma thought that her getting back into bed might have messed up his sleep pattern and now she was the reason he was late.

"Baby?" She shook him this time.

"Mmm. You feel so good in my arms," he whispered into her hair.

"It's 7:30, honey. You are late."

He chuckled at this. "I forgot to mention that I hired an assistant manager."

Emma half-turned so she could see his face. His eyes were open and looked like ice on a frozen lake at sunrise. "When?"

"I hired her when I started designing with Diane. Her name is Brandy."

"That's great, baby," she finally responded, recognizing the name and instantly feeling like a heel.

"Yeah. And I took the day off so I can help you at the studio or stay out of your hair. Whichever is best."

Emma turned over to face him. She ran her hand over his chest, mapping the topography of his torso with her fingertips.

"What if I don't want to go to the studio?"

He chuckled. "I'm yours to do with as you wish."

"Oh, I think you know my wish."

He started kissing her neck. "Your wish is my command."

David

CHAPTER FORTY

The loud barking hammered me awake and I lay there breathless at 4 a.m. Whether a passing car, jogger, or some nighttime scavenger, I couldn't be sure what had pulled Houdini downstairs.

Hours later, while scrounging for some painkillers and making coffee, my internal to-do list was growing. Find out the reasons I never knew my wife; look up the rules for modern dating; call Kellyn; and try to get my life together.

I was pondering this when the phone rang. Seeing Kellyn's name on the screen, I wondered if I'd already broken a rule by not calling sooner.

"Wyatt and I were wondering if you were free for dinner tonight," she said.

"I am completely free. What time?"

"How about 5:30?"

"I will be there. Should I bring anything?"

"Just you. Wyatt is very excited about seeing you." She paused. "And so am I."

"I've been thinking about you both," I said.

I heard her smile. "I'm headed to a meeting but I'll see you at 5:30."

After I hung up, I realized that I had no idea what to expect from this. What were the rules for dating a woman with a child? I had no one to ask. Houdini popped his head up as if to offer assistance. That gave me an idea but I'd have to wait until later to ask her.

Grabbing my laptop and collecting the leash, Houdini and I headed for a small café called Hitch & Hound for breakfast. It was located near a popular trail that attracted runners, equestrians, bikers, and families.

There were hitching posts and troughs for horses, and it was okay to bring your dog inside on a leash. All the locals called the place H2.

Two horses were tethered to a long-split rail fence. The black and white paint was idly munching on grass, while the bay took several gulps of fresh water. Neither of them seemed to mind when Houdini checked them out.

An aged, red-framed sign hung to the right of the doorway at the entrance invited guests to seat themselves. Usually, the place was bustling but today that was not the case. An older guy with an excitable Shih Tzu sat in the far corner. The equestrians were both female and looked to be in their 40s. Both wore riding pants and boots and had helmets on the floor beside them. They smiled as Houdini and I made our way to a quiet corner near some large bay windows with a view of the city.

It wasn't two minutes before a perky young woman popped up beside the table. She had naturally curly hair and a huge smile. From her nametag, I saw her name was Katrina.

"And who is this?" she leaned over to pet Houdini.

"This is Houdini."

"Great name. Houdini's a good boy," she said, still stroking the dog's head. Houdini looked like he was in heaven, his eyes half closed.

"What can I get you today?" She finally straightened and met my eye.

"I'm thinking eggs benedict, side of fruit, and a toasted English muffin."

"And for Houdini?"

"I've never actually ordered for a dog before since he's my first. What do you recommend?"

"We have a sampler platter of treats that are homemade, grain-free, and made with organic beef, brown rice, veggies, and fruit."

I looked at Houdini, who licked his lips as though he understood. Katrina and I laughed as the dog continued his performance by sitting up and pawing the air.

"We'll take that," I said finally.

"Good choice. What a great dog," she said. Then, as she walked away, she looked back. "Coffee?"

"Yes, please."

Houdini put his head on my lap but was clearly watching for the waitress to return. She did return shortly with a cup of coffee, cream, and a container of sweeteners. In her other hand, she had a bowl of chilled fresh water for Houdini.

The dog and I both savored our beverages for a long moment. I looked out the window while I sipped the steaming hot java and powered up my laptop.

I started with Asian symbols. The doodle was too plain to be Asian, I discovered after I started looking at them.

Typing in the search box "symbols with lines and dots" netted multiple images and publications but none of them looked like Emma's. It was entirely possible that she had made it up but the precision of the rest of the cypher convinced me that it was a real symbol.

Clicking on the link "Ideogram ciphers" took me to a gaggle of ads and offers for a free decoder. There was no way to enter the symbol with the keyboard so I dismissed the notion of getting the decoder. In addition to other links, there were numerous questions, but the answers proved to be a dead end.

Our food arrived and I kept scrolling through language pages. Arabic had some dots but flowed into much more complicated strokes than simple vertical lines. Stopping long enough to savor my meal, I mused over Houdini eating slowly as though he was also savoring.

Returning to my search, I tried zodiac symbols next and found tons of interesting reading but nothing that explained the mark on the outside of the wheel. Although I'd never really given much credence to astrology, it was undeniable that the profile of the different signs was accurate.

Two hours of searching and reading all manner of things got me nowhere. I'd had a gallon of coffee. After leaving Katrina a huge tip for keeping her table occupied for so long, Houdini and I got in the truck to head home. It was time to call Kellyn and ask her about my idea.

Emma

CHAPTER FORTY-ONE

She felt bad asking him to work on his impromptu day off but she needed a few things done. Despite his brain injury, Nick didn't have trouble with his balance.

Surveying his muscular legs and derriere from the ground, she watched him go up the ladder without hesitation. There were several bulbs that needed changing and she wanted a few canvases hung.

Watching him and holding her hands up involuntarily, as if she'd catch him if he fell, she suddenly felt panicky. To distract herself from worry that he might fall, she asked him a question.

"If you could do anything, what would it be?" She smiled at the splendor of the powerful muscles in his legs as he climbed down the ladder.

"Well, it wouldn't be changing lightbulbs," he teased. Stepping off the last rung, he kissed her. "I'd like to travel and see the world, presuming that money wasn't an issue. I'd also like to go back to college since I bombed out. Then, after all that, I'd design my own furniture and planters."

"Wow, that's a lot. What would you study?"

He shrugged. "I think that's what the problem was before. There were too many choices. I mean, I like history, biology, and I'd enjoy anthropology and philosophy."

At this, he looked into her eyes. A slow smile crept across his face. She knew his looks but this one wasn't desire or amusement. His eyes were like the flames of a Bunsen burner.

"What I want most is to share my life with someone. To travel with a person that I love and who loves me. Regardless of money or success, the most important thing is right in front of me. You are what I dream of."

She found herself somewhat breathless at the unexpected intensity. She told him she felt the same but felt a pang that fragments of Jake and David were still drifting through her mind while Nick was declaring his love.

The gallery was 'by appointment only' and there were a couple appointments set up with potential buyers. All that it entailed was a meet and greet, standing by for questions while the client browsed, and taking their money. Emma wanted to paint so she asked Nick if he would mind playing shopkeeper. Nick was better at talking to people than she was, she rationalized. He didn't know much about art but he was genuine and a natural salesman. He sold two pieces by discussing the emotion that the images made him feel. It wasn't lost on Emma that Nick's physical appearance had aided his salesmanship.

Waving the second sales receipt as he entered the room, he teased.

"I've made $1000 for the gallery today. What have you done?"

It was something about how the light was draped over him that made her hold her breath. Golden fingers touching here and there but not engulfing him made him look otherworldly.

"Can I paint you?"

She could see it took him aback. He chuckled.

"Are you serious?"

"Yes."

He rubbed his jaw, which was his tell for those moments he felt self-conscious.

"Okay," he said finally. "How does this work?"

She curbed her enthusiasm, afraid that her exuberance might make him feel uncomfortable.

"Well, I'm going to pose you. Then take some pictures. Then sketch. And finally, I'll paint."

"How long will that take?"

Everyone always conjured up images from history where models stood for days or weeks while a painter worked. Digital cameras had ended the need for that.

"You won't be here while I'm painting. You only have to stand for the pictures and sketch. And it won't take that long."

"Okay. Where do you want me?"

"Actually, right where you are. And," she bit her lip, "will you take your clothes off?"

This made him relax. Nick was very comfortable in his skin.

"Oh, I see. You want me naked in the middle of the room?"

Trying not to blink, she had to remind herself to breathe as Nick slowly, tantalizingly, pulled the shirt up his belly and chest, raising it up his long arms, and finally discarding it on the floor. He never took his gaze from hers. As she watched him undo his belt and unbutton his jeans, the last thing she wanted to do was paint. She'd seen this man naked countless times but she focused like a hawk on its prey. As if he'd been an experienced stripper, Nick slid the denim down over his hips, the material gliding languidly over the lean, taut muscles as if reluctant. She caught the tiniest curl of a smile on his lip as he hooked his thumbs into the waistband of his boxer briefs. Blue eyes darted down and then back to her, as if to ask her if she wanted him to continue.

Emma tasted blood and realized that she was biting her lip with too much force. She let her eyes drift over him and then nodded.

The stark white of his hips stood defiant in contrast to the rest of his tanned skin. Nick covered his crotch with his hand and let the underwear fall to the floor. He then stepped out of them and resigned the gray briefs to the pile of discharged clothes.

Light cascaded over him, traveling like a downhill skier, touching here and there but leaving places in shadow. It surged into the crevices between his fingers, illuminating the exposed hair, as if even the light was prying for a look at forbidden skin.

Emma picked up her camera. He moved his hand. Watching her like a panther waiting in silence as its dinner wandered ever closer to its clutches, Nick captivated her. It was exhilarating and unnerving. She almost hated to cover her eyes with the lens, to break the tangibility of eyes to flesh. Nick stood completely still as she captured all of him and all of the light.

There was no room for anyone else in her brain. The flashbacks and fragments pressed together like boxes caught in a trash compactor. She wanted only to observe Nick bathed in sunlight, naked and unguarded, like the first Adam.

Had Eve felt tentative or daring? Had there been arousal before the fall? Emma sketched him and wondered what this feeling was called. Perhaps it was lust, love or joy. Maybe they were the same feeling defined only by context.

The moment she finished her sketch, she went to him. Removing her clothing with much less fanfare, they spent the afternoon rediscovering Eden.

David

CHAPTER FORTY-TWO

Kellyn loved my idea, and I was relieved. Some people might think me ridiculous but I felt guilty when I had to leave the dog alone. It didn't take any convincing. Kellyn immediately said that Wyatt would be ecstatic if I brought the dog.

I was no closer to deciphering what had happened to Emma when she was 17 or what the strange symbol meant. I still didn't understand what had happened to my marriage, who my wife really was, and who I had become. But I had a dog and a truck. And I was going to have dinner with an attractive woman and her adorable child. That would have to be enough.

Wyatt spotted us from his post at the window. I could hear him yelling to his mother as we approached. Taking a second to compose himself, the boy opened the door.

"Welcome to our house," he spoke cordially with a big smile.

"Thank you. This is Houdini."

"Who-deen-nee," he attempted.

"Yes, that's right."

He practiced softly under his breath while letting the dog sniff him and then slowly stroked Houdini's head. I watched as the child and dog accepted each other and Houdini's half-closed eyes told me that he wasn't planning to bite the boy. The child's face lit up.

"Please come in. Momma doesn't like me standing here with the door open."

I glanced up as Kellyn approached and nodded at Wyatt.

"Hi," I managed.

I'd spent the afternoon contemplating a provocative ice breaker so I felt lame uttering the simple greeting.

"So, this is Houdini," she said, crouching down beside Wyatt and the dog. Then, turning to Wyatt, "Go look under the counter and get the bowl we use when grandma brings her dogs. We'll put some water in it for Houdini."

Glad to be tasked with something important, the child ran in the direction of the kitchen. Kellyn stood up and looked me in the eye.

"Come on in." She turned and we both followed.

Wyatt had the bowl filled when we arrived in the kitchen.

"Momma, can I give him a treat?"

His face was earnest, and his hazel eyes kept darting to a small ceramic dog on the shelf. I assumed the head of the dog statue lifted.

"You'll need to ask David, baby."

"Mr. David, Houdini looks hungry. We have yummy snacks. Can I give him one?"

"I'm sure he'd love that. Are they in here?" I pointed at the ceramic dog.

"How did you know?"

Kellyn giggled behind me as I carefully removed the Bassett Hound head. There were a variety of treats inside. I watched in fascination as Wyatt carefully selected the treats. There was no way to tell what his thought process was but he obviously had criteria for the perfect snack.

Finally, he chose a large yellow-colored bone-shaped biscuit, two smaller green ones, and a medium-sized black one.

Astonishingly, Houdini stayed seated and waited patiently. Each time the boy reached into the jar, the dog scooted closer.

Wyatt presented a green bone first. I had no idea if Houdini would snatch it from his tiny hand and I was suddenly worried that little fingers might accidentally clash with teeth.

"Hold on, man."

I set the jar back on the shelf and replaced the head. Then, I walked behind the boy and squatted down.

"Hold your hand flat and put the treat in your palm."

I repositioned the treat and placed my hand under Wyatt's. We extended the bone to Houdini and, to my relief, he gently extended his muzzle and took the offered prize. Whether he'd been taught or knew that his prize master was a child, there was no way to know. Either way, I was delighted with my dog's manners.

Wyatt leaned back against me and repeated the process. Each time Houdini took one, the boy praised him. When all the treats were gone, he turned to face me.

"Mr. David, can Houdini and I play in the backyard?"

I glanced up at Kellyn, who nodded from the stove.

"Sure, buddy. But one thing."

The boy's brow furrowed.

"We're friends, so you can call me David."

Launching forward, he clutched my neck with his little arms and hugged me so tightly I couldn't breathe. Without another word, he released me, called the dog, and the two shot out of the back door.

As I stood up, I watched them from the window. I probably should trust the dog more but every horrible news story of dog attacks replayed in my head. Seeing the child throwing a ball, and then both of them running after it, I decided it was okay.

Turning, I found gray eyes watching me. She didn't hide her amusement or affection.

"You're a natural," she said, adding pepper to something simmering on the stove top.

"How can you tell?"

"You weren't sure how the dog would take the treat from Wyatt so you got down there to protect him. But you let him take his time choosing the treats and feeding them to the dog. And I could tell you weren't doing that for my benefit."

"Thank you. I've always wanted to be a dad but worried whether I'd be any good at it."

She touched my arm. "You have no idea what a relief it is for me. Dating is hard enough but even more so when you have a child."

The words soaked in like water on a new sponge. It took a second for them to permeate the surface of my consciousness. She'd said "dating" and that cleared up any questions about what we were doing.

"I'm sorry about the other night," I blurted out.

She giggled and turned back to her food. "You have nothing to be sorry for. First dates aren't the source of numerous movies or TV shows because they're smooth and blissful."

"I started feeling bad and was embarrassed to tell you."

"Don't worry about it. I had a lovely time and you're here now."

"Can I help you with anything?"

She nodded. "Reach in the fridge. In the vegetable bin you'll find stuff for a salad. The salad bowl is sitting by the sink."

Later, after a meal of baked chicken breasts, couscous, squash casserole, salad, and cornbread, I offered to help her clean the kitchen while Wyatt and Houdini played.

"You are our guest," she insisted, but her smile told me she would concede.

"I can load the dishwasher," I offered.

She handed me a plate in response. The look she gave me took my breath. I didn't even notice that Wyatt and Houdini had come into the house.

"David," the child pulled my attention from my thoughts.

"Yes, sir?" I stopped to give him my attention.

"Can Houdini spend the night with me?"

Both the child and dog looked up with sad, pleading eyes. It was both compelling and adorable.

I glanced over at Kelly, who was suppressing a laugh. She shrugged and I understood it was up to me. Turning back to the boy and dog, I sighed. I hated to say no.

"Not this time, buddy. I didn't pack any of his stuff, and plus, I'd miss him. But. I promise to bring him over again. Maybe earlier next time, so that you'll have more time to play. And," I paused, "if I ever need a place for Houdini to stay the night, I'll ask you first."

Both faces before me seemed dejected. Trying to soften the disappointment, I continued.

"Will you promise to give him food and water?"

Wyatt's face shot up and he nodded vigorously.

"And let him out to go potty?"

"Yes."

"And pet him?"

"Yes, and brush him."

"Okay, next time I need someone to keep him, you are hired."

The boy wasn't letting me off so easy.

"But how about tonight? Please."

I slipped down on one knee. "I'm sorry. Not tonight but we'll pick another."

"Okay," he said reluctantly.

"We're about to watch a movie. How about you take Houdini on a tour? Show him your room. Get into your PJs and brush your teeth. Then the two of you come down and choose a movie."

"Okay, Momma," the boy said, running out with the dog in tow.

We both watched them go. When I turned around, she was looking at me.

"Not many people could look into the 'please-oh-please' face and say no."

"Was that mean?"

She snickered. "No. It's necessary. And you handled it like a pro. I'm impressed."

"Did I read your shrug correctly? Were you saying it was up to me?"

"Yes." Her voice was soft.

Good to know, I thought. I'd already misread one woman for thirteen years. I didn't want to start a new relationship with misunderstanding.

Later, we had hot chocolate and cinnamon rolls. The dog nabbed at least two when Wyatt tipped them off his plate. Together, all four of us piled onto the couch and watched three animated episodes of five animal friends who go on imaginary adventures in their backyard. Wyatt and the dog were wedged between Kellyn and I but it was cozy. Eyes fixed on the TV, there were moments where the boy would rest his hand on my shoulder. Perhaps feeling replaced, the dog edged closer and dropped his head on my knee.

Kellyn and I exchanged looks of amusement and delight. The desire I'd seen earlier had now been replaced by something primal. I could feel her eyes on me when we weren't looking at each other. I watched nature shows. All female predators got this same look when sizing up a male. It didn't bother me. She had much to consider.

I thought of Emma and her journals. It had definitely shattered my confidence to see she'd only written about me a few times. There was a coded journal that I still had to decipher. I wasn't trying to win her back anymore but I still needed to understand. Maybe that would help me understand myself and why I didn't see us falling apart.

I looked back up. The boy was falling asleep. Kellyn smiled but something in her face had changed. I didn't know what it was but she had just decided something.

Emma

CHAPTER FORTY-THREE

The next morning, she looked at her sketch of Nick, considering her palette. It had been a long time since she'd painted anything other than children, animals, or landscapes.

There were only a few pieces left to be finished to fulfill her contract with her benefactor. She was ahead of schedule, although Mr. Aroosian didn't know that.

Other than her painting of Nick, she had too much on her plate with all the memories. How much had she actually forgotten? How had she lost so much of her life but remembered with stunning clarity the scariest night of her life or the devastation that came after that? Emma could have let some of those images slip into the shadows forever.

It wasn't that she wanted to forget Jake. It was just that she didn't want to relive him. He was gone. No number of painful walks down memory lane would bring him back.

For that matter, why did she have to remember the good times with David now?

Truth was, she felt angry but she wasn't sure where to direct it. Should she be mad at herself, God, the universe, the ECT, or her father? Where did it all start? She knew the answer to part of it.

And when was her penance served? When was it okay to forget and forgive, or feel free?

In addition, could she trust her mind? It had turned on her, after all. Like a family dog mauling its owner after years, her mind had viciously attacked her present, past, and left her future uncertain. Had she simply been overloaded with emotion? Were her emotions the enemy? That didn't feel right because she'd also experienced complete numbness, and that wasn't any better.

While she was in the hospital, she'd felt nothing. She remembered lying in bed and staring at the ceiling. She couldn't feel anything and imagined herself a zombie.

She imagined a lot of things. The doctor would come in, with his bushy eyebrows and scowl, shake his head, and write little notes. Then, he'd leave and shortly thereafter a nurse would replace him, same worried expression, and try to get her to drink something. They seemed to magically appear and disappear and she had been convinced they were trying to poison her.

It was like lying on a slab of ice. Her limbs were paralyzed. Her mouth wouldn't work and her throat seemed sealed together. Her eyes were open but she couldn't turn her head.

Her mind had been a different story. It was very much alive and active. She counted the ceiling tiles, imagined the face of Jesus in a cobweb, and debated over which was the best shade of purple.

That was what worried her. How long before her mind turned all of it off again? She had medication but she didn't always remember to take it. She had not gone to see her therapist in several months. Her medicine made her feel numb, but she had continued to take it. Why couldn't that be enough? She didn't want to talk about losing a baby or whether she felt it was her fault. Those were the top two topics that all counselors rushed to after reading her file. She didn't want to delve into her abusive father and docile mother either. No one knew about Jake so she couldn't talk about him.

Emma wanted to exorcise her demons but it wasn't going to be through talking. Art had always been her therapy. She'd just have to paint until the heaviness subsided.

Deciding to make some coffee, Emma saw the divorce papers on the counter. She had brought them up to look at them but had not even pulled the neatly folded sheets from the envelope once. She pulled them out and let her eyes drift over the legal verbiage that seemed like a foreign language.

Emma had no idea how David had turned out like he was. They shared one thing in common. Both had one drunk parent and another parent who tried to shelter their offspring. The biggest difference in their childhood was that David's good parent had died.

David had called her when his dad died. Her own father was home that weekend, which meant she couldn't talk on the phone any longer than to tell him she was sorry. Emma felt a pang in her chest remembering how broken and scared he'd sounded.

She felt sorry for him. Even when her father was abusing her, she thought of how hurt David must be. She thought of how lonely he must feel having lost his shield from his mother's abuse.

David actually wanted a relationship with his mother. He wanted to help her and be close to her. Emma, on the other hand, prayed every night that her father would go out on one of the Navy ships and never come back.

David was still taking care of her as he had when they were kids. The terms of the divorce were proof of that. He could have grown up cruel and entitled. Instead, he was taking great care to make sure that things were fair. Considering she had been the one who had left him for another man, he wasn't trying to punish her. That spoke volumes about him.

This inevitably made her think about herself. Ever since her episode, she'd struggled with feeling like a horrible person. As if, somehow, she'd brought this on herself. Maybe she should have spent less time numbing herself to her father and more time fighting him. She had even prided herself on being able to take his abuse and shield her mother from the brunt of his rage. How deranged was that? David's abusive mother had made him more caring. What kind of person had her bastard father made her?

The phone broke her reflection. She stared at the image of palm trees and ocean waves for a second before answering.

"Hey, Mom."

"Hey, honey. Sorry to interrupt your day."

"It's no problem. What's up?"

"I got a call from the people who bought the old house. They were remodeling and found some letters and a book hidden under the floorboards. I haven't looked at them but I can tell they are yours. Do you want me to mail them to you?"

She knew the book they had found. It had a plain red cover and the words "2 legit 2 quit" embossed in gold on the front. She'd recorded the whole summer with David and all the things she wanted to tell him. The letters were the few that she'd kept because they had been so sweet.

Looking at the divorce papers on the table in front of her, she realized that there was no real point to keep the journal and letters now. She almost laughed aloud at the fact that her "treasures" had stayed hidden for so long and what the owners must've thought in finding them squirrelled away under the floor. What secrets did they now know? She still needed to get into David's place and try to remember where her other treasure was buried.

"No. You can just throw that stuff away."

"You sure?"

"I'm sure but thanks for asking me. How are you?"

David

CHAPTER FORTY-FOUR

W yatt insisted his mother read one book but then me the other two. He nonchalantly called Houdini onto the bed and both fell asleep before the end of the second book. I didn't want to risk waking the boy so I let the dog stay.

"I think your son's just played me," I said when we were downstairs.

"Like a violin," she replied, laughing.

Despite her amusement, I could hear something serious in her voice. My anxiety only increased when she opened the back door and I followed her to the deck. We sat down on the wicker love seat. There was no moon tonight so the only light to see her with was shining out from inside. It left her partially in shadow. It reminded me of the night on the swings. Since I couldn't read her tone and could only partially see her face, it gave me a strange sense of foreboding.

The day after I got into a fight with Emma's dad, I lied to my dad about my black eye. I knew he'd notice right away and nervously chatted with him trying to distract him. I couldn't tell if he was angry at me but something in his voice sounded like there was some underlying feeling. This moment felt like that one. I took a preemptive sip of beer. I didn't have to wait long.

"I met her once," she said quietly, watching me with those eyes.

I knew whom she meant. Remembering the painting in the living room, I simply nodded.

"She was almost other-worldly. There was something so genuine and dynamic about her, and I felt like I had been put under a spell. She's so beautiful."

She continued and seemed restless. I took another sip of beer as she crossed and uncrossed her legs.

"Watching you with Wyatt warmed my heart tonight. He is so taken with you, and has been since the first time he met you. He's asked about you almost every day since."

"He's an amazing kid and you have done an incredible job," I said.

"Thank you. Only my job is not even a fourth of the way finished. There is so much left to teach him and guide him through."

"It must be overwhelming but I have no doubt that you'll make it look easy."

A brief smile touched her lips and she took a sip of beer. I felt a surge of adrenaline and knew something was coming. Swallowing slowly a big gulp of beer, I steadied myself as she chose her words.

"Earlier, when Wyatt was trying to talk you into letting the dog spend the night, I was thinking you both could stay."

Her eyes met mine and neither of us were breathing.

"But now?" I ventured.

"I've no doubt that the experts are right. My son needs a father figure in his life. But I have to be careful, David. Dating for single people is different than it is for single parents. It isn't about breaking your own heart but risking breaking your kid's heart too. He already loves you."

"Kellyn, I get what you're saying and I agree we should move slowly."

"David, you aren't divorced yet. You still love your wife and I don't blame you. I don't want to be a rebound and, even though my son needs a father, I don't need a man to complete me. I've already had one man who needed to find himself. See where that led. I cannot risk breaking Wyatt's heart or my own."

"What are you saying? You don't want to see me?"

"I do want to see you but I think we should limit it to seeing each other in the park. I also think you should go and figure out whatever you need to figure out before we move forward. Go find yourself and, if you're still interested, then come find me."

"I've been attracted to you since we first met. Up until then, I'd never thought of another woman. I felt guilty, and I guess I still do. Then, there's Wyatt."

I fearfully plunged on, sucking down some beer in hopes it would imbue me with eloquence.

"I lost my son. Until I met yours, I couldn't really tell how deep that hole in my heart was. All the things I'll never get to tell him or teach him. So, I agree. I have a lot to sort out before I could offer either of you more than brokenness. I care about you both but if we're going to give this a try, there are a few things I need to do first."

"You know I'm not telling you any of this because I'm not interested, right?"

That made me smile. "I saw the look earlier. I'm pretty sure I read it right."

This made her laugh. "You caught me. Please promise you won't stay away."

I glanced toward the house. "Well, I can't. Your child is holding my dog hostage."

We both burst into laughter, immediately trying to control the volume since it was late. When we stopped laughing, we were facing each other. Our eyes locked like magnets. She reached out and touched my face, rubbing my cheek and running her thumb over my lips. We didn't speak but I could see the desire in her eyes and feel it boiling through my body.

A scraping sound from the door made us both jump. We turned to see that Houdini was pawing at the panes. She turned to me.

"This is what it's like, you know?"

"What?"

"Trying to have a moment when you have kids."

I leaned closer. "At least this one won't talk."

We kissed and it was like a rainbow exploded in my brain. I saw fireworks. It may have only been seconds or years, I couldn't tell. All I knew was that her mouth on mine, her face in my hands, was the most bliss I'd felt in longer than I could remember. It took several minutes before either of us realized that the dog was still at the door and was now barking.

"So much for him not talking," she said ruefully.

We had another kiss when she walked me out. Part of me was relieved and the other was disappointed. She slipped her arms around me and we held on for a long moment.

"I appreciate your honesty and I heard what you said," I said.

"Thank you for understanding and please don't run away."

"We'll see you soon."

The dog whined all the way home. I wanted to join him. While I understood and agreed with her logic, it was hard to get a taste of something and then immediately go on a diet. Her words kept playing in my mind.

I let us in the house and went straight to bed. I found no comfort in my new bedding and welcoming mattress. The dog seemed to locate all the comfort I couldn't and his loud sigh indicated he was okay with that.

I felt elated and discouraged in the same breath. It was maddening that I felt guilty.

Emma had left me. She didn't mention me with any affection in her journals, yet I felt like I was doing something wrong. Kellyn had laid it out with a bow wrapped around it. She'd not been over-dramatic, nor had she held back. All I had to do was confront my feelings about Emma, go find myself, and then come back to her unfettered. Although it sounded like a straightforward plan, I couldn't help but feel overwhelmed.

"Emma left you," I said out loud, startling the dog and hoping my guilt was listening. As if expecting trouble, Houdini popped his head up.

"Sorry, boy," I said and laid my hand on his head. "It's okay."

The dog grumbled, repositioning. I wondered if he missed Wyatt. The two had been inseparable all night. To have all that attention and then have to leave was a hard pill to swallow. Now, I had something else to feel guilty about. In a small way, it helped drive her point home. The last thing I wanted to do was hurt her or Wyatt. But, did anyone set out to hurt others? Well, some people certainly did. My mother came to mind.

It was like the universe wanted me to learn a lesson in irony. No sooner had I thought about the woman than my phone rang. The explosive hum scared me and the dog. I flipped my phone over since there was no ring tone to tell me who was calling. The screen read "Mother". She had called before and I'd ignored it. Curiosity got the better of me.

"Hello?"

"What made you decide to answer this time?" Her tone was even and without mirth.

"Curiosity," I answered just as calmly, despite the fact that my palms were getting sweaty.

"David, I'm selling the house and settling some of my affairs. Your father left you a huge piece of land. Some developers want to buy it."

"What land?"

"I doubt you'd remember it, although I'm sure he took you there. It's north of San Francisco. Seven thousand acres."

"Why is this the first I'm hearing about it?"

"Because I kept it from you."

"And you're telling me now because?"

"I can't sell it because it belongs to you."

"And what if I sell it and don't give you a dime, Mother?"

"I don't need the money. I'm in liver failure. I need a liver transplant."

Some cosmic force punched me in the throat. I sat up, disturbing the dog, and put my feet on the floor for grounding.

"When were you going to tell me that?"

"Honestly, I wasn't. I figured you had your hands full with Emma. How are you?"

"Well, let's see. You aren't one for small talk. Emma miscarried our son, had a psychotic episode, got Electroconvulsive Treatment, forgot our marriage, and left me for another man. You and I will soon have one thing in common when Emma and I are divorced."

"Probably for the best," she said finally.

I shouldn't be surprised after all these years. She'd never shown me an ounce of warmth. After my father died, countless bike crashes, and the ordinary fears that plague childhood, my mother had never once tried to soothe me. Usually I held back, but I was a new man.

"Thanks for the compassion, Mom," I added the pronoun because I knew she hated it when I called her that. "You've got a lot of nerve. You keep my inheritance from me for twenty years and then try to appeal to my emotions by telling me you need a liver transplant. Yet, you can't spare a single kind thought for me after I tell you I lost my wife and child. Why did you even have me? What could I have possibly done to you to cause you to hate me so much?"

"I'm selling the house and having the tree house torn down. If you want to see it before it's destroyed, you will want to get here before Thursday."

Nothing could have prepared me for that cut. My dad and I had built the treehouse. Emma and I had spent countless hours there. Finding out that my mother had hidden land from me was not as big a betrayal as destroying the last piece of my childhood happiness.

"I'll catch a flight. Don't let them take it down before I get there."

She simply hung up and I dropped my phone on the floor.

Emma

CHAPTER FORTY-FIVE

As she sipped her coffee, Emma studied her ring and wished she had someone to talk to about it. She admired the marquise diamonds set on a nature-inspired, entwined gold band—two strands of gold that looked like vines. She understood why Nick had chosen it.

Emma did not remember much about her friends but she was sure having some girlfriends to *ooh* and *ahh* over the ring like in the movies would be fun.

She couldn't call David. He would definitely not want to hear about her ring.

The canvas hanging in her office was one from Maria's collection. That gave her an idea.

She needed to see Maria anyway. All of her grandmother's art had sold, including the piece in her office that she had bought for herself.

"Maria?" Emma spoke hesitantly when someone answered.

"Yes. Hello, Emma. How are you?"

"I'm good. I wanted to ask you to lunch."

"Okay. When?"

"When would be good for you?"

"Today or tomorrow will work."

"Today would be great."

After everything she'd contemplated this morning, Emma decided that new friends were the way to help her feel less isolated. Nick was her everything and he was good at it. But she needed other people too. No one had to tell her that she and David had been joined at the hip. During her counseling sessions after the episode, there was much discussion about codependency. Of course, she had no idea if she and David had been codependent but it seemed possible. Now she found herself in a new relationship that could easy be defined in those same terms. She and Nick called each other several times a day. They met for lunch. And only recently had they socialized with anyone. She was going to change that.

It was like a war cry. The feeling that welled up in her chest, tightening her throat, and drawing tears to her eyes. The words of her new mantra formed in her mind and radiated through her body. ***I don't know who I was but I know who I want to be.***

David

CHAPTER FORTY-SIX

I didn't sleep much, and what little sleep I did get was infested with nightmare fragments. I finally got up after countless times waking sweaty and breathless. The shock and pain of my mother's words were still so raw that I couldn't touch my phone.

It was enough to hear that she was very ill. My heart hurt at the thought of her having to navigate an illness severe enough to require an organ transplant. What was more devastating is that she didn't want a relationship with me, even though she was facing her own mortality. She had not even planned to tell me about it. I wondered whether anyone in her social circle would know to call me if she died. Had it not been for the land my father had left me, I might have lost the only mother I never had.

I didn't know what game she was playing but I knew I had to go. I pulled the laptop out of my backpack. The thin, cold aluminum felt harsh and unyielding in my hands. I'd bought it for Emma but she had left it when she moved out. It booted up fast. A few keystrokes and curse words later, I was booked on a flight to San Diego for the next day.

My next order of business was to find suitable arrangements for my dog. I didn't want to board him because that would seem too much like the pound. I didn't know if dogs suffered from PTSD but I didn't want him to relapse into a depressive state or think I'd abandoned him. Kellyn and Wyatt were the obvious choice but I worried that it might be too soon to ask such a huge favor.

During the time we'd spent outside while I was reading journals, Houdini had dug a small hole by the fence. I guessed that he didn't get his name by faithfully staying by his master's feet. It would be a travesty to see holes appear in Kellyn's yard, and I didn't want him to escape.

I typed in "boarding alternatives" and got several entries about doggie daycares. I clicked the first one because I recognized the name. The description sounded perfect. The place was called 'Diggers Daycare for Dogs' and featured outdoor places to play, a sandbox to dig in, supervision and positive socialization with other dogs. The place also offered grooming, obedience training, and tons of organic treats. It was located about a mile from Kellyn's bank. I picked up my phone and found her number.

She answered on the first ring. "Hey, you."

"Hey. I hate to ask for a favor but I've got to go to San Diego."

"We'd be happy to keep Houdini."

"Are you sure?"

She chuckled. "I woke up to a crying child wailing about how he didn't get to say goodbye to his best friend."

"Oh, man. I'm sorry."

"You and me both. But seriously, it's no trouble. What's in San Diego?"

"My mother."

I could tell she wanted to ask but must've thought the better of it. I explained about the doggie daycare. She was moved over my concern for her yard.

"That's very considerate of you," she said. "I know the place."

"I really appreciate this. I'll bring all his stuff."

"Don't worry about toys or treats. We're good on those."

"I'm going to come back to a fat dog, aren't I?"

"Probably. How long do you think you'll be gone?"

I winced. "I don't know. I can board him."

"No, that's not an issue. We're not going anywhere and it will be nice to have a dog. If nothing else, he'll keep Wyatt entertained. I just wondered..." She paused. "I just didn't know if what I said... If you were still..." She paused again, swearing under her breath.

"You didn't scare me off. I've got to deal with some things with my mother but I'm also working on me."

"Don't worry about your dog. Take as long as you need."

"I'm only worried he won't want to come home with me when I get back."

"Well, that's a possibility but we'll cross the bridge when we get to it. I look forward to seeing you, David. I should be home today by 3:30, so any time after that is good. You know where we will be."

"Me too. See you soon then."

I looked at the stacks of journals. Basically, I was negative step one at this point. I had more questions than answers, and an entire book written in nothing but numbers that seemed to contain the missing pieces. It wouldn't tell me anything about us but it might explain her.

I opened the cover and stared at the drawing with its strange symbol. I'd swear that the book vibrated every time I held it. Some mystery imprisoned in these pages was begging to be solved. There had to be a way to break this code, and I was determined to find it. Sliding the book into my backpack with the laptop, I decided I'd have plenty of time on the plane to puzzle over it.

It dawned on me that it wasn't just that I didn't know her. It was that she felt like she needed to hide parts of herself from me. Did she not trust me at all? Clearly, she had trusted me with her body and with her time, the years we spent together. That led to another series of disturbing questions for which I had no answers. What parts of me had I hidden? Do we ever truly reveal ourselves to another? Can we know another person fully?

Before all of this, I would have been able to answer those questions with certainty. Now, I wasn't sure about anything. Perhaps the trip home would help me uncover truths about both of us.

I also still didn't know about the tiny onesie. Had this been for our son? I didn't want to ask her. That might upset her and might also make her ask about the journal. I would return them but I wasn't ready just yet. I didn't want to just leave the onesie lying around.

When we bought the house, the closet came with an Ikea bookcase that to the casual observer looked like the perfect place for sweaters or shoes. The previous owner had mounted it and hidden the release latch on the back so that the whole unit swung out. The built-in cubby in the wall behind the shelf was perfect for a 17 x 13 safe, which featured a biometric fingerprint sensor and LCD screen. We both laughed when we bought it because it seemed so extravagant even though it wasn't expensive.

I didn't keep much in there. I still had her passport, which rested in the back of the safe with mine, and a stack of emergency cash. The important papers like our mortgage, life insurance policies, and birth certificates were also neatly stacked inside. A small black box stood in the back corner by itself. I reached and pulled it out, opened it, and admired a pair of my dad's cufflinks and my watch. I don't know why but I pulled the watch out and put it on. Then, I took off my wedding ring that I was still wearing and put it in the watch's place. I should have done it sooner. It was too late to chide myself for forgetting about it during my date.

The watch felt cool on my skin and, even though it had a history related to Emma, I decided it was time to reclaim my time piece for myself.

I placed the bag containing the onesie in the safe and closed the heavy door.

A short time later, the dog and I drove the small span of asphalt to the edge of the park. Wyatt was wearing jeans, a Mets shirt, and a full Batman mask with an attached hood. Kellyn shrugged as we approached.

"Hoodeeni," the boy exclaimed and threw his arms around the dog's neck as though they'd been apart for years.

The dog pranced in place, whined, and pulled on his leash with the strength of a tractor. When the tiny caped superhero rushed me, the dog wrapped his leash around us. Hug solidified, we crashed to the ground, which seemed like a ride to Wyatt.

"David! That was so fun! Let's do it again!"

My backside begged to differ and my side ached for good measure. I helped him up but not before the ecstatic dog had the chance to topple the child again. Kellyn was laughing helplessly. I picked the child up, commanded the dog to sit, and removed the grass that was stuck to the mask.

"Thank you, Batman. You don't know how much it means that you'd take care of Houdini for me. I hope this won't get in the way of your crime fighting."

The child shook his head so vigorously that the mask got out of alignment with his face. He straightened it, fixed me with a serious expression, and in the Batman voice said, "Every superhero needs a sidekick."

"Well, Batman, I think Houdini will be a good sidekick and you'll teach him the ropes."

He laughed and ran over to a small bag by Kellyn's feet, extracted a rope bone, and dangled it out to the dog, who barked with pleasure.

"See if he wants to play, baby. Don't just tease him with it."

I managed to get the leash unhooked as both the boy and the dog took off. In less than five seconds, they were tumbling and wrestling over the bone. The child managed to wrench it from semi-clenched jaws and fling the tattered bone a few feet. Kellyn and I watched for several long seconds before turning to each other.

"What?" she said smiling.

"How do you do it?"

"Handle a four-year-old? It's not easy."

"Make an ordinary park feel magical," I replied.

She caught me with keen gray eyes. "The same way you make the sun seem brighter."

"May I hold your hand?" I asked, passing a glance at the boy and dog getting farther away.

Her response was slipping her hand in mine, our fingers instinctively interlacing. She looked down, I presumed because she noticed I had taken off my ring. She didn't say anything but smiled at me.

We turned wordless and started in the direction of Batman and his shaggy sidekick. It took me several seconds before I realized I was holding my breath.

Emma

CHAPTER FORTY-SEVEN

Her lunch with Maria had been just what she needed. The two women had talked about the ring and Nick. Maria offered suggestions for the wedding.

They chatted for an hour before Maria had to leave to start collecting her children from school. For someone heavily pregnant, Maria had an amazing amount of energy.

"Oh, one more thing," Emma said, reaching into her bag. She pulled out an envelope that contained payment for the art she'd sold.

Maria opened it and stood transfixed as though she was trying to comprehend the numbers. She was saying something in Spanish that Emma decided must be a prayer.

"This is for all of the pieces?"

Emma felt a jolt. What if Maria had expected more? She hadn't considered that. The heat rising over her chest and neck made it hard to breathe. She swallowed.

"Yes. Is that less than you expected?" The last thing she wanted was her friend to be disappointed.

The woman's dark eyes shot up to meet Emma's anxious gaze. "I didn't know what to expect, but this," she paused and swiped the corner of her eye, "is amazing."

Emma took a breath of relief. The collection of Estella's art had been over a hundred works in various sizes. She worked to promote the fact that the artist was blind and priced them higher than most of the contemporary pieces to drive home the rarity.

It had worked. People who bought art regularly are more likely to spend more if the work is exclusive. The total after the gallery's cut was over seven thousand.

Maria held onto Emma for a long moment and both women cried. She thanked Emma in English and Spanish.

"You have no idea how you have helped my family."

"Your abuela would be proud to know that her paintings are going to be displayed all over the country."

It was true. Several pieces had been purchased by online buyers. One man visiting his family purchased a large canvas for his home in New York.

"She was very humble but I think you're right. It would make her proud."

Emma watched her friend drive away still smiling and crying. It felt good to have delivered on her promise that the work would sell. It felt better to know she had a friend.

She drove around until she ended up at the park and didn't know what had led her there. It was comforting to see the usual patrons walking on the track. She spotted two older ladies she'd nicknamed Thelma and Louise. Then, the mother in her LuLu Lemon pants watching five children, two of which had to be her own since they were dressed just like her.

Her attention went to a small boy in a Batman mask and cape playing with a dog. The dog was brown and white, with a brown spot over one eye. She caught herself laughing as the dog grabbed the cape and spun the little boy around like a rag doll. It was just then that she noticed a man and woman running toward the child. She was shocked to see that it was David and a woman she assumed was the boy's mother. They were holding hands. Given the fact that this was the same park across from the house she'd seen him at, Emma figured the woman was the mystery friend.

Emma watched as they both helped the boy up, subdued the dog, and stood there beaming at the boy. David lifted the child over his head. Lifting her camera, Emma got a picture of the four of them perfectly framed in sunlight. They looked happy. They looked like a family.

The past few months had been happy for her but she'd worried that her own bliss had destroyed David. As she now watched, she was glad to see David laughing.

Emma's father had had a knack for making his family think that he knew where they were at all times. It was not just regular stalking. He was so good at it, at showing up out of the blue, that it seemed he'd sold his soul.

She rejected the thought that she was like her sire. She'd had no idea that David would be here. Her father never seemed happy about people laughing or enjoying themselves. She was enjoying watching David play with the boy and dog. It was strange to see him holding hands with the woman. Even when she was leaving him, it made her feel safe that he still loved her. Then, his distress over her leaving became too heavy a burden to bear.

Karmically, it was probably bad that she was a little jealous of David. He knew exactly what he wanted. He wanted a family. Once upon a time, she had wanted the same but now it was too painful to imagine. The only children she would ever have were captured in her paintings, static and safe. Emma liked it that way.

In a way, she'd done David a favor by leaving. If they were still together, he would have come to resent her for not wanting kids. This way he stood a chance. Maybe there was a chance that the hurt she'd caused David might undo the devastation she'd caused Jake. Emma hoped so. She wanted to be free of the past.

The other thing she resolved was to see her therapist.

David

CHAPTER FORTY-EIGHT

I told Kellyn everything about the conversation with my mother. I didn't have the courage to tell her that I was reading the journals yet. She listened without interjecting any commentary. When I finally stopped talking, she simply nodded.

"Sounds like she is scared."

"You think so?"

"Well, it also sounds like she doesn't want much to do with you—aside from the sale of the land. But yes. She sounds scared. I don't really buy that this was all to let you see your childhood treehouse again."

"I like the way you just call things like you see them."

She shrugged. "What else can we do? I'm not saying it'll be a happy reunion but I do think it will give you some closure."

"That sounds good. Any closure would be welcome. I don't really know what to expect. As awful as she's been, she's still my mother. I've always loved her. Obviously, I knew one day she would have health issues."

"Well, look at it as a gift. This land she kept from you is valuable and she is giving you a chance to see your treehouse. Maybe going there is a bridge to your mother as much as your treehouse is a connection to your father."

"Maybe. I'm sad about my treehouse and how she told me. And I'm angry with her but I'm terrified that she still won't want anything to do with me."

"I'm glad you're going. And don't worry about Houdini. Wyatt started doing drills after I told him. He had to see how long it would take to jump out of bed, run downstairs, open the back door, and put food in the bowl. Plus, he wanted to set a record so we did that twenty-seven times."

We laughed and turned to watch Batman and Houdini resting momentarily. The dog was on the ground, legs splayed out like he was broken down. Using the dog as a pillow, the boy was looking up at the sky. I could tell that he was talking about the shapes of the clouds because he kept pointing at them.

"Thank you for this. I hope it won't be too much trouble."

"Do you know why the Darling children had a dog for a nanny in Peter Pan?"

"No."

"The dog is the only one who has the energy to run around and keep up. It can't talk so there's no chance of inadvertently passing on curse words or negative judgments. And they can go to sleep easily for five minutes here and there and then do it all again."

"So, it'll be good for you that Houdini can watch over Wyatt is what you're saying?"

"I think he'll run his little behind off and it won't be so hard to get him to bed. And he'll wake up easier and happier because he's excited about taking care of Houdini."

"You're welcome," I said and we laughed.

The boy had lifted his mask so he could kiss the dog on the nose. We looked at each other and shook our heads. Kellyn looked at my left hand.

"You took your ring off."

"I did. I should have before. I, well, I don't know why I didn't."

"Yes, you do. It's okay to admit you had hope. It's okay to still care about her."

"I don't want to hate her. I just need some closure. I want to understand what went wrong. Who was it that said that 'those who do not learn from the past are doomed to repeat it'?"

"George Santayana."

"Did you really just know that? Wow."

She laughed with me and touched my arm. "George also said, 'when men and women agree, it is only in their conclusions; their reasons are always different'. Maybe it isn't about what went wrong but understanding the reasons you two came to this conclusion." She paused and squeezed my arm. "And yes, I did just know that. My minor in college was philosophy."

"You scare the hell out of me."

"Good," she said with a wink.

I didn't hear Wyatt approach so I was surprised to see him standing beside me.

"We want you to come play with us," said the caped crusader. The dog added a whine.

I didn't have to look at Kellyn to know she was suppressing laughter. I could feel her shaking beside me. Without taking my eyes off the dynamic duo, I reached deep into my memory vault and pulled out my best Superman imitation.

"Wonder Woman. Batman and Houdini need us."

"Come then, we have much to do," said the tiny Batman.

Kellyn placed her hands on her hips and thrust her chest out. "I'm ready, Batman."

He gave us the Batman scowl and then turned and ran toward the playground. Soon, all of us were climbing, sliding, and swinging. Houdini sneaked away and used the time to rest.

All of my earlier anxieties and questions disappeared. There was only room for saving the world from the invisible horde of bad guys by swinging higher, climbing faster, and sliding down to begin again. Wyatt missed a rung on his way up for the fortieth time.

"Superman, use your super strength and lift me up."

After I boosted him to the platform, he turned grinning, gave me a wink and said, "Thanks for the lift, buddy."

I laughed because his commitment to the character was absolute. It also kept my throat from closing up. Now there was way too much at stake. Having had a brief glimpse of what a family looked like, felt like, I was even more determined to find my answers and get on with my life.

Emma

CHAPTER FORTY-NINE

When Emma was finally discharged from the hospital, she was assigned a therapist. She had no choice in the matter but, after a few sessions, discovered that she was comfortable with Rosalyn.

Rosalyn was a short woman with sharp features and pale blue eyes. She looked to be in her forties, had barely an ounce of body fat, and a smile that displayed all of her teeth.

"It's good to see you, Emma. Won't you come in?"

Emma followed the counselor into her office and chose a comfy leather wingback chair near the window. The woman sat across from Emma on a small sofa.

"I haven't seen you for a while. Mind filling me in on the last few months?"

Emma gave her the abbreviated version of moving in with Nick, asking for divorce, her business arrangement, and Nick's proposal. She left out that she had not signed the papers yet.

"Wow. You have had an eventful few months. How do you feel about all this?"

"Honestly, all of that is no problem. I'm having flashbacks and I don't know how to reconcile all the feelings. I go from happy to feelings of guilt and thinking that I'm a horrible person. How do I deal with all of that?"

The pale eyes looked at her so intensely it was like Rosalyn was looking into her soul.

"Okay. There are a couple of things that I think we need to address. First, we need to talk about the memories that might be repressed. The flashbacks, are they of your life with David?"

"Some. Others are from childhood."

"And these childhood flashbacks, what are they about?"

Emma explained that she had experienced arousal over David, and anger and repulsion over her alcoholic father. She didn't mention losing Jake. She didn't want to delve too deeply into that well. The water was already bubbling too close to the surface.

Rosalyn listened without interrupting, jotting notes, and acknowledging with short nods. Finally, she looked up.

"Why do you think you only paint children and yet you don't want any?"

Emma thought it was a fair question. She'd told the counselor that one of the reasons she'd left David was because he wanted kids.

"I'm actually branching out artistically."

"Sounds interesting. What have you painted?"

"I did a nude. Now I'm working on a family scene."

The woman sat forward and put her notebook down. "You have many extremes in your life. That is not surprising given all you've gone through recently. But you did not answer my question."

She didn't want to answer the question, though Emma knew she would have to make some offering.

"One of my first memories of my dad was him getting mad about all the stuffed animals I had. I was three years old. He was packing my stuff and suddenly became enraged. He ripped the heads and limbs off all my stuffed animals because they wouldn't fit in the box. When my mom came to see why I was shrieking, he slapped her and then spanked me for crying. I remember standing in a sea of bunny and bear heads, with stuffing falling like snow around me. I'd see other kids with their dads and remember that scene. I think I've always painted what I wished my childhood had been like."

"That certainly would affect most people the same way. Why do you feel you agreed to have a baby with David if you didn't want kids?"

"I don't know."

"Is it possible that you actually do want them but are afraid you'd become like your father?"

Emma shook her head, but becoming like her father had always been one of her fears. "I could never hurt a child the way my father hurt us. I'd rather die."

"Do you think a part of you is not dealing with the death of your baby because you were relieved?"

"No. I just don't want any. Why is that so strange? I had a shitty childhood and there is no telling how warped my mind is because of it. But I wouldn't want my baby to die."

"It's not strange to not want kids. I'm just concerned about repressed memories. You haven't mentioned any flashbacks to being pregnant or the miscarriage. Somewhere you have repressed something about kids, and it haunts you."

Silently, Emma agreed with the therapist. The wounds were deep and painful. She wasn't ready to talk about what might have been.

David

CHAPTER FIFTY

The flight was at nine a.m. I'd have to get up early and be at the airport by seven a.m. My side hurt from all the activity but I couldn't take the pain medicine since it would make me oversleep.

I pulled a backpack out of the closet and began filling it with my phone charger, laptop, pens, the mystery journal, and a notebook. I grabbed a couple of t-shirts, underwear, shorts, and planned what I'd wear on the plane. The only thing left to do now was sleep but I was pretty sure sleep wasn't ready for me. After a cursory check on doors and windows, unloading the dishwasher, and taking out the trash, I got into bed.

I was up by five-thirty, which was just enough time to roll out of bed and into the shower. After grabbing my backpack, wallet, and keys, I got in my truck and headed to the airport. Luckily, the airport was only fifteen minutes away. I would have time to park, check-in, get through security, and then get a coffee once I was on the concourse.

To my delight, I had no difficulty finding a good parking spot in the deck on the end of a row that was a little wider than the other parking spots. I didn't know how this trip was going to end up but it started well. After cruising through check-in and security, I headed for the closest coffee shop and purchased a double expresso latte, and ham and cheese croissant.

With time still to kill, I ended up in one of the airport stores. Picking up a magazine on Oahu, the latest David Baldacci novel, a bottle of water, and a neck pillow, I found a quiet spot at my gate and waited.

I'd never been one to fly first class, but I upgraded since I wanted some space. Having trailed behind a family of five, stroller, carry-ons and kids in various stages of meltdowns, I was glad for the upgrade now. I found my seating station, with its 27-inch TV, retractable tray for work or eating, and a luxurious leather seat that would convert to a bed.

The flight was bumpy and I kept looking at my watch as if that would somehow make the plane go faster. I tried to sleep, read, and watch a movie but the hours seemed to drag.

After we landed and I deplaned, I strode up the concourse toward the rental car counter. The rental clerk, a pimply faced college kid with long fingernails, suggested I upgrade to a convertible. I took his advice.

It had been thirteen years since I'd been to San Diego. Although all the familiar landmarks were still there, the place had changed. A multitude of restaurants and coffee shops had grown up in the abandoned parking lot that my friends and I skateboarded in every summer. A tech company had taken the corner where my favorite donut shop had been.

Some things were the same but had improved. The pair of concrete lions at the entrance of my mother's neighborhood had been sandblasted and looked brand new. The houses along the main drive had all been updated with new paint or new gates across the driveways.

Tall and imposing like a giant guard, a shiny new black gate stretched across the refurbished driveway of my childhood home. My father never wanted a gate because it made him think of prison. The first thing my mother had done after he died was install a gate.

The access system had also been updated. Instead of the previous metal box with yellowed intercom button and small camera, the housing had been upgraded to marble. A sleek, LCD touch-screen and large camera lens made me wonder if I was at the right house. I pressed the digital intercom button.

A woman's voice answered immediately but the heavy accent clued me to the fact that it was not my mother speaking.

"Yes, may I help you?"

I looked straight into the camera so that it would get a good capture.

"David Campbell to see his mother."

The gates opened quietly and I wondered how much you had to pay to buy silence from metal. The first gate Mother had was whining and bumbling but this gate seemed to glide along as though operated by magic. I experienced a sense of foreboding as I pushed the accelerator.

Emma

CHAPTER FIFTY-ONE

S he met Nick for a picnic at the club after her therapist. Ordinarily, she would have been glad to see him. Today she felt like she couldn't breathe.

He greeted her with a smile and kissed her.

"How did it go with your therapist?"

"Well, it wasn't fun but I'm glad I went."

It was true. Even though the woman had locked onto her like a heat-seeking missile, she had given her some things to think about.

After they had danced around her repressed memories, Rosalyn had talked about damage from childhood abuse.

"Victims tend to find themselves repeating the cycle by getting involved with abusive people. There are many kinds of abuse. People always hone in on the physical and sexual kinds but emotional abuse can be just as damaging."

It wasn't the first time Emma had heard that. The problem was discerning the difference between relationships with other humans who were also flawed and the ones who were actually abusive. She didn't feel qualified enough to determine someone else's mental state.

"There is also parental neglect. How do you feel about your mom in all of this?"

Emma thought about that before she answered. During the terror years, her mother had taken the brunt of her father's rage. Sometimes she would deliberately instigate a fight by dropping things.

One particular evening, her father came home and flew into a rage because dinner was not on the table. He immediately began yelling at the children for their rooms not being clean enough. Ruth had rushed to begin preparing dinner and instructed Emma to set the table. They both busied themselves, ignoring the yelling and insults from the other room. When they heard a loud pop, they knew that Bob had just hit Daniel. Ruth sprang into action. Emma watched her mother rake all the pots and pans onto the kitchen floor. The clatter interrupted the tirade but she knew it would bring the monster into the kitchen.

Ruth gave Emma a little smile. "When he comes, you and Daniel run."

Like a crazed bear, Bob roared into the kitchen, and the minute he passed Emma she ran, grabbed Daniel, and they bolted out of the door.

They ran until their legs cramped and forced them to stop. They ended up on the beach and stayed there until dark. Emma felt both relieved and guilty that her mother had given them a chance to escape. She both loved and resented her mother for her sacrifice.

"So, you felt glad it wasn't you or your brother getting the beating. This made you feel guilty and resentful?"

"I guess I just resented that she repeatedly risked him killing her but wouldn't leave him."

Emma realized she had never said that aloud. She felt bad for saying it but equally felt lighter.

"Hey," Nick interrupted her thoughts. "Where did you go?"

"Sorry," she said and picked up her fork. Dabbing at her salad, she realized the past wasn't ready to let her go.

"Still thinking about your session?"

She looked up to find the blue eyes searching. Nick was not a stranger to abuse or alcoholism. He'd told her many times about his own father.

"I've just realized I'm really angry at my mom. I've always been, but then I'd felt bad for it."

He didn't interrupt and she could tell he was listening to every word. She recounted the story of the deliberate distraction and how they'd stayed at the beach and then snuck back into the house after dark. They found their father passed out in his chair. Their battered mother was cleaning the kitchen. She had saved them supper and acted like nothing was wrong, asking them to tell her about their adventure.

"Her face was swollen and bleeding and she told us she was fine. She said she bled easily and made up a story about falling. She wouldn't even admit that it was him that did it."

"Do you think she was ashamed that she couldn't prevent it?"

"I don't know. I never asked her."

"I don't know if I've ever said this but you know you can tell me anything, right?"

Emma nodded but silently laughed. You say that, she thought, but only because you don't know. You don't know what happened because of me.

She thought again about the book and the other treasure. She had to find it.

David

CHAPTER FIFTY-TWO

The house was still French provincial, with fifteen windows visible on the front. The exterior was now painted a light beige with white trim and a frosted glass front door. As I climbed the few stairs to the entrance, I noted that the design of the black, metal door matched the design of the gate.

I didn't recognize the woman who admitted me. She was short and squat, with thick black hair and bushy eyebrows over fierce brown eyes. I estimated her to be in her fifties though she might have just looked worn in by life. She stepped back.

"Mr. Campbell, please come in." Her voice was the same one that greeted me at the gate.

The foyer was still magnificent, with its sweeping double staircase, crystal chandelier, and hardwood floors. The walls had been beige when I was growing up but were now a pale yellow with white crown molding.

"Your mother is in the library."

I thanked her and started forward on my own as she shut the door behind me. Unless Mother had done a complete renovation, I knew my way.

Walking past the enormous living room, with its floor-to-ceiling stone fireplace, I turned left and admired the art that lined both sides of the hallway. At the end of the hall, I turned right and came to some French doors.

My father had designed and built all thirty-six bookcases that lined the walls like knights in armor. I was shocked to see that she hadn't replaced them. Despite her affinity for alcohol, my mother was an avid reader and my father had gone to great lengths to buy books to fill the shelves with other worlds to which she could escape.

Not seeing her, I ventured deeper into the space. The air was cool and smelled of oranges. The library had always been off limits to me. Leather chairs and sofas, cedar tables, and several chaise lounges in rich burgundy offered visitors plenty of places to sit and read. Sunlight cascaded through the skylights, revealing the rich mahogany finish on the smaller bookcases and tables arranged throughout the space. The drapery and a medieval-themed tapestry were new. Not seeing her, I walked toward the only place she might still be found.

Perched off the left side of the house, the terrace was small but had its own fireplace and an amazing view of Mission Bay. A single, multi-paned door stood between me and her. My hands were shaking as I reached the knob. I forced myself to take a deep breath. Her back was to me but I could tell by her rigid body posture that she knew I was here.

Mother didn't turn or greet me. I felt awkward but pushed myself forward and around the small table where she sat with a book, tea kettle, and a steaming cup of something I didn't recognize.

She was dressed in a lightweight gown and matching robe, the material dancing in the breeze. I turned around to face her and almost gasped. Gaunt and emaciated, she looked nothing like the woman I'd known but rather a shrunken, yellowed version of her. Her green eyes were dull and receded into deep sockets. I must have looked shocked because she laughed suddenly.

"You should see your face," were her first words.

"I'm sorry, Mother," I stammered and struggled to find words. "I didn't know what to expect."

"Here." She pushed the kettle and an empty cup toward me. "You may need this more than I do."

"What is it?"

"Green tea with turmeric, lime juice, honey, and CBD oil," she offered without malice.

I poured the tea and sat in the chair opposite her. It smelled good but the dark liquid didn't look pleasant. I added extra honey just in case. Lifting the cup to my lips, I expected it to taste better than the conversation.

"Does it help?" I wanted to know.

"I don't know. Connie keeps fixing it for me so I keep drinking it. I don't think it hurts."

I could taste the lime first. It wasn't awful but the lime was bitter. The honey only improved the taste by offering something sweet. Assuming that the woman who'd admitted me was Connie, I wondered if she had been with my mother for a while.

"You must have questions," she said, reading my mind.

"I do," I replied and retreated behind a sip of tea.

"Let me save you some effort," she offered and poured another cup for herself.

I waited patiently as she precariously poured the bitter brew, returned the kettle to the center of the table, and added honey.

"I was young when I met your father. I hadn't experienced much of the world outside of the farm. He was rich and dashing, a gentleman with means, and my parents were so taken by him," she began, stirring her tea as though transfixed on something I couldn't see.

"I was in love with a local boy—a poor farm boy with big dreams. He asked me to marry him and we made plans to elope. And then, one sunny day, your father showed up, lost and charming. My parents had forbidden me from seeing Micah because his father had been to prison. I suspected their real objection was that he was poor and their own farm was in jeopardy. They got one look at this young oil tycoon, who was clearly fascinated with their only daughter, and saw a way out."

"I've only ever heard his version. He said you were the prettiest girl he'd ever seen. I thought you were probably equally taken by him."

"I didn't care about your father's money. He was handsome and kind but my heart already belonged to Micah, who saw me as his soulmate, not as a damsel in distress. I thought the interest would pass but your father kept coming back. I'm not sure whom he was courting because he spent so much time talking to my father. Soon, he was making small investments into the farm. Micah and I were trying to wait to elope after the fall harvest. He didn't want to leave his family without help, despite the fact that he had eight other siblings. Your father came by in September and took me to the county fair. He kissed me on the Ferris wheel, and when I told Micah we moved up our plans. The next night I was in my room pretending to be preparing for bed when my mother burst in and demanded that I come downstairs. I told her I was tired and she slapped me. She said I was ungrateful and listed all the reasons it was lucky I was pretty. She said I couldn't hack it as a farmer's wife. I didn't have any choice but to go with her. Downstairs I arrived to discover my father and Edward laughing and toasting each other. In hindsight, I should have known what was about to happen. When your father slipped to one knee and put a giant ring on my hand, all I could think was that Micah was waiting for me and I couldn't get to him. It wasn't until after the wedding that I found out that your father bought my parents' farm and gave it to them for my hand in marriage."

"What happened to Micah?" The words felt like betrayal as they spilled out. I should be defending my dad and the fact that he loved her and wanted to help. All I could think of was the poor farm boy shivering in the crisp fall air, waiting for a girl who would never show.

"He married another girl, worked hard and carved out the life he promised me."

"I never knew," was all I could say.

"Your father was a rescuer. He had some sense of nobility that required him to help those who had less than he did. He thought he was giving me a better life. He felt sorry that I was this beautiful girl living in a drafty old farm house. But he never once asked me what I wanted. I would have been content to be a poor farmer's wife."

"Why didn't you leave him?"

"The man I loved had already married and Edward could've taken my parents' farm. He gave it to them but held the deed. Perhaps he wasn't trying to hold it hostage but it felt like he was. My mother cried and cried, falling on him like he was a savior. I'd never seen my parents so happy and, even though I was miserable, I couldn't ruin everything for them. Your grandmother had already drilled in my head that she'd lost all the other babies who might have been more grateful than me."

"All the others?" I was confused. I knew my mother was an only child but I thought that had been a conscious choice.

"Six children. Three boys and two girls before me and another boy after me. One of my first chores on the farm was to weed around their graves. My mom told me it was to remind me that I was the lucky one."

"Oh God. I don't know what to say. I don't know what to think, because everything is completely opposite from what I thought. I'm so sorry, Mother. I guess it makes sense now."

She sipped her tea. "You asked me what you ever did. Your father was on a mission to undo the relationship he had with his father. He wanted children so badly. I knew if I gave him a child I would be trapped forever. But he persisted. He built this library, having already picked a house with this view. He never struck me or threatened me. I had a new car every year. He showered my parents with gifts. So, I finally agreed." She paused and reached with shaky hands for the tea kettle.

I reached out and took up the kettle, poured her a cup. She looked at me for a second with dull green eyes so much like my own.

"Thank you."

"Did you love him?"

"When you were born, he cried. He kept thanking me, and it was so precious to see the joy on his face. I've painted a different view of him than what you knew. But you should know that he loved you more than anything. His gratitude and humility made me feel something I'd never really felt. I think I loved him at that moment."

"And me? Did you ever love me?"

The answer terrified me as much as the question but I had to ask.

"I have been a monster. Consumed by my bitterness and pain, I pushed you away. You were the living personification of the chains that bound me to him and pulled me away from Micah. I've given you no reason to believe that underneath it all there was a warm heart. But," she placed her bony hand on mine, "I did love you. I was terrified that if I was around you, I'd say those horrible things that my mother said to me. I thought I was protecting you by pushing you away. And, of course, my present circumstances are all the result of how I coped with it all. It's my fault, and I brought you here to tell you I'm sorry."

I was already crying so hard that I couldn't breathe or respond. Whether the earth moved beneath me or the bones of my body pitched forward in unison, I couldn't tell. I was on my knees, my arms around her and my head in her lap. The words falling from my lips were inaudible as I sobbed them but she seemed to understand. I'd never felt my mother's hands stroking my hair. Nothing was reversed but everything had changed. Now I finally understood.

Emma

CHAPTER FIFTY-THREE

Emma had never worked a nine-to-five job in her life. After her father had died, his life insurance had been enough to keep them going and provide a way for Emma to go to college without worry.

She knew she'd been lucky. She watched people from a small balcony perched over the gallery's front door. Business women and men made their way to their offices. A gaggle of women in designer workout clothes got their daily steps together while sipping on coffee and pushing strollers. One such group gathered across the street and Emma wondered if this could have been her life.

A tiny boy in the midst of the women caught her eye and she got her camera out to capture the child's watchful eyes. He quietly wrestled with a bag in the bottom of the stroller while his mother talked. The child continued his efforts and was finally rewarded as he popped a treat in his mouth without incident.

She already knew that this boy, with his red, curly hair and tongue sticking out in concentration, would be the subject of her next painting. She only had to complete two more to fulfill her contract.

Despite all the positives in her life, Emma was still struggling. She had not signed the divorce papers, had no clue how to uncover her repressed feelings, and was stymied by the relentless floods of flashbacks. Still, she was sleeping better and had been able to focus on her work.

Looking at her photos of the boy, she decided on the one that would be her painting entitled "Furtive Glance".

After sketching the photo and completing a few other chores, Emma decided to go for a hike at the local state park. She always felt close to Jake when she hiked.

The air was crisp today and she noted the footprints and pawprints of previous visitors. There had been many, and Emma wondered if they had felt the need to connect with nature or just wanted to disconnect from everything else. She was glad to be alone but equally content not to be blazing a new trail. Uncharted territory had only been fun with Jake.

She spotted an outcropping of rocks that made her think of the temple ruins they'd discovered together.

"Kaniakapupu," Jake announced, extending his arm out as if announcing royalty.

He'd gone on to explain that the site had once been the summer palace of King Kamehameha III and his wife, Kalama.

"Are we allowed to be here?" she asked nervously.

"They don't patrol here," Jake replied with a grin.

They had hiked from there to Lulumahu Falls. The 50-foot waterfall had been worth the effort.

"No telling how many people have been standing on this exact spot. Sometimes when I get out in nature, I can feel their spirits. Many people believe that the Maya came to Hawaii."

He turned his hand to show her the tattoo on his wrist.

"What does it mean?" she asked, tracing the ink with her fingertips.

"It's a Mayan symbol. I wanted it to remind me to live bravely."

He was brave, Emma thought. Along with surfing the North Shore, he dove from great heights and never seemed daunted by the risk.

She told him that he was the bravest person she'd ever known.

"No. You are. You live in a house with a monster. Yet you sneak out to be with me. You're much braver than I am."

Emma sat on the rocks and let her tears flow freely. He'd promised to take her away and hide her from her father. Hesitant to leave her mother and knowing that Ruth wouldn't come with her, she had decided to wait on their plans. Emma could see he was disappointed but she insisted that she couldn't leave her mom alone with the devil.

All that had happened after that weighed on her, as though she was under these rocks instead of on top. Rosalyn was right. She had repressed memories and was angry with her mom. If the woman would have left her father, she would still have Jake. She might be in Hawaii now, lying amongst the bamboo with her own children. She was responsible for Jake's death because she'd refused to leave her mom.

Scrolling through her contacts, she pressed 'call' before she could see the screen.

Ruth answered on the third ring. "Hey, baby. I was just thinking about you."

"Why didn't you leave him? I didn't leave with Jake because I didn't want to abandon you. Then, that bastard—" Emma cut herself off.

There was a long silence and Emma could hear her mother crying. It was too late for regret now. They had never spoken about that night. Emma could feel the fists slamming into her body. She could feel the man looming over her and hear his voice yelling in her ears.

"You were young and probably don't remember. All the times we played hide and seek. All the times I had you put your things in a bag as fast as you could. You probably thought they were games but I was training you. So that we could escape and you wouldn't be afraid." She paused to blow her nose. "He caught on. I don't know how but he figured out what I was doing. He told me that if I left him, he'd find us. Then, he said he'd kill you and Daniel before my eyes. I believed him. Maybe it would have been better to risk it but I was afraid."

Emma, laid back on the rockface, tried to focus on what her mother was saying. The jagged edges pressed into her body but it didn't hurt as much as her heart did at hearing the misery in her mother's voice. She'd never known why her mother suddenly stopped playing hide and seek with them or why her father got so mad when the children played it.

"Honey, I prayed every night that he would die. I even thought about killing him. But then I worried what would happen to you and Daniel if I went to prison."

The beatings, terror, the weight of it all pressed Emma down, as though some giant had placed a foot on her chest. She'd blamed her mother and never once thought that her father might have threatened them. Why hadn't she thought of that? After everything he did, why would he draw the line at threatening to kill his own children?

"I've been so angry with you for all the times he beat you nearly to death. We never knew if we'd be coming back to find you dead and be stuck with him. But I should have known. Oh God, Mom. I'm sorry. I'm so sorry. Of course he threatened to kill us."

"I'm sorry I failed you," the woman replied, sobbing.

"You didn't fail me, Momma. You saved us. I'm just sorry we couldn't save you."

They both cried for several long moments and Emma knew nothing she said could take away her mother's guilt.

"Do you think he killed—" She stopped herself again.

"I think he did. I still wonder what…" Ruth trailed off.

"I'm so glad he's dead," Emma whispered as much to God as her mother.

"Me too, honey. Me too."

David

CHAPTER FIFTY-FOUR

The exchange had been emotional and exhausting for both of us. I offered my mother my arm and helped her to her bedroom. Not wanting to leave her alone, I pulled a chair over to her bedside, questions swirling in my mind.

Finally, I asked, "So, you are selling the house. Where will you go?"

She smiled briefly and squeezed my hand. "I didn't really finish the story, did I?"

"There's more?"

She nodded with a chuckle. I had never heard her truly amused and was momentarily spellbound by the sound.

"Before I got sick, I started playing on social media. It was curious to me that so many people I saw had their faces in their smartphones. So, I gave it a try. And I found him."

"Your farm boy?"

"Yes. Micah is a widower and lives not far from where we met."

"Oh wow. Did you contact him?"

"Not at first. I was afraid he was still angry. When I married Edward, he called me a few choice words and vowed he never wanted to see me again."

I sat forward. "What happened?"

"Time softens nevers. He was glad to hear from me, and before long we were talking every day. Then, I went to see him."

"So, the poor farm boy made good."

"Very good. Both his parents died young. He and his siblings inherited the farm and divided it up. Micah sold some timber and leased out his portion. He started making money and then started buying other businesses. I don't fully understand how all of it works but he built a good life. Turns out he had a good mind for business. He owns hunting lodges, an ATV business, adventure trails, and countless other things. When he finds someone struggling, he partners with them and helps them turn a profit. He has six children and they all do the same thing."

"He sounds like a good man."

She blushed despite her illness. "Yes. He is. He always was."

"So, you are selling to move there?"

She nodded. "I was going through all the papers and came upon your land."

"Wait. It's real?"

"Oh yes, it is real. There have been offers over the years but this one is the most promising. David, I..." She paused and reached for a glass of water.

I handed it to her. "It's okay, Mom. I'm not mad that you didn't tell me anymore."

She sipped the water without taking her eyes off me. Handing it back, she studied me for a long while and then took my hand.

"You're like him, you know. That was the first thing I thought when you started seeing Emma. You have your father's rescuer gene. She had a rough childhood and you wanted to fix it."

"You knew about that?"

"Everyone heard the rumors. The girl always looked frightened. Who could blame her? I can see why she was drawn to you."

"Clearly, her being drawn to me was what I mistook for loving me. Maybe she just needed a rescuer."

"She may not know what she wants. Childhood trauma can lay dormant for a long time and then spring up like a jack-in-the-box. She seemed to love you."

"Well, now she loves Nick," I replied more bitterly than I meant to.

She squeezed my hand causing me to look up. "I can see you have a big heart and might be somewhat clueless, like your father. You weren't wrong for loving her and wanting to rescue her. Your father felt best when he was needed and I'll bet you feel the same way. But some people don't want to be rescued. Circumstances sometimes require them to accept help but they end up repressing what they really wanted in taking the hand up."

"I'm finding that out the hard way."

Without preamble, I told her about the journals. Then, talking for an hour straight, until there was nothing left, I let all my fears, anger and questions spill out like a levee breaking.

Then, I told her about Kellyn and Wyatt and how she was the opposite of what I'd ever known. She didn't need me and I wasn't sure what to do.

"I don't think I'll trust my judgment until I understand what happened to Emma and me."

"Probably not. She definitely went to some trouble to hide what happened. What are you hoping to find?"

"I don't know. I guess I need to see if she just lied to me or if she loved me. Was I just stupid in thinking she did? But it's more than that. Maybe, at first, I just needed some proof of one thing or another. Now, I don't know exactly what to hope for. I just know I have to find out."

She yawned and I realized that I had used up all her energy purging my soul.

"I'm sorry, Mom. I've been going on and on."

"Feels like you needed to talk."

I nodded. "I did. I haven't had anyone I could talk to and I was really lonely. Thank you for listening."

She was withering and I knew I needed to let her rest. I'd never seen her so fragile. Part of me wanted to stay and watch over her. Forcing myself up, I carried the chair back to the desk.

"Look there on the desk. You'll find the deed and contact information for the interested buyers. Your father bought that land with the intention of developing it. He would want you to sell it, even if you're tempted to keep it for sentimental reasons. But it is yours. You do as you see fit."

"Maybe it's time to stop holding onto things for sentimental reasons."

"I'm glad you feel that way. The treehouse is in a diseased tree and will need to come down. It's rather decrepit now. I'm sorry it can't be saved. I know you and your father built it."

She was drifting off before I could reply. I'd seen her asleep only a few times in my life but I had never seen peace on her face.

Leaving the room as quietly as I could, I headed for my room. The developer would have to wait. What I wanted more than anything right now was to talk to Kellyn.

I grabbed the journal from my bag and headed to the tree house. The hike to the back of the yard seemed farther when I was young. The tree was located on a landing just beyond the highest point of the yard. It set nestled out of view of the main house but with a stellar view of the bay. Warily, I climbed up the wooden rungs bolted into the trunk and with some effort crawled into my treehouse.

The inside was smaller than I remembered but still intact. My dad had built me a bench, desk, and bookshelf. There were still books in it, although the elements had damaged them. Most of the outside wood was dry-rotted and I questioned whether the structure would hold my weight. There were no loud pops or groans as I settled onto the floor. Pulling my phone out and finding her name, I forced myself to breathe so it wouldn't sound like I was panting.

Kellyn was glad to hear from me. I told her about everything that had transpired.

"So, she is going to move in with this Micah guy, huh?"

"Yes. I guess she is."

"How do you feel about that?"

"I guess I'm glad she has reunited with the man she loved. He sounds like a nice man. I'm not sure how I feel about six siblings. I've just found my mom so I'm not sure I'm ready to share yet."

"I don't know how I'd handle six instant brothers and sisters either. Yikes."

"Two brothers and four sisters, to be exact. It doesn't seem real. Of course, now I'm really worried about her health. How strange it must be to finally have some happiness and find out you're critically ill."

"Where is she on the transplant list?"

I shook my head, realizing I had not asked. "I don't know yet."

"Well, regardless, David, I'm glad to hear that you're healing things with your mom. Did she say anything else?"

"My brain is mush. She told me an entirely different version of how she and my dad met. I'm trying to absorb it all and not change how I remember him. She said I'm like him."

"Oh? How so? Ruggedly handsome?"

That made me smile. "Well, sure, that... and apparently we're both like the medieval knights roaming around looking for damsels in distress."

There was a long silence and my heart jumped into my throat. Mentally I started backpaddling.

Finally, Kellyn spoke. "Maybe to her that seemed like a bad trait. You are a gentleman, and it is obvious that you conduct yourself with honor. Not all women would run from a knight in shining armor."

"And what about you? Do you like chainmail and white horses?"

I heard her smile. "I'm no damsel in distress but I can appreciate a man with a big heart and principles. And I like horses of all colors."

"Good, because my days of being a rescuer are over but I'm not sure I can shake the armor off. I've got to confront this need-to-be-needed thing. I'm working on it."

"You know, David, it may not seem like it now but your vulnerability is a strength. Just because a woman doesn't need you to save her from life it doesn't mean she doesn't need you to be a partner, soulmate, or friend. The problem comes when your need for someone to need you overshadows the equality in the relationship."

I thought about that. Had my need to protect Emma, and give her a better life, become a greater priority than just loving her? Was that why she couldn't reveal herself to me?

"I know you're right. I've never thought of vulnerability as a strength. I've always been told I was too sensitive and thought it was a bad thing."

"You're a Cancerian, right? The sign known for sensitivity."

I laughed and lay on the hard decking. Having recently found the zodiac chart in Emma's journal, I remembered the last time I'd talked to anyone about being a Cancerian.

"I don't know much about the zodiac," I replied as I looked up at the roof. I could see where water had leaked in and followed the dark brown stain with my eyes.

And then I stopped breathing for a few seconds. There was a circular zodiac drawn there. It was still clear, having been drawn in ink. It was not as carefully rendered but I could still make out the signs.

I still remembered that summer night. Emma had been fascinated with astrology. She'd found a book and brought it with her that night, and read it to me.

"You're a Cancerian and I'm a Piscean," she'd stated, as if I knew what that meant.

As she continued to read, she explained what the biggest strengths and weaknesses of each sign were. I confessed that the description sounded like me but I didn't fully get the concept. I was mostly impressed that she'd understood it all.

"It says Cancerians are the best kissers."

I had blushed so hard it felt like a shiver. Somehow, I managed to reply that it was undoubtedly true.

"Let's see," Emma suggested.

We kissed, and the best-kisser reference would follow us throughout our entire marriage, our own zodiacal private joke. The kiss had been brief and, since it was my first, I didn't know if I did it well.

After that she'd stood and drawn on the ceiling of the treehouse to leave something to commemorate the night of our first kiss. I lay on my back watching in titillated silence as she drew the entire circular chart with a pen and marker.

Kellyn was talking about how she was a Scorpio and that the Cancer-Scorpio combination was one of the most compatible.

"They say that Cancerians are the most romantic and best kissers."

I tried to make myself breathe. Until this moment, I'd forgotten all about Emma's drawing on the roof of my treehouse. There it was above me. It was somewhat different from the one in the journal and there were no extra symbols. Clearly, though, the symbol set beside the sign for Cancer was the key. If only I knew what it meant.

"Good to know," I replied finally, trying to act like this was the first time I'd heard that.

"Yes. I'd say they were right about that."

I felt guilty talking to Kellyn about kissing when I was thinking about kissing Emma. "Thank you. I would say we Cancerians do try our best but, as you know, we're already born that way."

"Do you know what Scorpio is the best at?"

I didn't but from her tone I could make a good guess.

"Gardening?"

She laughed heartily, and momentarily the rest of the world slipped away. I loved her laugh. For a moment, I let myself forget about journals, clues and summer kisses.

"We Scorpios have many talents," she said quietly.

"It's no wonder the Cancer-Scorpio combo is so powerful. Most romantic, best kissers, and beasts in bed. I feel sorry for the other combos, really."

She laughed. "As much as I'd love to keep talking, I have a meeting to attend."

"Are all Scorpios huge teases too?"

"We are. But we're always worth the wait."

"I've no doubt about that. I'm glad I got to talk to you. I miss you." It slipped out and I panicked. "Now, get to your meeting, slacker. I'll let you know when I find out more."

"I hope you find your answers and I hope your derelict treehouse in the diseased tree brings you joy and not broken bones."

I thought about the joy I'd found here as we hung up. This tiny refuge had been the place of my first kiss, was time spent with my dad, and had been the place I cloistered myself in when the world got to be too much. Still looking at the zodiac drawn on the ceiling, with its sun and moon character in the middle, I realized that my treehouse wasn't through with me yet. I curled up, closed my eyes, and prayed as I had as a boy that the treehouse would whisper what I needed to do next.

Emma

CHAPTER FIFTY-FIVE

She and Jake had been dating for a year when Emma got pregnant. Not even their closest friends knew they were a couple and none had expressed suspicion. The only ones who knew were the couple's close family and Jake's best friend, Kekoa.

Emma had been sitting at the breakfast table when she experienced her first bout of morning sickness. Despite spending increasing amounts of time on the ship, her father would come home and expect everyone present at all meals. Her brother Daniel had already left with the Peace Corps so that meant she and Ruth bore the burden of sitting through meals no matter what.

Her father would not allow them to skip eating and would rail against wasting food. She'd sat there cutting her food into tiny bits and forced herself to eat. Ruth had tried to distract Bob with questions but he preferred the quiet and soon became angry.

"You think I work all the time so that you can turn your nose up at the food I provide?" he turned to Emma.

"No, sir. I'm not turning my nose up."

"Then eat your food."

She took a bite of eggs and bacon, regretting it immediately, but forced it down.

"That's better," he sneered and handed her another biscuit.

She grabbed the biscuit and pretended to savor its aroma before taking a bite.

Her mother recognized the wave of nausea and jumped into action. "Can I get you more coffee, dear?"

No one was allowed to leave the table without permission. He consented and Ruth got up to get the pot. She made a big show of carrying the pot of coffee, pouring slowly, and jabbered to keep him focused on her.

He turned around so quickly he almost caught Emma swallowing food and bile.

"I like that you're not dressing like a slut in those tight jeans you've been wearing."

He said no more and both women sighed in relief when he retired from the table to watch TV in his study.

After he shut the door, Ruth leaned in. "I have some tea that will help, honey. We need to get you on vitamins."

"He'll find them," Emma said, tears brimming in her eyes.

"We'll hide them where he won't look. I have a friend who can help. We won't have to use the base doctors."

Emma nodded, glancing nervously in the direction of the study. She didn't know how they would pull this off. Her father would comment on the slightest imperfections and she knew that he'd be the first to complain she was getting fat. Turning back to her mom, she smiled.

"Thank you, Momma."

"Does Jake know?"

Emma nodded, batting tears away in case her father emerged.

"And he's supportive?"

She nodded again. "He's already picking names."

They giggled together quietly but Emma's tears came harder and she couldn't suppress them.

"He will marry you?"

"Yes."

Her mother nodded and took a sip of coffee. Emma could tell her mother was thinking but she hadn't the courage to ask if Ruth would come with her. Jake had a family that would absorb them and keep them safe. She'd already thought of how they'd move things out slowly to avoid discovery.

They didn't talk anymore and Emma finally got to throw up.

She had heard some banging but had been too sick to wonder what was going on. Her father was standing outside the bathroom door. He had a cruel grin. She panicked thinking he might have heard her vomiting.

"If I find you with any local trash, I will kill him, Emma. Do you understand?"

Emma managed to nod. "Yes, Father, I understand."

She and Jake didn't go to the same school. That was a good thing because it made the relationship easier to hide. Although he made a convincing demon all on his own, Emma knew her father also had a network of spies, so it was too risky for anyone to see them together. They met in secret even when the bastard was on the ship. Emma's mother didn't mind when she spent weekends with Jake.

Jake asked her questions about her art and her dreams. They got into discussions on philosophy and politics. He challenged her to look at everything at a deeper level. He knew everything she could bear to tell him about her childhood. It was hard for him to understand why they didn't go to the police.

"He's a God on base. He's decorated and respected. Nobody cares that he drinks too much, and they won't listen to us about the abuse."

"Have you tried?"

"So many times. My mom confided in one of my dad's commanders. The guy not only told my dad, but shortly after he asked for reassignment. Someone called the police one time and, as soon as they got there, they saw my dad in uniform. They shook his hand and left. We have no one."

"Why don't you fight back?"

Emma sighed. "If we do, we'd have to kill him. Otherwise, he'll just find another way to punish us. The man is the devil incarnate. He figures things out and is always one step ahead."

"So, why can't you just leave? Your brother did."

"My bastard father was glad to see Daniel go after he refused to go in the military. Plus, he was always calling Daniel a fairy. When Daniel stopped denying it, my father told him to get out because he didn't want anyone to know his son was gay. He told Daniel that he was dead to him."

"Yeah, but he didn't beat him or kill him. You could leave," Jake pleaded. "We could go to another island. My family is spread out and they'd help us. We could take your mom with us."

"I know you would protect us, and your family too. But somehow he'd find out and it would end in disaster because she will not leave him."

"So, what are we doing? If you won't leave your mom and she won't leave your dad, what does that mean for us? For our baby?"

She touched his face. "Do we have to decide everything today? We're young and have our whole lives. I love you and want to be with you. I just need more time to talk my mom into leaving."

Jake placed his hand on hers and smiled despite the conflict showing in his eyes. "I'm sorry, Em. You're right. I just cannot stand the thought of that man…" His voice trailed off.

He didn't have to finish. She knew what he was saying.

Every time that they did not get caught, Emma felt less afraid. Jake commented that she looked more relaxed. It should have concerned her that she was letting her guard down but she ignored the sensation of impending doom, opting instead to trust in the invincibility of youth and love.

That was a mistake.

David

CHAPTER FIFTY-SIX

I woke with a feeling of euphoria that I had not felt in years. Something had shifted, though I wasn't sure what, and had drained away the heavy feeling that had made it hard to breathe.

The drawing caught my eye again and I stared at it until my eyes watered. What I knew was that she liked astrology and had learned about ciphers at a young age. I still had no idea what the extra symbol was or how any of this tied into the neat rows of numbers.

Pressing myself upwards, I ignored all the memories begging to be relived. I could probably spend all day in here recalling all the hours it took to build this haven. It had been the first time my dad let me cut boards with the saw. We both smashed our fingers with hammers. Somehow, despite that, we had laughed and talked. Sitting here now, cramped and sore, I could still feel the love.

When I had arrived, I'd entertained the idea of taking the treehouse apart and relocating it but now it seemed extreme. The love and fun would remain but it was time to let the treehouse go. On my way down, a rung turned suddenly sideways, pitching me straight down the tree like I was sliding down a pole. It wasn't the first time I'd scraped a hand or knee on this bark. Giving the trunk a pat, I accepted that it would be the last time.

"I miss you, Dad, and I'll always be grateful for this."

I made my way into the house quietly because it was early. My mom was still sleeping peacefully when I peeked into her room.

After a much needed shower, I shaved and dressed and surveyed myself in the mirror. I didn't look that different but I felt like a new man.

There was movement in the house so I checked on my mom again on my way to the library; not awake yet. I grabbed the journal, notebook, pen and the magazine I picked up at the airport. After a brief exchange with the housekeeper, I netted me some coffee and an orange-cranberry and goat cheese scone.

The breeze was cool and playful and the view of the bay looked like a painting. Ropes of sunlit waves looked like a laser light show. The sky was crisp and cloudless and filled with various gulls that looked like paper planes from this distance. As I sipped my coffee and took a bite of the scone, I knew I was stalling. The thought of staring at numbers on a page seemed cruel and painful in comparison to the brilliant palette of color before me. I made myself focus on what I had read during my research.

Julius Caesar used ciphers scratched onto the heads of slaves. In order to decipher them, the recipient would have to shave the slave's head. He used simple substitution and replaced letters by moving three places forward in the alphabet.

The numbers glared back at me from the page like rows of soldiers guarding a treasure. Using the pen and pad, I wrote the alphabet with the corresponding number for each letter. I had the brief thought that maybe the letters weren't encrypted with any substitution.

This theory turned out to be false since the first line made no sense. I tried Caesar's method and shifted three. Still nothing useful emerged, and I soon found myself surrounded by crumpled pieces of paper. Frustrated, I turned to the zodiac component.

In Western astrology, the order of signs starts with Aries. The symbol was drawn on the outside of Cancer. Since Cancer was the fourth sign from Aries, I hoped that the substitution was four. That method produced even more gibberish than my first attempt.

Next, I listed all the astrological signs and wrote the corresponding number beside them. Emma was smart but I didn't think she had created an unbreakable cipher. There was something that I wasn't seeing, although everything was right in front of me. Staring at the page until my eyes watered wasn't helping either.

I decided to take a break and picked up the Hawaii magazine. I'm not sure what I thought I'd glean from those pages but I leafed through them, stopping to look at the pictures and ads. The entire periodical was a marketing brochure for lavish resorts and overpriced products. Of the 120 pages, the articles made up less than a third, and I was about to toss it when something caught my eye and stole my breath.

The writer was obviously British by her choice of words and affinity for tea. She had stumbled across a theory that the Mayans had braved the seas and sailed to Hawaii. Interviewing surfers, she'd traveled to a site that many claimed were Mayan ruins.

"Many of the surfers claim Mayan heritage and have adorned themselves or their surf boards with Mayan symbols."

My heart was beating so loudly in my ears I had to read aloud. I had no interest in Mayan ruins, surfers or Oahu. What had pulled me like a tractor beam to the page was a tattoo on the first boy's wrist. Speeding through the article, I prayed that the writer had captured its meaning.

"The Western culture regards the number thirteen as unlucky. For the Maya, thirteen was a sacred number. The year was divided into 365 days, which was thirteen moons consisting of 28 days each. The symbol for thirteen is two horizontal lines with three circles above them. Many of the surfers have this symbol tattooed to remind them of their proud heritage and oneness with the creator."

I looked at the drawing in the journal again. She'd drawn it on the side so that it looked like two vertical lines with three dots beside them.

Thirteen was the key.

Emma

CHAPTER FIFTY-SEVEN

She hadn't slept fully since she talked to her mother. When she did momentarily drift off, her nightmares clawed their way through the veil and made her relive her trauma over and over.

Nick was making breakfast when she finally pushed herself out of bed. The house smelled of bacon, toast, coffee, and butter. Part of her wanted to run away to the isolation of her studio but she was hungry and she knew Nick would make her feel better.

"Good morning, beautiful," he greeted her and paid her a kiss.

"I woke up hungry," she replied, slipping her arms around his waist.

"You didn't eat much dinner. Did you sleep?" he asked, cracking an egg into the skillet.

"Not much. You?"

He paused to tend the food and she could see him choosing his words. "Who is Jake?"

Hearing the name almost stopped her heart. She saw something in his eyes she had never seen before today. She could hear her heart hammering and she was sure that the distress showed on her face.

"Where did you hear that name?"

"You."

Emma laughed nervously. "Me? What do you mean?"

"You called out the name Jake in your sleep."

Emma had not only dreamed about the night Jake died. She'd also dreamed about the last time they'd made love. She wondered which memory had made her cry out. Nick's face was not giving any clue.

"He's just someone from the past."

She watched as he put their breakfast on the plates, poured her a cup of coffee, and gathered everything to take to the table outside. He didn't say anything as he walked past her. Emma followed cautiously. She had never seen him like this and didn't know what would come next.

Outside the air was crisp and cool. The smells of earth and flowers greeted her in the breeze and she welcomed the grounding. Nick set the plates down and sat in his usual spot facing the house. He didn't wait for her to join him.

"Em, I know you are dealing with a lot of memories. But you've been so withdrawn. You don't talk to me like you did. I've tried to give you space but I'm worried. I mean, you did wonder if I'm cheating."

Emma sat down and picked up her fork. Suddenly feeling ravenous, she began eating. She could tell he wasn't done.

"I asked you if you were sure you were ready to get divorced and you said yes. Then, I planned the garden so I could propose. But you haven't mentioned signing the papers yet. So, I need to ask. Have you changed your mind?"

His voice was even and soft, without any hint of anger. He was genuinely concerned.

"No, of course not. It's just all the memories and feelings coming back. It's just a lot. But no, I haven't changed my mind. I love you," she added and reached across the table to touch him.

"And there isn't anyone else? Jake?"

Her father had forced her to endure abuse whenever his demons took over. Jake had pressured her to leave her mother and then died leaving her to deal with all of it. David had pressured her to get back to "normal" after her episode. She knew that all of these things were the product of her own perception but, in this moment, they were her only reality. She was tired of adjusting to someone else's timing.

"You know what it's like to lose memory and then have it flood back like a tsunami. You know it causes you to relive the past and deal with the grief like it's fresh. I haven't changed my mind. There is no one else. But I feel like you're pressuring me to sign when you told me that there was no hurry. I'm not sure what has changed. But I don't want to feel pressured."

He looked up and she could see the hurt in his eyes. After two deep breaths, the hurt burned away and pale blue hid his emotions like sea ice over a churning ocean.

"I meant what I said. I won't ask you again and I'm not trying to pressure you. I'm just worried."

"I'm okay. Just please trust me and give me time. I promise I won't make you wait too long."

He nodded. "I love you more than anything, Emma. All of you. Your past, your present, and your future. I can handle all of it so I'm here when you want to talk. But at some point, you're going to have to trust me with all of you."

He was telling the truth. She could see it. But was she ready for him to know all of her?

David

CHAPTER FIFTY-EIGHT

T he unexpected discovery of the symbol had left me panting and in shock. It also gave me a greater appreciation for how smart Emma was. The zodiac chart and placement of the Mayan symbol on the outside of Cancer could not be a mistake.

Since Cancer was the fourth sign, I counted four places and landed on the letter 'D'. From there, I shifted thirteen spaces forward and thirteen back. Writing down the result, I ended up with two Qs. Using the same method, I tried the first line, ending up on the same letter going forward or back.

Chiding myself for not breaking this sooner, I looked at the letters I'd amassed. No matter how I scrambled the letters, nothing formed a word. I tried another line but came up again with nothing.

There was still some other component that I was missing. I'd already spent so much time on this. What if it was a secret confession of a teenage crush?

Something jingled behind me and I turned to see the housekeeper standing in the door with a carafe of coffee and another scone.

"I'm sorry to interrupt you, Mr. Campbell. I wanted to bring you this before I went to the store."

I could see the source of the jingle sound in her hand. Her keychain was a metal letter "C" with the glyph depicting the Cancer sideways "69". I stared at it.

Undaunted by my zombie-like reaction, she placed the plate and carafe on the table before me. Then, patting me on the shoulder, she asked if I needed anything.

"Call me David. And I'm sorry I didn't ask for your name."

"It's okay. It's Connie."

"C for Connie and Cancer, eh?"

She blushed. "Yes. It was a gift from my granddaughter."

"That's sweet. No, I don't need anything but thank you for this. The scone is amazing. Is my mom awake?"

"No, Mr. David. She'll sleep a bit longer, I think. But her nurse is here so you needn't worry."

"Thank you, Connie."

Savoring the next bite, I took a sip of coffee to wash it down as a realization dawned. I'd gone years without hearing or paying attention to anything zodiacal. First, it was the chart in the journal. Then, Kellyn brought it up without knowing what I was doing. The drawing in the treehouse had watched over me all night. Now, the housekeeper with the Cancer keychain had brought me food.

I turned back to the journal. This time, I started at "C" for Cancer and then applied the thirteen-letter shift. One by one, I worked through the first line.

When I had finished, I stared at it, disbelieving. There was no need to unscramble any letters because they screamed out from the page.

"Pregnancy is not as hard to hide as I thought it would be."

I slammed shut the book to stop the screaming in my head. The questions swirled like a tornado until the roar was deafening.

How could she have kept from me that she had been pregnant before she married me? What had happened to the baby?

And, if that was the opening statement, I was not ready for whatever else came after

it. Everything I wanted to know was on the table in front of me but I found myself unable to focus.

I was glad when my Mom emerged from her room and I assisted her to a seat on the deck. She looked tired but she smiled as she sat down.

"Thank you, David."

"What can I do for you?"

She squeezed my hands. "Forgive me. I don't know if I'll survive this mess. I don't want to die without asking forgiveness."

"I forgave you. A long time ago. But I understand better now."

It sounded cheesy but it was true. There was no way of taking back the past and equally no reason why the future should be defined by it. I smiled briefly, remembering what Sophie had told me about living my truth and forgiving nostalgia.

Mom sat back abruptly as though she'd been released by a tractor beam. She took a deep breath and let it out, wiping her eyes on a napkin.

"You have no idea what a relief that is." She eyed the journal on the table in front of me. "Have you had any luck?"

I gave her a brief rundown of what I'd discovered. My voice sounded flat to me and I wondered if I was actually speaking.

"So, you think the rest will explain this baby you never knew about?"

I nodded. "Probably. She was seventeen and it must've been before her father died. I guess she was hiding it from him. I hate him."

"You probably don't know why they moved to Hawaii in the first place," she said simply.

"Emma told me that her father got a promotion or something."

Mom chuckled. "He got a promotion because your father called in a favor from a friend."

"What?" I was baffled and not sure I could take many more mysteries.

"You came home with a black eye and your father went and confronted Bob Roberts. He'd figured you got into a fight defending Emma. Anyway, your father threatened him and told him that he'd arranged a transfer and that Bob had better take it."

"Dad? I don't know if I even ever saw him raise his voice. And how did he know about the fight?"

"He just knew. And that man might've been a big deal in the Navy but your dad had two things he didn't."

"Money and...?" I searched.

"A strong desire to protect his son."

"Wow. I don't think... I mean, it's like hearing a story about your life in the third person. How did I know none of this?"

"You were just a boy. And you were heartbroken over her situation. I suppose I contributed to that."

I knew what she was saying but I stayed quiet. Instead, I picked up the kettle to refresh her tea. She shook her head.

"I think I'm going to go lie back down."

I stood and helped her out of her chair.

She patted my hand.

"You stay. You need to find out what the journal says."

I started to protest but she shot me a glance that I recognized. She was stubborn and the look meant that I shouldn't question her. She might be sick and had asked for forgiveness but she still needed some independence.

Emma

CHAPTER FIFTY-NINE

J ake had said all the right things when Emma told him she was pregnant but she still cried all day. She couldn't explain her worries or accept his reassurances. Her father's abuse had taken on a new form a few months before she'd met Jake. She'd snuck in from an outing with friends to find her father still awake. She managed to creep silently past the living room and was almost in her bedroom when she heard him coming down the hall behind her. He didn't say anything before he grabbed her and pushed her onto the bed. Emma struggled but he outweighed her by a hundred pounds.

It was over quicker than it began but for weeks the smell of whiskey made her feel nauseated.

How could she explain to Jake that the baby might not be his?

She considered abortion. Emma had never had strong feelings on the subject. There were other ways, herbs and such. She knew that there were people on the island who knew about those things.

Strangely, though, after all the tears had dried, she felt protective over the baby growing inside her. It wasn't even the size of a golf ball but she could imagine its face. How could she hold the baby responsible for who the father might be?

Ruling out abortion, she considered adoption but she already knew she couldn't give her baby away.

Every time she considered her options, Jake would talk about the future. He'd already decided what he'd have to do to support a family. He was more responsible than anyone she knew.

He was also a daredevil, which gave her pause. Jake would never stop surfing, cliff diving, or any of the other dozens of things that could get him killed.

In the last month, an experienced surfer had been killed. A miscalculation had caused him to be crushed and ravaged. The water tossed him like a rag doll and broke his neck.

A month before that, another guy they knew had been attacked by a 12-foot tiger shark. He'd survived the attack but would probably struggle his entire life since the shark took both his left arm and leg.

Emma was terrified that the same thing would happen to Jake. He was not afraid of anything, and that scared her.

Marrying Jake would mean taking on the risk. Not marrying him and not escaping her father held a treasure trove of unknown horrors. She decided the risk of being a widow was not as scary as being under her father in any capacity.

Aside from her fears, she loved Jake more than she thought was humanly possible.

It wasn't that he completed her. Instead, it was a knowing, an acceptance, a surrender that she felt. If they were not a couple, they'd still love each other. Their relationship went well beyond explanation and defied conventional definition.

Emma feared for Jake's safety but she trusted him. She'd never trusted anyone completely. Other than the one thing, she knew she could tell Jake anything. Some things, however, she only told her journal.

Having devised the perfect cypher, she documented every day. It was clever and she was proud of it. The encryption involved substitution, replacement, Mayan symbols and used the zodiac.

After breakfast with Nick, Emma made up her mind that she would go to David's and look for the journal. Although she was pretty sure that David wouldn't be able to break her code, she needed to find it and the onesie.

She told Nick she was going to stop by David's on her way to the studio. That wasn't the lie. The part she omitted was the piece she felt guilty for, and she couldn't bear the thought that she'd spent her life speaking only half truths. Nick walked her to the car and gave her a kiss.

"I'll be at the club for a bit but maybe we can go out to dinner and a movie tonight?"

"That sounds nice," she said, not lying.

Unsure if David would be home and not ready to repeat the last time she tried to sneak in, Emma parked around the back. Both the front and back doors were keyed the same but the French door offered a view inside. This way she might be able to ascertain if David or the dog were around without them knowing she was there if they were.

Jogging up to the deck, she put her face against the door. There was no guard dog growling on the other side. The house was clean, with everything in its place.

Not wanting to risk a dog attack, she didn't just use her key to get in. First, she rattled the door knob knowing that the dog would be able to hear that if he was here.

"Houdini?" she said softly. How much sharper was a dog's hearing than a human's? She didn't know but tried again a little louder.

When nothing growled, barked, or crashed down the stairs, Emma stuck her key in the lock.

"Here goes nothing."

She shut the door roughly, just in case the dog didn't hear that well. This way she could still run out. Nothing followed but silence.

Emma laughed at herself silently. She had a key. This was not breaking in, she rationalized as she walked upstairs. The hall closet was across from the bedroom. A cursory glance in the room revealed that David had a new comforter. She presumed that the old bedding folded neatly and placed in the corner was the dog's bed. A few days earlier she'd remembered working with the designer to pick the fabric for the bedroom drapes and matching bedspread, decorative pillows, and bed skirt. There was no sign of the pillows or skirt.

"Good for you," she mused.

Opening the closet, she found a wedding dress, several coats, a box of frames, and ski gear but nothing that would hide her journal or the tiny bodysuit. Maybe she had hidden it in the bedroom closet. Still somewhat trepidatious, she shut the door, turned around and walked straight to the closet in the master bedroom.

There was nothing there but David's immaculately organized clothes. She briefly considered the safe behind the Ikea bookcase but couldn't imagine finding anything there. Besides that, David had explained a few months ago that the biometrics kept up with who had accessed it. She didn't want David to know she'd been here.

Turning around, her heart nearly stopped when she saw it.

The box of journals seemed undisturbed. She doubted David would bother to read them, although she already knew that there wasn't much of interest in them. She had recorded silly and trivial things and used metaphorical language to capture real events. Her father read her journals so Emma's strategy was to make him so bored that if he actually found her real journal he wouldn't bother.

The Kona coffee bag on the top of the stack was what caused her distress. Rushing forward to grab it, she could already see the contents were gone. In addition, the sight of the bag itself brought back to her where she had hidden her treasures. Had he thrown them away?

Sitting down hard on the bed, she looked at the rough-hewn fabric in her hands. Maybe it was for the best. She would never need the onesie anyway. David was smart but Emma had taken great care to come up with her cypher. She was sure he wouldn't be able to break it and that gave her peace.

David

CHAPTER SIXTY

Using the key, I slowly began to transfer the numbers to letters. As I did, the words leapt from the page and told the story about the boy I'd noted in earlier journals.

"I live in fear that he'll show up when I'm with Jake so I'm glad when we go far into the wilderness. Jake wants to build a house far enough out here where he can't find us. "

I thought about how awful that must've felt. She had to sneak away to see me too but I never thought she was afraid her father would show up.

It was midnight by the time I'd finished deciphering the whole journal. I hadn't been consistently reading so that I could concentrate on decryption. My eyes were hurting and I looked at my watch. Hoping Kellyn was still up, I sent a text. She answered in under a minute.

When my phone rang, I answered it without delay.

"So, how's it going?" she asked cheerfully.

"I don't know. I'm somewhat in limbo. How's Houdini? I'm sorry I haven't asked.

The doggie daycare will board him if it gets too much."

"Well, truthfully, I didn't take him to daycare today."

"Oh? Is something wrong?"

"No. We were running late today so I wasn't going to have time. I left him in the house."

"Is the house okay?"

She laughed. "He was the perfect houseguest. Not a single thing was disturbed. I came home at lunch to let him out and then went back to work. He didn't even get on the sofa as far as I can tell."

"That was intense. I didn't know if it was gonna start with 'and everything seemed to be fine, and THEN I discovered he'd chewed up all my shoes'," I teased in a falsetto voice.

"I do not sound like that and I don't have a lot of shoes within reach."

"Thank you for taking care of him. I guess I am really worried because I don't know him well yet."

"Even if he had eaten all my shoes and the dining room table, it would be fine. I grew up with dogs. He's a good one. I wouldn't have offered if I thought otherwise. So you can concentrate on things there and stop worrying."

"Well, I'll think on that and let you get to bed. I'm glad we got to talk."

"Me too. Is your mom okay?"

"About the same."

"Talk tomorrow?"

"Count on it."

We said our goodnights and I hung up. The journal sat on the table before me like an angry demon. Part of me wanted to swat it away or drive it to the coast and throw it in the ocean. I got up to get a beer but decided on coffee instead. This was going to require caffeine.

Emma

CHAPTER SIXTY-ONE

She met Maria for lunch and the two sat down at a small sandwich shop, eager to catch up.

The walls were swamped by framed inspirational quotes. Six tables were covered by clean linen tablecloths and tiny vases full of seasonal flowers. We headed to a corner.

Her belly massively swollen, Maria plopped down in the chair opposite Emma.

"Dios mio. This kid is going to be an acrobat or something. All the time flipping around. It's like having a trampoline on your bladder."

Emma laughed with her. She could remember now that both her pregnancies had been like that. She attributed the first to Jake's surfer genes, convinced that, somehow, he'd passed his daredevil tendencies to their child. The other baby would have probably been cautious like David, and she figured the tossing and turning was preparation for a lifetime of anxiety.

"How are you feeling?" Emma asked, adding honey to her tea.

"You know, not too bad. It's getting close now. The doctor says I may go another week but I think it's a few days."

"Oh wow. Are you ready?"

"As much as I can be. The nursery is stocked and clean. And I have always had pretty easy deliveries, so yes." She paused to sip her water. "How are you feeling? And I'm sorry. I talk a lot about this," Maria said, waving her hands over her belly like Vanna White presenting a new puzzle. "I don't want to be that friend who dominates the conversation and brings up bad memories."

"You're fine. I like hearing about all of that." Emma imitated the sweeping hand gestures over Maria's belly.

The women laughed and started talking about men and daily struggles getting things done.

"How are things?"

"I've been having so many flashbacks. So many memories and grief from the past. It has been hard on Nick because I keep weird hours and the other night I called out the name of my old boyfriend in my sleep."

"I hate it when that happens," Maria commiserated.

"Oh? You too? How did you explain it?"

Maria shook her head. "Jose is not as level-headed as Nick," she started. "I dated this boy, Taos, when I was young. He was a beautiful boy. Big." She paused, her hand gestures driving the description home. "It was a summer fling but nothing really happened; just messing around. One night, I was dreaming about him and my mind was filling in the parts that never happened. It's like two o'clock and I yell, 'Oh God, Taos, ravage me!' Scared Jose so badly he jumps out of bed and he is standing there naked with a garden tool as a weapon."

Emma was laughing so hard she couldn't breathe. "What happened then?"

"I wake up and see the shape of a naked man in my room, with what looks like a knife. I scream to Jose, 'He has a knife'. Jose is not entirely awake so he thinks that someone else is in the room. He comes over toward me to protect me, grabs me, and I punch him." They laughed uncontrollably for several minutes until Maria grimaced.

"I think I just wet myself." She groaned.

"You and me both."

"Needless to say, I have a lot of explaining to do when Jose finally stops bellowing about his nose. Luckily, he bought the story when I told him I was dreaming about a character named Taos from one of the soaps I watch. He was mad but mostly because I made his nose bleed."

"I told Nick it was someone that I used to know but I don't know if he feels better about it."

"Men are strange. They have all kinds of dreams and wake up in all kinds of states. You know, they don't see any problem with that but if we dream something then it means something."

"I never thought of it that way before but you're right."

"Men always say that women are hard to understand. But would a woman have a gardening tool on her bedside table?"

David

CHAPTER SIXTY-TWO

I read until my chest hurt so badly, I prayed it was a heart attack. If Bob Roberts was not already dead, I'd want to kill him myself. I was wondering why she kept alluding to her fear of telling Jake the truth. A few pages in and I discovered why she was afraid.

Her words, like ice razors, cut into my soul as I read about her father raping her. He had whispered in her ear that she was saving her mother form a beating since she didn't satisfy him anymore. He said it like it was something she should take pride in instead of something that should cause him shame.

"I look up at his ugly, red bulbous nose and listen to his grunts and taunts as he does his thing. I smile the whole time cause I'm thinking that one day he will die and I'll never have to see him again. He won't be able to hurt us then. He asked if I like it since I was smiling. I laughed at him and he hit me but it was worth it."

I vomited over the side rail of the deck.

Returning to the journal, I glanced at my watch. It was 3 a.m. and I couldn't read any more. I wanted to see what happened to Jake and the baby but had neither the heart nor the stomach for the truth.

Moving through the house without turning on the lights, I stopped at my mom's room. The nurse was still there but I didn't want to disturb her. Instead, I crawled into bed and tried to block out the images in my mind, monsters looming in the shadows.

I'd always been that person who struggled with condolences. When someone was experiencing a loss, I didn't want to say something that would make them sad so I said nothing. It wasn't that I didn't care. Instead, I felt their pain so deeply that it was easier to not make them talk about things.

There had been many times in our marriage when I could feel that Emma was sad. I didn't want to make her relive the events that caused her sadness so I looked instead for ways to cheer her up.

The one thing that I knew from reading her journals was that I should've asked her to talk about it. It might not have saved our marriage but it might have helped her.

Regardless of what had happened between us, I was glad that she'd had Jake during this awful time. And even though her leaving me had ripped my soul, I was glad she had Nick now. How could I begrudge her any happiness after the childhood she had? It was just unfortunate that she couldn't find peace with me. At least, now, I understood why. I hoped that Nick asked and that she felt safe enough to tell him.

Emma

CHAPTER SIXTY-THREE

E mma was aware that her despondency was just feeding Nick's worry but she didn't know how to pull herself out of it.

She couldn't really say she'd slept since all the memories started coming back. Every time she closed her eyes, the memories came like a horde of zombies. She couldn't separate them or get any reprieve, as they came one after another, relentlessly, demanding she relive them.

One such memory was her first Christmas with David. They were still adjusting to each other as adults. He had just landed a job that would take them away from California. David was anxious to prove himself and she admired that. He had a trust fund but never wanted to rely on that money. It was important to work, so Emma didn't voice her sadness over leaving California just after the New Year. With him, she felt safe in a way she hadn't before. After all the cautious analysis of every angle, no one would ever accuse David of being spontaneous or reckless. Emma felt frustrated sometimes but was happy that his caution made him dependable and predictable. She'd had enough of wild flights of fancy.

They'd gone to pick out a tree and had driven out to a tree farm. Emma had never really had a Christmas tree. Instead, she'd decorated house plants or palm trees in the yard.

When she told David that she and her brother had strung shells to make a garland, he'd gone to every effort to give her the perfect Christmas experience. They'd spent a bundle on lights, ornaments, strings of beads, and multiple packs of bows. Neither of them spent much time at church but they picked out a small creche with wooden figurines of the nativity characters.

On the way to the tree farm, he asked her what her dream Christmas looked like.

Emma wasn't sure how to answer. How could she describe something she'd never dared to dream about? Imagining only invited disappointment.

"I don't know. What does yours look like?"

"Well, it is you and me decorating our tree. Wrapping presents for each other and our kids. Staying up all night and putting a bike together, then a dollhouse. Eating Santa's cookies or sleeping for two hours before the kids wake us."

"Your dream is to be a fat insomniac at Christmas?" she teased.

Laughing, he nodded. "Maybe. The best part is that I'd be doing it all with you."

Most of her childhood dreams had been about escaping her home and living on the land. She'd never really had time to consider what an ideal Christmas would be.

"Well, that does sound nice," she remarked, though she wasn't sure it really did.

In the end, they'd spent hours traipsing around the woods, got lost, and finally bagged a tree that turned out to be much too big to drag easily. They had laughed at getting lost. It gave them the perfect opportunity for a quickie, and there had been a hint of danger since they'd seen bear tracks on their hike.

Struggling to drag the tree out had been a different matter. Instead of laughter, there was frustration and multiple cuts, bruises, and expletives. Finally back at the starting point, one of them decided that rolling the tree downhill might save their new marriage. Both of them would later claim that the other let go too soon and loosed the mammoth Monterey Pine to become an avalanche. The tree and many of its friends slammed into a cider stand, destroying it, and decimated a hand-crafted Santa sleigh.

The owners were not pleased.

David paid for all the damages and also offered to pay the four guys it took to help get the tree strapped to the roof of their car. Driving home had been precarious since the tree extended past the front and back of the car. David's chin was bleeding from being slapped by a rogue branch. Emma had bruises on her shins, forearms, and was sure that the pulsing sensation on her cheek would end up being a black eye. For absolutely no reason, she started laughing and soon they were both laughing so hard that David had to slow down to keep the car on the road. They had only been traveling at 10 mph. When he slowed to 2 mph, they roared with laughter at the line of people behind them.

The twine came loose somewhere between the gasps, tears, and an unfortunate pothole in a deep curve. David nearly wrecked trying to pull onto the shoulder, afraid that the monster pine would fall onto the cars behind him. They watched as their pine prize shimmied off the car, sounds like fingernails on a chalkboard, and rolled down the ravine to rejoin the forest.

David was laughing but Emma could tell he was shaken.

"Clearly, it wanted to die amongst its own," Emma joked, hoping to cheer him.

David nodded. "Well, that was a waste of time, and I'm no closer to giving you the perfect Christmas."

"You are my perfect Christmas. The fact that you care so much is perfect."

He kissed her and she saw the mischief in his green eyes.

"You want to hike down there and retrieve it?"

She knew he was kidding but it was sweet that he tried so hard to make her laugh.

Later that night, with a small Douglas fir firmly set in a stand they'd purchased from a tree lot by the drug store, they donned hats and played Christmas music. Hours passed as they piled the six-footer with all the things they'd collected. At 2:30 a.m., they went outside to see the tree lit only to discover that the star had toppled and that none of the blue lights worked.

David put his arm around her with a grin. "Welcome to the perfect Christmas."

Emma thought about it now. At the time, she had nothing to compare the many experiences David gave her to. It wasn't that she'd just agreed to things she didn't want. The problem was that she had no idea what to want so it was easy to go along with things that were better than what she was used to. She didn't know how to explain that and she didn't want to disappoint him.

David

CHAPTER SIXTY-FOUR

I woke early the next morning but lay in bed for a while, thinking. The journal was on my bedside, on the top of the Hawaii magazine, beckoning me. Maybe I knew enough. Emma had survived an alcoholic dad who raped her and possibly had gotten her pregnant. I understood why she didn't tell me.

What I didn't understand was why she'd called out for her father after our son died. We'd spent the night in the hospital with a view of the mall. I couldn't sleep. The gravity of losing our baby was too heavy and I didn't know what to do.

After wrestling for a comfortable position in the recliner beside her bed, I finally dozed off. When she suddenly screamed, it scared me so badly that I almost fell out of the chair.

"Father, please don't go. Please don't take him."

I'd heard that people often called out to people who had died when death was near. She had no memory of it when she awoke, and I didn't want to upset her by mentioning her father so I said nothing.

After all I knew now, I couldn't imagine why she would have called out for Bob Roberts. I still needed to find out what happened. I picked up the journal and flipped it open.

"Whether I stay or go, I see no happy ending. What will become of me and Kai? What if he comes out pasty white and Jake realizes it can't be his? Jake would kill my father if he knew, and that would solve one problem but would result in Jake going to prison. But if my father finds out I'm pregnant, there is no telling what evil he will do."

There were pages of debate over abortion and adoption. I could feel the tears in her indecision. She was also worried about Jake.

"Jake is taking more and more risks like he's trying to prove he's man enough to take care of us. He laughs when I tell him I'm afraid he'll get killed. Then, he'll hold me and tell me he's sorry and that he just wants to be a father his son will be proud of. He did the 'Leap of Faith'. I almost threw up watching him up there. It's an 85-foot jump."

Reading as fast as I could, I learned that her father had started criticizing her for gaining weight. Emma wondered why he hadn't figured it out. Time was speeding up and her window of escape was closing. She had to get away, and finally there was good news.

Bob Roberts was a Surface Warfare Officer on one of the smaller boats. As Lt. Commander, he literally drove the ship. Emma wrote that his latest tour was supposed to be six months. She thought it would be enough time to convince her mom to leave. They'd pack, she'd have the baby, and the demon would return to an empty house. Sounded like a solid plan, I thought.

"Mom says she'll help me transfer to another school. If I graduate from my school, someone will see me and tell him. I can't risk that."

I already knew that this bliss would be temporary since she ended up marrying me but I kept reading as though there might be hope. Strangely, I wanted a happy ending to this horror story. I was invested in Jake and baby Kai. Turning the pages faster and faster, I raced to find out.

Hearing the details of her pregnancy, the subtle ways her body began to change, took me back to watching our own baby grow in her belly. I realized now that she'd slipped up a few times when she'd stand and look at her growing stomach in the mirror. It never registered when she'd comment on her stretch marks having stretch marks that she was comparing pregnancies.

I thought about the onesie with the tiny surf board in my home safe. At least that made sense now.

I adjusted myself in the bed and the book fell open to a different page. Trying to find my place, I turned the pages back and stopped as the words hit me so hard I couldn't breathe.

"My father is dead and he killed them both."

Emma

CHAPTER SIXTY-FIVE

Nick was working on a river table when she finally came home. She could see in his face that he was glad to see her.

She didn't explain what she'd been doing and he didn't ask. She was glad because she didn't want to lie if he asked specific things.

She watched him run the sander over the wood. Nick was deep in the throes of creating so she didn't interrupt.

Instead, she went into the house and got in the shower. It took a minute for the water to warm up but she stood in the cold deluge anyway. It reminded her of the waterfalls and all the times Jake had made love to her under the freezing cascades.

Emma half expected Nick to join her but he didn't. She took a long shower to give him time. When he still didn't appear, she got out and wrapped herself in a towel. She was hungry but chose instead to lie down.

An hour later, Nick woke her to say he was grilling some steaks. She waited until she heard the sliding glass door close to push herself upright. She had dreamed about Hawaii.

After they died, she and her mother had cleaned the house and removed all the remnants of Bob. His recliner, dozens of bottles of alcohol, smoking pipes, collection of miniature ships—all were placed in a big pile in the backyard. They had separated his military things to donate to his friends but not out of respect. The women had agreed that not showing some reverence might be viewed with suspicion. Neither of them wanted to answer questions about what had really happened. If people had not believed them when they were bruised for years, why would they believe now that he was a monster?

It was cathartic watching all his things burn.

At the last moment, Ruth threw her husband's favorite leather jacket into the pyre.

"You'll need this in hell," she said through clenched teeth.

They moved to a small place that Ruth's sister owned on the eastern side of Oahu. It wasn't updated and smelled musty from months of vacancy. The appliances were new and there was no fear looming within its walls.

Emma cried through the entire process. To the casual observer, they might have thought she was mourning her father but nothing was further from the truth. Emma was giddy that he was gone and caught herself excited to tell Jake. Then, over and over, she had to remind herself that both Jake and Kai were gone.

"Kai means 'from the seas'," Jake had explained.

Ironically, if he'd survived, he would be the age she was when she'd had him. She and Jake would probably be living like she and Nick were now.

Kai would be a surfer like his father and, by now, would have earned his moniker. In her dream, she saw him surfing on the board that she and Jake had made. She wasn't sure she really believed in heaven but she hoped that there was surfing there if it existed. She regretted that the onesie was lost too.

Joining Nick on the patio, she slipped her arms around his waist.

"Hey, you," he said warmly while flipping the steaks.

Setting the tongs down, Nick turned and wrapped his arms around her tightly. Emma couldn't speak. Fighting tears, she managed to whisper loud enough that she loved him.

"I love you too," he whispered back.

"The steaks smell good," she said.

"You hungry?"

Still buried in his chest, she nodded.

"I was hoping this would lure you out. I have salad and corn on the cob too."

"Rolls?" she pulled back to ask.

"In the oven," Nick replied with a wink.

During dinner, they talked about his table and her painting. Nick filled her in on the daily goings-on at the club. She told him about her lunch with Maria but she left out the story about calling out names during sleep. It seemed risky to broach the subject again.

After dinner, they cleaned the dishes together and then got into a hammock to look at the sky. Curled against him, she let all the memories recede into the shadows of her mind.

"There's the first star." He pointed.

Using his arm to sight the shiny spot he was pointing out, she corrected him.

"That's Venus."

"Oh yeah?"

"Yeah. It's the most visible at sunrise and sunset."

He was grinning and paid her a kiss on the forehead. "It's so cool that you know that."

They watched the sky bloom into as many stars as could be viewed in the city. Nick didn't ask her how she knew so much about stars, planets, and constellations. Jake had taught her but star-watching always made her think of David. How many nights had they climbed up into that treehouse and tried to count the stars? Emma didn't know but the memory made her smile.

"That's a pretty smile," Nick's words jolted her from her memories.

She looked up at him. "I'm so happy here with you."

It was a true statement but also a lie.

$\mathcal{D}avid$

CHAPTER SIXTY-SIX

I stared at the words for a long time.

It wasn't immediately clear if she meant her father had killed Jake and himself or Jake and the baby. Emma was convinced that her father had killed Jake. Was that why he hadn't made it to the birth? Had Bob already murdered the boy?

The next section was about the pains of labor. The numbers were etched harder into the page, which I attributed to writing to distract herself from the contractions.

I went into labor in the afternoon. When the midwife got here, she told me that I was doing good. Jake is still not here and I'm freaking out. I know I should be focused on having a healthy baby but I'm so afraid it won't look anything like Jake. I wanted him to be here. He says he's working on something to prepare for our escape but it's not like him to not check in knowing how close I am.

The impressions on the paper got lighter after she recorded the birth.

He's perfect. The actual last pushes were so painful I thought I'd die. But once I saw his face, I knew it would be okay. Ten fingers, ten toes, and a tiny patch of dark hair. He's got Jake's nose.

Her words were raw and uncensored as she laid out the plan that they had hatched. Once it was safe to travel, they'd load up their belongings and Jake would take them to Kauai, where his uncle had a surf business. They would hide in Oahu until the baby was ready for the move. One of Ruth's sisters had moved to Kauai after she and Ruth had lost touch. They reconnected through a mutual friend, which would make it harder for Bob to find them. Ruth would move in with her sister and all of them would be away from Bob. It was a well-thought-out plan and almost infallible. Except it wasn't.

I couldn't begin to understand how courageous Emma had to have been at seventeen. It wasn't enough that her father was an abusive alcoholic. He was also a rapist, tormentor, and captor who had a spy network working for him. Emma reported that random Naval vehicles drove by regularly and that several of his "friends" had stopped by under the pretext of checking on them. Clearly, he intended to keep tabs on them in his absence. In an earlier passage, I read about how they avoided her father's spies.

I leave before dawn to go to school. Jake picks me up in a boat so that we can stay off the roads. Strangely, being on the water helps my morning sickness, so baby Kai is definitely his father's son.

Given all I knew, it was excruciating to see the words of excitement as she went on to imagine introducing Jake to his son. She wrote at length about breast feeding. Jake was still missing in action and she was concerned.

It was hard enough to know that she'd rather be with Nick than me. I'd spent our entire marriage trying to give her back all the joy that was taken from her, even though I clearly had no idea how horrible her life had been. Now, I was forcing myself to accept that, before me, she had been with the man of her dreams. She'd chosen me after he died, and I doubted it was because I was a dream. The picture was starting to take shape and I wanted to close my eyes. I forced myself on.

I love his little face. So perfect. His life is ahead of him finally.

She was writing about her hopes for the child and their family when the narrative was suddenly interrupted.

The next words were the ones I'd read before but I broke into a sweat reading them again.

My father is dead and he killed them both.

It would be hours later when she heard it on a local news report. Jake had fallen and was pronounced dead at the scene. Had Bob pushed the boy off a cliff? I needed to know what happened to Kai. How had Bob killed the baby?

I was holding the journal like a baby against my chest. The depth of despair and the pain were intractable. I felt every word and wished I could console her. My poor Emma! The only justice was that the bastard's heart had exploded but why couldn't he have died before all this happened? Why did she have to endure abuse, the loss of her soulmate, and then lose their baby? My chest hurt over the knowledge that this perfect boy, just like our son, did not survive.

No wonder losing our baby had triggered an episode. I got that now with greater clarity. Losing a child to miscarriage was traumatic enough to send anyone to the hospital. But, in the context of her story, I could not truly understand her anguish. Even if I had known, I couldn't possibly comprehend her sense of loss.

After what seemed like hours, I read the rest.

I didn't go to the funeral. They must hate me. It is my fault that Jake is dead. The school called and told my mom that my grades were high enough to let me out of exams. They heard about my father's death and extend their condolences. I don't care about graduation. Nothing matters anymore. My sweet baby Kai and my soulmate are dead. I will never love another like I loved Jake. I will never have another baby to honor Kai.

Her last words cut my soul in half. I guessed my mom was right. Time softens nevers. Or was Nick right? Had she just lost herself and agreed to have a child to appease me the way my mom had appeased my dad? It was baffling. She seemed so resolute in her journal. Why had she changed her mind? More importantly, why hadn't she told me from the beginning that she didn't want children? As I had so many times in the last few months, I inventoried my memories. I did not remember her saying anything about not wanting kids. Instead, we teased about how our kid would be serious and stable like me and messy and creative like her. We talked about names and Christmas time putting things together. Was she just playing along? All of this could have been avoided if she'd only been honest with me.

That wasn't the whole truth. I should have asked her. I just assumed that everything was fine because she didn't say anything to the contrary. I assumed a lot of things. If I had known how bad things had been, I would have still tried to give her peace, security, and joy she'd never had. The reality is that I had given her that and she stayed with me because of it.

Laying the journal down, I handled it as though the souls of Jake and Kai were housed between its covers. Staring at the worn cover, I wondered how Emma had survived all that and managed to keep it a secret. It was still so unbelievable. No one had corroborated her suspicions but she just knew.

Pushing myself upright, still unable to take my eyes off the journal, my gaze was drawn to the Hawaii magazine that lay open beneath it. The water, sand, and palm trees framed the journal like an altar. I must've disturbed something when I moved my leg to get out of bed.

That was when I saw something that nearly stopped my heart.

Emma

CHAPTER SIXTY-SEVEN

Jose had called Nick in the afternoon to let him know that the baby was on her way. Emma had to push hard to keep the memories of her own delivery away. Nick asked her several times if this was bringing back memories. She told him that it was but she was okay and couldn't talk about it yet.

That part was true.

The next day, they showered and dressed and headed to the hospital to see the latest member of the Suarte family. Emma was grateful that the hospital was not the same one that David had been in. Something about that place gave her an unsettling feeling and she was sure it was related to her miscarriage.

The facility wasn't as big as some of the others in town. There was no parking deck so they parked in the front of the brick building and walked through the front doors. Maria was on the third floor so they rode the elevator up, followed the room signs, and found the couple without difficulty.

The baby wasn't in the room yet so they had a chance to visit with Maria and Jose. They both looked like they hadn't slept but neither of them could stop smiling.

"Congratulations," Emma said, hugging her friend.

Maria held onto her for an extra second. "You okay?" she whispered.

Emma nodded. "I'm fine. How are you?"

"Tired, sore, but happy. We'll have to talk later. All the family will be here soon."

"Okay." The women hugged again.

The men were talking about something that had happened at work. It must've been quite an ordeal because it kept them busy and animated until the nurse arrived with the baby.

"Here she is," she announced, wheeling the mobile bassinet.

To the most astute observer, Emma looked like any other person nervously holding a newborn. Beneath the façade, she was anything but that. The memories always flooded back when she held babies. They all had the sleep-drizzled faces and skin like silk. This baby had dark hair and Emma forced herself to look into the baby's eyes instead of looking at the door. The memory of her father bursting into the room would pass, she knew that. A huge crowd of well-wishers started arriving and Emma was glad. She wasn't sure how much longer she could hold back the tide of emotions.

"Here, I don't mean to hog her." She turned to the other people waiting.

Emma handed Estella off to Maria's cousin, Angela, and then turned back to her friend.

"She's beautiful and you look tired. We're going to go and give your family a chance to congratulate you."

Maria smiled. "I know this must be hard for you but I'm so glad you came."

Emma leaned down and the two hugged. "I'm glad too," she whispered.

She and Nick waded through the crowd to get out of the room and off the ward. Emma was surprised that none of the nurses objected to the horde of people. She was glad when Nick took her hand and whisked her away.

The tears started before they reached the stairwell. Nick opened the door and turned just as Emma's knees gave way. He caught her and swept her up without effort. She buried her face in his neck, fully confident that he would safely convey her down the two flights of stairs to the truck. It took him not time to get her into the cab and she let him help her with the seatbelt. She was already back in Hawaii before he started the engine.

The bellowing came first, just like a hurricane inside the house.

Emma instinctively clutched the baby closer, making him cry. Polly and her mother were sitting at the foot of the bed but rose and formed a shield between Emma and the door. All of them watched the door as the storm moved closer.

It was locked but that did nothing. The frame exploded, wood splitting, and the door twisted on its hinges.

His eyes were red. His mouth was so twisted in rage that he looked like a possessed gargoyle.

To Emma, it all happened in slow motion. Polly and Ruth leapt up to keep him away from the baby. Bob grabbed Polly by her shoulders and pushed her into the bookcase. Her face bounced off a shelf and then books rained down on her. She didn't move when she crashed face-first into the floor. Next, he turned all his hatred on Ruth with a fist to the face and then a kick to the stomach. She flew backwards like a rag doll and slammed into the closet door.

The baby's shrieking and her own voice were so loud that she couldn't hear what he was saying at first. Having just given birth, she had no strength to fight him but she gave everything and it wasn't enough. He ripped the baby out of her arms and punched her in the stomach.

Like everything was in a vacuum, the room went silent because the excruciating pain diverted all her other senses. He was speaking, his mouth frothing like he was rabid. It would be much later before her brain would relay their meaning.

Emma watched in horror at him holding the baby. It wasn't gentle or soothing. He glared at Emma with such intensity she was afraid he'd kill Kai before her eyes.

"You'd better be glad you're a whore."

Later, the meaning of his words punched her again. He was aware that he had raped her. It wasn't something he'd done in a drunken state. He remembered and feared the child was his.

She promised him anything he wanted, to save her baby. It was excruciating to push herself up, her hand stretched out like she was reaching for something to cling to before a fall.

He laughed at her as he turned. Emma had to watch him walk out of the door with her baby. She couldn't move. She hoped that the darkness taking her was death.

There was no way to know how much time had passed. Polly and Ruth had managed to get up and were attending her. She was vaguely aware of them cleaning and examining her.

A boulder blocked her throat. She couldn't move her limbs. The boulder in her throat made it impossible to push words out. Emma could hear them talking in hushed tones. She knew they wouldn't call the police. Home deliveries with a midwife were illegal, Polly was saying. The police would arrest Polly and overlook Bob's abuse, as they always had. And, one of them was saying, it was probably too late.

Emma felt numb, as though she was paralyzed. Yet, the greater cruelty was that her hands could still feel Kai's soft, warm skin. She was angry that Jake wasn't there. The one time she would have unleashed him on her enemy and he was nowhere to be found. How would she tell him that his son was gone?

When she heard a car door, something stirred in her that propelled her out of the bed. All of the rage, pain, and hatred rose inside her like lava. There was a baseball bat in the hall closet and she grabbed it on her way down the hall. He was going to tell her where her baby was or she was going to bash his brains in. If she failed, he'd probably kill her. She didn't care.

His shirt and undershirt were torn and covered in blood. His face was gnarled but pale like a zombie's. Emma raised the bat.

"Where is my baby?"

He opened his mouth and then fell as if an anvil from space had landed on him. She knew he was dead. Somehow, she knew that Jake and the baby were dead too. There was no need to hurry. They needed to clean up before they called 911.

David

"Wait, you're going to Hawaii?" Kellyn asked over a broken line. I had to come clean about the journals and tell her what I'd found. My heart sped up every time I thought about it.

"Yes, I'm about to board. I'll call you from Oahu."

"David, are you sure this is the best idea?"

"I know it seems crazy, Kell. But I have to see this through. It makes sense why she hid everything but there is a chance that I can find some answers. I have to try."

"Are you doing this to restore your relationship?"

"I'm not trying to win her back. But if I can give her some closure, I would feel better."

"I trust you, David, and I hope you find what you're looking for."

"I'll be home soon," I said.

My mom understood. I rushed in and told her everything. She waited until I finished to tell me that she had received the call about her transplant.

"Oh my God, Mom. You let me go on. This is great news. I can cancel my flight."

She shook her head. "There is nothing you can do here, David. You need to go to Hawaii."

"But, Mom. What if…?" I couldn't finish the sentence.

"Sweetie, your being here will not keep me from dying if that is what's going to happen. We've had a chance to undo some of the wrongs in our past. You have to go find your answers. I'll be fine. Plus," she paused and giggled, "Micah will be with me."

"He's going to think I'm an awful son."

"No, he won't. I've told him the truth about how awful I was. And I've told him that we've talked about the past and that you've forgiven me. But, regardless, you cannot live your life based on what others think. Just like defining yourself by the past, worrying about what other people think will cripple you. Go find your closure and to hell with anyone who tries to stop you."

I understood that she needed to face this her own way. We finally had no walls between us, and now I was going to confront the barriers that kept me from knowing my wife for the entirety of our marriage. I didn't care who understood or approved. Even if I couldn't find all the answers, I knew it was the right step.

Hastily shoving newly laundered clothes into my bag, I skipped the shower. Driving to the airport, returning the car, and getting through security were all a blur. Once on the concourse, I got a coffee and biscuit and sat down to wait.

The article had not mentioned the location of the photograph. Scouring the magazine for any visual clues, I finally turned to the end of the article for the acknowledgments. To my chagrin over spending so much time looking at pictures of beaches on Oahu, the writer's email and Twitter handle were neatly listed. I didn't bother to explain why I was asking but emailed her to see if she still hand the name of the beach and the tattooed surfer.

I checked my email once more before takeoff, hoping the writer had responded. Shortly after reading the article in the Hawaii magazine, I'd emailed the writer hoping she still had some notes. There was no email in my inbox, so I put my phone on airplane mode and tried to relax.

Like a TV detective, I started recording everything in a small notebook. Reviewing my notes, I inventoried what facts I had. I knew the approximate date when Jake and Bob Roberts had died. Would there be a birth certificate for Kai, I wondered. I made a list of things I needed to search for, including the office of vital statistics. When it was safe to use devices, I powered up my laptop.

I turned my research to finding Jake's last name. Emma had never mentioned it in the journal, and that surprised me. She didn't want to inadvertently give her father a clue about the boy she loved.

Typing "death of Jake in Oahu" netted me nothing. I tried to search the local obituaries but there wasn't another named Jake. After following multiple leads, I finally typed "local boy dies from fall in Oahu." This scored several articles so I added the date range.

Like a kick to the ribs, I inhaled sharply as the top article loaded. The story was about a 17-year-old named Iakopa Mokulehua, who'd fallen from 400 feet on Mount Olomana. The article simply noted that the teen was hiking on a non-sanctioned trail and fell to his death. Bookmarking the article, I turned the search to Mount Olomana. The pictures were stunning and it wasn't long before I found the exact match for the front cover of her journal.

Entering "Iakopa" in the Hawaiian boys' name search engine told me the proper pronunciation and that Iakopa was the Hawaiian equivalent to Jacob.

My next search under the full name produced an obituary where I learned the names of the boy's mother, Keikilani Mokulehua, brother Kale Mokulehua, and the pall bearers. Morbidly, I wondered how much of his body they'd been able to recover and bury. There were a large number of pall bearers. One of them had showed up in the article about Jake's death. Apparently, Kekoa Mano had been there when Jake fell. This was the man I wanted to talk to.

After a few hours, I had some good leads. Pleased with myself, I shut down the computer and closed my eyes.

When the plane touched down, the first call I made was to Connie to inquire about my mom. Connie didn't know much but she told me that the surgery was underway.

With my backpack on one shoulder, I headed straight to ground transportation. My adrenaline prevented me from lingering to admire the cultural gardens, pagodas, and water features of the airport. My stomach was growling but my eyes were set on the car-rental counter.

I guesstimated the clerk, with dreadlocks and tattoos on both arms, to be about 21. He walked me through the paperwork and explained the GPS upgrade I got for free on my 2018 Ford Mustang convertible. A small part of me wanted to drive a Ferrari like Magnum P.I.

After typing in the address into the GPS, I pulled out onto Aolele Street and headed for my destination, Haven Inn. The pictures had been quaint, with stunning views of Mount Olomana. I didn't really care about the luxurious outdoor lounge, updated rooms, close proximity to the beach, or the large pool. This was the first place I'd found with a vacancy and, like the convertible, it would have to do.

The Haven Inn was spectacular and the grounds covered in the expected exotic flowers. The décor theme seemed to hint at Oahu's history of royalty. A host of birds sang me to my bungalow. From my front door I had an amazing view of the mountain and access to the pool.

Opening the door, I was pleased to discover that the room was clean and cheery, with a king bed and fresh-fruit basket. I dropped my bag and lay down on the crisp white bedspread with its teal floral pattern. Even though I had my list, I honestly wasn't sure where to start. Deciding to close my eyes for a few minutes, I sprawled across the bed.

An hour later, after I woke from an unplanned nap, my first order of business was to call and check on my mom. It took a minute to command my limbs but I finally found my way outside. My phone was in my pocket, and I suddenly panicked again when I saw that I had missed a call from Micah. I took a deep breath, and with shaking hands I pressed send and steeled myself. It went to voicemail and I couldn't help but feel a mixture of relief and impatience.

To keep my mind busy, I contemplated the next steps in my investigation. I needed to check my email to see if the writer had responded. After that, the list got jumbled. Should I call Ruth and ask her if I could see her? Would she be alarmed that her son-in-law was in Hawaii without her daughter? It was weird, I had to admit. And if the writer never answered, how would I find the answers about the photos?

I called again and Micah answered on the third ring with a deep, warm voice that disarmed me.

"I'm sorry I missed your call. Is my mom okay?"

Emma

CHAPTER SIXTY-NINE

Emma cried herself to sleep. Nick was great. He didn't try to get her to talk. Instead, he held her and got her water and tissues.

She was glad he didn't ask questions. She knew that he was thinking that seeing Maria's new baby had brought back some memory of her miscarriage. Truth be told, she still had no memory of that. Emma had already given herself grace for not being sad over something she couldn't remember. One day she'd probably have to deal with it but not now. It was too much now anyway. She wasn't in a hurry to set the record straight.

Nick was gone when she woke up. He left a note that said he loved her and he'd see her later. Although she missed not seeing him, she was glad he wasn't there.

Earlier that morning, she pulled the divorce papers out of her purse and signed them. The law office wasn't far away so her first order of business was to drop them off.

Solomon Aroosian called her while she was on her way to the lawyer's office. He was brief, if not mysterious, as he always was. She imagined him as a Godfather type who always seemed to be sitting in a shadow. Explaining that he wanted a painting focusing on a baby's face from the mother's perspective, he gave her the dimensions and described the chapel where the painting would be displayed.

"Can you finish it in that short time?" Aroosian asked.

"I think so," she said, although she knew she could.

"I know it's last minute. There was a question about when the contractor would be finished with the chapel but evidently, they caught a second wind. It will be a beautiful prayer chapel in the maternity ward."

"It won't be a problem. I'll get right on it."

He thanked her and they disconnected. The man was not one for small talk and Emma was glad. She didn't have much use for it either. His last comment was simply that they didn't care about the ethnicity of the baby but wanted to capture that connection from the mother's point of view.

Emma knew exactly what he wanted. The first time she had held Kai and looked into his face, it was magical. She'd memorized every line, angle and the way the light spilled over him. They had been transfixed on each other, although she knew she probably looked like a blob to Kai.

She didn't trust her memory for accuracy, and that gave her an idea. Picking up her phone, she selected her friend's name and waited for her to answer.

David

CHAPTER SEVENTY

S training to hear over my heartbeat, I listened carefully as Micah reported my mother's condition like a news anchor. His tone was serious and did not give me an impression of the man. There were medical terms I didn't know but the summary was that she was doing well so far.

"I'm glad you both had a chance to talk. I know it may not seem like it but she does love you. And I can tell that you love her too."

"I always have," I tried not to stammer.

"Forgiveness is a tricky thing, son, but there is nothing more freeing than being forgiven and offering forgiveness."

"I appreciate what you said. Will you tell my mom that I love her? I look forward to seeing you both soon."

"Will do. I look forward to meeting you in person, David. And don't worry. I'll keep a watch over her and let you know how she's doing."

I thanked him and said goodbye. I was sitting in a chair by the pool barely remembering how I got there. The dark face of the mountain loomed like an angry Polynesian god. Staring at the summit for a long moment, I wondered if Jake's spirit still roamed the cliff. A sudden chill caused me to jerk, and I took a deep breath to calm myself. Still disoriented and somewhat hungry, I pushed myself upright and wandered back into my room.

After turning on lights, securing the door, and snagging a protein bar from the welcome basket, I unloaded my laptop and set it on the table. My phone was dying so I took a minute to plug the charger into the bottom of my android. I finally sat down and logged in.

My heart was still racing and I tried to take a few deep breaths while logging into my email. When I saw a notification marked "About your Inquiry" from Astrid Walford, I closed my eyes to prepare myself.

Mr. Campbell, thank you for your inquiry and lovely comments about my article. I don't have the names of the other guys but I can tell you that the primary subject works at a surf shop on Kailua Beach, where the picture was taken. His name is Kale Mokulehua, Jr., and he is the surf shop owner's son. I think the other people in the picture are cousins and mates. I hope you enjoy your trip and thank you again for your inquiry. Cheerio—Astrid.

It was hard to breathe as I looked up the surf shop. It was owned by Jake's brother, Kale, who had been mentioned in the obituary. If my suspicions were correct, most of the answers I was looking for were only a few miles away.

A few keystrokes led me to the website for Kanaloa 13. It was bigger than I imagined. I guess I was expecting a grass hut with a few boards, beach chairs or umbrellas for rent. Instead, I found a 5,000-square-foot store that sold everything from boogie boards to Sea-Doos. The website described the merchandise for sale, equipment for rent, custom boards, and lessons for anything you wanted to do in the waves. In addition, they also designed and built their boards on site. The picture of the front of the store boasted a barrel. In surfing terms, a barrel is the hollow of a breaking wave and the most iconic surfing image. This barrel was made of fiberglass in shades of blue and green and was probably enough to draw tourists if only for selfie opportunities.

Out of curiosity, I looked up the meaning of Kanaloa and was not surprised to find that Kanaloa was the Hawaiian god of the sea. I already knew the significance of the number thirteen although I was somewhat disappointed that they had not used the Mayan symbol in place of the numbers.

Growing up in San Diego, I knew kids who surfed. Skateboarding had been much easier for me because of immediate access to places we could practice. The mean streets and cul-du-sacs didn't harbor any sharks or riptides, so that was a plus. I'd never really had a proper surfing lesson and I was in Hawaii. That would probably be the best way for me to find answers so I scheduled a tour of the board shop and a beginner lesson.

The notification said that the instructor was TBA. I was hoping for the tattooed surfer in the picture. I was also hoping to find someone who knew Kekoa Mano.

Staring at my computer, I typed the name of the only witness to Jake's death in the search bar. This guy had no social media presence, and that surprised me. Although I didn't post much, I had several social media accounts. Where was this guy?

I'd already looked up the meaning of "Kekoa" and knew it meant "brave". The surname "Mano" meant "shark". While staring at the mountain earlier, it dawned on me that Jake and Kekoa weren't up there being reckless. They were planning something for Emma. After losing his friend, I couldn't imagine that Kekoa would want to be hiking those trails but it gave me an idea.

I searched for hiking guides on Mount Olomana. There were several with pictures and reviews. Scrolling through them hurriedly, I stopped on the fourth one and was sure this was my guy. The picture alone would have convinced me. It was the view that had been seared into my brain from the front of the journal. Ultimately, it was the place where Jake had died. Within seconds, I'd booked an adventure hike and hoped that Land Shark Adventure Tours was a one-man operation.

Emma

CHAPTER SEVENTY-ONE

When Emma arrived at the hospital, her friend was walking around the ward, still tethered to an IV.

"Hey. Are you trying to escape?"

Maria was disheveled, in a lumpy, badly tied hospital gown. Her hair looked like bats had taken up residence in it, and her face was puffy.

She answered something in Spanish. Emma only had a vague idea of its meaning but the brusque tone was enough to convey the message anyway.

"No. I didn't sleep much and they won't let me go home until I finish this and go to the bathroom." She pointed at the solution bag and called it something ugly in Spanish under her breath.

"Who tied your gown?"

"That would be Jose. He says he don't want nobody looking at my culo." She whispered "ass" as if her pointing to her butt had not been enough.

"How's Estella?" Emma asked, hoping to lighten her friend's mood.

Maria smiled. "She is good."

"She's beautiful. Your abuela would be pleased, I'm sure."

"I'm not so sure she'd be pleased with me," Maria said.

"What do you mean?"

Her eyes were wide as she whispered as though she was giving up top-secret information.

"I had my tubes tied."

The reason for the concern was not immediately obvious to Emma. It finally dawned on her that Maria was Catholic. Birth control and voluntary sterilization were considered sins.

Maria continued. "We have five children and struggle to make ends meet. I don't know which one is a bigger sin, being sterilized or not being able to buy shoes or food for five kids. We'll have to find a new church."

"Well, you know you'll get no judgment from me. I actually wish they had tied my tubes when I had the miscarriage."

Maria looked at her for a long moment. "You're sure you don't want kids?"

Emma nodded slowly. "I'm sure." She paused to take a breath. "I've been pregnant twice."

"Twice?"

They stopped at the end of the hall where there was a cushioned window seat big enough for two.

Emma felt like she was on a roller coaster. Her head was floating above her but her stomach plummeted. She was glad there was a place to sit down because she felt dizzy as she spoke the words aloud for the first time.

"I had a son in Hawaii."

"What happened to him?"

"My father was abusive my whole life. My mother helped me hide the pregnancy from him and I had the baby while he was on sea duty in the Navy. We thought we'd have time but somehow, he found out. He attacked us and took the baby. When he came back later, he was covered in blood. I found out later that my boyfriend was dead. My father pushed him off a cliff and, I believe, threw my baby off with him."

"Oh my God," Maria whispered, tears running down her face. She hugged Emma so tightly that neither could breathe.

It was then that all of it came crashing down. Jake and Kai were lost to her again. She could not hold back the tears or take back the words.

Maria was whispering in Spanish and holding Emma like a child. Emma's head was on her shoulder and Maria was stroking her friend's face. It took Emma a few moments to realize that her friend was praying.

The pain was excruciating. Reliving each event with each word. Yet, she felt something she had never known before now. It started at the crown of her head, traveling down through her limbs like a mountain stream, and ended at her toes. She wasn't sure if this was what freedom felt like but she liked the feeling. Reluctantly, Emma admitted to herself that it was time to tell Nick.

David

CHAPTER SEVENTY-TWO

Waking up nervous, like someone with an important interview, I showered and got a good breakfast of eggs, bacon, bagel, and fresh fruit.

Later, dressed in board shorts, t-shirt, and Tevas, I grabbed my keys and wallet and headed to my car. My side was hurting some but I thought moving might soften the pain.

Like a dork, I stood at the entrance of the store, grinning. Halfway through the 20-foot structure, there was a surf board bolted to the ground. A small TV allowed visitors to see themselves on the board. I'd be willing to bet that no one bypassed the temptation to put their arms out and pretend they were on a real wave. I had to do it and, to my delight, a message appeared on the TV screen that told me to hold the pose for a picture. Positioning my feet for balance, like I actually knew what I was doing, I stretched my arms out. Was it my imagination or did I feel like I was moving?

Moments later, I entered the shop and heard a male voice call out.

"You looked legit."

I turned to face the speaker. "Thank you."

My words nearly caught in my throat. It was all I could do not to stare at him.

A younger man handed me the photo of me on the wave. I noted the Mayan symbol for thirteen tattooed on his wrist.

"For most first-timers, this is the best surfing they do, so we take it before going to the beach."

I looked at the image. The words on the bottom read, 'First Surfing Lesson at Kanaloa 13'.

"Good idea," I mused.

The young man laughed and smacked me on the shoulder. "Well, come on in. Let me show you around the shop and then we'll hit those waves."

I felt giddy and teary at the same time. It was unbelievable to have just seen his picture in a magazine days ago. He was bigger than I realized. I guessed him at six feet and one hundred and eighty pounds. He was all muscles and suntan. His golden eyes and dimples gave him an otherworldly look and his smile was full of straight, white teeth.

Leading me to a small room, he indicated an open locker. "You can put your stuff in there. Pick any 4-digit code." He explained how to enter it in the electronic pad as he stepped into a small closet and retrieved a wet suit.

"I think this will fit," he said, handing me the black suit with orange trim around the arms and across the chest.

"Are you my tour guide or instructor?"

He smiled a dazzling white grin that looked so familiar I wanted to cry.

"Both, actually." He held his hand out to shake mine. "I'm Kai."

Emma

CHAPTER SEVENTY-THREE

" I 'm sorry to dump all this on you."

Maria shook her head. "No, it's okay. You needed to say it and I'm honored you trusted me."

They arrived at the room just as the nurse returned Estella. Emma quietly removed her camera from her bag and snapped a few pictures of the tiny baby. She was glad to have something to hide her face behind since she was feeling exposed and raw.

"I think my time has come," Maria announced with a frown.

Maria shuffled unceremoniously, dragging the IV pole, and hurried to the bathroom. Emma watched the baby sleeping. The tiny eyelids fluttered as Maria released a stream of Spanish expletives from behind the closed door. Estella began to cry before she opened her eyes. Emma put her camera in the bag and reached for the baby just as real tears began to gather in the corners of the infant's eyes.

Cuddling the baby, she spoke softly to soothe her.

"It's okay, sweetie. Mommy is okay and you're okay."

Emma loved the feel of the warm silky skin. She sang softly to get the child back to sleep. It was a song that she'd only sung to her son once.

Twenty minutes later, Maria emerged triumphant and was able to climb into bed despite the tangle of gown, IV tubing, and disheveled bedding. Once settled, Emma handed her the sleeping baby.

"I'm glad I will be home soon. I miss all my babies."

Emma nodded with a smile. She had already explained she wanted a few pictures, and now lifted her camera silently. Standing in a tight corner at the head of the bed, Emma shot a few from over Maria's shoulder. Satisfied with the shots and exhausted from her confession, she put her camera up just as Estella roused again and started making little sucking sounds.

"I'm going to go," Emma said. "I'll check on you tomorrow. Do you need anything before I go?" Maria shook her head without taking her eyes off Emma.

"It was not your fault. You have to find a way to forgive yourself and even that horrible man. I know it is hard. I have some abuse in my past too. If we don't forgive, it eats us like cancer. I'm praying for you, my friend, that telling me was the first step to healing."

"Thank you," was all Emma could say.

The women hugged as best they could.

Driving back to the gallery, Emma thought about her friend's advice. She wasn't sure she could forgive her father or herself, but she accepted that her friend was probably right.

Parking in the back and letting herself in quietly, Emma sat down to look at her pictures. She wasn't ready for any more conversation. Words were like barbells and she still felt their weight in all her limbs.

The phone rang and she set her camera down to answer it. It was Nick.

"Hey, baby," he started. "I'm going to be late tonight. One of my guys got hurt and I need to finish the job."

"I'm sorry. Is he okay?"

"Yeah, he'll be okay. Are you okay?'

"I'm good. Tired but good. I was visiting with Maria and Estella."

"Oh yeah? How are they?"

"They're good. Looks like they might go home today."

"I hope so. Jose is in a terrible mood."

She could hear his concern. "I know I've been..." Emma started. She wasn't sure what word fit the blank.

"It's understandable, babe. Don't be hard on yourself."

It would all make sense soon, she wanted to say. Pushing away her anxiety, she took a deep breath.

"Do you need me to bring you something to eat?"

"Nah, I'll get something on the way home. Will you be there?"

She thought a moment. "Solomon gave me a new project. I think I'm going to get started so I'm not sure."

"Okay. I'll check with you on my way home."

"I love you," she said and heard his smile.

"Love you too, Em. I'll see you soon."

As she put the phone on the tabletop, she remembered that those were the words David always used. She remembered that now. She couldn't help but wonder what would have happened if she had told him the truth.

Maybe Maria was right. Maybe it was time to forgive and ask forgiveness from David. She just hoped that David didn't hate her as much as she hated herself.

David

CHAPTER SEVENTY-FOUR

I'm not sure I'd ever loved Emma as much as I did right now.

"Mind if I go to the bathroom first?" I asked, trying to fight the emotion.

"Sure. Right through there." Kai pointed to a short hallway.

I nodded and shot past him for a tiny bathroom just larger than a closet. Managing to turn on the fan and the water in case the walls were thin, I gripped the sink as though bracing for a beating.

In the back of my mind, I knew there was a possibility that he was not her son. Maybe Jake's uncle had had a son and named him Kai in tribute. But in reality, I knew this was her son. He had her eyes and smile. He even had her laugh and some of her mannerisms. It was overwhelming. The child that she had mourned her entire life was alive.

Forcing myself to breathe, I doused my face with water and flushed the toilet to perpetuate the deception. I was glad that I'd thought to bring board shorts; they didn't bunch as I wrestled into the wetsuit. Whipping off my shirt, I opened the door and practically ran to shove it into the locker. I felt like a scarecrow caught in a tornado as I shoved my arms into the wetsuit, while trying to shut and secure my locker. I finally whirled around.

The young man was waiting with Emma's smile on his face. "Ready?"

I nodded. "Can't wait."

With Kai leading me through a pair of swinging doors, we entered the workshop. It smelled of wood and resin, paint and oil. Pointing to a board encased and mounted on the wall, Kai explained.

"That was my dad's board."

It was about eight feet long and painted a deep orange that made me think of the sunrise. The symbol for thirteen was on the top end and some smaller writing on the bottom. I stepped closer to decipher it. There were initials, neatly carved, polished and stained into the surface.

"It's beautiful," I said finally.

"This is one of mine." Kai indicated a work in progress on a pair of saw horses.

I came over and let him explain the process and how much longer it would take.

"I've never understood the sizes," I admitted.

Kai nodded. "That's probably the most asked question. It really depends on your experience, fitness, size, and what kind of waves you want to surf."

"Wow, it must be a popular question because you came right back with that."

"Seriously, all the time. Like with you, you haven't surfed much but you're in reasonably good shape. You're about six feet tall and around 170, right?"

"Wow, if this surf gig doesn't work out you might want to take a job at a carnival."

We laughed but Kai continued, obviously serious about his craft.

"We'll try you on a 7 or 8-footer, 22 inches wide, and three inches thick. I want to give you a lot of volume and stability."

"That sounds comforting."

The boy laughed. "Don't worry. I've got your back."

Seeing Kai before me gave me a glimpse of the 17-year-old that Emma had described as her dream man. He was handsome, affable, charismatic, and genuine. I couldn't blame her.

"Does your dad still make boards?" The pit of my stomach cramped as I waited for his response.

"Oh yeah. They're heavenly."

I must've looked startled because the boy laughed heartily.

"My dad died the day I was born. But I know it wouldn't be heaven to him if he couldn't still surf."

"Oh man, I'm sorry," I exclaimed, silently not sorry. In fact, I was ecstatic to have confirmed one more detail that corroborated Emma's story.

"It's all right. You didn't know."

"Do you mind if I ask how he died?"

The teen shrugged, as though I'd just asked if the sky was blue. "He fell off a cliff."

I had to know if he knew about Emma. "What about your mom?"

Shrugging again, he indicated a long rack of finished boards. "Here, you get to pick the one that speaks to you."

I nodded, disappointed. The TV detectives made it look so easy to get confessions and facts. Perusing the boards, I hoped he hadn't seen my face.

"They say she died that day too," he finally said. "I never met her."

I wanted to whip around and tell him the truth right now. I wanted him to know that his mother thought he was dead. *She still loves you.* I wanted to say it and almost grabbed the boy. Then I realized it wasn't my story to tell.

"God, Kai, I'm two for two. Sorry to dredge up sad memories."

He surprised me with a huge smile. "You're okay. Technically, they aren't memories for me. My grandmother and uncle loved me and raised me not to live in the past. I'm not mad or traumatized that my mom left. If she had stayed, she would have been broken every time she saw me. They tell me I look like him. Well, I have his nose, height, build, and charm."

"You have her eyes and smile," I said, and then realized I hadn't phrased it as a question.

Kai laughed. "If this surfing gig doesn't work out, you might want to try one of those psychic lines."

We both burst into laughter and I rested my hand on a board. It was white with teal and green flowers.

"Looks like you picked your board," Kai said, pointing to my apparent choice.

"Is it a good one for me?"

"Well, let's go see."

Emma

S ipping a glass of pinot grigio, Emma stared at her blank canvas. As she began to sketch, Emma closed her eyes to reach into her memory vault. She'd spent so long trying to bury the images deeper so they wouldn't hurt. Emma knew that she'd been successful for the most part. But now she wanted them back.

She spent time on the baby's eyes. Imagining her own, she roughed out an almond shape. From there, she created a small version of Jake's nose.

The lips were next. They were a combination of his full ones and her thin. She fought to remember the tiny smile she only saw once. If he had lived, Kai would have had his father's dimples.

She worked without breaks. The night had arrived without her acknowledgement. By the time she looked up from her canvas, it was eleven. She'd been so consumed that she'd forgotten to call Nick. It struck her that he hadn't called either.

Setting her brush down, she sailed to the table, swept up the phone and scrolled to her last call. What if something had happened? She felt lightheaded and her chest hurt.

As the ring started, she heard a sound coming from outside. Emma walked closer to the door, hearing the sound again at the same time as the ringing on her phone. She opened the back door, spotting the phone first and then the shape of a man asleep just beyond the threshold.

Emma didn't need an explanation. She already knew what he would say. Nick understood when she got into the zone. He didn't like to break her concentration but wanted to be near her. The man could sleep anywhere so he had just lay down outside the door. To anyone else, it would be strange.

To her, though, it was dear and appreciated. She got on her knees and gently stroked his face until his eyes unraveled and eyelids flew wide open.

"Hey, dude, if you show up at someone's back door and pass out, they're going to think you're a psycho or a drunk."

"I didn't want to interrupt."

She kissed him hard and fast, suddenly overcome with gladness to see him. He returned her ferocity, pushing himself upright as he did. Emma straddled him and they continued kissing, each holding the other's face like they had been apart for decades.

She didn't know how he stood up with her on top of him. He took them inside and headed to the couch. Resuming their former position on a softer surface, they let the passion intensify. Hands roamed fabric and skin, and they wordlessly undressed each other as though the world would end if they didn't make love.

It was midnight before they came up for air.

"Oh crap," he said so suddenly it startled her.

"Buzz kill," she muttered, slightly irritated for being roused from her euphoria.

"I left food in my truck."

Emma's stomach growled on cue and they both laughed.

"What was it?"

Nick crinkled his nose, clearly thinking of all the reasons the food was no longer viable.

"Sushi."

"Your truck is going to smell," she teased.

"Yep."

"We probably have crackers and cheese up here if you're hungry."

"Nah. I was just worried about you."

She traced his eyebrows, then let her fingers drift down over his temples, cheeks, and then teased his lips. "You don't have to worry about me."

He looked at her for a long moment. She wanted to say something but he suppressed her urge with a smile.

"You want to see my painting?"

He nodded and they got up, walking hand in hand and naked to the canvas.

Emma liked to paint with her back to the wall so the painting had been turned around. Nick took several minutes, seemingly studying each stroke. He finally looked at her with an expression she couldn't interpret.

"The eyes," he said quietly. "This is your baby."

She nodded silently, waiting for the moment. Her heart thrashed in her chest and a knot formed in her throat. It was time to tell him.

"I have something to tell you," he interrupted her moment.

"What is it?" She saw him shaking and the anxiety rose like lava from her toes.

Tears welled up in his eyes and Emma was helpless to stop him walking away. He stood there, his shoulders and back tight.

"When I saw how you were the other night. With the baby. And then you went back today. The way you cried. I knew I had to tell you."

"Baby? What is it? You're scaring me."

He turned and looked at her. Pale eyes bored into her as though he was expecting a fight but had no plan to resist.

"I lied to you."

David

CHAPTER SEVENTY-SIX

We started on the beach with me repeatedly trying to pop up into a standing position. More than once, I sprang up and fell into the relentless sand. I had grains in my ears, nose, hair, and embedded in the stubble on my face. Kai found this particularly hilarious.

"You're psyching yourself out."

"Think so?" I questioned.

"Don't overthink it."

I put everything out of my mind and concentrated on the mechanics of pushing myself upright cleanly. After a dozen more tries, I finally did it.

"That was the best one. I think you're ready for the water."

I was relieved to hear that. At least now I'd have a new medium to fall into and perhaps extricate some of the sand.

Kai kept me focused but also distracted, telling me stories of his childhood. It was so natural talking to him that I stopped thinking about Jake and Emma.

"Your poor grandmother. She must've been a nervous wreck," I said after hearing a story about 5-year-old Kai stealing a kayak and being swept out in a current and having to be rescued by a fisherman in a boat.

"She was pretty mad because I wasn't supposed to be on the water alone. She told me that being lost would teach me more than being found."

"Wow. And at five you understood that?"

"I was probably just glad she didn't spank me for disobeying. But her words stayed with me. I get it now." He was smiling but I saw sadness in his eyes for the first time. "When you're lost, you can't think about your fear. You have to focus on how to survive. How not to fall in and drown, how to find your way back, and how not to psych yourself out about what danger might be lurking around you. When you are found, it's hard to think of anything other than what could have happened or how grateful you are to have survived it. Lost is focused. Found is reflection."

"Your grandmother is a wise human," I said. It was then that I recognized why there was sadness in his face.

"She died last month. Complications from her diabetes," he replied quietly, surveying the horizon.

"I'm sorry, Kai." I meant it this time.

The boy poked me and pointed toward the vast sea. "Here comes your wave."

These words were followed by frantic paddling on my part. There was maneuvering and swearing as I got into position. Truth be told, I'd looked where he was pointing and saw nothing but water. Sure enough, though, the wave he promised came. I paddled as hard as I could with Kai right beside me.

"Now," he yelled.

I sprang up with all my might and found myself the master of my board for about fifteen seconds.

We tried this several more times and I fell on all my attempts. The sand had been a much more generous medium. The water was much crueler. The good news was that the sand in my nose and ears was gone.

After the fifth time paddling out, I thought surfing may not be my thing. I'd also started thinking about sharks.

"Aren't you afraid of sharks?"

Kai laughed. "It's taken you longer than most. I respect them but I don't fear them."

"What's the difference?"

"To respect something is to acknowledge that it is powerful. When you fear something, you aren't respecting your own power."

I didn't have time to take in the wisdom. He didn't have to poke me. By now, I knew the expression and immediately started paddling. For a brief second, I felt as though my arms were merely flailing in the water and that the wave building behind and beneath me was going to crush me. Suddenly, Kai was off to my left.

"Now, David, now," he yelled, and I obeyed.

It might have been my imagination but it felt like some force helped me explode upwards. Then, it seemed like something was holding my feet firmly to the board. I had no illusions that I was racing along, zigging here and there, without some help. My board was possessed with me on it. Some of my earlier skateboarding experience came back and I was able to stay upright. It was terrifying, exhilarating, and strangely calming all at the same time. I understood now what Emma meant when she said that surfing made her feel closer to God. The smell of the sea, the sun anointing me in warmth and light, and the majesty of the roaring waves were better than any church service I'd ever attended. Here I felt God. Here I felt like I knew Him better.

In the end, I finally fell off and splashed hard into the shallows. The board surged on toward the beach and gave my right ankle a good pull. It hurt and I had a welt where the tether around my ankle had been. I was happy though.

"David! That was amazing. I've never seen any newbie catch and ride a wave like that. I mean, I pointed it out but I didn't really think you'd be able to do it. It was a big wave. You must have some seriously cool guardian angels." Kai patted me on the shoulder and then hugged me.

It was so brief and innocent but I suddenly realized that the tragic story I'd come here with wasn't all sad. Here was Emma's son. He was alive and celebrating in my face. He was happy and balanced.

"I've never felt…" I tried to explain.

"So close to God," Kai finished my sentence.

I nodded. "And free. I've never felt so free. But, I swear, it felt like I had help. Like someone hoisted me up and held my feet to the board."

"Maybe someone did. Maybe it was my dad. He and my mother made this board together. Maybe he was helping you. It was cool that you put your hand on it right after we talked about them."

My mouth literally fell open as Kai held the board proudly with a huge grin. The words would not come. I had just surfed the same waters that she had on the board she and Jake had made together. What were the chances? Maybe Jake really was here.

"Wanna try again?"

I stood up nodding and he handed me the board.

"My grandmother surfed every day until about a year ago when they had to take her leg. I miss her but I'm glad she doesn't have to watch the waves knowing she won't be riding them anymore."

"Maybe she was the one who yanked me up," I suggested.

Kai laughed so hard he snorted. Emma could emit a snort big enough to make a warthog proud when she got really tickled.

"Gram was about four-foot-eleven. It's more likely she was the one holding your feet to the board."

"Well, let's hope she does it again."

Emma

CHAPTER SEVENTY-SEVEN

Confused and breathless, Emma stared at Nick as he put his clothes on. She didn't know if he was planning to leave and she was terrified over what he needed to say.

"When we first got together, I knew you didn't want to talk about babies. We both agreed that we didn't want kids," he started.

Emma felt her body cramping like a marathon runner in need of electrolytes. Nick sat down heavily, still shirtless, and fixed her with a stare.

"But seeing how you held Estella and then how you cried, it hit me that you might've only said you didn't want kids because you were grieving the loss of your baby. And that made me think."

She started to speak but he held his hand up to stop her. Emma was suddenly cold, goose flesh spreading across her body. She usually left a sweater on the floor for the occasions when she got cold painting. Careful not to take her eyes off Nick, she squatted down and felt along the floor for it. She snagged it and pulled it around her shoulders as he started again.

"I lied when I said I don't want kids. I've always wanted them but my wreck made it impossible."

"It's okay, Nick. You didn't lie."

His head shot up. "Yes. I did. I told you I didn't want them because I was afraid to tell you I couldn't have them. I realized while you were crying that you might want kids at some point."

"I don't," she said more defiantly than she meant to. "So, if you're telling me that you do then this isn't going to work."

He grabbed his shirt and stood up, putting it on.

"Maybe it's not. I don't know what to think. You're calling out names in your sleep. And I'm feeling inadequate. I don't know if you're crying 'cause you are mourning your baby or want more. You aren't talking to me, sleep here or somewhere else for days. And what do I do? Like some puppy, I'm falling asleep on the back porch. Afraid if I say something, I'll lose you. Afraid if I don't, I'll still lose you. Feeling bad that I lied when I know there are things you aren't telling me. Either you trust me with all of you or trust me with none of you. I love you and I can handle it. I cannot handle not knowing."

If there was ever a moment, it was now. She pulled her sweater tighter around her to cover her nakedness. Had this been what Eve had felt when she had to tell Adam she took a bite of the apple? She knew she was making him suspicious, because every time she looked at the door his head turned. It was an old habit from the panic attacks from which she suffered. She knew it was irrational to expect her evil father to burst into the room, red eyes and mouth full of hateful words, but the fear he'd left in his wake was eternal.

"Oh my God," Nick said slowly. Looking once more at the door, he turned back to her. His eyes were cold. "You're expecting someone."

She started forward as he turned. "No, I'm not," she called but in seconds he was gone.

She wanted to chase after him but felt paralyzed. Her limbs became heavy as the panic took over. Reaching for her phone, she fumbled to call him but midway through scrolling she dropped the phone. The numbness started in her chest, as it always did, and then poured into her extremities like ice water. Her mind wouldn't let her separate her thoughts or turn off the montage of memories playing like a video loop in her brain.

Ordinarily, there would be tears but even her tear ducts were malfunctioning. She felt the burn of tears but nothing came. She felt helpless to stop it. The panic was her master.

His words were still ringing in her ears.

"Trust me with all of you or trust me with none of you."

No one had ever said that to her in her entire life. Emma breathed as slowly as her lungs would allow her. She had been taught meditation techniques to combat the attacks. As she worked to slow her thoughts, she closed her eyes and recalled the sound of Nick's voice. As mad as he was, she knew he meant what he said. He really wanted to know all of her. It wasn't out of a need to control or rescue.

Pushing herself upright, Emma clawed at the table to use it as leverage. She had to go after him. It was a struggle to get the rest of her clothes on and find her keys. Finally dexterous enough to scroll through her phone, she tried to call him but got a message that he was not accepting calls.

First, she drove home but didn't get out since his truck wasn't there. It was the middle of the night but she drove to the service entrance to the country club. Nick had given her a key card to get into the gate. She could see that there were no cars or trucks in the small lot designated for employees.

After several long moments, she turned back toward the gallery. A small detour allowed her to drive by their place again but he was still not there. The parking lot at the back of the gallery was still empty and she chided herself for wishing this was a Hallmark movie and he'd be there waiting for her.

Locking the door behind her, she tried to call him again. Wherever he was, Nick did not want to talk to her.

And then she finally found her tears.

David

CHAPTER SEVENTY-EIGHT

Whether Keikilani was helping me or muscle memory from skateboarding kicked in, I stood more than I fell for the next hour. Kai showed off some of his skills and taught me a few surfer terms.

Since we'd gone beyond the lesson and he didn't have any other clients, we just hung out. It was fun and I was sure I'd never had this much fun hanging out with a 17-year-old, even when I was that age. It was humbling in places as he spoke. I had to remind myself that he was younger.

"So, you are living with your uncle now that your grandmother passed?"

He nodded. "My uncle and grandmother and a couple other cousins have houses all in the same place. They're connected by a lanai. So, my uncle is technically next door. He's technically listed as my father."

"Technically?" This was news.

The boy nodded with a smile. "It's complicated. When I was born, a midwife delivered me and that was illegal. I didn't have a birth certificate. About that time, my aunt had miscarried her baby but no one knew. So, my uncle and aunt registered me as their son so I'd have a birth certificate. They knew my dad wanted to name me Kai, and the last name was the same so it just worked."

The picture was becoming clear. Bob must've snatched the baby and took him to Jake's mother.

"You're in school?"

"Yeah. I'm a senior. I'm planning to go to University of Hawaii in the fall."

"That's cool. Do you know what you want to study?" I chided myself for sounding so adult.

"Marine Biology and Atmospheric Science. I'm planning to minor in Disaster Preparedness and Emergency Management."

"Wow. You've got it mapped out. I don't think I settled on a major until I was already in college. That's impressive and practical."

"I've been saving for college since I was ten. Everything I make off my boards and lessons my uncle lets me keep."

"You got enough?"

"I'm good for the first two years. Course, I plan to keep working so I can save for the last two years."

"I wish I'd been more like you when I was your age. I lost my father when I was thirteen but I never got over feeling lost. I mean, I went to college and got a job. But I still longed for his counsel and approval."

"I wonder how my life would be different if my dad hadn't died and my mom hadn't left. But then, if they hadn't, I wouldn't have had the life with my grandmother, uncle, and cousins like I do now. We'd still be close but we might have moved away. My uncle has been a good father and I've never heard him complain about having another mouth to feed. He taught us to appreciate everything we had and to work hard. My grandma was the same way. They never put my dad on a pedestal or spoke ill about my mom."

"Do they know how your dad fell?"

"My godfather was with him and only ever said that dad slipped."

"Wow. That must've been really traumatic for him. Is he still on the island?"

"Oh yeah, he's still here. He has an adventure trail company on the same trails where my dad fell. I guess he could never bring himself to leave dad up there alone."

"It isn't Land Shark Adventures, is it?"

A broad smile stretched across Kai's face. "Is that who you're booked with?"

I nodded, hoping my surprise was convincing. "What are the chances?"

The boy shrugged. "Pretty good, actually. All the surf and adventure outfitters on this side all know each other, grew up together, or are related. That'll be a good hike but you won't be able to move tomorrow between surfing and hiking."

"You've been on the tour?"

"I grew up on it. We go up there all the time, and especially on my dad's birthday. I help Koa keep up the trails."

"Well, I hope I'm up to it. I'm excited to see the views."

"They are amazing," he said quietly.

I felt a pang in my heart for him. "Do you ever feel your dad up there?"

Kai looked up at the mountains and then back at me. "No. I feel my dad here on the water. When I go up there, I feel my mom. I know it sounds weird. I don't think she's dead but I think her sadness lives there."

"What would you say to her if you saw her?"

"I don't know the exact words but I'd want her to know that I'm okay. And that I understand. And," he paused and looked back at the mountains, "I want her to know that there is nothing to forgive. I think she feels guilty. I would want her to know I love her."

"Wow. This has been one of the best days of my life."

"Next time, you need to try windsurfing. And you really need to see the surfing on the North Shore."

"I'll definitely be back. And I will take a drive up there. I'm guessing I'm not ready to surf the North Shore."

He laughed but it wasn't cruel. "You need a few more lessons. I'll get you a towel."

He jumped up and disappeared briefly, returning with a rolled-up beach towel. I could see the logo as he unrolled and handed it to me.

"Hey, man, show me some of your boards for sale. I'd like to buy one."

"Seriously? Cool. Come on. I think I know the one you need."

I changed my clothes and then came out to find the boy waiting for me on the storeroom floor. For the next thirty minutes, Kai showed me the boards that would best suit my weight and skill. To his credit, he spent equal time explaining the virtues of the boards his uncle had made. I settled on an 8-foot orange and black board with the Mayan symbol in the middle. Kai explained its meaning and I pretended that I knew nothing about it. I also purchased a smaller board that his uncle had made, a hat, three t-shirts, a key chain, and flip-flops.

At the register, I noticed other patrons for the first time. It was like all the rest of the world had fallen away. Kai was explaining the shipping charges and delivery guarantees but I didn't care. I wasn't sure how much surfing I was going to do but I wanted to help him. I included a tip for the lessons.

"Wow, are you sure about this, man? That's a big tip."

I smiled. "Least I can do. I feel like a new man. You gave me much more than surfing lessons. Thanks for sharing your stories and wisdom."

He blushed. "I'm sorry if I talked too much. I don't usually talk about all that." He paused and then brightened. "Let's get a selfie."

He came around the counter while I got my phone out. Arm in arm, we got a couple of pictures in various degrees of serious and silly, like we were old friends.

When he walked me out, the boy gave me a hug. It wasn't awkward, and my heart strings pulled so sharply I fought tears. I didn't want to leave but I knew I'd be tempted to tell him everything if I stayed. It wasn't my place. Maybe he'd never know that his mother didn't leave him. I remembered his words and knew he'd be okay either way.

"Until next time," I said when he released me.

"I'll be here. Tell Koa to go easy on you."

Emma

CHAPTER SEVENTY-NINE

He had not come back or tried to call. Emma stared at her phone. It made sense. He thought she was with someone.

Emma drove over to their place, found it empty, and took a shower. She didn't want to be alone so she drove to Maria's place. Her friend was clearing the dishes from breakfast.

"Are you hungry?"

Emma picked up a left-over piece of buttered toast.

"This is fine. Thank you."

Maria nodded and continued clearing dishes. "What's wrong?"

She told Maria the condensed version, chewing her toast in between. Maria came to join her at the table with a cup of coffee.

"You have to tell him."

"I went everywhere looking for him. I want to tell him."

"Good. Where do you think he is?"

Emma shrugged and took a sip of piping hot java. "I don't know."

Maria wasn't satisfied. She picked up her phone and called Jose. After a brief conversation in Spanish, she looked at Emma with a sad expression.

"Jose says Nick took a few days off."

Emma nodded. "I've already cried and panicked over this. I'm just going to have to wait."

"Well, I'm glad you came."

Emma looked around. The house was trashed.

"Want some help?"

Maria shook her head. "No, you didn't come here to work."

"Actually, that sounds like the perfect way to keep me calm. And," Emma paused to take her friend's hand, "it looks like you could use some help."

For the next two hours, the women split up to conquer the chaos. Emma extracted 32 tiny dinosaurs from the sofa, having already sucked one of them into the vacuum. She gathered discarded shirts, socks, and an unused pull-up from the family room. After starting a load of laundry, she scrubbed the Hershey's syrup out of the bathtub.

Sitting down later with Maria and Estella in the freshly cleaned house, Emma drank the last of a bottled water she'd started midway through the cleaning journey.

"How does one get gummy bears on the ceiling? Good grief."

Maria laughed. "If you turn your back for one second, there is no telling what kids will do."

The women laughed for a long moment and then stopped to watch the baby, who emitted grunting sounds as she breastfed.

"It's worth it, though." Maria looked up. "And I'm sorry you didn't get to experience it."

"I got to breastfeed Kai one time. I can only remember little shreds of the second pregnancy but none of them seem real to me. I feel bad for that baby and like a horrible person for not missing him."

"You shouldn't have to feel bad because you aren't more devastated or because your treatment wiped out your memory. Grief comes in stages. First, there is denial. Then, anger, depression, and acceptance. It sounds so neat and clean. But," she got up and extracted another small dinosaur wedged between couch cushions. "grief is like dinosaurs hidden in the couch. It looks like the coast is clear but then you wonder what sharp thing is poking you. Just because you don't feel the pain now doesn't mean you won't. Don't be hard on yourself."

Emma listened, amused and somewhat embarrassed that she'd missed the mini stegosaurus. Perhaps she would talk to her therapist about all this. She didn't know what stage she was in or what to expect. All these years she'd kept her secrets, and now the one person she wanted to tell was missing.

David

CHAPTER EIGHTY

Still euphoric, I drove to the meeting spot for my hike. The directions had promised that it would be easy to find. I was relieved when they turned out to be true.

The man waiting for me was a big guy, approximately 6'4" and 250 pounds. He was pure muscle without an ounce of body fat. His biceps were bigger than my head. If he had not been wearing a bright yellow Landshark Adventures shirt, I wouldn't have gotten out of the car.

"You David?" the man asked in a deep, booming voice.

"Yes." I held my hand out and he shook it with huge hands.

"I'm Kekoa."

"Nice to meet you, Kekoa."

"Call me Koa. You ready for your hike?"

My legs and torso were already screaming their disapproval but I smiled. "I am."

He handed me a small, lightweight sports pack with the Landshark logo on the front. "This is yours to keep as part of your package. There are snacks and water inside. All of the snacks are organic and locally sourced."

Putting the pack on without looking inside, I thanked him. He handed me a clipboard with a waiver on it. The language was the same as the one I'd signed at Kanaloa 13. Basically, it just said that if I died during this excursion it was all on me. I signed it and handed it back.

It was fascinating watching him collect his gear. His pack was much bigger than mine and full of ropes and harnesses. Silently, I was trying to remember the description of the adventure and if it involved rappelling. Then I decided it was easier to ask.

"Are we rappelling?"

"Not exactly. There are a few tricky spots, and it's safer if you're harnessed."

I followed him in silence for twenty minutes. He was not a talkative guy so I had my work cut out for me.

"How many of these do you do a day?"

"Depends. Could be as few as one or as many as four."

"Wow. I can't imagine four of these a day."

He laughed a big jolly laugh that made him sound even bigger. "You do what you have to do to pay the bills."

"True. You got kids?"

"Oh yeah. Married for fifteen years, two kids, and lots of bills."

"I'll bet. Do your kids come out and hike with you?"

"All the time. My son is the oldest. He's thirteen and thinks he knows the trails better than I do. He's my daredevil. My daughter is the one with the business mind. She's the one who is always thinking of marketing and gimmicks. She is the one who suggested Groupon. I'm hoping that between the two of them they'll take the business to the next level when they take over."

"They sound like cool kids."

"They are. They call me a mountain goat, so if I'm going too fast, let me know."

"I'd say they gave you an accurate nickname," I said with more conviction than I meant to express.

"You need to stop?" He turned and gave me one of those arched eyebrows and a big grin.

"Not yet. I'm good." I was lying.

"Okay, well, let me know."

We kept ascending for what seemed like days. Koa pointed out various landmarks, native plants, and told me stories about previous clients. I was hoping he would mention Jake but this guy wasn't letting anything slip. Basically, I was just trying to keep up.

At the first peak, I sat down on a rock and wished I had the balls to just ask him what I wanted to know and head back down. Surveying the view, though, made me momentarily forget my mission. There were shades of green I had never seen before today. The trees spread out over the mountains and valleys so thickly that it was impossible to see the ground. There are few moments when witnessing a place makes you feel like the first person to see it. This was one of those moments. All around me were tangled branches, exposed roots, and reddish clay blended with rich, dark soil. It was breathtaking.

Koa was watching me. I didn't know if it was the sheer size of him or his hawk-like eyes that made me feel intimidated. He handed me another bottle of water.

"It gets harder from here so you need to hydrate." Reaching in his backpack, he handed me a small packet. "Here, put this in your water. It's electrolytes in the form of a cherry-orange-flavored powder."

"Thanks," I said, pouring the powder in the water.

It tasted more salty than citrus, and the fact that the water wasn't cold made it worse. I didn't complain. My muscles were already fatigued. Koa was pulling out harnesses and ropes. After a short demonstration, we were harnessed and tethered. Koa had explained that the tether would ensure my safety. *Unless you fall*, I thought.

Grappling with rocks, ropes, and mud, I was glad that I was tied to Superman. Several times my foot slipped on mud and the rope between us was taut and sure. By the time we got to the second peak, we started scaling steep inclines. I kept my eyes on the narrow path before me, aware that a misstep might not send me plummeting but the jagged rocks would leave an impression. In some places, there were frayed ropes and loose tree roots to assist. I tried not to think of Jake.

Emma

C oncentrating on her work had always been her salvation. Emma could tune anything out when she painted. She was grateful for that.

There had been no word from Nick, and her brief excursions home revealed nothing to indicate that he'd been there.

So, she painted. What else could she do? She finished painting Kai and started the one of Estella she intended to give to Maria. She sketched a series of babies and had multiple easels set up. Emma had never before worked on simultaneous pieces before now. She was curious if she could finish several works at the same time.

Hours later, she knew she needed to get outside. The state park was a short drive. She paid her entry fee then tried Nick one more time and wondered if he hadn't blocked her. Where could he be?

Fighting the mounting anxiety, she pulled into a small parking lot next to a trailhead. After gathering her phone and her water bottle, she charged off down the trail as though she was meeting someone.

Usually hiking made her feel better because she was forced to take deep breaths. Today she wasn't hiking vigorously enough to raise her heart rate. Meandering through trails, she took deep breaths and tried to clear the panic that was holding her by the throat. Was everything going to be okay? She didn't know but she hoped her mom would have some answers. She pressed the call button and waited.

"Hey, Momma."

There was a pause. "Are you okay, honey?"

Emma briefly explained the fight and the fact that Nick was nowhere to be found.

"Momma, you're happy, right? And Glen knows everything?"

"Yes. I am happy and I told him everything. He needed to know that certain things trigger reactions."

"I've never told anyone until recently. I should've told David. But I didn't. I didn't tell him when I didn't like things. He deserved better. I want things to be different with Nick but I'm scared that if he knew…" Emma sat down on a rock and let the tears flow.

"My poor, sweet baby. I know it is hard to trust people with all this. The past is a wicked master and it isolates you. You don't have to tell everyone or even tell everything. But you do need to trust the person you want to spend your life with. You need to tell him."

"I know. I will." She paused. "If he talks to me again."

"Either way, please come see me, Em."

"I will. I promise."

Emma hung up more determined to find Nick. She couldn't wait to see him and tell him she loved him. His absence was triggering her and she knew she had to face this.

Practically running back to her car, Emma decided to go home and wait for Nick to show. Surely, he would need clean clothes. Since she no longer had her journal, she decided to make a stop and pick up a notebook and a pen. She'd start fresh and write down all the things she wanted to tell Nick.

An hour later, she sat down at the picnic table outside with two notebooks, pens, two bags of pretzels, hummus, and a couple of chocolate bars. After she'd written her first words, she opened the chocolate. This wasn't for Nick or Jake, David or Kai. She was writing down her story. It was for her. And that called for some celebratory chocolate.

She wasn't too worried about David finding the journal anymore, although she was still desperate to get the onesie back. She'd never gotten to put that on Kai but she still could picture him wearing it. Maybe when all this was over, she'd tell David the truth. Would he even want to know now that their marriage was over? He had never asked. Emma couldn't help but smile. The two things she knew about David were that he was not spontaneous and that he didn't like to delve into the past.

David

CHAPTER EIGHTY-TWO

This was what I got for being spontaneous and delving into the past. Every single muscle in my body was hurting now. This was no ordinary hike.

The view from the second peak was even more breathtaking than the first.

"This is Paku'i. That," he pointed at what could only be described as a shark fin sticking out of the earth, "is Ahiki. It looks like a shark fin, which is what inspired my business name."

"Oh yeah? I wondered. I thought it had something to do with your name."

"Good guess. My name does mean 'shark'. Ahiki is my favorite peak, so between that and my name, Landshark seemed perfect."

"It definitely stands out. I saw several outfitters but yours stood out. I didn't even know there was a Groupon."

We pressed on, and getting to the third peak was the most terrifying thing I had ever done in my life. The cliffs and trails were relentless, with sheer drops and trail space no wider than a loaf of bread. I slipped a few times, and skin met with sharp rocks, so that by the time we got on the summit, I was bleeding, breathless, and glad to be alive.

I didn't know exactly where Jake had fallen from but I thought of him on every part of the trail. The final climb was thirty feet that presented me with another frayed rope anchored with a tiny nail. I had never had a moment of such profound realization about the fragile veil between life and death. A single misstep could result in my death. Part of me wanted to cry and the other wanted to shout out in defiance when we finally reached a clearing big enough to sit down.

Koa instructed me to get another electrolyte packet out of my supplies, along with a piece of jerky and a protein bar. I slammed another 20-ounce water before attempting to speak.

"Amazing, isn't it?"

I looked around. I looked down. It was amazing, and the fact that my entire body was shaking, bruised, and bleeding was a small price to pay.

"I've never seen anything like this. In fact, before a few months ago, I wouldn't have even tried to do this."

"What changed?"

Where could I start? I'd come here to get his story but now was confronting my own.

"Everything. I married my childhood best friend. For nearly thirteen years, everything had been great. Or so I thought. Now I find out that she loved someone before me and had a baby with him. Then, he died." I paused to see if this was ringing any bells. "She left me after miscarrying our baby. And in the wake of all that, I realized that I didn't know myself any more than I knew her. I don't do things like this."

"She left you for another man. Man, that's cold."

"See? That's the problem. She wasn't trying to hurt me. After the miscarriage, she ended up in a mental hospital and had electric convulsive treatment. It restarted her brain but stole her memories of us."

"So, she didn't even know who you were?"

"She remembered me from childhood but not as her husband. We were best friends in the sixth grade and then she moved to Hawaii."

This surprised him. "Is that why you came here?"

"Yes. I'm trying to figure out why she didn't tell me what happened here."

"We need to start back. These trails are too treacherous when the light begins to fade."

I nodded, deflated that I was no closer to finding the truth. When a large hand came down on my shoulder, I looked up. It was impossible to know what he was thinking but his eyes were misty.

"I don't know if you believe in hell but it sounds like you're in your own hell right now. I know about that. You came here to reconcile the past and maybe understand the place where she really left you. It hurts but, for what it's worth, I respect you for doing it."

"Thanks, Koa," I said, hoping he would expound about his personal hell.

He didn't. Instead, he snapped the tether in place and handed me the other end to do the same.

"Ready?"

"Let's do it."

I should have been thinking about every step I made but I couldn't quit thinking about what he'd said. I'd come to the place where she'd really left me. Maybe it wasn't ever about finding out if she had just settled for me. Maybe it was just to see this place that took her away from a broken-hearted boy who loved her more than anything. Frankly, I'd never thought of that.

We were going back and I had plenty to contemplate but I still had no answers. Koa had been quiet, only providing instructions as we weaved through roots and rocks. He had just pulled himself up a cliff face and negotiated a large tree. Standing on solid ground, Koa turned, waiting for me to follow. The tether was the only thing between us and I started to panic. It wasn't the sheer drop below me that was causing my fear. The adventure was ending and we were almost to the first peak when my mouth rebelled.

"Koa, I know you were the last one to see Jake Mokulehua alive. I need to know what happened that day with Jake."

His eyes flew wide and mouth dropped open. Whether it was the shock or realization that I'd just played him, Koa was clearly disoriented because he stepped back.

It happened so fast. He tried to grab onto something to stabilize but I knew what was coming next. He fell and I flew.

Slamming into the tree felt like being hit by a bus. The pain was immediate and searing. Blood was gushing from somewhere near my eye and I couldn't breathe. My ears were ringing and I had dark spots in my vision. I heard yelling but I wasn't sure it was coming from me. When I turned my head, the sobering terror overtook me as I realized that I was probably going to die.

We both were. Koa was unconscious and bleeding badly from a wound on his head. All 250 pounds of him were pressing me to the tree, which was the only thing that had kept us both from plummeting to our deaths.

I'd heard stories of super-human strength in times of crisis. Right now, I couldn't move my feet enough to plant them against the rocks. My right arm was around the base of the tree, shoulder firmly planted. Disregarding the immense pain, I grated my left arm up the face of the cliff. My plan was to pull the tether so that I could dislodge myself from the tree enough to get my legs in front of me.

It didn't work. Koa was still unconscious and outweighed me by 80 pounds. I couldn't breathe from being crushed against the tree. My left arm was the only part of me that was free but there was no super-human strength hidden amongst the abrasions and contusions on it.

"Koa," I yelled, although I couldn't tell for how long. I was sure I had a concussion. I tried again, and this time he jerked some but not enough to rouse him. At least I knew he wasn't dead.

For some bizarre reason, I started laughing. My chief fear earlier had been falling to my death. How could I have known that my death would actually result from being crushed against a tree by 250 pounds of dead weight?

I must've blacked out. The pain radiated from my chest to my limbs like someone had poured gasoline on me and threw a lit match on my sternum. Somewhere, from the void that was swallowing me, I heard a voice. It was calm and quiet, familiar, and yet I couldn't quite make out who it sounded like. Was it the voice of God?

"Get your feet planted and use your legs."

I roused from my stupor to a new spasm of pain but, somehow, I moved until the balls of my feet where firmly planted against the rock face. It might have been my imagination but, at the same time, I was slowly shifting and moving up. If I didn't act fast, Koa's weight was going to pull me around the tree and we'd both fall. Taking the deepest breath I could, I squirmed and ground my knees into place. My feet slipped but I ground them into place.

"I can't do it." My own voice shocked me.

"You can. Push back with your legs."

My toes were cramping and my knees were going numb but I used my free arm to help me push away and then pressed with all my might into the balls of my feet.

It worked, albeit only a few inches. Intense pain spread through my every cell and, for a moment, I thought I might pass out. Again, pressing through my feet, I managed another inch. My arm was in front of me now, though I couldn't fully extend it. My right shoulder hurt so much it took my breath. In my head, I yelled at my useless limb like a drill sergeant and forced it to join the fight. With a small space between me and the tree, I could breathe deeper. It hurt to breathe but I forced myself to inhale as though I was going to dive under water.

The next push gained several more inches. As I looked down at Koa dangling unanimated over 400 feet of death, I knew I needed his help. My legs and arms were shaking so hard that I felt they'd buckle at any moment.

"Koa. Help me," I yelled despite the burning in my chest.

Whether it was my plea for help or the same voice that I heard was working on him, he jerked awake. The sudden movement almost caved my desperate limbs. He looked down and then up at me.

"Hold on," he said.

Blood covered half his face, which gave him the appearance of some ancient warrior. He kicked his feet forward and I thought the gyration would snap my spine. The harness was already biting into my skin. I knew what he was trying to do and I prayed for strength as he strained to swing toward the rocks.

"I can't hold on much longer," I told him.

The first time his feet touched the rocks, I slipped back a few degrees. I looked like someone who was about to rappel. The new angle gave some relief to my cramping legs and allowed me to anchor us even more. The second swing hurt so much that I screamed.

He caught a gnarled root with one hand and rock with the other. For a second, we were balanced. Then, he started to climb up, and it hit me that I'd end up dangling if I didn't hold on. One hand pulling on the tether to help him and the other grabbing a small clump of roots, I prayed.

It seemed like hours but was probably less than a minute. Despite the gash on his head, Koa seemed to have all this strength. He scrambled up with much greater speed and agility than I expected. I opened my eyes just as he rolled onto the small edge and belly-crawled to my side. I saw his head pop out over my side. Then, his massive arm snaked out and grabbed my wrist.

He didn't have to tell me. Exhausted and shaking, my legs instinctively began to push me up as Koa pulled my arm and the tether. Passing a glance at the certain death below me, I grabbed the tree with my bad arm and cranked a leg up to get a better foothold for the last heave upward. The ground beneath my face was cool, musky, and tasted bad when I kissed it.

Both Koa and I crawled away from the edge and collapsed against a small embankment. He wrestled his backpack off and got out a first aid kit and some bottles of water. I looked at how enormous the backpack looked and realized that it had to weigh at least fifty pounds. It was a miracle I hadn't been whipped around the tree in the first second. Suddenly the pain in my shoulder and chest didn't hurt as much.

Koa handed me an instant cold pack and a clean rag that he had wetted with the water bottle. I wasn't sure where to start. There were too many places bleeding or bruised to count. He must've read my mind.

"Start with the gash on your eyebrow."

I'd forgotten about that wound. For several minutes, we both dabbed at the cuts and then winced simultaneously while applying the cold pack. I thought there would be one of those buddy moments like in the movies where the guys, who almost died, shared a boisterous laugh. This was not that moment.

"Who are you?" he growled.

"I'm Emma's husband. Jake's Emma," I added, wincing.

Koa was staring at me in disbelief. He looked more shocked over what I'd just said than he was when he realized he was dangling 400 feet in the air.

"What did she tell you?"

I shook my head, suppressing a laugh. "She didn't. It's a long story but I just found out about Jake and Kai. I met him earlier."

"You didn't—" he started.

"No. I didn't tell him anything. I found an article about Jake's fall and it said you were the only witness. I know that's not true. I need to know if Emma's dad killed Jake."

"Jake fell. That's all you need to know."

"Koa, Emma has believed her entire life that her father killed him. She thinks he killed them both. She has no idea that Kai is alive. Please?"

"We were afraid he'd killed her when she didn't come looking for Kai or come to the funeral."

"Please, Koa. I need to know the truth. Her father is dead and Emma believes that it is her fault that Jake died. She has spent her life painting children because she was mourning the loss of her son."

He took a deep breath and punched the ground. I could see him wrestling with something and, even without being slammed into a tree, I had to force myself to breathe.

"It wasn't her fault," he said quietly. "It was my fault."

Emma

CHAPTER EIGHTY-THREE

It was surprising to Emma how quickly she had filled the first notebook. As she focused her thoughts, the story flowed from her with ease.

The words weren't the only things that flowed. She didn't try to stop the tears. They came with the territory.

After hours of recalling the smallest to the largest details, Emma finished her second notebook. She had just gotten to the part where she'd told Jake that she was pregnant.

Perhaps a sliver of sunlight got in her eye or maybe the flashback literally blinded her for a moment. Just as she wrote the words, "I told him about the baby," she remembered another moment in the not-so-distant past.

She had waited all day for David to get home. They were supposed to go out with clients and she was pondering how she could keep her news off her face.

Emma was in the studio trying to get the neighbor's cat, Constantine, out after he snuck in while her back was turned. He had clawed one of her canvases and his long hair got everywhere. She'd even found a few strands in the refrigerator.

Neither she nor David had pets growing up. They had both been terrified of a feral cat that would get into the treehouse. The children had named him Ashes because of his smoky color and an uncanny ability to re-emerge in another corner after having been swept away.

Emma was having that same struggle with Constantine when David showed up in the doorway. She was momentarily startled but breathed through the feeling of panic.

"Hi," he said. His tone was warm and his smile melted her anxiety.

"Hey you," she replied, walking over to give him a kiss.

His lips were warm and inviting. As they slipped into each other's arms, Emma hoped David wouldn't be able to tell that she was trembling. She knew he had noticed when they parted and she looked up into his face.

His green eyes were alert and searching. Emma could tell he wanted to ask but was being polite.

"I'm pregnant."

"Really?" He was smiling and placed his hands so gently on her stomach that it made her cry. "Oh wow, honey. I mean, really?"

"I was going to wait until after dinner to tell you."

"Are you scared?"

"A little. A lot. Are you?"

He nodded but had not stopped smiling. "Maybe we can give this baby the childhood that neither of us had."

Emma was sure that they could do that. Neither of them was an abusive alcoholic and they loved each other. She put her hand on her belly and David put his hands on hers.

"I'm glad he'll have such a wonderful father."

"He?" David was wide-eyed.

"It feels like a boy," she said.

"I love you, Em."

"You always have. I love you too."

Somewhere behind her, a dog barked and pulled Emma back from her memory. She was momentarily disoriented and grabbed the table for grounding. David had not coerced her into having a baby. She had made a decision to try and move on, to honor Kai in a different way. She had been in the studio because she had hidden the Kona bag and its contents in the false bottom of one of the bins. Emma had been contemplating telling David the truth.

With tears dropping onto her notebook, she pushed herself back to the past and to her task. It was too late for her and David, although she was glad to recall that she was going to tell him. Right now, though, she had to focus. *Trust me with all of you or none of you.* She could still hear Nick's words.

"I hope you're ready for all of me," she whispered and prayed that Nick would come home soon.

David

CHAPTER EIGHTY-FOUR

"What do you mean?" I asked more boldly now.

Koa sat on the ground like a defeated demi-god. He was mortal and vulnerable. For a second, I got a glimpse of the boy he'd been.

"Jake had this idea to build a small place up here, away from everything. Basically, he wanted to squat out here where Emma's father couldn't find them. Then, he'd move them to a house on another island."

"Near his other uncle."

Koa nodded. "Anyway, I'd gone down to get some more stuff. I didn't see Bob. He must've been watching, because he knew which trail to take."

We both took a sip of water. I could picture Bob watching the boys from the shadows somewhere, waiting for his moment. Koa laid his head back against the rock we were propped on and stared out at the mountains. For a second, I thought he might pass out. It was obvious that he was distressed. He took another sip and continued.

"I was tired and not very strong. The boards were heavy, and when I first heard the yelling, I thought it was hikers on another trail. Then I heard Jake's voice."

I felt sorry for this giant man who began to shrivel before my eyes. He covered his face with his massive hands. Tears were forming in his eyes.

"I dropped everything and started running but I was struggling. They were fighting when I got there and the asshole had Jake in a headlock and was beating him. Blood was everywhere. I punched the guy as hard as I could and that made him let go. Jake laughed and teased him. There were two of us and one of him. That's when he pulled out a gun."

"Did he shoot Jake?"

"Jake turned and started running and the bastard turned on me. He told me he'd kill me if I followed them. Then he took off after Jake. I stayed there crying for a few minutes until I heard a couple shots. I got mad. You know? Fear becomes anger and I got mad and got up to go after them. Jake was way out in the front but he was getting to some dangerous spots on the trail. The old guy was having trouble keeping up but he pushed through it. His face was so red. Then, Jake came to a spot he thought he could get away. That's when the man raised the gun. It was like slow motion. Jake turned and jumped and the old man fired. The bullet missed Jake but he miscalculated his jump. I got there just in time to see the look on his face as he went over. He was surprised."

"Oh my God, Koa. I'm sorry." I meant it. The man was sobbing now and I didn't care if he pummeled me. I put my arm around his shoulders.

"The demon turned on me and shoved the gun barrel in my mouth. He told me if I told anyone he'd start with my mother, then sisters, and then everyone I loved. There was evil in his face. He left and I never saw him again. When the cops got here, I was scared so I just told them that Jake fell. I didn't find out until much later that Bob Roberts was dead."

"It wasn't your fault, Koa."

The man looked at me with liquid chocolate eyes. "I was weak and afraid."

"You were a boy, Koa. Anybody would have been afraid."

"Jake was laughing when he jumped. He really thought he could get away."

"It was Bob Roberts' fault. Not yours. Not Emma's. Not Jake's. Maybe Jake thought he was invincible. Maybe he was reckless. But if Bob hadn't gone after him, if he hadn't abused his family, none of this would have happened. It wasn't your fault."

"Maybe. That's why I've spent my life on these trails. That's why I got into the best shape possible."

"So, your business is really your punishment for how you feel you failed Jake?"

He nodded. "I've tried other jobs but I can't leave him here alone."

"Jake lived life to the fullest. He wouldn't want you to torture yourself because of him. Would he?"

"No," Koa sobbed. "But if I hadn't failed him, he'd be here with me."

"Bob Roberts came here to kill him. Even if he hadn't fallen, he'd still be dead. You might be dead too. If he hadn't died himself that same night, he might have killed you to keep you quiet."

His head jerked up and his eyes flew wide. Clearly, this scenario had never dawned on him. He didn't have words but stared at me, horrified. His eye movements told me he was thinking. I continued.

"You couldn't have saved Jake. He probably knew that and that's why he ran away, to draw Bob away from you. Maybe he thought he could outrun the guy. Maybe he thought he could jump to a spot that Bob couldn't get to. But what if he knew he couldn't? Maybe the look you thought was surprise was something else. Or maybe he was surprised that his life was ending this way. Either way, Koa. It wasn't your fault. But I do have a question."

"What?"

"Why did no one tell Emma that her son was alive?"

He looked down. "I wanted to tell her. Jake's mom was devastated to lose her son. She didn't blame Emma but I don't think she could give up the only part of Jake that was left. Maybe she, too, was afraid of the evil. He threatened her too when he brought Kai to her. I don't know. Maybe she did blame Emma. Maybe she was afraid that she had evil inside her too." He swiped his eyes. "If it weren't for you, I'd be dead."

"If it weren't for me, you wouldn't have slipped."

"True. But I can't blame you for wanting to understand." He clapped a huge hand on my shoulder. The bad shoulder. "Maybe she didn't love you like she loved Jake. But she stayed with you for thirteen years. She was pregnant with your baby. She loved you. You have to believe that and move on. I'm sorry you lost your son and your wife. But, take it from a guy who has spent every day in Hell on trails that remind me of the worst day of my life. Not letting go of the things you lost will only bring more pain."

"I do understand better now," I admitted.

"And you have the bruises and scars to prove it." Koa laughed.

"Thank you, Koa. For everything. I hope we both can move on now."

The big man smiled, although his eyes were far away. He finally turned and looked at me for a long moment.

"Thank you. For forcing me to say all that out loud. This is the first time in seventeen years that I don't feel like a weight is on my shoulders.

I love this place and I don't want to give up being out here. But it will be nice to not have to carry all the guilt, fear, and pain with me."

"Your backpack is heavy enough," I said.

He laughed hard and slapped me again on the bad shoulder. I felt something pop back into place. It was excruciating but I made myself laugh.

"Okay, let's get you back to your car and maybe the hospital."

Gravity seemed extra needy as we made our way back. Everything felt heavy. I knew the whole story but I still didn't know why she had married me. Maybe Ruth would have some answers.

Emma

CHAPTER EIGHTY-FIVE

E verything was neatly written. The entire story was on the table in front on her.

Still no Nick. She'd stopped trying to call him. Briefly, she thought about calling the police. Breathing through her fear, she almost laughed. What would she tell them? Emma could imagine how the cops would react to her recalling a fight and a boyfriend that stormed out.

She didn't want to bother Maria. Calling David was out of the question. Besides, what could she offer now? He was moving on with the family in the park. There were no answers she could give him that would help.

Her phone began to rumble from underneath a bag of garbage. She ripped it up, praying that Nick was calling. The number on the screen was one she didn't recognize.

"Hello?" Emma was imaging all the places Nick could be calling her from as she waited for a response.

"Mrs. Campbell, this is Bill Nichols. I'm calling to give you some good news. The judge signed your divorce papers today. You are officially divorced."

"So soon?" She didn't know why she'd said it.

"Yes, ma'am. I'll admit that even I was a little surprised at how quickly this happened. Uncontested divorces are usually faster anyway but this is remarkable. I'll be calling your ex-husband as well but I wanted to let you know."

"Thank you."

"You're welcome. Have a good life."

She clicked off without responding. "I keep trying to," she said to herself.

She looked at the notebooks full to the brim with her efforts at a good life. Her own personal heaven and hell lay on the table before her and Emma wondered if she was trying or if she'd ever stop punishing herself.

David

CHAPTER EIGHTY-SIX

I called Ruth on my way to my hotel and asked if I could come see her. She agreed without hesitation.

"Emma doesn't know I am in Hawaii."

If she thought that was odd, it wasn't obvious. "We'd love to have you for dinner. Glen thinks he is an amateur chef and he's made enough pork loin, slaw, and grilled veggies to feed an army."

"Are you sure it is not an imposition?"

"Not at all."

She gave me the address and told me to come at six o'clock.

Climbing into the shower with difficulty, I let the hot water find all the torn and sore spots. Ruminating over all that I had discovered, I realized that my reason for coming here wasn't just to understand. I was still trying to give Emma a life she never had. If learning the truth might give her any peace, then I could feel good about moving on.

Driving to Ruth's, I debated telling them. It should come from Emma, I decided.

They spilled out of the house with open arms. I'd met Glen only once before, when Emma was in the hospital. They both stopped short when they noticed my cuts and bruises. I had not been able to pull long pants over my knees, and the button-down shirt revealed just enough of my chest to frame the dark bruising.

"What happened, man?"

I smiled. "I went hiking."

"Do you need to see a doctor?" Glen seemed concerned.

"Maybe. Or maybe just a visit with Dr. Jack Daniels."

"Paging Dr. Daniels," he sang out.

The two of them ushered me into the house and out to the back patio. Glen brought me a drink and I welcomed the burn as I took a few sips. This was probably the last thing I should be drinking but it was the only one that came with the promise of numbing pain.

"How are you, David?" Ruth finally asked.

I knew she didn't mean the injuries. Her eyes were practiced in seeing the wounds that weren't on the surface.

"I still miss her, and sometimes I'm still angry. I haven't properly mourned our son's death. It's still somewhat shocking that all this has happened."

She nodded somberly. "It will take time. What brought you to Hawaii?"

Momentarily, I fought the urge to tell her. "I've been trying to figure out if she loved me and why she married me. Was I just the first guy after Jake?"

Her eyes narrowed but she kept control of her face. "How do you know about Jake?"

"Emma left all kinds of things at the house when she moved in with Nick. She couldn't remember us at all so her wedding dress meant nothing to her. There was a big box of journals. I was angry and hurt. I read them. I didn't want to confront her with the past. So, I guess I came to look for some closure."

"It's good you didn't confront her." She set her wine down and rose. "I have something that might help."

She beckoned me to follow, and we passed through a small living room, down a long hall, and finally arrived at a guest room decked out in floral patterns and bright colors. She opened the closet door and pointed at a box on the top shelf.

I grabbed the box and lowered it down to her. Reaching in, she withdrew a thick book. The dusty cover bore the title of her favorite MC Hammer song and the yellowed pages were littered with old envelopes. Returning the box, I turned to see her leafing through the fragile pages.

"She told me to just throw this away but I couldn't." Ruth handed me the book and I must've looked confused because she chuckled. "You've read the others. That one is about you."

Staring at the faded cover, I fought the urge to laugh and cry at the same time. Another damn journal.

"I will admit that it hurt me that she only mentioned me a few times in all the other books. I thought I didn't matter enough for her to write about."

"Maybe that will answer your questions."

My chest hurt to breathe but I took a deep breath and opened the book to a random spot.

"David loves me and I love him. I feel safe in our treehouse."

"Thank you, Ruth." I choked back the emotion and closed the book.

Glen sang out from the kitchen that dinner was ready and we both laughed.

"He's thrilled to have someone else here to witness his creations."

"I'm so happy for you. No one should have had to go through what you did. I'm glad you have someone who treats you with respect and love."

She looked at me and I saw the tears forming. It hurt when she slipped her arms around me but I hugged her back.

"You are a good man, David. Thank you for the way you've always loved Emma. I'm sorry she hurt you but I hope you find love again. You deserve to be happy."

For the first time since the miscarriage, ECT, Emma moving out, I not only believed her words but I had hope. Glancing at the book in my hand, I realized that I didn't need confirmation that she loved me. The fact that she kept a separate journal about me was enough to tell me that I was significant to her. The other books hadn't been about me. Reading this one, though, would feel more like betraying her trust.

When Ruth stepped back, I handed her the book. She was confused.

"I read the others looking for something about me and I found the truth about her life instead. This one is personal. I can't read it."

"The truth," she said ruefully. "The truth is a tricky thing."

My heart was pounding. It dawned on me that Ruth believed the same thing that Emma did. The two sides of my consciousness weren't whispering their pleas in my ears. They were in a full-out brawl. Should I tell her? How could I come to her home and tell her she deserved to be happy and then not tell her the truth?

"Yes, it is a tricky thing," I said finally.

After replacing the journal and box in the closet, we rejoined Glen. He had set the table, refreshed the drinks, and had heaping platters of food everywhere.

Despite being hungry, my mind wasn't on food. I couldn't hear over my heartbeat, and my words stumbled out of my mouth like I was a drunk out of a bar at closing time.

"Oh my God," Glen said simply after I told the story of why I came and what I'd found.

My eyes were on Ruth, who was transfixed and staring at something neither of us could see. The pain and shock were evident but there was something else hidden amongst the lines of her face.

"Kai and I took a selfie." I paused, handing her my phone. "Here."

Ruth blinked at my phone as she studied the picture. I was prepared for tears; it was logical that seeing her grandson alive might bring them. But it was me who cried when a slow smile stretched across her face.

"He's beautiful and full of joy. Oh, he's beautiful." Her hands were shaking as she held the phone like it was fragile.

I couldn't speak. Ruth couldn't quit smiling. Glen was crying like a baby.

"And you say he works not far from here? Teaching surfing?" She looked up from the picture, seeking reassurance that she'd heard me correctly.

"Yes, ma'am. He's working there to save for college, although he's already saved enough for the first two years, he says. He's an amazing young man."

"And you figured this out from a picture in a magazine?" Glen asked through his blubbering.

"It almost gave me a stroke. I mean, he looks like a male version of Emma. It's the eyes. The whole time I was telling myself that I was crazy. I mean, there could be a lot of people with eyes like hers. Especially here. But I had to know."

Ruth quietly handed me the phone. Now I could see the tears forming but she couldn't push any words out. She was wringing her hands.

"I should have known."

"Honey, how could you have known?" Glen asked.

Ruth stood up and turned her back to us. "He took great pleasure in torturing people. I should have known that he'd take the baby and leave him a few miles away but let us think that the child was dead. All this time, my grandson was growing up miles from me. I might have seen him at the market or the beach. Right in front of my eyes but still unreachable. That is something Bob would do. It wasn't that he had any compassion or mercy, even for a baby. He just wanted to choose the cruelest thing."

She turned suddenly, alarmed. I knew what she was thinking.

I shook my head. "I haven't told her yet."

Ruth started pacing as though she was wrestling with something. I recognized the same mannerisms in Emma. I'd seen her pace like this.

"I probably shouldn't tell you this and I'm not sure you want to know. She and Nick have had a fight and he left. Emma is worried and can't find him. She's having flashbacks about all this. I'm not sure now is the right time to tell her."

"Left as in never coming back? What happened? I'm not his biggest fan but it's obvious he loves her."

"I think so too. The fight was over her not telling him things. She called out Jake's name in her sleep and Nick thinks she's seeing someone else."

"Well, I can understand why he would think that," I conceded.

"This might be too much," Ruth said, wringing her hands.

"Yes, it might be, honey, but she has to know her son's alive," Glen piped up.

"I agree. She's spent her whole life thinking that Bob killed Jake and Kai. She deserves to know the truth. It will be hard to hear that someone else raised her son but maybe it will relieve that pain," I added.

They both nodded but I could see Ruth's apprehension. I got up and went to her.

Stepping into her pacing, I put my hands on her shoulders and she looked up.

"Ruth, she was raised by a strong mother. The miscarriage triggered all her memories and that shut her down. I don't think that would have happened if she'd known the truth—that Kai is alive. She thinks Bob threw them both off a cliff and she feels like it's her fault that any of this happened. Finding out the truth will bring some pain but it will also bring some peace. I have to tell her, and it should come from me because I need to explain why I read her journals. You know I don't want to hurt her. I would never do that. But she has to know."

"It wasn't her fault. I am the one to blame. I should have left him or killed him."

She began weeping and I put my arms around her. Glen didn't move from his seat. He was crying too and simply nodded. I could see the trust in his face. Waiting until she stopped, I lifted her face gently. Her eyes were liquid gold and I could see the pain in the shimmering pools of tears.

"Bob Roberts was an abusive asshole. He already knew who Jake was and who his family was. He would have found them. I don't know how he got all his information but this was all him. It wasn't your fault. If you had killed him, then you would have gone to jail. Part of the problem is that everyone except Bob has accepted blame. And then, no one told anyone what happened."

"So much fear. He caused so much fear. If I'd been stronger..." She started crying again.

"Ruth," I gave her a gentle shake, "you are one of strongest people I've ever met. I don't know how you endured it. Beating after beating, you still managed to love and protect your children. He threatened to kill you if you left him, didn't he?"

She shook her head. "No. I figured he would kill me at some point so I wasn't afraid of that. He threatened to kill the children."

"What else could you have done? He would have found you. One of his demons would have told him where you were. And," I paused to suppress the bile rising in my throat, "he would have kept his promise. I'm so sorry. I'm so sorry that any of this happened. But, if you failed, then we all failed. I knew about the abuse before you left San Diego. I was a kid but I should've told someone. We're all guilty for not telling but that is all. The rest belongs to that evil man. You have to forgive yourself."

She stepped away. "I thought I had. All this with Emma... My poor, sweet girl."

Glen got up and crossed the short distance with his arms open. Ruth's sobs intensified but Glen soothed her by gently stroking her head and whispering soft words into her ear. I didn't really know this man but I loved him. It wouldn't undo her childhood but I hoped that Emma would get to know her stepfather and see how he treated her mother.

They parted and Ruth nodded in answer to something Glen had asked.

"You're right, David. She needs to know. And I trust you to tell her. Will you do it soon?"

"As soon as I get back home."

"Okay. Now, we should eat this dinner that my wonderful husband has been working on."

Later, they walked me to my car and gave me multiple hugs. Glen had packed me a few pastries he'd experimented with earlier in the day.

"You never know what they'll have on the plane," he said, and hugged me again.

"Thank you, for everything. The food was fantastic but thank you for being a good person."

He looked into my eyes. "Takes one to know one. Not many people would handle divorce like this."

I shrugged. "I still love her and always will."

Ruth stepped in and hugged me tightly. "Don't be a stranger, David. You will always be part of this family." She looked up and I could see something in her expression that confused me at first. "I know it hurts but you have to move on."

I smiled thinking about Kellyn and Wyatt. "Actually, I've met someone. I meant what I said. I do love Emma. She was my best friend for a long time. But I've accepted what's happened. I didn't want to like Nick but the guy is un-hateable."

We all laughed and Ruth asked me again about the journal.

"Are you sure you don't want to take it?"

I was tempted to see what she'd written about me but I knew all too well the familiar pull of nostalgia. I knew it would only weaken the resolve I'd already accepted.

"I'm sure. Thank you."

I drove to my inn feeling both relief and anxiety. Grabbing a beer, I took it out to the pool. Sitting down heavily, I pulled my phone from my pocket. Micah had texted me to say that my mom was doing great. Dialing the airline, I listened to hold music for twenty-five minutes before I finally got through. It took another ten to change my flight. I was ready to get back and see my mom and then go home. My body ached more than my heart, but it still felt heavy in my chest.

Even though I wasn't divorced yet and it had only been a few months since Emma had left me, I thought our relationship had shifted before she got pregnant. It wasn't drifting apart exactly. Maybe we wrote it off as distraction, but something started being different. If I stretched my memory, and found the courage to be honest, I'd have to admit that there had always been a tiny disconnect.

This experience helped me inventory everything. When she suffered her episode after losing our baby, I wanted us to get back to normal. But neither of us were true to ourselves. The problem wasn't that I didn't know her well enough. I didn't know myself well enough either.

Uncovering all her secrets and picking apart the layers of our lives had laid bare the fabric of my own life. Having a distant mother had made me want to rescue and fix people. That had become my identity and kept me from pushing myself into the unknown. Trying to shelter Emma was exhausting, and playing it safe had prevented me from growing. Basically, I'd been walking on eggshells my entire life to keep others from getting upset.

My head was swimming from all the emotion and the alcohol. I crawled into bed knowing that sleep crept in with me.

The next morning, I overslept. Then, pushing out of bed I thought I would die. Every single part of my body hurt. There was no rushing. There was only gathering things, groaning, and thinking I needed to hurry. I felt bad for not calling Kellyn, but the events of the past day needed to be relayed in person.

Skipping the shower and breakfast, I headed to the airport with my backpack and small bag of things I'd purchased at the surf shop. The same kid was working the rental counter when I returned the car.

When I finally sat down in my first-class seat on the plane, I ignored the pain in my body and concentrated on how good my soul felt. I was asleep before the flight attendants went over safety.

My first order of business when I landed in San Diego was to see my mom. After ordering an Uber, I rode to the hospital with a guy named Ping in his 2019 Kia Tucson.

She was alarmed by my appearance and even more concerned when I told her the story of my hike in Olomana. I was surprised to see how good she looked, despite still being in ICU.

"How do you feel?" I asked.

She laughed. "Better than you."

We were holding hands and swapping stories when Micah arrived. I had been unsure what this first meeting would be like, but Micah alleviated any apprehension I had by skipping the formal handshake and hugging me.

"It's good to finally meet you in person," he said.

I agreed and thanked him for looking after my mom. Micah waved dismissively and turned to her. His expression held such love that it made me teary.

"She has been a great patient, so my job was pretty easy. You've just missed the doctor.

They're moving her to a regular room."

"Oh wow. So soon? Way to go, Mom."

She was still holding my hand but reached out and took Micah's with the other.

"I'm so happy to have my two most important men in the same room."

This choked me up and I leaned down to pay her a kiss.

"I love you, Mom."

"I love you too. Now, tell us what you found out."

It took nearly an hour to recall all the events of my trip. In the end, they both sat wide eyed and smiling. My mother cried and squeezed my hand throughout the tale.

"So, you have closure for Emma. How do you feel?"

I thought for a moment.

"Free. It doesn't hurt less that my marriage collapsed or that we lost our son. Finally, though, I understand what really happened. I know who I am and what I want. I feel a confidence I've never felt before, and I'm happy. Really happy to be able to give her back her son. I don't know how she'll feel but I know it's the right thing to do."

"I am so proud of you. Your father would be proud too," she said softly.

"You helped me more than you can ever know. It wasn't just reconciliation and hearing your story. What you told me about being a rescuer like my father and my need to be needed really caused me to think about myself and my relationship with Emma. It's helped me to make some decisions about how I can keep from making the same mistakes. Thank you."

"I'm glad I finally did something right."

"There's been so much sadness. Here's to some happy," Micah interjected.

"I'll second that."

It was hard to leave but I had to catch a plane. I thought about her words long after I had left. We promised each other that we'd talk and visit more. The thing that made me smile the most was knowing that it was not an empty promise.

I slept through another flight and called Emma to set up a meeting as I walked down the concourse in Birmingham. Right before I called her, I'd listened to a voicemail from the lawyer telling me that I was divorced.

Afraid I'd just blurt everything out, I decided to wait and call Kellyn later.

Emma

CHAPTER EIGHTY-SEVEN

T he phone rang while she was re-reading her confession. It was David.
"Hello?"

"Hey, Em. I was hoping I could come by in a bit. I need to talk to you."

She thought about saying no. There was no excuse. Her paintings were complete and Nick was still missing. Plus, she owed him some answers.

"Okay. Is it about the divorce?"

She heard him hesitate.

"No but it's important."

"Sure. I'm at home."

Something was different in his voice. Emma couldn't put her finger on it but she was relieved that he wasn't glum. She had a fleeting thought that he'd deciphered her journal but quickly dismissed it.

Regardless of what happened with Nick or what David had to say, Emma was tired of hiding. Her art had been the best way for her to hide her pain. She had made rash decisions to keep from having to face her fears or think too deeply. She had loved David but his consistency and devotion had allowed her to hold him captive in a stable little box to keep herself feeling safe. David needed to protect her and had done from the first day.

He had on a Superman t-shirt the first day they'd met. In so many ways, he had been her superhero their whole lives. If she had told him the truth about Jake and Kai, he probably would have worked even harder to comfort her.

Emma didn't want to depend on an external source for safety anymore. She no longer needed a knight to slay her dragons. Life was not fair and inflicted its cruelty equally on everyone. She would not allow her past to define her anymore. At some point, she would talk to Nick and tell him the truth. If he was able to handle it, then they would build a life together. If he ran away, she would be okay.

She was crying now. It was not because she was sad or scared. For the first time in her 34 years, she knew who she was and what she was capable of doing. No one was around to see it except for a tiny finch perched on a nearby tree. Her thoughts turned to Jake and Kai.

"It's time to let them go, isn't it?" she asked the bird.

The bird answered by flying away.

The problem with nostalgia, she thought, was that cherishing it too much caused a person to live in the past. She hoped the painting she'd done for David would evoke joy instead of nostalgia. Unlike nostalgia, joy was evolving.

$\mathcal{D}avid$

CHAPTER EIGHTY-EIGHT

My own vehicle felt foreign for the first five minutes. Driving I-59 felt cramped compared to the pristine highways in Hawaii. The exit onto I-65 was affectionately called 'malfunction junction'. I didn't have time for the traffic that was bunched in the area that had been under construction longer than anyone could remember.

I pulled into the driveway, shut off the engine and gathered my bag. Letting myself into the house, I noticed something out of place. There was a soda can sitting on my coffee table. I was about to drop my bag when I heard a noise coming from upstairs.

Looking for a weapon, I found nothing deadly unless my intention was to make the burglar die of laughter by brandishing a throw pillow and lamp. Remembering my golf clubs in the hall closet, I crept to the door and eased it open. The hinge whined, of course.

Grabbing the first club I could reach, I ascended the stairs as silently as I could. My knees were still swollen and they groaned and popped as I climbed. My heart was roaring in my ears and I was sure that the intruder had to have heard me by now.

I tripped and fell up the stairs. There was no time to curse myself. It sounded like someone was rifling through my stuff, heard me and paused, and was now awaiting my attack just beyond the door.

Mustering all my strength and fighting nausea, I sprang up and ran into the bedroom, bellowing like a caveman with my club raised for battle. What I saw before me stopped me in my tracks and I vomited in the wastebasket near the door.

The intruder was wearing nothing but a towel and was holding a pair of my favorite boxer shorts. There was little mystery as to what he planned to do with them.

"What the hell are you doing in my house? And why do you have my underwear?"

He smiled brightly. "It's not as bad as it seems." He pointed to the lettering on the front of the boxers. "No guards, no gates, just me and my jewels. I like that. I met the guy that started Royalty in Exile. He's a cool dude."

"He is a cool dude. Please explain to me how it's not as bad as it seems. See? I thought the guy my wife left me for was in my house, wrapped in my towel, and about to put on my favorite Royalty in Exile drawers."

He let the towel drop and pulled the boxers on. "I can explain, and I'll buy you some new underwear."

"Yes, you will, but right now I need to know why you are in my house."

"What happened to you? You look like you were hit by a truck," Nick asked, thankfully pulling on his pants.

I knew Emma had a key and I knew they had fought. It wasn't hard to figure out that he had been staying here to be away from her.

"I nearly fell off a cliff."

"Dude, what were you doing on a cliff? You aren't feeling suicidal, are you?"

"What? No. I was hiking."

I waited as he stepped into the bathroom, hung his towel—my towel—and retrieved his dirty clothes. He was pulling on one of my shirts when I realized that all of the clothes, dirty and clean, were mine. I felt foolish standing there holding the golf club, although I was still considering hitting him with it. Nick sat down on my bed. It was still made so I didn't think he'd been sleeping here. Putting on his shoes, he looked up.

"I've got some beer in the mancave. Do you want one?"

I was dumbfounded. Was this guy inviting me to my own mancave for a beer?

His eyes weren't full of his usual mirth and his face looked tired.

"Sure," I said and put the club down.

I followed him down the stairs toward the back of the house. He pointed at my bag in passing.

"Where did you go?"

"California and then Hawaii."

"Where was the cliff you almost fell off?"

"Hawaii."

He made a sound of acknowledgment. We walked together out of the backdoor, crossed the lawn, and he opened the repaired mancave door to admit me. I was surprised to find things tidied up. Nick had removed the debris from my tirade and swept up. He walked over and retrieved two beers from the fridge.

"I can help, you know?" he started, taking the chair opposite the sofa.

"Help me do what?"

"Finish this place. What are you wanting to put here?"

"Pretty much this is it. I have my saws and tools. There needs to be a big screen TV up there." I pointed to the wall behind him.

"That would be awesome. What about some cabinets over there?"

I looked where he was pointing and nodded. "I was thinking about a workbench too." "Have you been sleeping out here?" I asked, noticing a folded blanket on the sofa to my right as I sat down.

"Yeah. Emma and I had a fight. I didn't want to sleep in your house uninvited."

"You draw the line at sleeping in my house but borrowing my underwear isn't a problem?"

He laughed. "I'm sorry, man. I really needed some clean ones."

"Why can't you go to your house?"

He shook his head and his expression made me think of all the recent times I'd looked in the mirror.

"I think Emma is seeing someone else."

"Why do you think that?"

"She's been sleeping in the studio a lot, or somewhere else. She's always distracted, like she's thinking about someone else. Then," he paused to take a sip of beer, "she's been calling out other men's names in her sleep. I asked her about it and she kept looking at the door behind me like she was expecting someone. That's when I realized it."

"Realized what?"

"She had been expecting someone else. I got upset and left and haven't been back. I didn't know where to go so I came here."

"You said she's calling other names. What were they?"

"Jake and Kai. I've never heard her mention them before so I don't know where she met them. But it really unnerved me and I felt stupid for thinking we had something special."

"Look, Nick, it's not what you think. Jake and Kai are from her past but she will have to tell you about them herself. She was looking at the door because that's what she does involuntarily when she gets anxious. You were confronting her and it triggers her anxiety. Her father was really abusive. So, confronting her and standing between her and the door triggered her fight or flight. She doesn't even realize she's doing it."

"She was afraid of me?"

"Not exactly. But you were probably mad or accusing. You'd have to know her bastard father to understand."

Nick sat back heavily like a child about to throw a tantrum and covered his face with his hands. "I'm an idiot. All those things I said and then just stormed out."

I wanted to agree but there was no need to beat Thor with his own hammer.

"That was a bad idea but I understand. She keeps things to herself. When you sense them and say something, she always says she is thinking of a painting and pulls back."

"So, she did the same to you?"

"Yes, but unlike you, I stopped asking. I figured whatever it was would come out later. I thought if I loved her enough, she would trust me."

"See? I don't know if I believe you can truly love someone and not trust them."

"I didn't think of that before, but I agree now."

Nick skewered me with those pale eyes. I felt pity for him. No. It was more than that. I was starting to like him.

"What do I do now? I love her, David. I know that may not be the thing you want to hear but I do. I don't want to lose her."

I looked at my watch and felt a pang in my chest. There was no telling how panicky she felt and I didn't want to be late.

"Let me talk to her. And go home. I believe that you love her, and I can see she loves you. You guys need to talk. Don't ever walk out mad again. I mean it. Never do that again. But don't quit asking questions. That's where I failed. Don't be like me."

Nick stood up with a nod. "Thank you, man. I'm sorry for the pain I caused you. I know everyone says this but it wasn't my intention."

When I stood up, he hugged me so tightly I thought I'd die. The pain was excruciating and tears sprang to my eyes. He was still holding onto me, noticed my tears, and patted me hard on my bad shoulder.

"Don't cry, man. It's okay."

"My ribs are broken."

Nick released me so fast I almost fell. "I didn't think of that. Have you been to the doctor?"

Shaking my head, I resisted the urge to punch him. "I don't have time. I'm meeting Emma to talk to her. Oh," I looked at him, "our divorce is final."

His mouth fell open. "I didn't know she signed the papers."

"Take care of her."

"I will if she'll have me back."

I couldn't stand up straight without something hurting. "And I'll take you up on your offer to help me with this place."

I actually let Nick carry the box of journals to my truck after I collected the onesie from the safe and grabbed the cyphered journal from my bag. He didn't ask but I could tell he wanted to. He slid the box into the other side of the cab. For a moment, I thought he was going to go with me.

"You'll call me when you're done."

"Will do."

"Thank you, David."

"Thank you."

He cocked his head like a dog. "For what?"

"Asking me a question I couldn't answer."

Emma

CHAPTER EIGHTY-NINE

H e looked like hell, with bruised and scraped skin on his knees, torso, and face. He was carrying a box.

"Can we sit down?"

"Sure," she said and led him to the picnic table.

Emma could tell he had something on his mind. She had something to say too. When they both spoke at the same time, they laughed.

"You first," he offered.

"No. You called this meeting."

David took a deep breath. "Are you sure?"

Emma nodded, noticing that he was trembling. "Are you okay?"

First, he held his hand out and she gasped. Taking the journal from him, she stared wide eyed at him, unsure of what he was going to say. Then he handed her a clear bag with the onesie inside.

His eyes were vibrant green. "I know about Jake and Kai."

Emma tried to speak but the words stuck in her throat.

"I read your journals and deciphered the code in this one. I know the whole story."

He reached over and took her hand to continue. "I started so I could understand how I could've missed how unhappy you were in our marriage. I wanted to know if you loved me or if I was stupid and you just lied to me."

"I didn't lie. I just couldn't—" she started. Emma could feel the panic welling up and the tears burning her eyes.

"No. You didn't. Not exactly. I didn't ask or rather I stopped asking. I should have asked, Em. I'm so sorry. It's like we were still sitting in that treehouse. Suspended somewhere between innocence and reality. Maybe that's why it was so hard to let go. We were safe there. We didn't talk about things but had these imaginary adventures and talked about stars. But I should have encouraged you to talk about it. I understand now why you didn't tell me. I'm so sorry your dad—" He paused and squeezed her hand. "I'm glad he's dead."

"I should have told you. Maybe you would have understood why I was nervous about having kids. You've always been good to me and I know you wouldn't have held all that over my head. It's just so…" She sobbed. "It just hurts so much that I never got to say goodbye to either of them."

Tears were streaming down his face. "I need to tell you what really happened."

"What do you mean? How could you know?"

"I went to Hawaii. I talked to Kekoa. Your dad didn't push Jake. Jake fell running from your dad."

Emma was trying to process. "But the blood."

"They got into a fight and the blood was the result of that. He pulled a gun and Jake ran from him. He was trying to jump to another part of the trail and fell. And…" David paused. He was crying as hard as she was. They both took a breath. "And your son is alive."

Emma heard the words, but they wouldn't form a coherent thought. "What?"

"Kai is alive. The bastard dropped the baby at Jake's mother's house. He threatened her not to ever tell you. But, Emma, I've met Kai. He's alive and well."

Her brain sped up and then slowed down like she was in a speeding train and someone was pumping the brakes. There were spots in her vision. David must've sensed that she was faint because he suddenly shook her.

"Emma, stay with me. I know it's a lot of information but I have proof," he said.

"Proof?" She blinked hard.

Her world spun under her and for a moment she thought she was falling. It was like she was trapped on a carousel. She saw the faces of her father, mother, David, Jake, Nick, and Kai. What was happening? She couldn't hear through her own beating heart. How could this be true? Kai is alive? No, her father took him. Jake was dead. Kai was dead. Then, David was holding her up.

"Look," he said, holding his phone up to her face.

Emma knew the boy instantly. The shape of his golden eyes like her own. He had Jake's nose. A face she had only seen for a few hours so perfectly framed in her mind's eye on the screen in front of her.

"I thought…Oh God, I thought he was dead."

Her face hurt. The weight of realization, guilt, grief, and disbelief felt like a wave had just knocked her off her board and was crushing her. Her baby was alive? And she had abandoned him. How stupid could she be? She didn't even go looking for him. She couldn't breathe and the spots in her eyes started getting bigger. *Let the darkness come. Let it take me.*

David was holding her as she cried. "He's okay. You're okay. It wasn't your fault. He doesn't blame you."

She was ready to let herself fall into the abyss but his last words were like a hook that drove into her heart and hauled her back. The pain gave way to fury.

"What did you tell him about me?"

David obviously recognized the fire burning in her eyes. He backed away slowly, his eyes round and mouth hanging open.

"I didn't tell him about you. I didn't tell him anything. But I talked to him, and he told me his story. He was raised by his grandmother and uncle. Kai says they never said a bad word about you."

"You're lying. They must've. I left my baby. I never went looking for him. He must hate me." She could barely get the words out.

"He's amazing, Emma. He's so like you and Jake. He's not angry and he specifically said he would tell you that he loves you. He didn't know that I know you so he wasn't just saying it, Em. And I know that this is hard but you've kept this secret to yourself for too long. I understand why now. But you needed to know the truth."

She sat down too hard, but she was glad for the pain. All the what if scenarios circled her like hungry sharks. All this time. Her eyes swept up to David.

"I should have told you. But I…" She paused. "And now Nick thinks I'm cheating, and he's gone. Maybe it's better that he is. I'm a mother who abandoned her child. I can't even remember the other baby. Our baby."

Tears streamed down her face but Emma didn't wipe them away. She was looking at David, who was crying too.

"I'm sorry. I'm so sorry," was all she could say.

He reached out and stroked her face. "It's okay. I forgive you if you will forgive me. I'm sorry I didn't help you face it. But," he paused and kissed her forehead, "I know someone who will."

"Who?"

"Nick is at my house. He's been there the whole time. I haven't told him but you need to. He loves you, Em."

"I didn't even think of that." She rolled her eyes as she spoke.

"The guy is pacing the floor. I'm supposed to call him when we are done."

Emma looked at David for a long moment. For a second, she could see the face of her childhood friend. The same kindness and love still remained in his smile.

"I cannot remember everything about us, David. I love you, though. I always did and I always will. You've always been my best friend. Thank you. I keep saying it because I don't know what else to say."

He was doing something with his phone. Then he looked up. "I love you too and always will."

They both turned as a truck came barreling down the drive. Nick must've been waiting out in front of the house.

David

CHAPTER NINETY

I expected a superhero to open the door but instead found a sad boy and equally sad-looking dog.

"Hey, buddy. What's wrong?"

I got on my knees when I saw Wyatt's eyes brimming with tears and his lip quivering.

"I don't want Houdini or you to leave."

"You know what? You're going to see us a lot. I'll talk to your mom about Houdini sleeping over."

"What about you sleeping over?"

Kellyn was standing in the hallway just beyond them. She looked beautiful in jeans and t-shirt. Her eyes were somehow darker.

"I'll talk to her about that too," I said to Wyatt but never took my eyes off Kellyn.

"I love you, David, and I love Houdini. He's my best friend."

The child stepped forward and put his arms around my neck. I was already feeling emotional but this choked me up.

"I love you too, Wyatt."

I had to lighten the mood. Reaching out, I pulled the dog into our hug.

"And I love Houdini. And Batman."

Wyatt started giggling and I tickled him. He managed to get free of the tickle monster and took off with Houdini, still laughing.

I stood up to face Kellyn. She reached out and touched the places that were bruised.

"So, you're back. And you want to sleep over."

"I found myself. And," I slid my arms around her waist, "I know what I want."

"Oh? What is that?"

There were too many things to name so I kissed her.

Two months later, we were all together in Hawaii. At my wedding with Emma, I'd been a nervous wreck. But today, the groom playing dinosaurs with Wyatt was the farthest from nervous.

"I'm bringing these dinosaurs to your wedding," Nick said, looking up.

"Beer and stegosaurus sound good. What time is it?" I asked.

Nick peered at the watch I'd given him. "Fifteen after one."

"Okay. We're in the home stretch."

The wedding was at two.

A knock on the door caused us both to look up. Kellyn stuck her head in. "Everyone decent?"

"Houdini has no pants on," Wyatt announced and we all laughed.

She came bearing a message. "Emma wants to see you."

I nodded and slipped out, and found Emma waiting in the hall. She was in a simple A-line, knee-length dress that seemed more lace than fabric. She was holding a canvas.

"I promised to paint you another piece when the treehouse painting tried to kill you."

She turned the painting around and I recognized it immediately. It was a beautiful image of the day in the park with Kellyn, Houdini, and Batman.

"A new happy place," she said.

"I love it, Em. Thank you."

"You guys are next, you know. I wanted this to be a pre-wedding present."

"It's beautiful. As are you."

She blushed. "Thank you, Davy."

It was my turn to blush. "I'm so happy for you, Em."

She looked up at me and I saw the tears forming. "Do you remember all the times we sat in that treehouse and dreamed about our lives?"

I nodded. "Probably turned out a little different than I imagined."

"I'm so glad you are still in my life. In both of our lives."

"And I'm glad you're both in ours. Your future husband is playing dinosaurs with my son."

"Your future wife has been helping me with everything. She's amazing."

We both laughed and when we parted, she kissed me on the cheek.

I watched Emma go for a moment and then turned my canvas to look at the picture of my family. Kellyn was waiting for me when I opened the door. We were getting married in a few months, but Wyatt already called me Dad. I turned the painting around and she smiled.

"She showed me earlier. That was a great day."

Looking into her gray eyes was like gazing into a crystal ball. I wasn't sure exactly what I could see but I knew my future was there.

Kai and Ruth walked Emma down the aisle and I stood as Nick's best man.

"Oh my God," he whispered when he saw Emma.

"Breathe, buddy," I said, placing my hand on his shoulder.

It was short and sweet and everyone cried. I turned my face to dash away tears, and for a second, I believed I saw Jake surfing. When I turned back around, Emma was looking at me. I was pretty sure she saw him too.

At the reception, I looked around. We were all okay. My mom and Micah; Nick and Emma; Sophie and Joanna; Maria and Jose; Ruth and Glen; Kellyn, Wyatt, and me.

When the bride and groom were leaving, we all waved. My wedding present to them had been a sailboat. The couple named it *Forgiving Nostalgia*.

www.ingramcontent.com/pod-product-compliance
Lightning Source LLC
Chambersburg PA
CBHW030928260626
47169CB00002B/408